A Properly Conducted Sham

MOST IMPRUDENT MATCHES - BOOK SIX

ALLY HUDSON

Busy Nothings Books

This novel is entirely a work of fiction. The names, characters, and incidents portrayed in it are the work of the author's imagination. Any resemblance to actual persons, living or dead, events or localities is entirely coincidental.

A Properly Conducted Sham Copyright © 2025 by Ally Hudson. All rights reserved. No part of this book may be reproduced in any form or by any electronic or mechanical means, including information storage and retrieval systems, without written permission from the author, except for the use of brief quotations in a book review.

Digital Edition ISBN: 979-8-9918384-0-5

Print Edition ISBN: 979-8-9918384-1-2

Cover design by Holly Perret, The Swoonies Romance Art

FIRST EDITION

For Mariah, who always reads my messy first drafts with far more enthusiasm and kindness than they deserve.

This Monster, who is only one in form, has a heart so humane that he should not be persecuted for a deformity which he refrains from rendering more hideous by his actions. I will not repay his kindness with such black ingratitude.

— GABRIELLE-SUZANNE BARBOT DE
VILLENEUVE, *LA BELLE ET LA BÊTE*

A Properly Conducted Sham

Author's Note:

Dearest Reader,

Welcome to A Properly Conducted Sham!

If this is your first time entering the Most Imprudent Matches universe, you should know that events in my series are interconnected, and timelines overlap. Though this book takes place simultaneously with Angel of Mine, it is not necessary to have read that book to enjoy this one. However, this story does contain spoilers for previous books in the series.

A Properly Conducted Sham opens with main characters who are no strangers to trauma. Both find themselves in a dark place when the story begins.

Inside these pages, the heroine is dealing with the ramifications of an unwanted pregnancy. Additionally, she has endured spousal rape—though she does not think of it as such. There is no on-page depiction, but she is deeply affected by her past. If she were diagnosed today, she would be experiencing vaginismus.

The hero is scarred physically and mentally. He regu-

AUTHOR'S NOTE:

larly expresses feelings of guilt and self-loathing and has on-page panic attacks. Though the term post-traumatic stress disorder (PTSD) was not in use during the Regency era, that would be his diagnosis.

If you are not in a place to read such things, I urge you to skip this one and explore any of the other books in my series—they all function as standalones. While I strive to handle all of these situations sensitively, and my characters heal throughout their journey, the early pages may be difficult for some readers.

If you are in the right headspace for this book, you'll enjoy a story of perseverance, healing, love, and family.

Love,
Ally

Prologue

BOND STREET, LONDON - MAY 8, 1816

CHARLOTTE

The copper bite of blood kissed the air. My gaze flicked along the raucous stands surrounding the sweat-drenched boxing ring as I hunted for dark hair and eyes. A gentleman swayed into my side while pouring moonshine down his gullet. Its caustic scent dragged bile up the back of my throat. I swallowed hard.

I'd been here for more than a quarter of an hour with no sighting, but he would be here. He had to.

Of course, I ought not to be here. I should still be at home, drowning in black crepe, but that was no longer feasible. And Wesley had been unavailable every time I chanced the scandalous journey to his bachelor lodgings.

With the help of a few strategically placed shillings, my housekeeper had been assured of his attendance tonight. I would not leave without speaking to him—without his promise.

A jeering cry rose from the crowd as one of the men in the ring knocked the other to the ground. Mocking heckles followed. And then I saw him. Too handsome, sprawled across the bench seat and half-undressed in only his shirtsleeves and waistcoat.

For perhaps the first time in the years I'd known him, my belly didn't flutter with anticipation at the sight of him, but rather nausea.

Across the room, he clapped a hand on the back of one of the men accepting wagers—most likely from that damned gaming hell, Wayland's. Was every man in London determined to give that wastrel every farthing they had?

I ducked around the nearest drunkard, shoving through the crowd and down the stands with less ease than I was accustomed to. This was not a ballroom, and no one gave deference to my status as a lady. Many of the men in attendance were familiar, if only by sight. The women were not the sort I was acquainted with.

Though the distance was not great, the journey was perilous. A man backed into me, unseeing. He jostled me into another, even more unsteady fellow. His drink sloshed along my side. I was left soaked in a sticky ale with not even a hint of apology.

There was nothing to be done for it. If I left now, Mrs. C would have to bribe a maid all over again. I forged ahead, weaving around the swaying crowd. The buttery fragrance of ale clung to my bodice and skirts, leaving me even more queasy.

A lecherous hand made for my bosom and I smacked it away, pressing on. It did not warrant further thought. I could not afford to be missish. Not now.

Finally, after swimming through drunken masses over a floor wet with what I hoped was ale but rather suspected was something more revolting, he was within reach. And surrounded by others.

Gentlemen I had come to know through Wesley. Not

friends—ladies were not friends with gentlemen—but acquaintances. Acquaintances I did not particularly wish to see me in such a place.

I stared, a few feet away, desperately willing him to make eye contact. But it seemed nothing about me was as riveting as the sight of men beating each other and the sickening sound of fist on swollen flesh.

Swallowing my pride and the nerves storming in my belly, I approached.

"Mr. Parker," I said simply.

Five pairs of eyes shot to mine, brows raised to the heavens.

"Lady James, what in God's name are you doing here?" Lord Christiansen asked. He was a short, bespectacled man that I knew Wesley only tolerated due to his flush pockets and fine port.

I ignored him, refusing to relinquish Wesley's gaze. "I need to speak with you. Privately."

Wesley's attention shot to his compatriots.

"Now, please."

"But the match—"

"Result will be the same whether you're watching or not," Mr. Varley said quietly. "I think you'd best speak with her."

I broke my stare to offer him a grateful glace, only to be met with wide-eyed pity. I shoved my shoulders back. I had no need of pity. I would leave this cesspool with a fiancé.

Wesley grunted, wobbling to his feet. He grabbed me by the wrist and dragged, leaving me to trip after him below the stands.

The floor here was more revolting than the steps would have indicated. And the activities taking place even more scandalous.

So distracted was I by the sight of one man taking another's member into his mouth that I didn't notice when Wesley stopped abruptly, and I crashed into his back.

"Why the devil are you wet?" he demanded, whirling around.

I ripped my gaze away from the shocking display only to find a man and woman engaged in a more traditional but no less salacious activity behind Wesley's shoulder. Shaking away my prim, missish astonishment, my eyes found his dark, sharp gaze. "Someone spilled ale on me."

"And what the bleeding hell do you want with me so badly that you couldn't wait until the end of the match? Or better still, until we could meet properly?" The drink on his breath was so thick I could taste it. I beat back the answering swell.

A cheer rose from the crowd and his attention shot to the ring. His head bobbed to and fro as he struggled to peer between gentlemen's legs.

"Wesley, please."

"What?" he snapped, not turning back to me.

"I tried to call on you. You were never available."

"Perhaps you should have considered the implications of that."

"Why are you speaking to me like this?" Tears threatened to fall and I blinked them back. I did not cry. Not ever.

Years I had known this man. Years filled with teasing flirtation and lingering, lusty gazes. Years of promises of the future, the one we would have when Ralph's age and drinking made a widow of me.

True, our single tryst hadn't held a candle to the ones I'd seen in my dreams. But this wasn't the man I knew.

"What do you want, Charlotte?" he bit out between gritted teeth, finally facing me once more.

"I am with child," I blurted, the words slurring together.

He blinked slowly. Once, twice, a third time. "My felicitations," he replied, something nasally and viscous in his tone.

It was my turn to stare stupidly.

"I don't see what that has to do with me." His lips twisted into a cruel smile. It wasn't an unfamiliar expression on his handsome face. But it had never before been directed at me. My gut wrenched.

"But, Wesley..."

He raised a challenging brow and that was the moment realization washed over me. I knew what I should have known when he failed to call on me the morning after. What I should have understood when he was never available to receive me. Hell, a smarter woman would have known never to let him touch her.

I forged ahead, fueled by desperation and denial. "It is yours, you must know that. Surely you know that."

"I know nothing of the sort."

"Wesley, please. What about everything we spoke of? You said we would marry as soon as I was out of mourning. You—you said we were already wed in your heart."

The man behind Wesley climaxed with a groan, then pulled free from his paramour and swayed off, still buttoning his stained breeches. The woman was left to right herself alone.

It was a heartbreakingly familiar scene from my marriage.

Wesley's laugh was brittle and vicious, drawing my eyes back to his. His dismissal slid through my heart like a knife. "Charlotte, please tell me you are not that dim-witted. Do not make me lose the last shred of respect I have for you."

I floundered, grasping desperately for something, anything to force his hand. "If you will not take responsibility, my father will be forced to call you out."

This laugh was genuine, so full-bodied that he doubled over at the waist. "By all means, Charlotte. Please inform your father that his daughter is a strumpet. I'm certain this will be astonishing information to him." His voice dripped molten sarcasm.

"You will be ostracized by the *ton*!" I flung the words pathetically, bile pooling behind my tongue once again.

"Darling, please do be serious. They've all seen you. All these years... Dressing the way you do... Flirting with every gentleman you meet... And as a married woman too." He tutted. "They know as well as I do that there's absolutely no way to know who the father might be. You've certainly had enough paramours. It could be anyone."

"There was only you. Please, I love you." My voice sounded so small, so hollow, so pathetic, even to my ears.

Cheers and groans rose in equal measure as a bell sounded —signaling match end. Wordlessly, Wesley stalked off, leaving me alone beneath the stands.

Without warning, my stomach abandoned the fight. I doubled over and emptied its contents with great retching sobs. Sick landed on my slippers and spattered my skirts. That was the moment I lost the war against my tears. I was pathetic. Truly pathetic.

A warm hand found my lower back and rubbed it soothingly at the same time another pushed back the curls from my forehead. "There, there," a throaty feminine voice cooed. "You'll be well, duckie."

"Wha?" I asked blearily, not trusting my gut enough to turn to face whomever was touching me.

"You don't need 'im."

After another few heaves proved ineffectual, I felt confident enough to wipe my mouth with the back of my hand and turn to face her. It was the doxy who'd been taken against the wall only moments before. Her dress was righted, though she still looked thoroughly tupped with curls unbound and frizzed, cheeks flushed, and rouge smudged.

"What?" I repeated inanely.

"He's cruel, that one. Better off without 'im."

My stomach gave another threatening lurch.

"Come along now. There's a back way out."

That intelligence left me suddenly, desperately grateful for the bawd before me. I hadn't considered what it would take to escape this hell. Especially now that I was more repugnant than the floor.

"This way," she added, guiding me with a hand on my back as if I were a child. I couldn't complain. I felt like a child, simple and ignorant.

At last, we found a door and she pushed it open for me. It led into a back alley, stinking of piss and other things I didn't wish to consider. I gritted my teeth against more sickness and held my breath.

"It will be well, you'll see, ducks." She ushered me toward the street where the air was clearer. "Can you make it from 'ere?"

I nodded, searching for my carriage. I found it down the street and raised my hand to catch my footman's attention. When I turned back to thank the woman, she was gone.

And I was alone, facing a life entirely unlike any I'd ever imagined.

Chapter One

84 BROOK STREET, LONDON - JUNE 5, 1816

LEE

THE GLITTERING cufflink landed with a *plink* before skittering under the armoire.

"Damn and blast."

"If you would allow me to do it, as you should, it would already be buttoned."

"Brigsby," I warned with a sigh.

"I hope you don't think I'm climbing under there to get that. You're the one who insisted on dressing yourself as if you don't employ a perfectly respectable, handsome, charming, witty, exceptionally skilled valet. If you can dress yourself, you can sprawl across the floor and dig through the dust yourself."

"I employ a mediocre and impertinent valet. I know of none that match your description."

The man sighed as he fetched a second pair of gold cufflinks and freed one. With a raised brow, he thrust his hand out expectantly, waiting for me to acquiesce and allow him to do his job.

"You're going to leave that?" I asked, tipping my head toward the armoire where the cufflink hid.

"Of course not. I'm going to tell Eliza that I've lost one and beg her to help me search. Then I plan to appreciate the view," he explained with a waggled brow, finishing with one wrist and gesturing for the other.

"Brigsby... Why that girl encourages your flirtations, I shall never understand."

"I'm a delight."

"You're a pain in my arse."

He finished with the second cufflink and turned to fetch the black-and-gold half-mask he'd had commissioned for me.

"I am about to be. Turn around and bend down," he demanded. I bent at the knees, rather than the waist for a multitude of reasons. He handed me the mask. The cool ceramic was a balm as I pressed it to the right side of my face. The ribbon bit into my forehead as he tied it. Even crouched as I was, he had to rise on his toes to reach. The inconvenience of a tall employer was a small punishment for his usual audacity.

Of course, he'd also managed to distract me from the very reason I'd dropped the cufflink in the first place. My hands were astonishingly steady when I pulled them from the mask and rose, then turned to face the mirror with wary anticipation.

My breath escaped in a rush. It was perfect.

It had been years since I had been able to meet the looking glass with anything but trepidation. With half my face covered... Perhaps there was something, a spark, of the old Lee in there. Though, if I was honest, old Lee was in desperate need of a haircut as evidenced by the wayward strands I could tuck easily behind my ear.

I gripped the edges of the mask and gave it an earnest tug. It didn't give at all. "What sort of knot did you use?"

"The kind that must be untied with prayers and a pair of shears. I thought you might prefer that."

I swallowed a welling of gratitude, instead giving him only an appreciative nod.

As soon as I turned away the nerves returned. It was ridiculous, a grown man half shaking at the thought of a ball like a timorous debutant. The absurdity didn't lessen the fluttering in my chest in the slightest.

Brigs turned to leave and I filed after him, tapping the mask again before pressing it against my face. Still secure from hairline to chin.

I was still fussing with it when we reached the marble floor of the entry. He stopped short and I nearly crashed into him.

He spun on a heel before I could rip my hand away. "Enough. It'll stay just fine if you stop touching it."

"Need I remind you who employs whom?"

"Hardly. Leave it be," he retorted.

Crawford, my butler, sensing a circumstance that would not be improved by his presence, inserted himself. He opened the door in his self-important way before gesturing toward the open doorway as if I couldn't see it with my own two eyes. On Brigsby, it would've been cheeky, but Crawford, in all his obsequience, thought it proper.

I nodded my half-hearted thanks as I rolled my shoulders back, testing the stitching on the ebony brocade overcoat. It was an ostentatious thing, decorated with overdone gold cording and frippery, but it suited the evening's theme. And it would distract from anything that needed to be distracted from.

Lord, perhaps I shouldn't atten—

"Get in the carriage, *my lord*," Brigsby said, risking a lecture from Crawford for his insolence. The title held all the sarcasm the valet could muster, and perhaps a bit more he'd manifested from Lord knew where.

I needed a new valet.

Left with only two choices, face the *bon ton* and all the horrors that could befall me there or face Brigsby's judgmental stare combined with Crawford's moralisms on the evils of tardiness, I chose the former and approached the carriage.

The carriage.

I could usually abide them in town. In the daylight. If I had to.

There were always folks milling about and the streets were relatively smooth, after all.

But each time a wheel met a rut, jolting the carriage about, I was left shaken. And at night...

No. The club was not so far, a mile perhaps, less than two certainly.

"My lord?" Crawford urged.

"I think I shall walk tonight."

"It is not proper," he insisted.

"Neither is a ball hosted in a gaming hell."

"It looks like rain," he tried again.

"Hardly."

With a sigh, Brigsby cut in front of Crawford to pass me a hat. I donned it after running my fingers through my overgrown hair.

"Good luck," the man added with a vigilant glance toward the evening sky.

He held out a fist and waited until I aligned my open palm underneath before dropping a large handful of my favorite peppermints there for safe keeping.

I scoffed at his insincere well wishes and unwrapped one. Freshness burst over my tongue when it hit. I inhaled, allowing the cool mint to fill my lungs. When I swallowed, it hit my stomach, immediately settling one or two of the overwrought nerves.

I nodded at both men before setting off. I would need more than Brigsby's luck to survive the bloodthirsty gentry.

My pace was unhurried as I trailed down the London streets. Distractedly and nearly entirely out of habit, I tipped my head back to the sky. It was one of the things I found most distasteful about town. London nights were too bright. The ambient light drowned out the stars. Tonight's clouds may have been too heavy for gazing even from my observatory, but the lamps did not help matters.

Less than half an hour and several mint candies later, I caught sight of the fine carriages lining the pavement. Walking had certainly been the correct choice, all that fitful starting and spasmodic stopping... No. Better to walk.

I sidled between two families I did not recognize while their backs were turned and they were making conversation, and made short work of the receiving line.

I popped a peppermint just as I turned to face the evening's hosts.

"Champaign! Good to see you." Michael Wayland, a pale blue domino mask covering the top of his face, clasped my hand in his as I set foot inside his club. His other hand remained wrapped around the waist of the statuesque woman at his side, surely his wife. She offered a warm smile. He continued, "I'm glad you decided to attend. Hugh owes me a pound."

I bit back my instinctive irritation—he didn't mean it that way.

"If I had but known such an astronomical sum was at stake, I should have arrived earlier." I struggled to keep my tone light.

Michael bet on everything, and he would use any opportunity to take money from his brother. And he wasn't a cruel man. He didn't intend to mock the rumors of my reclusive nature.

Michael's wife gave a polite cough, her wide eyes cast on me. "Have you had the opportunity to meet my wife? Lady Juliet Wayland?"

"Lady?" The question slipped out before I could catch it and I had to shutter a wince.

"I know. Who would have thought it of me? I managed to seduce an earl's daughter."

"Michael!" she scolded, before turning to me. "It was all entirely proper, I assure you."

Over her shoulder, I caught Michael's self-satisfied grin. Anything but proper then.

"It is a pleasure to make your acquaintance, Lady Juliet. I should leave you to your other guests." I stepped away with a bow, slipping into the crush inside the club.

And it was a crush.

Hundreds of the *ton*'s wealthiest and most influential darted across the rich carpeting, the stately gaming tables, the polished dance floor, like ants at a picnic.

An overly perfumed lordling jostled me from behind. When I turned, I was knocked again to the side as a set of oversize skirts passed.

I made for the nearest wall, sidling between flirting couples and darting around wallflowers. Finally, I found a patch of plaster to call my own.

It was cool and solid against my spine and the back of my neck. I brushed a hand over my mask—still in place—as I swallowed against the knot in my chest.

I patted my pocket and dipped a hand inside. Only three peppermints left. Had I eaten that many on the walk over? I would need to ration them, but in this moment...

"Here," a warm masculine voice drifted over from beside me. I turned to see Augie Ainsley leaning against the wall, a glass of something clear in his hand, outstretched toward me.

"You looked like you needed something to take the edge off. Gin, right?"

He hadn't bothered with a mask tonight. The years since I'd last seen him had been kind to him. He'd filled out a bit from the scrawny thing he had once been and wore the roles of father, husband, and hell owner well.

"How did you remember?"

He shrugged. "I always marvel at anyone who likes gin, vile stuff."

I took a sip. It was a fine selection. Though that was to be expected out of Wayland and Ainsley.

"Thank you."

"Of course. I find the lot of them overwhelming too."

"Is it that obvious?" I tucked a loose strand of hair behind my ear, checking the mask simultaneously.

"No, not to them." He tipped his head toward the masses. "I should get back to the bar before there's a riot. If you need a breath or two, you can always slip upstairs. My office is the second door at the top. It's open."

I murmured my thanks and took another sip, enjoying the burn when it hit my center.

The chaos of the night drew my gaze once more. And, Lord, it was chaos. Everyone who was anyone clamored to see and be seen in the massive octagonal room. Cheers and groans spilled out from the gaming tables that encircled the hell.

More than one young lady spun on heels, amazement in their eyes at the opulence of the space. Likely witnessing for the first time the very room where their husbands, brothers, and fathers made and lost entire fortunes.

A half-dozen or so ladies had even braved the gaming tables. A little slip of a girl dressed as a peacock, feathers and all, was absolutely dominating at a high-stakes hazard table, if the cheers of delight were any indication—cheers from the other ladies. The gentlemen were left to groan in devastation and poverty.

Her Grace, the dowager Duchess of Rosehill, cleared a swath through the room in a gown straight from Marie Antionette's wardrobe. The skirts... She could probably hide several small children and a large goat under that dress. And the wig... Oh, the wig.

These were the things I missed about society. In general, I found the balls, musicales, whist parties, and dinners tedious. But the sheer absurdity of the *beau monde*... It could not be matched in the country.

I bit the inside of my cheek, fighting against the laugh that threatened to bubble up.

My wall was near one of the more serious hazard games, though this table held only gentlemen. Some of them I recognized but could not name and some were entirely unknown to me.

The gentlemen were well on their way to soused. They groused and jeered in that raucous, overloud, overenunciated way that spoke of overindulgence.

The loudest and most unruly was pontificating to his rapt audience. "I'm telling you, lads. She's increasing. The bitch tried to insist it was mine too. As if she hasn't enjoyed all of our company at one time or another."

"Speak for yourself, Parker," a shorter one retorted.

The jackass was Parker, presumably. I could only see the back of his dark head from my vantage, but the name was familiar. There had been a Parker a year or two behind me in school. The boy was untitled, and his family money came from manufacturing, though he had always tried to pretend otherwise. If this was the same Parker I recalled, he had been an arse then too.

The lout continued, "You mean to tell me you never once played old Baron James for a cuckold? A man like that, a wife with diddies like that—he knew what he was buying. Hell, it's a miracle this is her first by-blow."

"The man is dead. Have some respect, Parker," the bold one from earlier returned.

"He was a greasy old simpleton with loose pockets and one foot in the grave. And his wife was and still is a threepenny upright. Why should that change now that he's gone to meet his maker"

"She does have a mighty fine pair of bubbies," another added. He was more familiar, but I still could not place the name.

A long-forgotten chivalrous instinct rose in my chest. I chafed to confront them—to call them out.

I made it a single step before nausea crashed over me. I wasn't that man—not any longer. That man died years ago. All that was left was a wraith hiding behind a mask.

In desperate need of Ainsley's promised respite, I braved the fray and left the *gentlemen* to their game, dropping my glass on the bar as I passed.

That was the moment my gaze found her—a more appealing distraction.

Lady Celine Hasket, Marchioness of Rycliffe. Her golden curls were elegantly coiffed, and she was draped in purple silk. She was exactly as she had been when I last saw her.

Visually, time had not passed for her at all. But that was not true. Years had passed, and more than one spouse between us.

I approached her carefully, clearing my throat as I tapped on the ceramic hiding my shame. "If I remember correctly, a woman as graceful as you belongs on the dance floor. Not along the wall." The speech was rather more suave than I usually managed—closer to something I would have offered her all those years ago. And, I realized belatedly, easily mistaken for an offer rather than commentary.

She turned, her head tipping back until her eyes met mine. A smile bloomed over her face when recognition set in.

The lady's only concession to the theme of the evening was a delicate, flimsy little mask that banded across her eyes. It did nothing to conceal identity or natural beauty.

"Lord Champaign, it has been an age!"

"Best part of a decade. We last spoke on the eve of your engagement, I believe. I am sorry for your loss."

And I was. I had caught her and Rycliffe that night. Passion sizzled between them. It was something I never could have given her.

"I heard you suffered a similar loss. I am sorry for you as well." Celine's accent had softened over the years, nearly imperceptible now, but the sensual, husky tone of her voice remained.

I thanked her. It was the proper response to condolences, even if the circumstances of our losses could not be less similar. After all, she wasn't responsible for Rycliffe's death.

Those thoughts lay down a dark path, one ill-suited for a ball. Desperate to drag my mind from the bleak past, I floundered for a subject.

Without permission or conscious thought, another, less ambiguous offer to dance fell from my lips as the first strains of a quadrille formed.

"I would be delighted." Lady Rycliffe's smile was genuine, bright. I'd seen the false smiles cross her face in our youth—she distributed them freely, with no real consideration. But the real ones, they tugged at the corners of her eyes. I was proud to have earned one or two during our courtship.

I towered over her petite frame as she, graceful and confident as ever, took her place across from me.

Something in the way she moved spoke of maturity in a way it hadn't when she was but twenty.

"You seem to have misplaced your accent," I teased. It was

something to say, something less fraught than long dead spouses and courtships that ended wrapped in another's arms.

"Just for tonight. I think it adds to the mystery."

That drew a chuckle from me. As if a soul here would not know her. She had been the belle of the *ton* ten years ago, and I had no doubt she would be the star of tonight's ball as well.

"Oh yes, I'm certain there are two, perhaps three people in this room who do not know you on sight. Even in the mask." My raillery earned a raised brow and a half smile.

"Four at least. Do give me credit."

"I'll be generous and give you a half dozen," I agreed. "How have you been?"

She found something of interest to contemplate on my waistcoat.

"It wasn't meant to be a trick."

"No, I know. I just wasn't... I wasn't sure which answer you wanted."

That was a sentiment I understood in my bones. The question, so commonplace, yet so fraught, always left me unmoored.

I was not well. I hadn't been well in years. I might never be well again. But that answer was an unwelcome one.

"Whichever one you want to give me is fine." I tried to offer reassurance in my tone, but whether I was successful was unclear.

She sighed before catching her lip between her teeth for the space of a breath. "I am well enough. Most days, I am all right. Some days I'm fine, marvelous even. Other days... Well, you know."

"I do."

"And you?"

"The same. More or less." Probably less—almost certainly. She and Rycliffe had been a love match. "Mia—Amelia—and I, we were well suited."

"I cannot imagine you being anything else. I should have told you—I always meant to tell you—it was never about you... that night. I— Gabriel was... all-consuming. You were—*are*—a wonderful man. I never doubted that you would make a good husband. It was just..." Her rushed assurances filled me with astonishment. They spilled forth as if she had been nursing them for a decade.

I had never taken her refusal of my entirely practical proposal as a rejection. No one who had seen her in Rycliffe's embrace on that veranda could have. But it was nice to hear—even if she was entirely wrong in her assessment.

"I never thought that. But I appreciate it all the same."

Her gaze caught on something as I spun her, and she missed a step. In truth, I hadn't thought her capable of a misstep and my gaze instinctively sought her distraction.

I had to restrain a laugh when I realized it was a gentleman.

The man scoffed in annoyance, turning to stalk away. She slipped back into position, her expression unnamable but entirely reminiscent of the one she wore when Rycliffe had met her eyes over the roast chicken. The expression that signified the end of my pursuit of Celine.

I bit back a smile as I released her. "Enjoy yourself tonight, Lady Rycliffe. I think it's time for both of us to live a little," I offered with a bow.

She backed away silently before spinning on her heel. As if by a string, the man pulled her along after him.

My statement had been a lie, of course. I didn't deserve to live at all. But Celine, she most certainly did deserve to find happiness—love—again. And if I could offer any encouragement, well, it was something—something the old Lee would have done.

Chapter Two

JAMES PLACE, LONDON - JUNE 5, 1816

CHARLOTTE

IF I CAST up my accounts one more time, I was going to scream. It was not enough that the thing growing inside me was destroying my life, it had to ruin my luncheon as well.

Imogen offered a tight-lipped smile as she wound my hair into a delicate twist with golden ribbons dancing throughout.

My maid hadn't once verbally acknowledged my condition. But she knew. Everyone knew.

I sighed, considering her efforts in the glass as I swallowed back the nausea. My hair was one of the few benefits of my situation. It was lovelier than ever, shimmering filaments of bronze and gold glinted in the candlelight. The effect was enhanced by the addition of the ruby pins I handed to her one by one.

"Any rouge, my lady?" Imogen held the carmine crepon in one hand and the pomatum in the other.

"I hardly think it necessary tonight." My cheeks had retained an alluring flush for some weeks now in spite of my regular reckonings with the newly repurposed milk pail, morning, noon, and night. I'd heard rumors that the sickness was supposed to cease at some point, but that hadn't been my experience.

She nodded and turned to find my gown. *The gown*. The one that must fetch me a husband.

Tonight was my last opportunity. Every morning my gowns pulled a little tighter, betraying a roundness where once there had been none.

I'd attended every single soirée for weeks—no easy feat. My behavior was unseemly. It was not done, mingling in society a mere seven months after my husband's passing. As such, the invitations required more than a little scheming to secure. I drew judgmental stares and whispers at every event. I should be grateful that, for once, they weren't directed at my bosom.

The glass top of my dressing table was cool against my hands as I pressed up. Wordlessly, Imogen moved to assist me into the corset. I turned to allow her access to the laces, my fingers clenching on the walnut post of the bed. The one I once shared with Ralph.

Imogen began to tug gently on the lacings—too gently.

"Tighter."

"Yes, my lady."

She commenced yanking. With a soft grunt, she pulled the laces taught. It was tighter than I normally would have worn it, certainly, but not tight enough.

"I said tighter," I snapped.

She gave a sincere wrench this time, and my breath shoved from my chest. Still it was not enough. The hints of *it* were still clear as day if one glanced below my bosom.

I resisted the urge to snarl at the girl—again—with a sigh. "Imogen, I need it tighter."

"Any tighter and the eyelets will rip."

The curse caught at the edge of my teeth before I could

scandalize her. With no other choice, I could only pray the dress would be sufficient.

"Very well. The gown, if you please."

The gown. My savior or my damnation.

I wore the latest fashions. Always. Even when I had to squirrel away shillings in the cellar with the potatoes to keep Ralph from drinking or wagering. I may have been forced to wed a decrepit spendthrift. But I refused to look it.

Tonight was to be my exception. Because this dress—it predated me.

Blessedly, for once in her miserable life, Lady Juliet Wayland had done something right. She had chosen a masquerade theme for tonight's fête. And a masquerade allowed for a more dramatic gown—even one a few decades out of date. This frock was one of my late mother's. It required all the absurd underpinnings of the era and disguised anything that required disguising.

Imogen held the gilded silk aloft for inspection. I suspected Mother was with child—with me—when she had it made. The strategically placed ruffles and panniers concealed exceptionally well.

The creamy golden robe à la française was festooned with delicate swirls. They were embroidered, climbing up the split skirt and hem. It was breathtaking.

At my nod of approval, Imogen set the gown aside and helped me into the underpinnings. Not for the first time, I was grateful I had debuted when slender silhouettes were in fashion. In fact, I had remained grateful for that fact up until two weeks ago when *it* started pulling at my dresses when I moved the wrong way.

Ridiculous underthings donned, I braced against the bedpost as Imogen helped me into the skirts, then pinned the stomacher into place and fluffed the engageantes at my elbow.

They brushed distractingly against my forearms when I moved. Good, they would draw the gaze.

I studied the silk taffeta with a critical eye and pressed my hands against the layers of petticoats and panniers, searching for evidence of my condition.

Ordinarily, I would have paused to admire the impeccable stitching and fine weave—straight from Lyon certainly—but that was hardly a concern at present.

While I noted the increased fullness, I was fairly confident it wouldn't be obvious to all. And I could only hope the men of the *ton* would be so distracted by the generous display of my assets that they wouldn't notice anything amiss.

My normally remarkable bosom had grown even more impressive in recent weeks. That alone should have been enough to entice an offer of marriage, but I'd had no interest at all.

Imogen handed me the mask I had commissioned to match the dress. It was impossibly fine, with golden metalwork forged to resemble lace. It covered only my left eye, leaving the other free. It did little to hide my identity but emphasized my whiskey irises and dark lashes in a way I hoped was tempting.

Imogen fretted with the ribbon as she tied it, concerned it would muss my carefully pinned curls.

A last glance in the looking glass gave me hope. Tonight was without a doubt my last chance.

If I did not find a husband at this masquerade, I never would.

Breaking away from my reflection, I dabbed a bit of the lavender-and-orange-blossom perfume behind my ears and in the crevice of my breasts—best engage all of my future husband's senses while he was admiring. My stomach nearly revolted as the fragrance reached my own senses, and I reached hastily for the—now cold—ginger tea I'd abandoned some time ago on my dressing table.

Imogen gave a sympathetic smile at my wince, but my gut settled.

"Beautiful, my lady." She handed me the matching gloves. I slid them on and up, up all the way past my elbows.

"Thank you."

She trailed after me as I set out down the fading crimson carpeted halls and descended the tread-worn staircase.

"Good luck," she breathed as I slipped out the double doors into the night. Though I didn't acknowledge it, I appreciated the sentiment.

I would need it.

~

My insides lurched as yet another gentleman turned away at my approach. This time, the jolt had nothing to do with the leech inside me.

Danforth—a man who once salivated at the sight of me—scurried to request a dance with the nearest insipid spinster.

He has told them.

Wesley had told them all. He couldn't rest after saddling me with a parasite and leaving me to deal with the consequences. He also had to ensure I found no hope from any quarter.

My corset, too tight, left my breaths shallow and ineffectual. That was the reason the room was dimming—no other.

As soon as he'd arrived, Wesley had commandeered one of the high-stakes tables. Drink after drink, round after round, he toyed with sums large enough to bankrupt anyone else.

He was surrounded by the same four men who'd been at his side that day at the boxing match, along with a few others.

When I finally allowed myself a glance his way, I found

him lounging in his seat, legs spilling out in front of him, dark hair tousled and unkempt. He'd forgone a mask in favor of ensuring there wasn't a soul who mistook him. Confidence hung over him as he rolled the die. Luck must have been his tonight.

It certainly wasn't mine—and that was his doing.

Christiansen looked up, catching my eyes with something between a sneer and a smirk curling on his lips before he nudged Wesley's shoulder. A burst of laughter came from the table as I spun away.

My innards churned uneasily and my blood chilled, ice forming along my veins. I pressed my eyes closed, inhaling as deep as my corset would allow before exhaling through my mouth. Desperation, despair, and panic warred for purchase in my chest.

When my lashes flicked open again, I glimpsed Mr. Ellsworth across the room. He was a decent sort, if exceptionally dull. Hope rose in the space of the breath or two it took to catch his gaze across the floor.

As soon as I managed it, he looked away and devastation crashed over me once more.

Another one slipped through my grasp, grains of sand through the hourglass.

I cast another frantic, futile glance around the room, only to be greeted by the sight of a familiar black pompadour by the bar. Clad in his usual sharp black and stark white, the sight of Alexander Hasket, Duke of Rosehill, never failed to cause a pang. Even masked, he was unmistakable.

In my less charitable moments, I blamed him for my situation. If he had simply proposed as he ought during our courtship my first season, none of this would have happened. I wouldn't have been forced to marry Ralph. I wouldn't have found my way to Wesley's side in search of something more.

And I would not now, months after my husband's passing, be in this wretched condition.

Even years later, Rosehill's rejection stung. That season, I had been perfection. A diamond to be spoken of in reverent tones, I was the very portrait of a proper debutant, demure, accomplished, coquettish without being forward, with a pleasing form and delicate manners.

For one brief moment, I had my pick of suitors. And who better than Rosehill? Handsome, fashionable, and titled with the wealth to support it.

Our very polite courtship lasted three months, during which I was all but certain a proposal was imminent.

And then, without the slightest warning or explanation, he ended our courtship. Days later, my father secured a match with Baron James. Elderly, with a sagging neck and a fondness for drink that bordered on obsession, my husband was no Duke of Rosehill.

After Ralph had rolled off me on our wedding night and his quaking snores began to fill the room, I comforted myself with the knowledge that I had been perfection itself. If Rosehill was not pleased with me, then there was no pleasing him.

The problem was that he seemed pleased with everyone else. Two years ago, he even offered for mousy Juliet Dalton, now Wayland, and only released her in the face of unendurable scandal. Even now, he chatted amiably with her at his side. He didn't avoid *her* gaze.

But me, he threw over with no explanation, no apology—nothing.

And now I was in an even more shameful position that grew more precarious every day. The future turned bleaker with each member of the *ton* who gave me the cut, and my hope dimmed.

My throat tightened uncomfortably. Struggling for breath

within the trappings of my underpinnings, the edges of my vision darkened.

Tears threatened to escape but I couldn't—wouldn't—allow it. Just before I lost the fight, a flash of black and gold caught my eye from against the nearby wall.

Hope bloomed once again.

The gentleman was impossibly tall—the tallest man here by far—with overgrown dark blond locks. He wore a half mask covering one side of his face.

And I did not know him. I was certain of it. It would be unthinkable to forget a man of that size, even behind the mask.

His shirt was a fine linen, the waistcoat a charcoal brocade, and the overcoat a heavy wool. It was several seasons out of date, but then, so was my gown. The gentleman was at least wealthy enough to have purchased decent, well-tailored clothing this century.

I could not afford to be choosy.

Better still, he was alone, propping up the wall with his tall, broad frame as he observed the play and dancing with a keen eye.

I *should* find someone, contrive an introduction. That was the proper way to go about these things. But an introduction would give that same someone time to inform him of whatever rumor Wesley had circulated.

This was a masquerade—the rules were relaxed, *surely*.

Squaring my shoulders, I plucked a single curl free from my coiffure to brush against my neck charmingly. A quick glance at my bosom confirmed it was still there and still magnificent. I glided across the floor with a grace reminiscent of my first season, even as the significant looks and whispers followed me.

A bare patch of off-white wall near his was available. I claimed it, angling toward him in what I hoped was an elegant manner. The ways of a wallflower were unfamiliar to me. If there was an enticing way to hug a wall, I did not know it.

The gentleman, of course, could not see fit to cooperate. His head did not so much as tip in my direction. Again, my heart plummeted deep into my gut, knotting painfully.

A jubilant cheer rose up from one of the high-stakes tables. Out of the corner of my eye, I caught a nearly imperceptible flinch from the man, so small it could have been a trick of the candlelight.

His chest rose on a sigh and an—astonishingly large and shockingly bare—hand dipped into the pocket of his coat. Something was trapped in his grasp when his hand emerged. Long fingers tugged on the item, unwrapping it before he popped it into his mouth. A sharp crunch caught my ear before his lips parted in a relieved exhale and appreciative inhale.

The brilliant scent of peppermint wafted my way. It curled around me, hovering in the air. The unending churning in my stomach lessened.

That sensation left me so rarely in recent weeks, I had begun to think it a permanent affliction. Whether it resulted from my condition or nerves was hardly relevant. But now, with a single breath, it dissipated.

Relief filled me and I allowed my eyes to drift closed as I inhaled, reveling in the sensation, or lack thereof.

"Do you want one?" A lilting tenor drifted to my ears.

Startled, my eyes flicked open to find a hand aloft before me. Dwarfed in the palm was a wrapped sweet.

"It's peppermint," the voice added. I followed the hand up the finely wrapped forearm along a broad shoulder to meet his gaze. The black-framed mask covering one eye contrasted appealingly against his icy, silver-blue irises.

"Thank you."

I plucked it from his open hand, allowing a fingertip to

brush the meat of his palm. Now empty, his hand remained aloft, waiting. With less eagerness than I felt, I tugged at the wrappings of the mint and freed it, then set the paper in his waiting palm.

The bright burn of mint bit at my tongue and crisped the air. Seconds later, my belly finally, blessedly ceased its endless churning.

"Thank you," I repeated, grateful to the man in a way he could not possibly know.

"Of course, Lady..."

"Charlotte. Lady Charlotte James."

It wasn't strictly my proper title. But I was not particularly interested in explaining my marital status to this unknown gentleman. Dead husbands were not an enticing topic of conversation.

He nodded, his eyes dragging down my form. The gaze was not lecherous, but appreciative.

"And you are?"

"A bit rusty at this." He chuckled half-heartedly, a hint of self-deprecation to the note. "Leopold Bennet, Earl of Champaign."

The name lit a spark. I'd heard it before, certainly. But we'd never been introduced. He had been out of society for some time.

An outsider. And a titled one at that. He was absolutely perfect for my purposes.

Finally, for the first time in weeks, it seemed my luck may turn. My heart jumped, this time with hope.

Chapter Three
WAYLAND'S, LONDON - JUNE 5, 1816

LEE

My second wall was a vast improvement over the first—quieter and absent jeering simpletons.

This one was behind the lower-stakes tables, where young bucks and debutants tried their hand at the games with helpful instruction from others. It also had the benefit of proximity to the door. The temptation to make an escape, to give myself permission to abandon the masquerade and begin the trudge home, grew with every passing moment.

I'd done well, I thought, though Brigsby would not be inclined to agree. When I received the invitation, my first instinct had been to pitch it into the fire. The astonishment of Wayland's name on it, paired with a wife no less, was enough to stay my hand. Curiosity had warred with instinctive revulsion at the thought until the former finally beat back the later.

And there was loneliness. I was man enough to admit to the sentiment. Brigsby and the staff had been my closest—my only—companions in the long days since Mia passed. The longer nights were devoted to the stars. Anything to escape the wrath that awaited me in sleep. Or worse, the devastating desolation when sleep would not, could not find me

No, the temptation of the masquerade found me at precisely the moment when my solitude reached an unbearable crescendo.

My fingers traced the edge of my mask in a gesture that had become habitual over the course of the evening. The ribbon that ground into the flesh of my forehead was a small price to pay for the brief conversations I'd had tonight. I would give far more for the moments when I felt like something other than the wraith I had become.

And, much as I could feel the exhaustion setting in, I wasn't ready to give up just yet. The bill for tonight would come due, sooner rather than later. I could already feel the edges of an attack closing in. I had pushed myself too far and too fast, and my tenuous hold on my nerves was sure to come crashing down. A smart man would know his limitations, would leave before disaster struck.

Generally, I considered myself sensible enough for pragmatism. I shifted on the balls of my feet, contemplating the door once more when a mound of golden silk spilled onto the wall a few feet from my side.

Out of the corner of my eye, I watched as the woman fussed with the fabric, arranging it artfully around her. She was lovely, with porcelain skin lit from within, a sharply angled jaw, and an arched brow. The left side of her face was masked, sparkling gold reflecting the light. It was difficult to make out the precise shade of her hair, but it glinted, flickering in the candlelight between rich honey and warm cinnamon.

Her masked gaze flicked in my direction, her full lips twisting into a pout. Likely at not finding my gaze devouring her shapely form. She shifted, angling herself in such a way to display her plentiful assets for my appreciation—and I did appreciate them. But her position was awkward and surely uncomfortable with those heavy skirts and underpinnings.

She was too pretty to be a wallflower, and far too unaccustomed to the wall. It was a wonderful thought, a lady making her way over to feign disinterest—in me. My stomach gave a flip at the realization. It was either elation or terror, or perhaps a combination of both. Regardless, I dipped into my pocket for a peppermint, unwrapping it and biting down with a distracted chomp, running my fingers over my mask.

The relieving bite of the mint gave me the courage to face her.

Her eyes had drifted closed and I watched, enraptured, as she inhaled, tasting the scent of my sweet between pouted lips.

A tension seemed to lift from her shoulders as she breathed. Perhaps I had thought wrong and she wasn't here for me. Perhaps the crowd was too much for her too. Instinctively, my hand dipped into my pocket.

Only two mints left.

Without giving myself time to consider the implications, I grabbed one and stepped forward, holding it out. Offering it to her.

Her eyes blinked open, lashes fluttering. I was met with a color somewhere between buckwheat and bourbon as they widened in surprise.

She accepted my bungled offer, her gloved fingertip brushing my palm enticingly. When she bit into the sweet, she inhaled the sharp, fresh essence. A half smile pulled across her cheek, just kissing one corner of her mouth and eye.

"Thank you," she breathed. Her voice was sensual and throaty, a clarinet in a sea of piccolos.

"Of course, Lady..." I realized too late that my approach was anything but proper. I'd never had to request a lady's name before—it was always provided with an introduction.

Nothing in her countenance indicated offense when she replied, "Charlotte. Lady Charlotte James."

Closer now, I could see that her eyes were a warm bronze, framed by thick dark lashes.

After a further cow-handed introduction, something of the old Lee seemed to claw its way to the surface and I managed to ask her for a dance.

She slipped her hand in mine easily, finding my shoulder with the other at the same time that I caught her waist beneath outdated skirts. A dip of my eyeline to the rest of her confirmed that this was no wallflower before me. Wallflowers did not dress like *that*. This was a gown to see and be seen, and she wore it so, so well.

The music began and I guided her through the first sluggish, unpracticed steps of a waltz. She moved easily, anticipating and softening in all the right places. There was no question in my mind that she was quite familiar with the dance floor.

What the devil was she doing with me?

Well, at the moment, she was looking at me expectantly, her eyes widened in question.

"I beg your pardon?" I blurted.

Her lips quirked again. "I was merely asking if you are often in town. I cannot recall having made your acquaintance."

"I've been... out of society for some time." Something about that response had a smile tugging at her full-bowed lips.

"Why have you returned now?"

"Wayland—he is an old friend. He invited me."

"Ah, so you are a gambler then? Too busy at the tables for the ballroom?" It could have been a reproach, but her air was casual and her smile never faltered.

"No, nothing quite so interesting I'm afraid."

"Oh no, sir. I do not believe you are the one who determines whether you are interesting." She dragged her eyes along my form with interest. That was... that was flirtatious. She was flirting with me.

Mouth suddenly dry, I swallowed pathetically. "And who does?"

"Well, I do, of course." She was good, practiced in coquettish smiles and enticing gazes. She reminded me of Lady Rycliffe in her youth. The girl she had been before her husband passed, when she could summon a man from across the room with nothing but a glance.

"Well, do be sure to let me know how I'm faring." Though my voice was strangled, the words were acceptable enough.

"Four," she offered with a coy note in her voice.

"Four?"

Her shoulder dipped in a playful shrug. "Out of ten. Room for improvement, certainly, but not dreadful."

A chuckle escaped my chest, loosening some of the tightness. "I shall take that under advisement. I do wonder, though, is it truly a benefit to achieve a ten? Surely, there is such a thing as too interesting."

I spun her with more ease. Now that I was no longer concentrating, the steps returned to me. Tentatively, I brushed a thumb across her waist—she wouldn't feel it through the layers of gown, chemise, and corset. But this was the closest I had been to a woman in years, and I couldn't help but take a moment to enjoy.

"That would depend entirely on the judge's opinion. But you, my lord, are being evasive."

"Am I?"

Her nod was definitive. "You are. You say you are not gaming but give no indication where you have been all these years." The words were demanding, but her tone was arch.

"Years?" I laughed. "How long have you been out in society? A quarter of an hour? You could not possibly know it has been years."

"Well, if I did not, that was surely a confirmation. And I shall not scold you for the impertinence of the question. All I shall say is that this is not my first season."

"No? I suppose that places you at a three and a half."

A laugh spilled from her, full and less studied than her manners had been thus far. "I am to be rated as well?"

"It is only fair."

"Very well. But your evasions grow tedious, my lord. Two," she popped the *t* between her teeth in a cheeky manner.

"I have been in Surrey. I suppose that takes me down to a one?"

This earned another giggle but it was less spontaneous than the last, more practiced. "Oh, at least. What is in Surrey?"

"North Downs, a river or two, Guildford, Box Hill, that sort of thing. Also my estate, Bennet Hall."

"Tell me of Bennet Hall," she requested.

I felt the smile curl up on the edge of my lip. "Ah, now that is interesting."

"What is?"

"You are very good with gentlemen."

She blanched. "I beg your pardon?"

"I just meant—you know men like to talk about their estates. I assume you would move on to horses next?"

"I had considered it," she replied pertly. The laugh from earlier had vanished from her countenance, leaving her stiff and lifeless in its wake.

My stomach sank and my hand twitched for a peppermint. I'd gone from sharing a mild flirtation to insulting her in the span of two sentences. I was fumbling this precisely as egregiously as expected.

"I have no interest in horses," I insisted, trying to ease the unintentional sting. I had been enjoying myself immensely, and I did not wish for this to end in disaster.

Why had I let it go so long? I used to be good with women.

I rushed to continue. "My vices lay... in other directions. And while I have a great deal of pride in my estate, it is not the sort of thing to intrigue a young lady in a ballroom. There is nothing scandalous about it at all. Bennet Hall is well maintained and profitable. The servants are paid well and loyal. And there is a tragic dearth of ghosts and other spirits." That earned me a giggle—feigned most likely, but I would accept what I was given gladly.

The last strains of the waltz faded, disintegrating into murmured chatter from the tables. Wordlessly, I guided her back to the wall where she found me, my hand hovering an inch or so off the small of her back.

"Is there an entail? Entails are always interesting," she asked, interest in her tone.

"There is..." I replied warily. Now, I could sense the beginnings of a fishing expedition.

"And who is to inherit? A son? Some hideous beast of a second cousin?"

"I do not believe the second cousin is any more hideous than the current occupant. Though I've not seen him in some years." My answer was carefully couched, but she didn't seem to catch it.

"Certainly a beast then," she insisted with a conspiratorial whisper. *So close to the truth.*

"I've no wife or children if that's what you were after," I said. It was sharper than intended.

Her eyes widened at my tone, a flush rising higher on her cheeks. And then, to my astonishment, she squared her shoulders, meeting my eyes. "It was, in point of fact. I see no reason why I should be reproached for it. We can continue to play coy, but to what purpose?"

"No," I blurted. "I suppose you're right."

"I usually am," she teased, her entire body sinking into the smile she offered.

I was strung too tight, an overdrawn bow. Her jest was not enough to release the arrow. I was, perhaps, pushing too much, too fast, straining unused muscles tonight. But she was stunning and sweet smelling—citrusy and floral. And better still, she had a backbone to her.

Tentative, testing, I pressed on. "And do you?"

"Do I have a wife and children? No." Her grin turned cheeky with that.

"That is disappointing—that would have put you at a seven at least."

The comment earned me another laugh, though something artificial remained. I hadn't yet made it back to the one real laugh.

"No husband either at present."

I opened my mouth to question the oddly specific nature of her words, when a shout rang out.

I jumped half out of my skin, spinning to find the source.

"Ten, nine, eight..."

What on ear—The unmasking.

My stomach dropped. How had I forgotten?

My gaze spun around the room. Ladies and gentlemen were fussing with the edges of their masks. Beside me, Lady Charlotte had already untied hers and was merely holding it in place. A strategic smile curved across her lips.

My heart hammered and my vision narrowed—darkness seeping in from the sides. Already, my stomach had found its way back from the floor, churning and swirling with agitation.

Instinctively, my hand found my pocket and I dipped inside, grasping the solitary peppermint. I pulled it free along with the wrapping papers I had stuffed there. It slipped through my trembling fingers to the floor. To the carpeted floor where someone promptly stepped on it, grinding it into the carpet.

"Five, four..."

"My lord? What is the matter?" That voice was soft and warm and too far away to reach me now. My empty hand found the edge of my mask, pressing it tighter still.

"Three, two..."

"I have to—goodbye." I wasn't entirely certain I hadn't offered those words to the door I was shoving my way through as I spilled out, the space between her side and the exit a blur.

I stumbled into an alley and leaned back against the wall, then slid down it to a crouch. There, in the stinking, filthy back alley, I dropped my head between my knees. I tried to concentrate on my breathing, but the stench threatened to upend my stomach just the same as the panic.

And then, to make the situation even worse, the heavens opened up. There was no drizzle, no forewarning. One moment the evening was muggy but dry. The next was a flood of biblical proportions.

Fortunately, the rain seemed to shock some of the panic out of my system, and I rose on shaky legs. Crawford was right. He would be horribly insufferable for it.

The rain seeped between the mask and my skin, leaving it even more sensitized and irritated than usual. With trembling fingers, I yanked at the knot, but it held fast. Frantically, I tore at the ceramic and yanked it over my head—scraping the skin of my forehead as I pulled it free. I tossed it to the ground where it shattered before me, shards spilling across the alley in a wretched mosaic.

I dragged my hand across the newly revealed mottled, gnarled flesh.

"Are you all right, dearie?" A well-used voice asked from

farther in the alley. Startled, I yanked my fingers through soaked hair, tugging it over my forehead and cheek. The sound of heeled slippers knocking on cobblestones echoed against rain-soaked pavement.

She stepped into the lamplight. Tangled hair, the kind that only came from a man's fingers in the throes of passion, topped a pale face with smeared rouge. She wore only a corset and chemise and might as well not have bothered for all it covered with the rain.

She approached slowly, tentatively. "Do you need—Oh, good lord! Your face!"

And with that, my stomach made its final rebellion. Peppermint and gin swirled in the sopping gutter droppings at her feet.

Chapter Four

JAMES PLACE, LONDON - JUNE 6, 1814

CHARLOTTE

"Could I have peppermint tea this morning, Imogen?" I begged pathetically between my early and midmorning reckonings with the recently repurposed milk pail.

"Of course, my lady." She scurried off with more enthusiasm than she usually had for her work. Sensitive stomach, that one.

My head pounded in irritation with each retch. Last night had been a disaster. Not only had I failed to secure a suitor but I had driven a man from the club in terror.

A knock signaled the arrival of Mrs. Courtland, not Imogen, with the tea tray.

"She didn't have the constitution for it?" I asked, self-deprecation dripping from my pores along with the sweat.

"Not this morning, my lady. I take it things did not go as you hoped last night?"

"Lord, does everyone know?" I asked, pathetic whining in my tone.

"Of course not. It is but a woman's intuition," she insisted as she crouched beside me. I'd half fallen out of bed in my effort to reach the pail in time and it had been easier to simply remain on the floor. At some point, I'd propped myself against the wall, and the cool plaster was soothing against my back.

"Intuition and requests for peppermint and ginger tea?"

"That as well," she agreed with a smile, running her fingers through my sweat-dampened curls, tugging them back from where they clung to my face.

"I need a husband, Mrs. C." It was a pathetic, indisputable sort of statement, but it was a relief to acknowledge the obvious.

"You'll find him. Someone kind, but strong enough to endure your mouth, and smart as you—smarter maybe." Her lips pressed together in something between a smile and a frown.

"Such a man could only be fictional. And, at present, my only requirement is alive."

"What happened last night? Surely there was someone?"

"There was, or I thought there was. I'd never met him before. The Earl of Champaign. Do you know of him?"

"I do not, my lady. I can make inquiries, though, if you think it worthwhile."

"It is certainly a wasted effort. But he is my only option at present. Be discreet, would you?"

"Of course."

My stomach gave a disgruntled lurch, and I took a quick sip of the tea. It settled for the first time in hours and I drank deep.

~

Mrs. C was a miracle worker.

It was the effort of a few hours at the market to discover

the mysterious earl who had recently returned to Berkeley Square. And to recover the intelligence that he was set to return to the country in but a day's time.

Apparently, he was the talk of the neighborhood. Lord Champaign had arrived in town for the first time in years only a few days previously, refused all visitors, and paid no calls. He was causing quite the stir and more than a few offenses. It certainly did not bode well for my scheme, but I was out of options.

After testing the strength of the lacings on my stays, Imogen helped me into the loosest gown I owned, a cream, floral thing with pleats at the front. I had never been particularly fond of it, and today was no exception, but it did the job credibly enough. Unfortunately, in the harsh light of day, my secrets were less easily concealed.

The entire ride, I fretted over how I might explain my impertinence. And then, once he accepted the explanation, how I might seduce him. And while I did that, how I was to hide the growing curve of my belly. I had no plan, and no time to form one, and no hope.

I arrived outside a bright red door, bold against the tan brick facade of the house, with no better scheme than the one I set off with. Seduce him. Somehow.

At my knock, the door opened to reveal a footman, quite young but well liveried. His astonishment at my arrival was plain in his dropped jaw and stammer. He was a pimply, bespectacled young man, and his gaping mouth revealed a chipped front tooth. He showed me into a well-furnished drawing room with a quiet plea to remain.

Youthful, feminine touches filled the room, and not an insignificant number of them. Powder-blue upholstery with gold accents covered the furnishings and curtains. The walls were painted a muted yellow with delicate blue flowers added near the ceiling. Lord Champaign had been very clear that he had no wife, but his drawing room disagreed.

My insides attempted rebellion at the thought. If he had lied about his marital status, my only prospect was well and truly gone. Surely Mrs. C's intelligence would have included a wife.

Afternoon sun streamed through the window, baking the chair I shifted to and fro on. It was too hot and my situation too tenuous. I could not cast up my accounts in the ficus beside me. It was unladylike, unbecoming of a future wife—and the scent was not conducive to a seduction.

Harsh whispers spilled in from the hall, an argument if the tone was any indication, but distant enough that I could not make out the words.

Abruptly, the drawing room door flew open and a servant stepped through. A tall, incredibly thin fellow of perhaps thirty with perfectly coiffed red curls.

"Apologies, my lady. It can be quite warm in this room in the afternoon. I will just close the curtains for you. Lord Champaign will be in shortly, he was just finishing some things in his study."

"Thank you," I replied, striving to hide the confusion in my tone. It mixed with relief at the intelligence that Lord Champaign would at least see me.

The man drew the floral curtains closed, casting the room into a darkness far more substantial than I had anticipated given the hour. But that was good, better for seduction.

Task completed, he busied himself lighting candles on the far side of the room. A few of them topped the mantel above the unlit fireplace. He found a few more on the bookshelves that crowded the brick hearth and lit them as well. The effect was a romantic glow. A convenient perfection.

"Perhaps you would be more comfortable over here, my lady? In the light?" He gestured toward a settee facing the fireplace. Even better. Why had I chosen a chair in the first place? Settees were much better for seduction—surely.

I settled as indicated and the servant slipped silently out of the room. One minute became five and staring at the candlelight grew tedious.

Eventually, I could stand it no longer and rose, approaching one of the bookshelves. Lord Champaign, or whoever had furnished this room, had exceptional taste. Everything from Homer to Sidney, Shakespeare to that authoress I liked lined the shelf. I pulled one, then two tomes out. All were well cared for, regardless of age, but clearly read. The spines cracked and the corners were worn, but no pages were bent.

"I must admit, I never thought to meet you again." The honeyed tenor of Lord Champaign rang from behind me. I spun, hand pressed to my racing heart.

He was even taller than I remembered, looming over me and half cast in shadow. His chin bore a full day's growth, adding to the angular, sharp picture he presented.

After nodding toward the settee, he took a seat himself, leaving the left side free for me. This was proving to be easier than I'd expected. I placed myself beside him, back straight and gown pulled away from my belly, hand glued to my knee to keep it that way.

"My lord. I trust you are well?" I began.

"Better than last night." He spoke into the fireplace. The corner of his mouth fixed in a crooked, wry sort of smile.

"May I—that is..."

"It had nothing to do with you. Do not worry yourself over it."

"All right..."

"I apologize for the rudeness of my leave taking. I was feeling unwell. May I ask what brought you to my drawing room?" Curiosity tinged his voice but not enough for him to turn to face me.

"Well, I enjoyed our conversation and dance, and I was worried after your abrupt departure."

A laugh escaped him, a single burst, sharp and bitter. "Of course."

"I did and I was." I sounded pathetic even to my ears. Somewhere in the last few sentences, I'd lost any ground gained by the flickering candlelight and lengthy furnishing. His tone wasn't at all receptive to a seduction and I hadn't the slightest notion of how to change that.

"Even before I left you standing there, I was coarse and unrefined." He continued to direct his speech into the cold coals. An overgrown lock of hair flopped down in front of his eye, but it didn't seem to bother him at all. "I do not mean to be, of course. But it has been many years since I was in polite company. Even longer since I was in the company of a young lady. I'm out of practice."

"I was not offended."

His answering laugh was cold. "Why are you truly here?"

With the kind of bravery that could only be born from desperation, I lifted a hand. Tentatively, I reached forward to brush the wayward strand of dark golden hair away from his face.

He gasped and caught my wrist in midair. His grasp was cool, firm, and unyielding and so, so *big*. Somehow even bigger than his hand seemed the night before. Where did he find gloves large enough to fit? Though, I suppose he had not the night before.

"My lord?" I breathed, my heart racing. I had pushed too hard and too fast. My plan, what little of it there was, balanced on the edge of a knife.

"The truth. Now." His words stung with anger and a slate note. But still he wouldn't face me.

"I enjoyed our time to—"

"I said the truth. You are trying to seduce me. Why?"

"I beg your pardon?" I was all bluster.

Even *that* accusation hadn't been enough to catch his eye.

"You are attempting a seduction. Why— Oh. Oh... You are her." His fingers loosened and I yanked my hand free.

"I beg your pardon?" I repeated, inane. It was the only question available to me that didn't include curses.

He knew. He had heard. Word of my condition had reached Surrey. My stomach swirled again dangerously.

"You are with child." He said it simply, plainly, as if it weren't the ruination of every dream I had ever had. And even that earth-shattering statement was not enough to earn his gaze.

"Look at me!" I demanded, a knot of frustration catching in my throat. "If you're going to have me bodily tossed out, you should at least look at me."

Still, his chin never moved, his gaze did not flick to mine. "Were you hoping I would marry you?" he asked, dipping his head to contemplate the hand in his lap.

There was no point in withholding the truth. As it was, he would surely throw me out when he regained his senses.

I sighed, a dramatic, pathetic sound. "Yes. And yes." It was difficult to force the words out through my pinhole throat.

My life, such as I knew it, was over.

"Do you know the father?"

I couldn't help the responding eye roll. "Yes."

"He was the one spouting off at the club last night?"

"Mr. Wesley Parker." He nodded, face still carefully studying the fireplace.

"You could have asked. It would have been much easier than whatever this sham was," he muttered.

My heart stopped.

"What?"

"You could have asked me," he repeated slowly, his tone mirroring the astonishment I felt.

"Truly?" I breathed. "I could have waltzed in here and spun you a story about a man that left me with child and is not only refusing to take responsibility but is actively spreading lies about me to the entire *ton*. I could have begged you to wed me, to save me and the parasite growing inside from utter ruination and destitution."

"Yes." He paused before continuing. "You do not wish to marry me, of course, so I will spare you."

"I do not—no, I rather think marriage would solve a great many of my problems."

"And cause you a great many more. At least marriage to me. You should know that now. I'm not... I was not a good husband to my late wife. And I'm not what I once was."

The speech was a great many words and none of them an outright denial. The intelligence that he was a widower barely registered among the astonishing implications. He couldn't be suggesting...

"You—that was not a no."

"It was a warning. You should not ask. Or throw yourself at me. You do not understand what you're asking for." His voice was thin and brittle, and his eyes remained fixed on his hand.

"You would consider it?"

"I— You do not wish to marry me," he repeated. My heart leapt, again, it was still not a denial. He could insist until he grew old and gray that *I* did not want to marry *him*. That could not make it so.

"I do not believe you grasp the precariousness of my situation, sir."

"Nor you mine." His tone dipped into something low and graveled, nearly a growl.

"So explain it to me." It would take more than his

whiskey-smooth voice raked over the coals to scare me away when there was even the barest hope he would agree.

With a great heaving sigh, he dragged long fingers through his hair. And then, slowly, as if he was afraid I would startle, he turned to face me. The candlelight, once so romantic, caught the right side of his face for the first time.

Air vanished from the room as I took in the sight of him.

Chapter Five

84 BROOK STREET, LONDON - JUNE 6, 1816

LEE

With a heavy exhale, I turned toward her. My skin crawled, tetchy and exposed. Not only the mangled, misshapen flesh of my forehead, cheek, and jaw, but all of it. Every inch of me.

It had been years, if ever, since I had *chosen* to show someone my face.

The staff had seen my scars while they were forming. The whole village learned the news before I woke and looked on me with pity, rather than disgust. Everyone else had been accidental viewings, people who caught me unprepared and unaware, like the poor woman last night.

The scars were, perhaps, the least of the horrors that Lady Charlotte should know about me before charging ahead with her ill-conceived scheme. But they were almost certainly the fastest way to convince her of the futility of her plot.

First I received the requisite gasp. That was to be expected. It was followed by a ladylike pressing of her fingers to her mouth, hiding her dropped jaw. Her eyes narrowed on the angry, twisted knot on my cheekbone.

I recognized, vaguely, while staring at the space between us on the settee, my gaze boring into it, that I was shaking. Just a little. I could only hope she would be too distracted by my face to notice. It would not do to be both hideous and cowardly, and only one of those was within my control.

Time had no meaning. This moment would last until the sun ceased to rise. It stretched into an agonizing eternity, while this beautiful woman starred in abject horror at the sight of me. Surely she'd had time to run by now. It had been longer than a second certainly. Was she frozen in terror?

Gathering my courage, I flicked my eyes back up to hers. She *was* frozen, her hand outstretched between us—as if she planned to—that could not be.

"What happened?" she breathed, a thready vibrato in the throaty tone.

"Does it matter? Surely you do not wish to press forward with this harebrained scheme."

"It isn't harebrained." Her eyes flashed in irritation. Without thought, I felt the corner of my lip rising. It was almost charming, the way she was more offended at the insult to her ill-considered, half-baked seduction than she was frightened at the sight of me.

I raised a skeptical brow above the unmangled eye. Something uncoiled deep in my chest. "Please explain the totality of it then. Because from what I've gleaned, you tracked down a man you met once, whose face you had never seen the entirety of. You presented yourself at his home, unannounced, to seduce him into marrying you. And you merely prayed he wouldn't notice when you popped out a child in—what—seven months? That might be the most ill-conceived plan I've ever heard."

"I was informed that you were returning to the country

tomorrow. I had limited time to work with." Her hand, the one that still hung between us, had unfrozen into a series of defensive gestures.

"And last night was what? Husband hunting? It was the right dress for it, I'll grant you that." It had offered her up as a masterpiece for appreciation. But she could hardly require my confirmation to know how effective the buttery cream and gold silk cupping her bust had been.

She pursed her lips to the side and shot me a look I was certain she intended to be fearsome. I bit back another smile before forging ahead, refusing to be distracted by kittenish irritation.

"And the father? The whore's pipe running his mouth at the gaming tables?"

"Mr. Parker," she repeated. At my blank stare, she continued. "He is tall—shorter than you, of course—but tall." She gestured between us, raising her hand to somewhere over her head but below mine, as if that was a useful measure. "With brown hair and eyes?"

"That describes half the *ton*. You could not have selected a less repugnant one?"

"I beg your pardon?" She was affronted, it was plain on her wide eyes and dropped jaw. It was actually quite amusing, she took offense in the oddest of places.

"They're all interchangeable, the lazy, degenerate lot of them."

"I hardly think that is—"

"And why hasn't he been made to take responsibility? Where is your father?"

"Well, he doesn't know!" she snapped. Her whiskey-colored eyes rolled in a brazen display.

"Oh, of course." I resisted the urge to roll my eyes as well. "Why would you tell your father? It's not as though he could offer you some manner of protection. You should throw yourself at the nearest stranger instead."

"My father already arranged one repugnant match. And that was when my reputation was spotless. I should hate to see what he came up with this time around."

"You are widowed?"

Her full lips twisted into a sneer. "No, I am still married. That is why I'm desperately throwing myself at you on this settee." She rolled her eyes skyward again. Impertinent thing. "Of course I'm widowed."

"How long ago was it? Could the child be his?"

"Oh, I hadn't thought of that! You are brilliant! I am saved!" The back of her hand found her forehead in a feigned swoon.

I raised a brow again. It was a growing struggle to contain my chuckle, but I did actually wish for an answer.

"He passed seven months ago," she added, taking my silent demand for a serious response as intended.

I glanced down at her stomach. The fabric of her gown settled around her waist, pulling just enough to hint at the rounding beneath. I wasn't an expert by any means, but I couldn't think that she was any more than four months along, likely less.

Dragging my eyes back up her form, they caught on the heaving bosom she had on full display once again.

"Are you quite finished interrogating me now?" A prim defensive note rang in her tone.

"Hardly. And there is no need to be so high in your instep. You're the one who came to me."

"You still have not answered my singular question. Do not think I've missed the evasion. What happened to you?"

Irritation snapped through me at the reminder. My stomach turned with it.

"I owe you nothing, in point of fact. You should go. Obviously, you won't be walking down the aisle—not with me. So there is truly no point in maintaining this farce of a conversation."

"No. Explain yourself." Contumelious, lovely little creature—she was. Demanding and fetching in equal measure. It was infuriating.

"I am not discussing it. You best entrap the next sorry candidate for matrimony."

"You are my sole prospect. These scars are old. How long ago was it?"

"Six years," I replied distractedly before remembering myself. "I do not understand why we're discussing this. Surely there is someone better out there. Speak to your father. He will find someone who will have you."

She forged on as if I hadn't spoken at all. "And you've just been hiding yourself away? Ever since?"

"I am not hiding. Half of Surrey knows. It is only that... I don't like to subject ladies to the sight of me. I avoid town."

"And what, precisely, is *your* brilliant plan then? Never return to London except for events where you can wear a mask? And *you* found *my* scheme wanting."

"It has been quite effective for years. And it's certainly no less poorly considered than yours."

"You are an earl. Surely you are in need of a wife. And an heir. How do you propose to achieve either if you refuse to be seen by ladies?"

"I hardly see what concern that is of yours."

"You need a wife. I need a husband." She said it simply, plainly. As if it were a fundamental truth I needed to accept. The sky was blue. The grass was green. I needed a wife. And she needed a husband.

I needed a wife.

She needed a husband.

She was already with child. We would never have to consummate. I could fulfill my duty without—

"I would have some conditions." The words escaped me before I had fully realized the decision I had made. My heart tripped before the words solidified in my mind. But I could not lament them once they were free.

Her eyes widened and she nodded, far too eager.

The idea took shape as the words poured free. "I—we would... I would require that you live with me. At my estate. Until after the babe is born, and for several months after. For plausibility."

"Of course." Her nod was persistent, never ceasing, likely sensing victory.

"I would expect discretion in any arrangements you made thereafter. Not this fellow—Porker?"

Her brow furrowed. "You do not expect fidelity?"

"This is not a love match—obviously. I would not expect faithfulness. I cannot expect you to... I expect prudence."

"Yes, of course." Her eyes grew brighter, and her nods surer.

"I will put off my return to the country for a few days. Take some time. Consider your situation. Let me know your decision, and I will approach your father with an offer."

"I do not require my father's permission."

"I will approach your father." I brokered no argument with my tone. This prospective marriage may be a sham, but it would be a properly conducted sham. "Are there any conditions, things you wish to add?"

"None that I can name at present. This did not go precisely the way I planned." Her cheeks had taken on a becoming flush, barely visible in the dark.

For perhaps the first time in years, I wished a room was brighter. I wished to see...

I had to clear my throat before beginning. "No, I'd

imagine not. Take a few days, a week. I can procure a special license without trouble."

"I-I do not know what to say. I am half worried that anything I say will have you revoking your offer."

Her fear was not unfounded. Even now, I could not believe I had rendered the proposal. It was a wretched, hasty, reckless, slapdash notion.

"You're not wrong."

Her eyes widened for a moment before her dark lashes fluttered. She straightened and leaned back, stealing the distractingly delightful curve of her bosom.

"I suppose I should be off then?" She asked, nodding seemingly to herself. She rose and thrust her hand before me expectantly. I stared at it a long moment before comprehension dawned and I took it. My hand dwarfed hers while we shook on our absurd little—potential—agreement.

"Good evening, Lord Champaign."

"Good evening, Lady Charlotte," I said. Escorting her over to the door. I pulled it open only for Brigsby to half fall into the room.

Rather than the screech the display deserved, Lady Charlotte chuckled softly and strode around him, then down the hall where Jack awaited to open the door properly.

Good lad, that one. Much more agreeable than nosey valets.

She stepped out into the late-evening setting sun, Jack trailing to help her into the waiting carriage.

"So, that was a gently bred young lady? I do not recall them being quite so... pragmatic," Brigsby commented with a smug smile, all but confessing to eavesdropping. I merely cuffed him over the ear in response to such impertinence.

"She may be my wife. Have a care how you speak of her." Even as I delivered the warning, my stomach churned uneasily at the thought. No man in the world was less deserving of a wife—well, perhaps the wretched Mr. Parker. But surely no other man.

"Yes, *my lord*," Brigsby added snidely. "Shall I have directions sent to begin preparing the countess's chambers at Bennet Hall?"

"Not just yet," I replied, then gnawed on my lower lip until the copper tang of blood filled my mouth.

What had I done?

Chapter Six

84 BROOK STREET, LONDON - JUNE 9, 1816

LEE

"Yes," Lady Charlotte—or Lady James, more accurately—nodded, bronze curls brushing the pale column of her throat with the movement.

She perched primly across from me in the same sitting room where I made my offer a few days ago. This time, she wore a fetching butter-yellow dress that did less to conceal her belly. I, too, made no efforts to conceal my scars. That choice left me peevish, uneasy.

"Yes?" I reiterated, demanding confirmation.

Her response was entirely predictable. I had all but expected it when I gave full consideration to her situation during each sleepless night since her attempted seduction. She had been desperate, truly desperate, to come to me. And to forge ahead when she had gazed upon my scars... She would not change her mind.

Still, I appreciated that she had taken the time I offered. She may have found herself in such lamentable circumstances, but she had considered this solution carefully. I would not complain about a sensible wife.

"Yes, I would like to marry you. We should marry. If you are still amenable to it, that is." She picked at her fingernails warily in a discomfited display that I suspected was uncommon for her.

I nodded. My education hadn't addressed this situation, and I hadn't the foggiest idea of the protocol for such a moment. And I certainly hadn't anticipated leaving London a married man. But it seemed I would.

"Very well." I dipped a hand into my pocket, pulled the ring out from where it was hiding, tucked away for days, and held it aloft on an open palm. "I suppose you'll be needing this."

Elegant fingers with feminine nails plucked the band out of my hand but didn't slip it on. Instead, she eyed the carved gold and diamond cluster thoughtfully. It wasn't the largest in the collection, but it was the least garish.

"There are others if you prefer something more ornate," I added.

"No, it's lovely. I wasn't expecting..."

"It was my mother's or grandmother's possibly." Speaking mostly to fill the silence, confusion overtaking me when she held the ring back out to me.

"You're supposed to do the honors," she explained, one corner of her mouth tipping up in a teasing smile.

I groaned. "Do not tell me you're one of those."

"One of those?"

"A romantic."

A little chuckle escaped her. "I attempted to seduce you on that very settee not three days ago. Hardly the actions of a romantic. It is only that I prefer things to be done properly."

"And properly involves the entire rigamarole? Do I need to get on one knee as well?"

"The ring will do." She held her hand out expectantly, and I slipped the jewel onto the appropriate finger. It slid on easily but fit securely. That was good. One less thing to worry over.

"There. That is taken care of. Is your father in town?"

She snatched her hand out of mine, a frown marring her lovely face. "Yes, but it is entirely unnecessary. I am four and twenty and widowed. I hardly require his permission."

"Lord, you are a child." I sighed. "*I* prefer things done properly as well. His name?"

"I am hardly a child. And you are what? Nine and twenty?" She snapped, still evading.

"Add six. And do not think you can distract me so easily."

She flicked her gaze to the window, refusing to meet mine. "He is Lord Francis Belleville—St. James Square, Belleville House. But should you find yourself regretting the decision to pay him a visit, you have only yourself to blame."

"I've regretted nearly every decision I have made since I returned to town. Why should this one be any different?"

She rolled her eyes. An irritating habit I would clearly need to accustom myself to.

I handed her the pile of documents from the side table. "Have a look through these and see if they meet with your approval before I show them to your father."

"You had settlements drawn up?" A divot formed between her brows as her head tipped to the side like a befuddled spaniel.

"I like things done properly as well. Of course I had settlements drawn up."

"My dowry is... not significant." Her head tipped down to the parchment clasped in her hand as she avoided my gaze.

"You have a dowry? I had a man look into your late husband. I presumed he lost the lot of it at the gaming tables."

"You—Why would you?" Her eyes shot to mine.

"I agreed to wed a complete stranger. You thought I

wouldn't look into your past? Confirm you were who you said you were? Speaking of, your Christian name *is* Charlotte, right? My solicitor had some difficulty confirming it.."

"Allow me a guess, Wayland?"

My lifted brow earned another eye roll.

"*He* takes great pleasure in refusing to learn my name. Or feigning ignorance. He could not rest with swindling my husband's entire fortune—he must mock me as well." Most of that speech was muttered under her breath while she flipped disinterestedly through the settlement agreement.

I refrained from listing the more amusing options that had been thrown about. Clementia was my favorite.

The exact moment she reached the section regarding pin money and funds to be settled on her child was apparent in the way her eyes widened. Leighton was right. I was being more generous than was common. I bit the corner of my lip to keep from smirking, waiting to see if she would protest the amount.

"This is..." She cleared her throat. "This is acceptable."

"I hoped it would be. Do you have any other conditions?"

"No, none."

"I suppose I should be off to your father then. Do you have a preference for a date?"

"As soon as possible. You said you can get a special license?"

"Yes, your father's house is near the bishop. It should be an easy thing. I assume he still has no idea of your... condition."

"He does not." Her cheeks flushed a pretty peach.

"And you would prefer it to remain that way?"

"I would, yes."

"Very well. I will do my best." She caught the corner of her lower lip between her teeth. "I will be off then. You are welcome to stay and tour the house with Crawford, my butler.

Or I can send you a note when I've finished. Whichever you prefer."

"I think I will stay if it is all the same to you."

With a nod, I set off. The day was nice enough to justify the walk, though I fully intended to use the carriage. Or I had, until the precise moment I was faced with it.

Instead, I pulled my hat low and my collar up, tucking my chin like an absurd turtle, and walked. It was closer to a scurry, truly—as quick as I could manage without drawing undue attention.

At Belleville House, I was shown in by a rotund butler who eyed me warily when I removed my hat. My fingers itched for a peppermint. How had I forgotten them?

The man collected himself admirably but nearly collapsed when I stated my purpose.

This was to be a long afternoon.

At length, I was led into a cramped, poorly lit study. The man, Lord Belleville, stood to greet me but his face sparked no memories.

He was tall with formerly dark, now graying, hair, and his eyes tripped along my scars. Fortunately, he gave no more overt reaction.

"Take a seat, Lord?"

"Champaign." I settled into the chair across from him, my back ramrod straight, legs crunched up beneath me, too long for the furnishing. This room was too small and too dim as well. Typically, I preferred the dark, but something sinister lurked here. Nothing I could identify, but I sensed it all the same.

"Higgins mentioned you would like a private audience. I must admit to some confusion, my lord." The man spoke carefully, measuring his words, his gaze still caught on the knotted skin of my cheek.

"Yes. I've recently made the acquaintance of your daughter, Lady James. I find her charming and I feel that we would suit well. With your permission, I should like to ask her to be my wife." I, too, spoke with caution, reciting the words I had practiced with Brigs that morning, and every morning since Lady James arrived at my door.

Desperate for a break from the eyes locked on my cheek, I turned toward the window, offering him the left side. The velvet curtains were closed, light streaming through only at the edges—the exact way they did in a carriage.

My stomach gave a tentative revolt but I swallowed and clenched my jaw.

"I see," he said, his gaze finally moving to examine the whole of my person. I fought back the urge to fill the silence with inane chatter. That inclination was unlike me, accustomed as I was to silence. "You find her charming," he repeated.

"Yes..." I replied tentatively, turning back to face him.

"You wish to wed her."

Was this man determined to rehash the entirety of my speech?

"Yes."

"Fine," he replied without the slightest indication of his opinion on the subject.

"Fine?" *Lord, now he had me doing it.*

"You may have her."

"You do not—there is nothing you wish to know? About me? About my situation?"

"Not particularly," he replied dully, his eyes tracing over my scars again, mouth twisted into something like disgust.

"Because I assure you, I am more than capable of providing financially for your daughter."

"Good for you." Condescension dripped from his voice and the curve of his upper lip.

"Do you wish to see a copy of the settlements?" I pulled

the folded parchment from my pocket and handed it over. He took it with an eye roll—the mannerism not at all charming on his visage. Flicking through the pages of the document with even less attention on it than his daughter, he, too, paused in the same place. His gaze flicked to mine with a raised brow.

"You're overpaying."

"It is what is due to my bride."

A derisive snort escaped him before he snatched a quill out of the nearby inkwell and signed his name with a disinterested flourish.

"My felicitations, my lord," he graveled, a sneer on his lips.

"You—I don't... You do not care—"

"I can see why she chose you. Best of luck." He folded the document back up and set it on the edge of his desk with a snap. "You may go now."

I snatched the document off his desk and strode toward the door. I made it all the way to the alley beside the house before my breathing turned ragged and desperate.

It was the work of nearly a quarter of an hour before I was in a state to visit the bishop. Of course, that was the moment I recognized I had forgotten my hat. Again.

Brigsby hadn't been pleased to have to retrieve it from Wayland's a few days past. If I asked him to fetch it from *that* house, it was entirely likely he would give notice. Nor did I particularly wish to walk the entirety of London without it, scars bare for the viewing.

With a sigh, I returned and knocked on the damn door again. The butler answered, my hat in hand, shoved it at me, and slammed the door shut.

At least I couldn't say that I hadn't been warned.

Chapter Seven

84 BROOK STREET, LONDON - JUNE 9, 1816

CHARLOTTE

I TRAILED a finger along leather spines of the books as I studiously feigned hearing loss. The collection lining the shelves was even more eclectic than I had first thought.

A man, presumably the butler, was arguing with the servant who had been listening at the door the other day. Their tone was a whisper, their volume was anything but.

"It's not proper. There has been no betrothal announcement." That was the butler.

"He is paying his addresses to her father as we speak."

"There is no chaperone! And the engagement isn't finalized. Her father could well throw him out." Well, the butler wasn't wrong about that. But it seemed unlikely. Father would be thrilled to be relieved of the burden of me. I wasn't a burden, of course. I hadn't asked him for anything, not since my marriage. And I wouldn't, not ever, not for anything. My father had made it more than clear that he didn't harbor any sentiment toward me, nor did he concern himself with my well-being. In truth I had not spoken to him since my mother's passing.

"Yes, and if she has seen the empty countess's chambers, she will be scandalized beyond belief," the other servant hissed.

I choked back a laugh. The former eavesdropper turned victim was certainly amusing.

"It is not proper!"

"Yes, you've said that. But his lordship said you were to escort her through the house. She may wish to make changes to suit her tastes. If you won't, then I will."

The butler scoffed. "You will do no such thing. That is my role. Go press a shirt or something."

"Show the lady the rooms. All of them."

"Fine, but I want my strenuous objections noted." The butler shooed the other one, a valet perhaps, down the hall and turned toward me. I kept my focus on the tomes before me, but out of the corner of my eye, I caught his startle at the open door. Yes, discussing me in front of an open door was also improper, sir.

"My lady, I am Crawford. I've served as butler for the Champaign family for nearly a decade. It would be my honor to show you around the house if you like. Mrs. Fitzroy, the housekeeper, would join us, however, she has remained in Surrey." I observed him as he gave an obsequious bow after his speech. He was a stout little man, with a sweaty forehead and mousy brown hair, and he carried himself with a self-importance that seemed unearned.

"Lady James," I said, pressing a hand to my chest. "I would be most grateful for a tour. If you think it would not be improper, of course."

From the hall, I caught a snort of laughter. The valet must be eavesdropping again. The man in front of me flushed, splotchy and peaked.

"Right this way, if you please." He directed me to trail after him, out of the drawing room and down the hall. Apparently, he deemed it improper to address my comment.

He indicated a study to the left but did not open the door. A few steps farther to the right was a music room. I was pleased to find that it was already outfitted with a pianoforte.

We turned a corner to a lengthy hall that served as portrait gallery. Family dating back several centuries stared down at me in disapproval. Crawford prattled on about their various heroic feats and relations.

Yes, I am about to sully your ranks. What of it?

The paintings appeared to be in chronological order, if the dress was any indication. Slowly the gown silhouettes shrank to something more familiar. Always light of hair and eyes, the family resemblance was stark.

And there at the very end was Lord Champaign, perhaps a decade younger than he was at present, unscarred and unbearably handsome. And he wasn't alone.

Beside him was an ethereal young lady. White-blonde hair topped her heart-shaped face. Her eyes were too big for her head, which should have been off-putting but instead it was becoming. Her nose was pert and her lips fit her face with a perfect bow, fuller on top than the bottom. Her frame was lithe and her gown was a lovely white silk that draped her form elegantly.

"—and of course you know Lord Champaign. This is the late Lady Champaign. This portrait was commissioned as a wedding gift from her parents."

I had a thousand questions, and I could not ask this man any of them. The valet, perhaps, but not Crawford. He guided me through a corridor and into a massive dining room. Someone, presumably the late Lady Champaign, had decorated using a shade of cream in every room. She had added a different accent color in each for variance. The effect was cohesive and elegant, without being dull. For the dining room she had selected a deep rose-pink shade. The breakfast room Crawford led me to next was a pale blue.

I followed the butler through empty halls and unused rooms all the way up the steps.

"—of course, there are fewer guest rooms here than in Surrey. We have six here, but there are twelve at Bennet Hall. Those are all down this direction and if you turn left, you'll find the family rooms."

He showed me guest room after guest room, each a different color for distinction. One thing was becoming readily apparent: Lord Champaign was wealthy, very wealthy. After years of economizing under my husband, the tasteful display of affluence was astonishing. And it was tasteful—nothing was ostentatious, merely of fine construction and considered for the situation of the room.

As we forged deeper into the house, the apprehension left by Lady Champaign faded to the background. I had been in an unhappy marriage where I survived rather than thrived. And one of the bigger points of contention in that marriage had been my husband's determination to lose every last coin at the gaming tables. If this house was any indication, that would not be a concern with Lord Champaign.

While some might call me mercenary, I considered myself practical. Marriage was a challenging enough prospect under the best of circumstances—which ours certainly would not be. There was no need to add financial concerns to the clutter.

Crawford turned back the way we came, traversing the landing at the top of the stairs to the family wing.

"Crawford? Does Lord Champaign have any living family?"

"I'm afraid not, my lady. His parents were not blessed with any more children. His father passed when he was quite young, when Lord Champaign was but four and twenty, I believe. And his mother passed a few years ago."

So much death... The poor man.

"I am sorry to hear it."

He nodded, pausing for a moment before proceeding with the tour as if our exchange was banal and inconsequential.

"This is the nursery, my lady." He opened the first door in the family wing. I peered inside. This room was decked in a pale yellow shade, slightly offset from the cream.

When I had first arrived at my late husband's home, I was shown a very similar room on an identical tour. That one had been a soft blue color before I had gotten ahold of it.

A few months into our marriage, when I was still attempting to make the best of things, my courses were late. Late enough that I found myself wondering, hoping even. On a whim, I had painted a forest scene that spanned the entirety of one wall. I was so excited to show Ralph that night, but he had scoffed and ordered a servant to return it to its appropriate state. The next morning my courses came.

I nodded at Crawford and backed away. He shut the door and escorted me past a few unused family rooms with nothing but a peek inside. "These are the countess's rooms, my lady," he said with a hint of pride in his tone. It seemed the man had overcome his trepidations.

The rooms were all very proper—a sitting room, a closet, and a boudoir, papered in a pleasing grayish green with accents of both colors. The bed was an impressive four poster carved in cherry wood with delicate leaves and vines etched into the posts and headboard.

And there it was, the connecting door. The bane of my existence. So unimposing in appearance while facilitating a husband's impositions on his wife.

"Through there, of course, are his lordship's rooms." I

nodded absently, feigning ignorance as to the function of said door.

The late countess had impeccable taste. If I learned nothing else today, that was clear.

Every inch of this household was spotless too, even the unused rooms. It was something of a surprise as I was given to understand that Lord Champaign rarely made use of this house. The staff surely ran like a finely tuned Swiss watch, like the one Crawford kept checking surreptitiously.

"Am I keeping you from something?" I asked pointedly.

"Of course not, my lady. I only expected his lordship back sooner."

I had too, come to think of it. Hopefully he had not met with trouble at Father's or with the bishop. I had barely secured the man's proposal—if one could even call it that—in the first place. I feared one too many challenges and he would give up on the concept entirely.

"Are you staying for supper, my lady?"

"I... do not know."

A cheerful voice from behind me added, "Of course she is. What kind of question is that, Crawford?" The eavesdropping valet had arrived, and Lord Champaign, in all of his impossibly tall glory, hovered behind him. Seemingly only a little worse—more tightness around the eyes—for having met with my father.

"Please do," he added. And just like that, I was attending supper.

Chapter Eight

84 BROOK STREET, LONDON - JUNE 9, 1816

LEE

WE STRODE to the dining room, her arm tucked in mine. Upon reflection, I was shocked to find that my offer to stay for supper hadn't been perfunctory or obligatory. I truly did wish for her to dine with me. Usually, after the company of others, I ached for the quiet.

She settled across from me, and it was as though I was looking upon her with new eyes. Her father... No wonder she hadn't wanted to involve him.

My parents hadn't been overly demonstrative with affection, but I could never imagine my father dismissing me so. And to think she had anticipated it. What had her life been?

"Did you meet with success today?" She asked politely between sips of white soup. She gave no outward indication of her enjoyment, and I was wound too tight to truly taste it. I could only hope it impressed.

"I suppose that would depend on your definition of success."

"I did warn you." Her brow raised pointedly.

"You did. I bow to your superior knowledge of precisely how repugnant your family members are."

Her laugh was quick and quickly aborted, covered under her napkin with a feigned cough. "He was that charming? You found him on a good day then."

Biting back a smile, I added, "I did meet with success with the bishop."

"That is excellent news."

"Yes. I only had to imply that my scars were marks from the devil twice before he was quite willing to offer me anything I wished for in order to be free of me."

It hadn't been nearly that difficult. I just had to allow the man to stare wearily at them for a quarter of an hour before he signed the necessary documents.

After the scene in her father's house, I hardly noticed the beady eyes tracing the lines from my forehead to my chin.

"Handy trick, that. I do not suppose you will tell me about them?" The causal disinterest in her gaze was belied by the curious note in her voice.

"It does come in handy. Had you considered a date for the wedding?"

She pursed her lips, her eyes narrowing at me over the table. I hadn't actually expected my dodge to work, but tonight was not the night for such conversations.

"Your subterfuge is noted and unappreciated. However, I would prefer to wed as soon as possible. For obvious reasons."

"Would three days' time be acceptable? We could wed from here? Unless you had something else in mind, of course."

"Three days will do perfectly well. And I have no objections to being wed from here."

"I will have Crawford tend to the arrangements. Did you enjoy your tour? Is there anything you would look to change immediately? I can have funds pulled, though substantive changes would be difficult to manage before we leave for Bennet Hall."

"It is all quite well situated. There are the most intriguing portraits in the gallery..."

I winced. I hadn't been strictly avoiding the discussion of Mia, but I wasn't yet prepared to admit the totality of my failings. Not at the table at any rate.

"Yes, they're lovely."

"Indeed, I found one in particular of interest."

"The one with Great Aunt Petunia—with the eye patch and peg leg and riding astride a large goat?"

"No, I do not recall that one."

"Perhaps it is in Surrey and I'm mistaken."

"Perhaps." She considered the second course thoughtfully and cut into her roast with delicate, ladylike bites before returning her discerning gaze to mine. I busied myself moving food around my plate.

When the silence stretched into the third minute, she could abide it no longer. Her fork clattered to the plate. "You are unwilling to reveal anything?"

"About what? Aunt Petunia? I rather think she was an eccentric."

A barely restrained irritation was apparent in her countenance and posture. Her spine was straighter, longer for her annoyance. Her brow furrowed, eyes narrowed, and her lips pursed. It took every ounce of good breeding I possessed to refrain from laughing outright. Such kittenish fury.

Moving into somewhat less amusing territory lest my restraint fail, I asked, "How long do you suppose you would need to be prepared to travel to Bennet Hall?"

"I believe the servants can have me readied by our wedding. My time in James Place was to come to an end sooner rather than later. The new heir and his wife are eager to take occupation of the place. Some of the process had already begun."

"Charming. Did they wait until he was in the ground to inform you of their choice?"

"They did not, actually," she stated, her prim lips pursed.

"Do you have any relations that are not repulsive?"

"I shall soon be able to write off that particular set."

"Ousting a widow... Whoever heard of such a thing?" That was directed primarily to my own plate.

I considered for a moment the second cousin I'd met only once who could one day inherit should Lady James be carrying a girl... What would have happened to Mia if she'd survived and I had not?

The roast turned cold and slimy in my mouth at the thought. I would need to check with Mr. Summers again. It was best to be certain my widow would be well cared for in my absence.

"I rather think a lot of people," she answered.

Her knife scrapped across the plate, slicing a potato before she speared it and popped it into her mouth. Oblivious to my turmoil.

I swallowed my mouthful and it hit my stomach like a rock, settling there, hard and unyielding. The room had grown quite warm, the urge to tug at my cravat nearly overwhelming. Sweat gathered at the base of my neck and pooled in the silk there, saturating it. The soaked fabric itched.

Yes, it was certainly too hot in here.

I glanced from my plate to the woman across from me, seemingly unbothered by the oppressive, swampy heat. Lady James was as unaffected as ever.

Perspiration bloomed across my forehead and temples, seeping into my hairline. I tugged a few strands behind my ear, needing the air on my face.

No one could feign that kind of cool countenance in the

face of the fever in this room. Yet no dampness appeared on Lady Charlotte's forehead, no beads of sweat on her upper lip.

My chest tightened with realization. It was just me. Again.

Wind rushed through my ears.

I was getting farther and farther away. Abandoning the table for horrifying places long gone.

Table. Table. My fork clattered to my plate and I grasped the edge of the table in my hand, pressing down on the wood.

Solid, immovable.

The tablecloth was rough, sliding against the smooth wood beneath. I ran my thumbs across it. My thumbnail caught on a loose stitch.

Sound returned next, the roar dying down. That was when the humiliation crashed in.

"My lord? Lord Champaign? Are you well?"

Lady James, frozen, half risen from her chair to reach my side.

Damn. I had one of my episodes in front of her.

For a brief moment, I wished it had been worse. That it had been one of the ones where I left this reality and found my own, years away. Yes, it was horrifying there, full of the copper tang of blood and the scent of charred flesh. But when I recovered from those, I never recalled anything from this world at all. Including any humiliation I may have suffered in the interim.

I fought through the shame, clearing my throat with a cough. Jack was at my side, peppermint-oil-soaked cloth in hand. I breathed deep and harsh. The metallic tang in my mouth was chased away by the mint's threat.

Confident, for the moment at least, of where I was, who I was, what I was, I finally looked up.

Disgust was etched into the lines of her face, her raised brow, her wide eyes, her flushed cheeks—it was clear to see.

And I couldn't manage it.

I should tell her. I knew I should. It was the only proper thing to do. I should have done before I approached her father. But damn it all, her solution was so simple. A wife and potential heir in one neat package. I could do my duty by my title.

And though I hadn't admitted it to myself until that exact moment, I did not wish to be alone any longer.

The truth would send her running—as it should. No sane woman wanted to be saddled with a half-addled beast of a man.

But for once in my life, I wanted to be selfish. As absurd as it was, I found myself enjoying her company. And I was so damn lonely.

So I lied.

And coughed again, harder. I coughed until even I believed I was choking. Until tears streamed down my face and my throat was raw. It was a clever bit of acting to convince her I had met with success. I managed a few more well placed coughs afterward.

"Apologies, Lady James." I rasped. "I merely swallowed wrong. I am quite well, thank you."

"Are you certain?"

"Yes, quite." I took a heavy drink of the wine beside me. In a cruel twist of irony, it burnt my ragged throat on the way down and I had another, sincere, fit of coughing.

When I regained control of my chest and lungs, I continued, "Forgive me. I do not know that I will be worthy company this evening with my throat so scraped. Speaking is somewhat painful at present."

She nodded thoughtfully, fortunately all but finished with her dinner. It was unpardonable to send her away without dessert, and unforgivable to send her off into the night unescorted. I hated myself more than a little for doing it. But that was precisely what I did.

I had Crawford bundle her off into my carriage. I did not even see her to the door, too afraid the sight of the conveyance would set me off again with nothing to excuse it.

Crawford looked in on me, still in the dining room in front of my half-empty, long-cold plate, after he had sent her into the night, alone. He gave a disapproving shake of his head before wandering off to scold some staff member or other.

Eventually, Brigsby stepped into the room. He pulled out the nearby chair and flopped down in it across from me. I had pushed myself away from the table some time ago, intending to do... something. Instead, my elbows had found my knees and my head had met my hands. Too trapped in the swirling hurricane of self-loathing, self-pity, and exhaustion to stand.

"It was perhaps too much today. Tomorrow will be better," Brigs murmured soothingly.

I didn't want forgiveness. I didn't want understanding. I wanted someone to hate me more than I hated myself. But I wasn't entirely certain that was possible. Perhaps Lady James would in short order, when she saw the shell of a man she had purchased with the rest of her life.

Something to look forward to.

Chapter Nine

84 BROOK STREET, LONDON - JUNE 12, 1816

CHARLOTTE

A MARRIED WOMAN AGAIN.

I had always assumed I would remarry after my husband died, and I did assume he would predecease me. But in my mind it had never been quite like... this.

Three years ago, I was wed in Saint George's. Though my wedding hadn't been what it would have if I had married Rosehill, there were attendants and flower girls and family in the pews. We were greeted with cheers when we stepped out into the bright sunny morning. An elaborate wedding breakfast followed the ceremony.

In my musings—fantasies if I was truthful—my second marriage had been a grander affair.

How wrong I was. Lord Champaign and I wed in a small chapel with no one to witness but his servants and mine. My gown was quite literally one of only three that concealed my growing belly. A meal for just the two of us and a bowl of punch for the servants was all that could be named a wedding breakfast.

And still, it was infinitely better than the first.

Lord Champaign was reclusive and elusive, scarred and marred, but unlike Ralph, he was the man I had chosen. I knew more about him, even with his evasive nature, than I had known about the first man I wed. And what little I did know, I liked so much more than anything I knew about Ralph, before or after the 'I dos.'

I hadn't wanted to wed again this quickly. I didn't wish to be with child. I hated that Wesley had forced me into this situation. But I couldn't help hoping, desperately, that this one choice, the only one of significance I had ever made, was as right as it seemed on the face.

It was a leap of faith, the trust I was putting on the word of Leopold Bennet, and I was left with nothing but prayers that he wouldn't forsake me, abandon me, or destroy me the way every other man in my life had forsaken, abandoned, and destroyed me.

It was a terrifying prospect to be sure.

Made all the more terrifying by the worrying way he eyed the carriage before us.

"My lord?" The weary warble in my tone escaped even as I strove to mask it.

He turned toward me, heaving a great sigh. "How would you feel about riding? We can send the carriage along with your things."

Absolutely wretched. I wanted to arrive with my things, to be able to change after my journey. Not to mention, my solitary riding habit did not fit particularly well any longer, and it was packed at the bottom of one of the precariously stacked trunks being loaded onto the back of said carriage at that precise moment. And I had spent the morning bathing and dressing with care so I would feel as beautiful as possible in spite of the growth in my belly come our wedding night. Currently, I smelled of lavender and orange blossom, I had no desire to smell of horse, manure, and sweat. What's more, my stomach was a tempestuous beast. Even now that I had discovered the wonders of peppermint tea it would occasionally rebel, and it would certainly be more manageable in a carriage than on horseback.

He must have sensed my hesitation because he reversed course. "I apologize, that was an impetuous request. I am not overly fond of carriages, so I usually ride. But I should not ask that of you."

There was something unnamed lining the undercurrent of his words. It was unknown, mysterious, and I suddenly knew that, as much as I wished to sit in the comfortable shade of the carriage, he wished to be out of it even more. And he wished for me to be with him.

"No. We can ride. I will need my riding habit though."

"Oh, right. I hadn't considered that..."

"Why would you? It is not a concern you are accustomed to." Imogen passed me, hat box in hand to be loaded onto the carriage. "Imogen, would you be a dear and pull out my riding habit? Lord Champaign and I shall ride."

Her eyes widened and flitted first to my stomach, second toward the carriage where I was almost certain my habit was in the trunk at the very bottom of the stack, and third to my new husband. It was almost comical, watching her thoughts mirror my own so completely and so transparently.

Brigsby, having overheard the conversation, began to unload the trunks without comment. Imogen went to join him, adding the hat box to the growing stack with minimal and almost entirely inaudible grumbling.

A quick glance at my husband showed something like guilt in his pinched brow but also relief in his easier countenance. He had asked for almost nothing in agreeing to wed me. I could give him this without complaint. Quietly, he directed the chipped-tooth footman, Jack, to have two horses saddled, and the boy complied without question or surprise.

No one from Lord Champaign's household was surprised, in point of fact.

In short order, I was bundled into a too-tight riding habit and assisted onto a brown mare by my new husband. We set off, leaving the carriage to be repacked in our wake.

I shuffled after him, immediately regretting every single choice that led me to this moment. I was aware that, in the grand scheme of problems one could have with one's husband, this was quite low. Lower, in fact, than nearly every single one of Ralph's foibles. But Ralph was dead, had been for months. And Lord Champaign was in front of me, the perfect target for every single imagined arrow in my quiver, and I had exceptional aim in such circumstances.

∼

LEE

I never should have asked. I had not intended to ask. This was a terrible thing to ask of a bride on her wedding day.

But the sight of her about to enter the carriage...

That she agreed to ride was something of a surprise in retrospect. In fact, she agreed with nothing but a longing look at the conveyance and a request for her riding habit.

Of course, now I could feel the glare burning through my back. She wasn't happy about the situation, but she was game and I could appreciate that.

It was a short ride to Bennet Hall, two hours at a walk, though I usually set a faster pace. But I had no idea how confident a horsewoman new my wife was.

The lane widened ahead, allowing for two abreast easily.

She angled Celaeno up next to my mount, cutting a fine figure when I glanced beside me.

A fine, slightly green-tinted figure. *Oh, good lord.* Women with child were known to have tetchy stomachs. And I plunked her on a horse.

"Oh damn," the curse escaped me without permission. "I didn't consider—I am so—I should not have…"

"I will require the whole of the sentence if you wish to convey some sort of meaning, my lord."

"I forgot."

"You forgot what?"

"A great many things. Would you believe I forgot you were with child? And that such a condition leaves one feeling unwell. And that riding might exacerbate that illness."

"I would indeed. I was all but certain you had forgotten at least one of those things when you made the request."

"Why did you not say anything?"

She merely shrugged. "You've asked for very little in this arrangement."

"Yes, but you should not agree to anything that causes you discomfort."

"Marriage is often a source of discomfort." She said it so matter-of-factly, almost unthinkingly. Of course marriage was an unpleasant thing. Whether that was her opinion on all marriages, or merely this one, was less clear. That I couldn't determine her meaning—that was a wretched understanding.

I considered my next words carefully. "It would mean a great deal to me—that is—going forward, I would prefer that you let me know if something makes you uncomfortable. I am afraid I have little experience with women in a delicate condition. While I expect I may make more than a few blunders in the coming months, I would prefer to make you as comfortable as possible."

She had turned from the path ahead, caught my gaze and

held it. Her expression was quite unreadable. The direct sunlight lent her eyes a more golden bronze coloring than the candlelight and firelight of our previous meetings.

"I shall try."

Even with the peaked undertone to her skin and the glisten of sweat below her hairline, my wife was a beautiful woman. Stunning. It had been painfully obvious the night we met, and it was an even more painful truth that she should have nothing to do with me.

We didn't *fit* the way the other couples of my acquaintance did.

Amelia and I had fit, once upon a time.

Mia had been an obvious choice, beautiful, poised, kind. Tall, fair with blue eyes and a heart-shaped face, she was everything a wife ought to be. And I was tall and fair with blue eyes and, though my face was longer and not shaped quite the same way, we were beautiful and bright together. Our life together had been beautiful and bright too.

Until the day it all turned to ash in that damned carriage.

Now I was hidden away in the darkness. My hair had darkened, no longer exposed to the sun. Most of my skin was still golden fair, except for the twisted, red-and-white marbled bits on my temple, cheek, chin, shoulder, and chest. Yes, I was still beautiful if one ignored half of me. My life was still beautiful, if one didn't mind hiding in darkened rooms alone.

No, Lady Charlotte and I did not *fit*. And that thought worried me more than it ought.

I didn't for one second believe she would try to tell me if I made a misstep. Whether it was her father, her late husband, or the prospect of marriage to me, she seemed convinced that discomfort was all her future had to offer.

I had saddled this woman with a broken man. My attempts to ease the burden—the time limit, the financial provisions, the return of her freedom—paled in comparison to what I asked of her. A year was a very long time to be uncomfortable at best, miserable at worst.

I would need to do better, be better, and anticipate her needs. It was unacceptable—I could not, would not be the cause of any suffering that was within my power to amend.

"We should stop, wait for the carriage. It cannot be more than a quarter of an hour behind us."

"No, that is not necessary," she said, swaying in her seat.

Her expression was so familiar to me, despite never having seen it on her before. I leaned over, pulling the reins to halt her mount.

I hopped off Poseidon, dropping his reins and steadying Celaena. Both horses could have their moods, but they generally heeded me and they were behaving well today. Lady Charlotte allowed me to pluck her out of the saddle and set her gingerly on two feet.

I reached into my pocket and pulled out a peppermint, then pressed it into her palm. She unwrapped it eagerly and popped it between full, pouting lips. Her cheeks pursed as she sucked on the sweet, emphasizing the angular cut of her jaw.

Her color returned, leaving only a fetching flush in its wake. Distractedly, she dragged the back of her hand across her brow before reaching to take the reins from me.

"We'll wait," I insisted. Her posture eased ever so slightly in relief. She would have traveled the entire distance on horseback, desperately trying to avoid casting up her accounts the entire way.

Mere hours into marriage, and I was already proving a poor husband. While entirely predictable, I rather hoped I could offer a better showing than this.

After slipping my hand back in my pocket, I snuck a peppermint of my own. I would need all the grounding relief it might offer.

A PROPERLY CONDUCTED SHAM

I *should* join her in the carriage. That was the proper way of things. But perhaps out here would be better. Even if we were farther apart than I would prefer... I could assist her better if something happened. Or would I be of more help inside? I was unlikely to be of any use in either situation if the tightening of my breath at the mere thought was any indication.

Before I could arrive at a decision, the carriage trundled into view, the wagon just behind it. They were making excellent time in spite of her numerous trunks.

They passed us before pulling to the side of the road. Brigsby popped his head out of the window, took one look at the two of us, and ushered a relieved Lady James—Lady Champaign, rather—inside. Me, he raised a brow at. With a jerk of my head, he followed my silent command and stepped out to join me.

"Well, that went as well as could be expected," he said. I didn't appreciate the inherent *I told you so* in his tone. He hadn't specifically told me so.

"I... can you?" Words were failing me now with a wife settled within the confines of a carriage once again.

He nodded in answer and climbed back inside the carriage to explain my absence... somehow.

I looped Celaena's reins to the back of the wagon. She might follow Poseidon, but it wasn't a sure thing.

They started off down the rutted path. Had it always been so uneven? My heart lodged in my throat as I watched my wife's conveyance jounce into various trenches and pits. The lantern swayed with every jolt, unlit for daytime travel.

It was, in point of fact, the finest carriage money could buy. Well sprung and maintained to perfection. At the cost a small fortune, I purchased it before I realized the extent of my fears. With gilded mahogany details and plush velvet seats and ornate lace curtains, it bordered on ostentatious. I only hoped my wife was too distracted by the luxury within to notice her wayward husband.

My pace was slowed by the necessity of remaining with the carriage. Leaving it was not an option, not with her inside.

And so we lumbered down the road, if such a holed, pitted thing could be termed as such. Wobbling along at a glacial pace, while every jolt, every bump, every shock, sent an icy knife through my chest, all the way to Bennet Hall.

Chapter Ten

BENNET HALL, SURREY - JUNE 12, 1816

CHARLOTTE

I PEERED out the window hoping for a glimpse of my husband. His valet had offered a scant explanation, and not one of his servants seemed to find his behavior the least bit out of the usual way of things.

The carriage was unbearably fine, bathed in velvet and silk, and so well sprung that my stomach actually settled. We drove on for another hour. I would not have survived so long on horseback, not with my uneasy constitution.

A gentle breeze wafted through the window, the scent of wildflowers dancing in. When I looked out again, the tall, broad form of Lord Champaign was still missing. Instead, I was met with a sprawling pond surrounded by well-manicured greenery. Small clusters of lily pads clung together on the water's surface. Two swans paddled lazily across the mirrored expanse.

The road ahead curved around the pond and there, on the other bank, was a house. Taupe brick with arched windows inset from the facade, the two-story home was settled delicately in the natural divot carved by the water. Only the back of the house was visible from my vantage with no entry to observe.

Rounding the bend, I saw a second two-story building, set off from the first. Built to suit the main house, this smaller, round structure had a domed ceiling—an observatory.

We pulled away from the lake, rounding the front of the house, larger than it appeared from first glance. It had an entire second wing jutting out to the west that had been hidden from view by natural growth.

At last, we turned down a long path toward the front of the house. The drive was gently sloped down to meet the double doors. Servants poured out from the entrance, forming a line to greet us. Finally, I found Lord Champaign, hurling himself off his horse and tossing the reins to a boy with a quiet word.

The carriage came to a halt, and Lord Champaign opened the door and handed me out. If any of the servants found our transportation arrangements odd, they gave no indication.

"Welcome to Bennet Hall, Lady Champaign."

Lady Champaign. I had quite forgotten my name had changed this morning. Lady James no longer. I found I quite preferred the new one to the old one, much less plain. I could only hope the marriage would be an equal improvement, even if the start had been less than auspicious.

Bennet Hall, though not the largest estate I had ever seen, was larger than any of my father's properties, and my late husband had no country house to speak of. For the first time, the task of managing a household left me with a hint of trepidation.

I turned to my husband to praise his home—men liked that sort of thing—when his scar captured in the sunlight. He had taken pains to hide it, donning a hat with a wider brim than was fashionable and a starched collar. But in the sharp, harsh light of day, there was no concealing the ragged, reddened flesh of his cheek.

Whatever injury had caused it was surely a grievous thing. Even now, clearly healed, it appeared shiny and tight. Could it pain him still?

He swallowed thickly, dipping his head lower. Guilt twisted in my gut, restoring it to its previously unsettled state. I hadn't meant to stare. He was just so... secretive about it and ensured he kept me on his left side, always. When he could not, he clung to the shadows and let his hair cover his face where a hat or collar could not.

Floundering for a way to ease the tension, I remembered my earlier intention. "It is beautiful." Men *did* love it when women complimented their homes. Wesley had preened and peacocked about the first time I expressed a wish to see his London house. I might as well have asked to see his roger for all the pride he had over it. The property was not overly impressive. Nor was his roger.

Lord Champaign nodded his thanks and turned back to the house.

I followed suit and saw the valet introducing Imogen to a woman, presumably the housekeeper. Crawford waited, clearly eager to introduce the staff to their new mistress and vice versa. And there were quite a few staff members.

That was a lot of people to conceal my condition from. It would be impossible, I supposed. At best, I had five months if my addition was correct. I couldn't help but hope to delay the inevitable. Anything to allow the staff to get to know me as someone other than the strumpet who had foxed their employer into marriage.

My husband slipped my hand into the crook of his elbow and guided me toward my new household. Tucked this close, I caught a whiff of peppermint and my stomach's dance slowed.

Crawford could hardly contain himself and bounced on

his toes before recognizing the imprudence of such action and ceasing, only to begin again seconds later. When we reached him, he began introductions without bidding. I spent the next quarter hour greeting no less than twenty people. I was quite certain I would be able to recall precisely none of their names.

The butler was eager to start a tour of the house and grounds as well. For a man who had disapproved of me, he was all keenness now. The thought of trailing him through room after unused room was wearying. I was exhausted, sore, and hungry and surely the guest rooms would all still be there in the morning.

"Perhaps tomorrow, Crawford," Lord Champaign interrupted. "It has been a busy day for us. I, for one, would adore if we could arrange an earlier supper."

"Monsieur Portier is already busy in the kitchens, my lord," the valet said from inside the open hall where he was directing the movement of my trunks.

My husband pulled me closer and directed me inside over the sputtering protests of his butler. "I hope that was to your liking," he whispered. "I always found I had little patience for exhaustive tours when I arrived somewhere new after a long journey."

"Yes, it was much appreciated."

"I will show you the important rooms. Just so you don't find yourself lost." I nodded and he gestured me on, stepping around a maid with a trunk in our path and into the entry. The vestibule featured a dark wooden staircase that split on the landing, one set of steps leading to each wing. The entryway was painted a rich, buttery yellow with cream accents, clearly matching the tastes of whomever decorated the London house.

He nodded past the staircase and down a hall. "Dining room and breakfast room are down this hall, both impossible to miss." He led me up the stairs and turned east at the landing, guiding me along.

"I've been residing in the east wing. The west is a mirror, at least on the second floor. I had them ready the chambers next to mine, but if you would prefer something else, just let Crawford know and they can arrange things to your liking."

"I suspect Crawford would find any other arrangement improper."

"Crawford finds everything improper. Do not pay him any mind. I do not."

I rewarded his deep, teasing tone with a low laugh.

He drew me down the richly carpeted hall to the end. "My rooms," he said, indicating the last door at the end with a nod. "And these are for you. If they suit." He released me at the door beside his with a respectful bow before slipping into his own rooms.

After turning the handle, I stepped into the rooms that would be mine. Imogen was already hard at work, unpacking my trunks and directing two maids.

"Oh, my lady. I thought Crawford would harangue you into a tour."

"Lord Champaign put him off." One of the maids tittered, then feigned a cough when she caught my eye. Right, best not disparage the butler in front of them. Particularly not after less than four hours as their mistress.

The sitting room was open and airy with the same cream to be found elsewhere, this time paired with a pleasant sage shade.

The windows in the sitting room and, as I peered through the door, the bedroom as well were massive and arched. That meant I was at the back of the house. I stepped farther into the room, trailing my fingers across the pale green floral settee before approaching the glass.

Directly below me was the lovely pond I had seen on my

arrival. The view was truly breathtaking. Surely the prospect was better here than any other room in the house.

"Would you like to rest?" Imogen interrupted my appreciative musings. "I imagine you're tired from your journey."

"That would be lovely. I understand that we're dining early tonight, would you wake me an hour before?"

"Of course," she said, drawing the other maids out. She returned to my side and fussed with my riding habit.

At last, I was down to my chemise, the bed calling out to me. Imogen drew the curtains and slipped out the door while I crawled into its welcoming arms, succumbing to its soft warmth in moments.

∽

LEE

Crawford's unending lecture was a worthy price for the relieved smile on my wife's face when I delayed his tour. As usual, he was content to recite his complaints while I attended to correspondence in my study. I offered him the precise amount of my attention that his comments required—one sixth.

Nodding as appropriate, I glanced over the stack of letters waiting for me. I hadn't intended to be gone this long. Nor to return with a wife. My steward was more than worthy of the title though and seemed to have everything in hand.

"—and another thing. It was entirely inappropriate for her to retire to her chambers with her trunks yet to be unpacked—" I favored the man with a contrite, wide-eyed expression.

A knock on the door startled Crawford out of his complaints, and Brigsby entered with tea. As always, Brigsby's natural ease overtook Crawford's performative manners, and he slid the tea tray on the desk, then rested a hip against the furnishing. He looked at me expectantly while I took a hearty sip.

"So, my lord…"

The look was utterly baffling. My gaze flitted to Crawford who was uncharacteristically silent and staring at me with a similar interest.

"Yes?"

Brigsby waggled a single brow up and down. It took far longer than I cared to admit for realization to crash over me.

My forehead fell to the rich mahogany of my desk without permission, landing with a solid *thunk*. "Go away," I mumbled into the wood.

"Tonight is the night," he said with a ridiculous singsong innuendo in his tone.

I groaned. Tonight was not the night. There was no night. It was one of the many benefits of wedding a woman already with child. I need not suffer the humiliation of a lady's horrified expression in a desperate attempt to procreate.

Precisely one attempt—that was all I could bear. One visit to a brothel, where I was met with a literal scream of terror, was more than enough for a lifetime.

Brigsby did not know the bruise he was pressing on. No one knew. Well, he knew that the scars on my face were nothing compared to those on my chest. He knew the weeks of pain and fever. But he didn't know that Lady Champaign and I would not consummate our wedding. Tonight or any other.

It was one of the many reasons wedding Lady Champaign had been, in fact, a terrible but impossibly tempting consideration. The possibility of an heir without the necessity of horrifying my wife with the sight of me.

"Monsieur has prepared supper using all of the finest… *aphrodisiacs* he could locate. He has oysters, pheasant, currants, and pine nuts."

Oh, good Lord. My head popped off the desk. Half of that was sure to have my wife casting up her accounts. Certainly the oysters would not sit well. They rarely did for me. But the staff could not...

"Oysters do not agree with me, would you be so kind as to have chef remove them from the menu?" Would pheasant be all right?

Brigsby eyed me suspiciously. I was not one to complain over a menu. Complaining would require one to care about the contents of a plate, and I rarely gave it that much consideration.

"Also, if you would, have some peppermint tea prepared for Lady Charlotte when she wakes. And see if chef can make some ginger crisps to have on hand." His eyes narrowed further at my uncharacteristic request before reading whatever he was searching for on my face. He nodded and sidestepped Crawford to relay my concerns.

"Brigs?" I called after him.

"Yes, my lord?"

"Would you have Lady Champaign's lady's maid sent in?"

His affirmative was tentative. The man had been with me my entire adult life. It was rare I surprised him, and I'd managed it at least twice in as many minutes.

Crawford's lecture resumed with alacrity, now with the additional complaints of my suddenly choosy stomach.

My wife's maid knocked on the open door, then lowered into a quick curtsy.

"That will be all Crawford." I rarely dismissed him, and I would pay for the choice at some later time. Still, he bowed properly with a clenched jaw and slipped out, shutting the door behind him.

"My lord?" the maid asked.

"I'm sorry, I do not know that we've been introduced."

"Imogen Talbot, my lord. But I prefer just Imogen."

"Imogen... I understand that ladies in a delicate constitution sometimes experience discomforts. I should like to mitigate that wherever possible for my wife." Her eyes widened before she nodded. Whether it was to my statement or the realization that I was aware of my wife's condition was impossible to say. "It has become clear to me that my wife is willing to sacrifice her own comforts to appease me. Or in a way that she believes will please me."

I let the statement land there and waited for some kind of confirmation or denial from the woman before me. Her jaw hung open slightly, but no sound escaped for a few seconds before it was clear that no response would be forthcoming.

"It would be a great help to me if you could let myself or Brigsby—Mrs. Fitzroy, as well—know if there is anything we could provide or do to give her comfort."

More silent staring. Was this woman addled?

"Are there any dishes I should have chef avoid?"

The direct question seemed to bring her back to herself somewhat. "At this point, everything has made her feel poorly at one time or another. There seems to be no telling what will cause it."

Nodding, I added, "You will let me know if there is something?"

"Yes, my lord," she agreed with a bob, then stepped to leave.

"Thank you. Oh, Imogen?"

She turned back to face me. "Not Crawford, if you please?"

The woman nodded silently and scurried from the room.

Silence enveloped me with her exit, leaving nothing but the whisper of the flickering candle and the scratch of my quill as I resumed answering correspondence.

Chapter Eleven

BENNET HALL, SURREY - JUNE 12, 1816

CHARLOTTE

I WAS TEMPTED to remain in the bath until my fingers and toes pruned and the water froze over. Every minute I remained swirling my hands through the sudsy water was a delay of the inevitable.

Supper.

Supper followed by marital congress.

The thought filled me with substantially less trepidation than it had on my last wedding night.

I knew what to expect, at least. And there was Lord Champaign, a significant improvement over my late husband by any measure.

But no one had touched me since Wesley. Wesley, whom I had longed for through the frigid months and years of my marriage. Wesley with his quick wit, bright eyes, and dimpled smile. Wesley, who promised me the world and then tossed me aside.

I was once a girl of silly fantasies. Memories that cut like swords had shredded that girl; Charlotte Hasket, Duchess of

Rosehill was never to be. Instead, I became The Right Honorable Lady James, long before I had finished mourning the duchess that never was. But The Right Honorable Lady James was married to a repugnant frog.

And there was Wesley, waiting in the wings with a quip and a look to save her from the frog who would never become a prince.

For two long years, Wesley Parker had been my confidant, my friend, and the love of my life. And when, finally, *finally* Ralph left this mortal coil, it was our time. I had waited two years, I could bear the requisite months of mourning before wedding the man of my dreams. The only man who had never disappointed me.

And when he pulled me away from the ballroom, offering me the most sinful vows of pleasure beyond my wildest imaginings, well... perhaps the waiting was not so essential after all. What difference would a few months make? This was *Wesley*. Wesley, who had waited years for me, years when there had been no hope at all. And Wesley would never reject me, take me for granted, or abandon me. He had *waited* for *me*. It would be cruel to make him wait a moment longer. Especially when he made such lustful promises of ecstasy.

Tonight I would feel another's touch. Lord Champaign had offered no promises of earthly pleasures beyond those required in the marriage rights. I couldn't say I was anticipating our joining. But it could not possibly be as awful as Ralph's touch—with his sweaty, sticky fingers that made my skin crawl, and the port heavy on his muggy breath raining over my face as he worked in and above me. Those would not be a concern tonight.

My husband... His hands had been soft and dry when he slid the ring on my finger that morning. And he always smelled of peppermints. Always.

He was quite handsome, as well, even with the scars. Or

perhaps because of them. They were real, human, in a way his ethereal eyes and towering presence were not.

Yes, he was quite handsome and quite strange. He never reacted the way he ought, the way other men did. It seemed he was petrified of crowds but made time for the social event of the season. The carriage discomfited him, but his conveyance was the finest I'd ever seen. He was seemingly immune to my charms, such as they were, but wed me all the same.

I could do this. I had to do this. That very morning, I had vowed to do this.

I had all but convinced myself to abandon the bath—I truly had—when a knock filled the room.

No, not a knock—digging or tapping? I thrashed round in the bath water, turning toward the door, toward the direction the sound came from. My heart slammed in my throat.

The mahogany door, with its intricate floral carvings I hadn't yet admired, rattled in its frame. It continued, three or four of the strange digging, tapping sounds while the door wriggled, then ceased before beginning again.

A gasp escaped me as the movement stopped and the door swung open. It was a few inches, nothing more. My scream caught in my throat, knotted there.

I waited, breath bated, for someone to enter.

And when they did, my breath escaped in a rush, spent air abandoning my lungs at once.

Less than a foot from the floor, a pair of yellow-green eyes blinked at me with interest. A cat, small and gray with black stripes and spots, twitched its tail at me.

A simple little barn cat of no particular breeding, it chirped a greeting before striding over to my copper basin. The thing hopped up onto its back paws, stretching impossibly long to rest its front paws on the edge of my tub. It was too short to see over the ledge, but I couldn't help but peer down at it, easing its curiosity with my own.

"Hello."

It chirped again, almost more birdlike than catlike. Seemingly satisfied with its inspection of my person, it dropped back down onto all fours and prowled the room. It made one circuit, then a second before approaching the screen where my evening dress hung. After a glance back at me, it directed its attention to the gown, hopped up on its back paws again, and sank its claws into the fine purple silk.

With a wordless shriek, I shoved myself to standing in the tub, wobbling precariously.

I was so distracted I never heard the clang of the other door, the one connecting my room and my husband's room. And I missed the panicked footsteps racing through the bedroom into the sitting room over the sloshing of the water.

I did, however, hear the masculine, "Char—Oh."

Unthinkingly, I spun toward him, heedless of my transparent shift.

And promptly slipped on the slick surface of the wet tub. My hands flew out to catch me instinctively and my eyes slammed shut as I braced for pain.

But it never came.

Rather, a massive arm found my waist and an equally massive hand caught my elbow. Blinking, I found my husband, eyes wide with terror, frantically searching my face for... something.

A beat. Two. Three. We remained frozen. And then the little urchin behind me dragged its claws down my gown once again, the fabric catching audibly on nails every few stitches.

His "Cass, no!" was nearly inaudible over my screech. Instinctively, his hand left my waist to stop the beast. My feet slipped again, and his hand slammed back onto my hip, gripping even tighter.

When I turned back, his attention was no longer on my face. Instead, it was drawn to the nearly invisible sopping fabric of my shift, clinging to my breasts. His eyes were wide with something, lust perhaps, at the swell of my bosom, or revulsion at the swell of my belly. There was no way to know.

He swallowed thickly, steadying me once again before loosening his hold. "Are you well?" His breath washed over me, cool and dry and peppermint-scented.

I nodded.

"In or out?" He tilted his head between the tub and the, presumably safer, ground before him.

"Out." He helped me over the tub's edge and steadied me before grabbing the thick woven linen that Imogen had piled nearby. He unfolded it and held it before him, then wrapped me in it and his arms by extension.

There we stayed for a moment, and I breathed in his fresh scent, enjoying the way my stomach's perpetual rolling ceased.

Scritch! My husband's arms abandoned me. He strode toward the cat and scooped it up in one arm. "Cassiopeia, stop that this instant."

"A friend of yours?"

"Something like that. I am so sorry. I'll give it to Brigsby, see if he can repair the damage."

There was no repairing that damage, not on shot silk. A sharp retort hovered at the end of my tongue, but something about the sheepish expression on the oversize man cradling a minuscule ball of fluff to his chest made it impossible to snap at him. I released my irritation in a sigh. "So you have a cat?"

"Sort of? I found her caught in a tree. Lord, it was probably a decade ago. I pulled her down and she just... never left. She's impossible to keep out of places. Doors are a personal challenge. Though, I thought this one secure. She's never tried her luck with it before."

"Possibly due to a lack of motivation, rather than capability."

"So it would seem. I'll just... take her." He nodded toward the adjoining door.

"All right then."

He paused at the threshold, arms still full of cat. "I'll... see you in a little while? At supper."

At my affirmation, he tipped the door open with a foot and slid in, before kicking it closed behind him. Through the door I heard him speaking to someone, his tone lecturing... Was he scolding the cat?

My husband was quite strange indeed.

Chapter Twelve

BENNET HALL, SURREY - JUNE 12, 1816

LEE

CASS PROMPTLY SANK her claws into my arm as soon as I shut the door to my wife's chambers. A curse escaped me before she bounded free, leaping from my arms to land on the bed.

"You cannot do that. I do not want her gowns ruined. What were you even doing in there anyway?"

The cat squeaked out her odd little meow in response before prowling to the top of the bed. There, she found a pillow and began to knead it with her feet, digging her claws into the fabric covering and yanking.

"Shoo!"

She paused to glare at me, then spun in a circle once, twice, three times before curling into a ball in place.

I collapsed onto the foot of the bed and Cass snapped a chirp before closing her eyes. I let out another sigh as I flopped back to lay half on and half off the bed.

This was an inconvenience I hadn't anticipated about having a wife—a beautiful wife at that. Separated from me only by a thin wooden door and a soaking wet shift that wasn't merely transparent but clung in all the best places.

The accident hadn't left me blind. I was still a man with eyes, and my wife was a stunningly beautiful woman. It was to be expected that I would find her attractive. It didn't have to mean anything.

Except that it did. I still reacted in all the ways I used to when presented with a beautiful woman. I still *wanted*. It was just that the wanting had no outlet. And I had signed on for a year of wanting desperately with no release in sight.

I would end up in the madhouse before the year was over. I glanced at the telltale traitorous tightening in my breeches. It was no help at all that every time I closed my eyes, the image of my wife's form in a soaked shift appeared, burned in my mind.

With an exhausted sigh of concupiscence, I considered the usual tactics... The mental image of Crawford in the same clinging shift seemed to do the trick.

Brigsby chose that moment to knock and enter without waiting for a reply. He froze at the pathetic sight of me wallowing on the bed. "Is everything well?"

"No."

"Do you... wish to talk about it?"

"No."

"Do you require a few more moments?"

"No," I sighed the word and pressed myself up to stand.

He began the process of collecting all the ridiculous accouterments required for a formal dinner. That would be another adjustment. No more solitary suppers in my shirtsleeves. Wives expected their husbands to be properly attired at the table.

"Is this about the very cross lady's maid I saw leaving your new wife's sitting room?"

"Not entirely, but that beast is responsible." I gestured at the little menace currently purring—and shedding—on my pillow.

"Oh dear…"

"Yes." I tugged my cravat loose, then pulled it free from my collar and unlooped it from my neck. "If you don't mind, would you see about assisting Imogen with it? Otherwise, we should see about having it replaced."

"Of course. Although… Your wife will soon require new gowns, if I'm not mistaken."

Damn, she'd want to go to a London modiste for that. My back ached at the thought of watching the carriage bounce along. Another trip to and from town, fretting over my wife, and I'd need to find the cane I used after my accident. I had no desire to hobble around the house like an octogenarian.

Brigsby held out the clean linen shirt I was to wear to dine, and I tugged it over my head distractedly.

"Can you discuss those arrangements with Imogen as well? Perhaps we can find a modiste willing to travel here?" The valet gave a dubious brow raise and I fought back an eye roll. My wife's habits were catching. "Ask please?"

"Yes, my lord." He draped a fresh cravat around my neck before tying it in a rather more showy style than I preferred. "Is there anything you wish prepared for tonight? Rose petals perhaps? Additional candles?"

"That will not be necessary." I hated myself as I said it. Those things ought to be necessary. My stomach clenched guiltily, and I longed for a peppermint.

"But, my lord…"

"No." He knew better than to press that tone. I gave Brigs a great deal of leeway and tolerated all manner of impertinences, but that timbre brokered no argument.

Lack of protestations did not signify a lack of opinion, however. Brigsby was more than capable of making his feelings known in the strength with which he tightened my cravat.

"Has chef made the changes I requested to supper?"

"I believe so." Still peeved with me then.

"Very good. How is Imogen settling in?"

"Fine."

At a loss and cursing imprudent valets the world over, I slipped my arms into the sleeves of the coat he held before him. Turning, I faced the mirror. Acceptable. I shook my hair loose and tugged a few strands free to conceal some of the scarring on my temple. It wasn't much, but it was the best I would be able to manage.

In the glass, my valet glared pointedly, arms crossed and hip jutted out.

"Brigsby, I will say this once. My marriage, such as it is, is neither your responsibility, nor your concern. I'll thank you to keep your comments about it to yourself. And the rest of the staff as well. If I catch one hint of gossip about Lady Champaign, the person responsible will find themselves turned out without a reference. There will be no warnings."

It was, in point of fact, the least kind speech I had ever delivered to him, perhaps to anyone. But I knew how gossip traveled. The child my wife carried was mine—as of this morning at any rate. Any rumors would damage not only my reputation but that of my wife and the babe as well. And I would not—could not—allow that.

His jaw had hinged open with the second sentence and hung there, open and overdramatic. I strode from the room, abandoning him, still pinned in place, in favor of the small dining room.

On the way, I found my wife in the drawing room, perusing the bookshelves with half-hearted interest. She wore not the purple gown that Cassiopeia had claimed but a sunshine-yellow frock. When she turned, I caught the whisper of a belly under the parted fabric.

It was astonishing, in truth, how an entire person could come from nothing. A child resided in there right that second.

Rather than share that inane thought, I floundered for a more appropriate topic. "Do you read?"

"Some. Are you the collector? It's quite a vast selection."

"The majority are mine. A few belonged to my parents and the others..." She nodded. There was no doubt in her mind where my thoughts had gone. "Do you..." I broke off, clearing my throat. "Do you have a preference?"

"I was reading a great deal of romance. But I may be in search of something new if you have recommendations." I considered thoughtfully before sliding *Belinda* free from its companions.

She took it and flipped through the pages with something akin to interest.

"I believe supper should be ready if you'd like to head in?"

My wife set the book on a side table for later perusal, then slid her hand into the crook of my arm. There, her ring caught the light, the glinting metal that called her third finger home astonishingly bright.

The family dining room was smaller, seating four comfortably, though six could be packed in if need called for it. The table was a rich mahogany with edges carved in intricate scrolls and vines. I helped my wife to her place before taking my own.

Three footmen filed in with dishes of greater variety and extravagance than I was used to—though I was pleased to find no oysters in sight. I had not escaped the pine nuts though. Nor the currants. The staff would enjoy the oysters at least.

I watched carefully which dishes my wife selected and which she took the smallest spoonfuls of. She seemed fond of pickled salmon but made no effort to touch the roast.

"Did... was your gown beyond salvage?"

"Imogen is looking at it."

"I apologize again. I had no idea Cass would break into

your room. She has never shown even the slightest inclination."

"It is no matter." Her words were perfectly polite, delivered in a perfectly appropriate tone. But there was an edge just underneath where her irritation lay.

"I should see about other locks. She's quite a magician."

"And she resides... indoors?"

"She resides wherever she wishes. Doors are no obstacle. Every attempt to keep her locked away or in the barn has failed within a quarter of an hour."

That earned me an indistinct hum.

I fought for something else to speak of, something to pull her thoughts away from her ruined gown. "Did you—do you—have evening rituals? For after supper?"

Lord this was stilted. Mia and I had known something of each other before we wed, our courtship and engagement having spanned nearly six months. The person across from me now was a stranger.

"I often play the pianoforte or read when I am at home in the evenings."

"If you like, after supper I can show you to the music room."

"That would be lovely, thank you." Supper continued in the same formal, laborious manner until the dishes were cleared away.

Her hand found that same familiar home in the crook of my elbow as I led her down the hall to the music room. The delicate touch was heavy there, a responsibility. For the first time in years, another person's happiness was mine to ensure.

"Lord Champaign?" I dipped my head down to her. "Do you, would you prefer I refer to you as such? Or..."

"I prefer Lee. And you?"

"Charlotte."

We entered the music room. It was spotless, despite having

remained untouched for years, and a fire was blazing in the hearth. I would need to determine which of the footmen overheard her and thank them. Charlotte broke away from me and trailed a hand across the harp before making her way to the pianoforte by the window.

She settled primly on the bench and lifted the fallboard. Her fingers whirled automatically through the notes of a scale. The piano was impressively well tuned for so long in disuse. I couldn't recall the last time someone touched it.

With seemingly no effort, but what was likely the result of decades of study, she shifted into the notes of a familiar jig. Even though her posture was impeccable and her technique flawless, her countenance was light and unaffected.

I settled in on the nearby settee to enjoy her performance. It seemed I had found an accomplished wife. It would be no hardship to listen to her play every evening. Not at all.

Chapter Thirteen

BENNET HALL, SURREY - JUNE 12, 1816

CHARLOTTE

IT WAS A FINE INSTRUMENT, releasing rich bass notes on command and mingling the tinkling, delicate highs. I kept the tunes jaunty and bright, displaying no hint of the turmoil within. This was already quite the opposite of my last wedding night.

That was, of course, a good thing. But the waiting... The waiting was interminable and agonizing.

Two songs became three, after which I turned away from the instrument and spun to face my husband, *Lee*.

The firelight cast the scarred half of his face in shadow. The left side of his face was beautiful, almost too beautiful. His eyes shone bluer in the dim light, the silver chased away by the fire. That side of his face wasn't merely unmarred, it was flawless. Only the shadow of his beard kept the ethereal descriptor from him. The stubble and overgrown blond strands atop his head were just dark enough to contrast his skin, kissed by the sun. From my perch on the piano bench across the room, his lips appeared warm and dry but not chapped, and a deep rose, a shade I tried to achieve with rouge—though I would never admit to it.

He really was too lovely. It was honestly a relief he had the scars. Perfection was a falsehood—especially in a man.

I hadn't the slightest idea how he would like to go about this evening. It had been an unbearably long day and my body ached for sleep. But surely my husband had expectations.

Yet he remained silent long after the last notes had faded away to nothingness.

Of course, so did I.

It seemed I must be the one to break the tension if I wished to retire. I stood, clinging to the quiet a moment longer as I gathered my courage. The evening's conclusion would not be any more enjoyable for dallying.

"I believe I should like to retire, unless you have an objection?"

"None at all," he stood and collected my hand, then placed it on his arm again. I could not imagine the motion was comfortable. With his height, he had to lean down or force me onto my toes, and he had chosen the former at every turn. But he seemed to take comfort in the effort, leading me to and fro through his home, my arm tucked to his side.

When he drew me down the hall to the staircase and guided me up, I knew it was time. My heart gave a nervous skip before I willed it into submission. It would be fine. He was, at the very least, not repulsive and had never been unkind in the slightest.

In front of the door that was now mine, he dropped my hand. His eyes trailed over my face, considering, searching for something. Then he squared his shoulders in a nearly imperceptible movement and leaned down to press a kiss to the crown of my head, atop the curls piled there.

"Good night." He turned for his rooms with lighter steps

than I had seen from him before. I blinked absurdly at his retreating form before slipping into my rooms.

I found Imogen at the ready, night rail laid on the bed. My husband had given me no notion of when to expect his attentions, and I was left to rush through my toilette lest Imogen still be there when he returned.

It was the work of only a quarter of an hour before she abandoned me. In want of an occupation, I explored the confines of my four walls for the space of several laps. The plaster had not increased in interest upon a second viewing.

I did, however, find the novel Lee had mentioned earlier atop my bedside table.

The servants were quite possibly magical here.

I perched in what I hoped was an enticing manner atop the chaise with my book to await the inevitable knock. One page became two became ten. For an entire hour, I read and enjoyed my selection. But it was not so interesting as to distract me from the rising frustration I felt at my new husband. It may be a husband's right to demand relations on his schedule, but it was entirely rude to leave me here with no indication of when he might return.

I had been awoken from sleep before by my late husband, returned from the gaming hell smelling of drink and smoke, and I loathed nothing more.

Perhaps he expected me to come to him? That was not how this sort of thing was done.

Snapping my book shut, I tossed it onto the newly vacated chaise. It was the work of but a few angry steps to knock on the adjoining door.

No response.

My knuckles rapped even more sharply on the wood, just shy of painful in their force.

Nothing.

Still flushed, I let my annoyance fuel my brazen grip on the doorknob and turn it. Light from my room poured into the empty, darkened chamber on the other side, illuminating the massive four poster bed. There, a form lay blinking in irritation at an interrupted rest.

Said form released a snappish, chirped *mrroow*.

The damned cat was curled into a ball on the pillow. And my damned husband was nowhere to be seen.

Awake and unhappy about it, the cat unfurled into a lengthy stretch before prancing to the end of the bed with another chirp. There, it—*she*, Lee had said—paced, releasing another agitated meow every few steps until I walked over to her.

I tipped my hand out for her to sniff. She gave my fingers a delicate whiff before rubbing her head against them. Taking that as permission, I flipped my hand over and gave her a quick scratch behind the ear. She was soft, softer than Angora.

Without warning—not even a chirp—the cat turned her head and sank her teeth into the soft flesh between my thumb and forefinger.

I cursed, and the cat merely meowed in response. It was impossible for a cat to smirk. I knew that. But that was precisely what her expression resembled, a smirk, cruel and self-satisfied.

Convinced my husband was nowhere to be found, and contemplating cat murder, I fled his rooms, slamming the door closed behind me.

I was done with waiting. It was late. I was tired. *He* could damn well wait until tomorrow to consummate the marriage.

The bed coverings had been turned down long ago and I slipped between them before blowing out the candle beside my bed.

I lay there staring at the canopy for minute after agonizing minute, nowhere near sleep, not while my hand still throbbed.

The only sound was the crackling of the fire and the tick of a nearby clock I hadn't noticed earlier.

Finally, I closed my eyes and turned to my side, curling my knees up. Sleep was approaching, so tantalizingly close.

Scratch... Scratch... Scratch...

My eyes shot open and found the adjoining door. In the dim light, I could just barely make out a tiny gray paw reaching underneath the door.

Damned cat!

Chapter Fourteen

BENNET HALL, SURREY - JUNE 13, 1816

LEE

My wife was peeved at me.

Oh, she was trying to hide it. But the snappish tone, pursed lips, and furrowed brow spoke far louder than her words.

Her knife clanged a touch louder than was polite after she spread the jam across her toast. She bit into it with a bothered chomp—as though she imagined it was my head.

It was, to be quite honest, most amusing. A good husband, a proper husband, would ask what, precisely, he had done to put her in such a foul temper. But she was so, so angry. And she tried so, so hard to conceal it. She made such a poor showing of it that a part of me was desperate to find out just how long she could maintain the charade. I wasn't particularly proud of that part of me, but it was winning at present.

"Pass the kippers, please?" They were perhaps half an inch closer to her than to me. I was a terrible man.

She stuffed the piece of toast into her mouth before

tearing it away, eyeing the dish. Then she grabbed it with one hand and half tossed it a few inches closer. It landed with a clatter, splashing up my arm.

I bit back a laugh. "Thank you."

The look she shot me would have had lesser men cradling their ballocks.

The silent evisceration of her breakfast did little to hide her temper. And I maintained my desperate efforts to conceal my laughter behind bites of the various offerings.

I ought not say it, I knew I should not, but it escaped all the same. "I trust you slept well?" I was barely able to mask the mirth in my voice.

All but tossing her fork to her plate, she pulled her napkin to her lips and wiped her face before throwing that atop her half-eaten breakfast. "I did not," she bit out between tight-knit lips.

"I'm sorry to hear that. Do let Crawford know if there are any changes you wish to make to your rooms that would allow you to rest easier."

"Will Crawford be able to transform you into a more polite husband?"

So the issue *was* with me. Her ire was only slightly less amusing when I was certain I was the target. Truly though, I could not imagine what I had done between her door last night and the breakfast table this morning. "I beg your pardon?"

"Never mind," she snapped, shoving her chair away from the breakfast table. Now I was annoyed too.

I caught her wrist before she managed a step. My irritation was such that I could hardly appreciate the silken skin and delicate bones of her wrist in my hand. "Oh, I think I very much mind."

"Let go of my wrist."

My grip slackened and her hand broke free. "I apologize. Did I hurt you?"

"Of course not," she scoffed, turning to leave once again. This time I watched her sweep out of the room, goldenrod gown trailing in her wake.

I dragged a hand through my hair, tugging the strands into place. Now I had thoroughly botched the first night of my marriage without the slightest notion as to how. And I successfully drove my wife from the wing. The morning began with the vague intention of returned correspondence and reviewing the ledgers. Now such a notion seemed untenable.

Perhaps I was overly familiar with her. The way I had placed her hand in the crook of my arm last evening. It was too easy, and uninvited. My father had taught me better than to touch a woman against her wishes.

Such perfunctory displays of gentlemanly conduct had never been unwelcome before. But I was not a scarred recluse before. Guilt twisted into a swirling amorphous mass in my gut.

The thought of remaining trapped inside my study with nothing but my own thoughts and a still peevish Brigsby for company was unendurable.

That left but one option. I slipped out the side door after catching a glimpse of the valet and leaving him with directions and a pinched expression in my wake.

∽

CHARLOTTE

"—and he is unbearably rude."

Imogen merely hummed disinterestedly while fussing with the pins in my hair. It was *possible* I was overreacting. But I was tired, drained physically and emotionally. And at the moment, I had only my husband and his viscous attack cat to blame

Distractedly, I brought the nearby teacup to my lips, hoping the ginger flavor would settle my stomach. As the cup reached my nose, I caught a whiff of not ginger but peppermint.

My eyes shot to Imogen's in the mirror. She must have read the confusion there.

"Your unbearably rude husband requested that for you."

I bit back a retort and took a tentative sip. The tea soothed all the way down, hitting my stomach in the midst of a discontented roll. Instantly the jostling ceased, settling. A second sip warmed something in my chest. It was unusual to have such pains so early in the day. That burning sensation around my heart was often reserved for night. But I found new gifts from the hanger-on inside of me every day. Fortunately, the sensation wasn't quite as uncomfortable as it usually was. Certainly not unpleasant enough to outweigh the easing of my stomach.

"It's possible I was a bit harsh with him this morning."

I caught a raised brow in the mirror, and she slid a pin into place sharper than usual.

"Something to say?"

"Not at all. It just seems that you would not have minded so much if the baron had absented himself from your bed chamber for any night." She smoothed another curl before slipping it to join its brethren.

"Of course not, he was horrid."

"Well, perhaps your unbearably rude husband was being considerate of the very eventful day and your delicate state and chose not to impose himself on you." She flicked her fingers through the hair accessories I had brought with me and pulled out a ribbon that matched my gown, smoothing it before me for approval.

I nodded before countering. "Then he should have said so. I waited up for him and then his horrid cat broke in."

"The cat is not so bad. Just give it a scratch or two behind the ears."

"It bit me."

"Oh no." Her tone indicated the true depth of her worry. If she cared enough to fill a thimble I would be astounded.

"Your concern is touching, truly."

"I know." Final curl in place, she pulled the chair free for me. "Charlotte—" She broke away. She called me by my Christian name so rarely I could count the instances on one hand. Imogen had been with me for years, since I entered society. And she never, ever used my Christian name without purpose.

"Charlotte. This is not your first marriage. Lord Champaign is not Lord James. Nor is he Mr. Parker. And you, my dear, are not the same Charlotte you were with either of those men. You cannot punish him for their sins. By the account of absolutely every member of the staff, your husband is a good man. Though your marriage has been but a day, he has been nothing but kind and eager to please."

Thoroughly chastened, I watched as she swept out of the room, puffed up on righteous indignation.

With a sigh, I flopped back into my chair. Imogen had missed a curl behind my ear. I certainly wasn't going to call her back for another tongue lashing, no matter how well deserved. A few pins were splayed out on the vanity, I tucked the curl back with one.

The tea was growing cold beside me. A sip confirmed that, unlike the ginger tea, the peppermint wasn't quite so unpleasant lukewarm. I downed the rest of the cup. I would need it for another one of Crawford's tours. Especially with a house this size.

"—AND THIS IS THE STUDY," Crawford drawled with an air of self-importance.

I peeked around the corner, hoping for a glimpse of my husband, only to be met with an empty chair. Objectively, I knew it was a rather large house. He wasn't avoiding me. Probably. Almost certainly.

I had often gone days living in a much smaller house with Ralph and managed to avoid him entirely. Except *that* had been entirely purposeful.

Still, my late husband lived in his study, particularly on days when his performance at the club had been less than exceptional—the majority of them.

Apparently, Lee did not live in his study, though evidence of his presence was everywhere, and a sharp burst of peppermint permeated the air. I took a few steps inside, approaching his desk while Crawford rambled on about the history of the furnishings or moldings, the same nonsense he had been babbling about for nearly two hours.

This room was lived in. There was a plate, bereft of all but a few crumbs, perched at the edge of the desk—surely some antique with a rich history that Crawford would relay. A half-drunk cup of tea, missing a saucer, left a ring on a hastily scribbled list. Ledgers were stacked on the floor in several piles, nonsensical to anyone except my husband I expected. Several books had been left open and lumped atop each other. Correspondence was also splayed across the mahogany desk in indiscriminate mounds.

It seemed my husband was something of a mess. For reasons I was incapable of explaining, that fact was endearing. Perhaps because he had been so practical about our entire arrangement. I needed a husband, and he needed a wife—of course we would marry. He would ask my father for permission—that was proper. A life together for a year, just long enough to stave off the gossipmongers—entirely well considered. If I was being generous, I suspected his absence last evening had an equally rational and reasonable explanation.

But this entirely sensible man was just a little bit of a mess, a little bit human like the rest of us. He was odd about carriages and had been claimed by a ridiculous cat and was just the tiniest bit irritated with me at the breakfast table this morning. My husband, a mortal after all.

Chapter Fifteen

BENNET HALL, SURREY - JUNE 13, 1816

LEE

Polishing a telescope mirror was always a tedious process with little room for error. Still, it was a worthy endeavor. If I did not keep up on it, the metal would tarnish and then the device would be out of commission until I could get it back to working order. I was forced to abandon a mirror a few months ago after the winter had been too harsh and I hadn't managed to replace it yet, so I had no backup.

Astronomy had once been a hobby, a passing interest. In the years after the accident, this room had become home. The stars never gasped or made comments. Planets never stared in horror.

The staff had learned to mostly leave me be here. Another thing that would need to change now that I had a wife. I couldn't very well spend all day and night out here, leaving Charlotte alone in the big house. I'd dragged her out to this secluded estate and insisted on her staying for a year. The least I could do was eat beside her.

Of course, if I managed to ruin another meal the way I had breakfast, perhaps I *should* live out here. Save us both the trouble of another stilted supper.

It hadn't been so bad being this large before the accident. The ladies seemed to enjoy it, and I appreciated their enjoyment. Men had generally respected me, likely because they knew they couldn't actually reach my chin to hit it.

After the accident... The same behaviors that were charming from a handsome man became terrifying from a hideous one. And when that man was three hands taller than a regular person... well, I could not blame anyone for their fears. I would be petrified of a scarred giant as well.

In my darker moments, I was quite glad I hadn't married Lady Celine following our courtship. She was more than a foot shorter than me and weighed seven, perhaps eight stone soaking wet.

Mia had been more substantial, though not by much. Eight or so inches shorter than me with a waiflike figure. I'd had to be careful not to injure her.

Charlotte was the tallest of the ladies in my life, half a foot, perhaps seven inches shorter than me. But she was still a little thing, even more so than she usually was if the cut of her gowns was any indication. Though tightening at her waist, the fabric hung loose around her arms and wrists this morning. It seemed the first few weeks of her condition had been difficult on her. I would need to make sure she didn't lose more weight.

A twirl spread through my gut at the thought of my delicate wife. Lord, I hoped I hadn't hurt her this morning. She said I hadn't. But she had also dismissed me when I asked what was wrong.

My back gave a token protest, as it always did when I worked on the mirrors. Too far to bend. It got worse after the accident. And worse still after I hit two and thirty. I straightened, bending back over the stool and twisting to one side, then the other.

That was the precise moment I heard Crawford's pompous rhetoric combined with two sets of footsteps coming up the path.

"And this is the observatory. His lordship had it built himself in—"

Charlotte! Here. Now.

I shot up, casting around frantically for something to do, something to put away, something to clean. There was too much, no place to start.

Why, oh why, had I assumed Crawford would know that my observatory was not to be part of his tour? The man had all the sense of a half-eaten scone.

The knob on the door rattled before it flew open. Crawford strode in filled with unearned confidence with Charlotte trailing wearily after him.

The man positively strutted, as if he'd built the observatory with his own hands, brick by brick. My wife's countenance was unreadable. Her pace slowed, abandoning Crawford's heels, as she stared at the room, her brow furrowed and lips parted. Upon catching sight of the telescope, her head tipped back, back, back. She spun slowly, wordlessly, in place, an implacable expression on her face.

Silently, she advanced along the walls of the hexagonal room, surveying my kingdom. When she reached the desk against the wall opposite me, she drew a finger along one of the star charts spread atop it.

In her position, she was bathed in the light from the opening of the domed ceiling. One of her curls had escaped her pins and brushed her neck with every movement. I had the utterly absurd desire to tug it, to see if it straightened and relaxed or coiled back like a spring.

She pushed aside the top chart and inspected the one beneath it. Then the armillary sphere caught her attention, she stepped over to it and traced it with a long finger.

Her lazy journey brought her to the workbench I had been crouched over moments ago and stopped before me. For the first time, I noticed her eyes had a ring of green around the perimeter of the mahogany irises. Little flecks of gold were there too. More notable for the bright sunlight caressing her face.

My butler, entirely oblivious to the rising tension inherent in her perusal, prattled on about the various construction methods of the building.

"Crawford," I broke in quickly, between two breaths. My eyes never leaving Charlotte's.

"Yes, my lord?"

"Get out."

He froze, speechless for an entire quarter of a minute, before protesting in disgruntled sputters.

"Thank you for the tour, Crawford. Your information has been invaluable," my wife added, head still tipped back to meet my gaze.

The man grumbled the entirety of the three feet he had to walk to the door and continued for some time, audible through the open ceiling. And through it all, neither of us breathed.

We weren't close, not scandalously so in any event. I had held her closer the night we danced. Our current distance had been halved the evening of her aborted seduction on the settee.

But this, now, something was in the air, thick and palpable, and I wasn't willing to be the one to cut it.

Seconds, minutes, hours later, her throat bobbed with a purposeful swallow. "So this is where you were last night?"

"Yes, I—did you need me for something last night?"

Something about my question had her expression shuttering as she took a step back from me. It was breakfast all over again.

I backed up another step, the backs of my legs hitting my work bench, and I half collapsed upon it.

Charlotte considered me carefully for a moment before gesturing to the entirety of my observatory. "What are you studying?"

"A little bit of everything. Stars, the moon, planets, anything, everything there is to see."

She nodded, though at what, I had no idea. "What are you working on now?"

"I'm polishing the mirror. It is prone to tarnish and can become misshapen. If it gets too off, I need to replace it."

"What is it for?"

"The telescope." I gestured to the massive golden tube occupying the majority of the floor.

"So you spend your nights here? Looking at the stars?" Devil take me. There was something about her tone I could not name, but it left me feeling uneasy, on edge.

"Yes—well, not all of them. Sometimes the weather doesn't oblige…"

"So if I wish to find my husband, I should begin my search here if the weather is fine?"

"I suppose. But I… is there something I can do for you?"

She shook her head and made another circuit around the room. The scrutiny was overwhelming as she examined my sanctuary with a critical but not unkind eye.

Her fingers were gentle as she trailed them over the various pieces of equipment strewn about the room. She bent over, inspecting the astrological clock on my desk. That motion displayed her pert derrière to great advantage, and I bit back a groan. I was, after all, celibate, not dead.

Finally, she turned to face me again, leaning against the desk, mimicking my position against the workbench. The gap between us spanned the entire room, and I felt every inch of it.

When she finally broke the silence, she didn't raise her voice, even in spite of the distance. Instead, her words were clear, bell-like, and in a practiced tone. "It is all very interesting. I can see why this would cause a man to abandon his wife on his wedding night."

Realization washed over me in waves. We hadn't spoken of it. In my mind, the conversation had been unnecessary. Obviously, I would not burden her with my desires. I could not risk it—could not have born it—not from her.

The muscles of my throat tightened uncomfortably. I swallowed, desperately hoping coherent speech wouldn't abandon me. "I... it occurs to me now that we never discussed... marital relations in our arrangement." My voice was thick and syrupy, and not in an attractive way.

Her only response was an arched brow.

I forced myself to continue, dragging each word out of my throat. "It had not occurred to me that you would expect or wish—that is—it is unnecessary given your current... condition. So I had assumed that we would... not."

"You assumed we would not?" She cocked out her hip, and her hand found it. The note of her voice was sharper, clearer. I could sense the pitfall in front of me. It was right there waiting, but I could not see through the mounds of brush and twigs and leaves. I could not find my way around the trap.

"Yes?"

She was silent. Unmoving. Eerily so.

"Very well." Her tone was thin, brittle. I had stepped right into that pit, and I had not even noticed the fall, the earth dropping out from under me, until I smacked the bottom with two little words.

Charlotte pressed herself away from the desk and exited the observatory without a sound. I was left with the understanding that I had said something very, very wrong.

And I hadn't the slightest idea what it was.

~

CHARLOTTE

Tears traced angry tracks down my cheeks, and I flicked them away with an irritated huff as I stomped away from my husband's observatory. Once again breaking my rule.

The reason that a cancerous, tangled pain grew in my chest until it stole my breath was a mystery. I hadn't wanted him in my bed in the first place—I truly hadn't. But that he did not wish to be...

This was all *its* fault, I was certain. It left me rounded and thick in all the wrong places and too thin in precisely the opposite ones. I was weak and sensitive in entirely unexpected ways.

Each and every interaction with my husband left me feeling more unappealing and unattractive than the last. Every time I thought he might... Every flicker of interest I thought I read in his eyes... It led nowhere, to nothing.

We had a purely practical arrangement, designed to suit both of our needs. And I should be thrilled—I was—it just seemed as if he had even fewer needs than I had anticipated.

Relief should be washing over me like a hot bath on a cold night. There was no reason to dread my husband's attentions because he had no intention of paying me any. At least three-quarters of the *ton* would be ecstatic in my situation. *I* would have been ecstatic in my situation less than a year ago.

And still the tears refused to cease, burning angry salty trails down my face and neck. I was not pretty crier, not naturally anyway. I could feign tears, lovely individual things. But the real ones were hot and ugly and left me a reddened, snotty mess.

I found myself in some sort of garden that was surely a future stop on Crawford's never-ending tour. Separated from the observatory by a large hedgerow, I was free to be hideous. Surrounded by flowers of every possible shade, I collapsed onto a wrought iron bench.

Bumblebees flitted from bloom to bloom relishing in their successful gathering. They paid me no mind, caring little for my flushed, swollen face.

Lee did not want me. Wesley did not want me. Rosehill did not want me. For all that men spoke in less than covert whispers about my face and figure, not one of them had shown the slightest interest in me when I was free for the taking.

This scene was entirely absurd. I knew that. Anyone with any sort of sense would know that. A few months ago, I would have told anyone that I was in possession of a great deal of sense. But I knew better now.

Wesley had pledged such words of desire and passion, interspersed with promises to love me. And he had kissed me with such enthusiasm, if not skill. His touches, too, were rough and desperate and even after they left me cold and uneasy I still wanted him.

And then came the day that my courses should have arrived. It came and went without my notice, actually. The day after as well. It was a fortnight before I realized they were late. The work of another fortnight to confirm they were gone and not merely tardy.

Several more weeks were spent in search of the suddenly elusive Wesley. But the day I found him—that boxing match—that was the day I understood that I had been a senseless fool all along.

I had vowed then, in the back of my carriage smelling of sick and piss, to be sensible, practical. I intended, from that day forth, to be the reasonable woman I had always believed I was.

Yet here I was crying in a hedgerow, just as pathetic as I had always been.

Chapter Sixteen

BENNET HALL, SURREY - JUNE 13, 1816

LEE

SHE WAS STILL upset at supper. Not cross, but there was something resigned in her countenance and the silent way she pushed the food around her plate.

A few of the pickled dishes received a secondary bite. Nothing else did. I knew little about women in her condition, and I reminded myself to investigate in the library tonight. The cloud cover wasn't ideal for stargazing. Also, the damned cat had claimed the observatory for her domain. This afternoon she bit my ankle repeatedly until I abandoned the place to her rule.

"Is the menu not to your liking?" I asked, desperately hoping for some sort of conversation.

"Oh, no. It's lovely." She took an enthusiastic bite of the roast duck. But then she chewed, and chewed, and chewed. I saw the moment the prospect of swallowing crossed her mind and precisely how unappealing that thought was.

"Oh, Lord. Spit it out." She shook her head, choking it

down with a revolted expression. Automatically, my hand dipped into my pocket, and I grasped a handful of peppermints, shoving them in her direction.

She assessed them warily before plucking one, unwrapping it, and popping it into her mouth. Her shoulders fell and she sank farther back into the chair.

"Charlotte, you needn't eat things that are not agreeable to you merely because they are on your plate. Chef can adjust the offerings until your constitution is less delicate."

"That would be rude."

"So?"

"So! I'm sure his skills are unmatched. I would not wish to offend him." Her expression was one of genuine horror.

"Offend him all you like. I do. He can and does grumble all day long to the scullery maids."

"But he will find other employment!" The tone of her protest was filled with distressed abhorrence.

"That is unlikely. I pay him well to cook for one—now two. And if he does... there are other cooks in the world."

"But you will be dreadfully bored. I can tolerate little with any flavor."

"Perhaps. But it is preferable to watching you waste away."

"I am hardly wasting away." She gestured vaguely toward her torso, where her child grew.

I caught the sleeve of her gown, too loose, between two fingers, and lifted her wrist in the process. The soft cotton of her gown ripped from my grasp as she yanked her hand free.

Yet another misstep. "Charlotte..."

"I am aware you find me unappealing," she snapped. "You needn't comment on it as I can hardly change it."

"I do not find you unappealing," I blurted. The response escaped me without thought, but as I parsed the words, there was no lie in them. Far from unappealing. She was too appealing, and that was the entirety of the problem. Because I could not *do* anything about it.

A half-snorted scoff was the only response I was to receive.

"I do not. You are beautiful—you know that, of course. But in your condition... I just worry."

She considered me with downturned eyes. I hadn't the slightest idea what she was searching for in my expression, but she merely shook her head and took another bite of pickled cauliflower. She made a face, but I suspected that was due more to the unholy combination of peppermint and vegetable than the actual dish.

A thought needled its way into my head, hovering there and refusing to leave.

"Charlotte?"

"Yes?"

"Is-Is that why you were cross this morning? Because you believe I am—that I do not—that I did not come to you?"

"I was not cross," she insisted, not glancing up from her plate.

The bites of my meal turned to lead in my stomach. "Because if you were cross—and that was why—I should like to apologize. Well, I'd like to apologize regardless of the reason, in truth. I had thought—perhaps I was overly familiar when I walked you to your rooms, and when I showed you the house. But that is not entirely congruent with your earlier comments."

Her fork clanged against the plate as she brought the napkin up to dab her lips. "I merely misunderstood the nature of our arrangement. Now that you have clarified, there will be no confusion going forward." Never once in the entire speech did her eyes meet mine.

"Oh... That is good." My voice was hollow for reasons I could not explain.

"Indeed."

"Did you—did you wish for a different agreement?" My heart twisted at the thought, even as I voiced it. "Because I suppose a discrete arrangement here in the country would not—"

"No! That—no, that is not what I was—no." Her eyes finally met mine, beseeching me to leave the subject.

"Right." The skin of the right side of my face was tight and angry with the flush of embarrassment creeping up along my cheeks.

Charlotte, too, was flushed but hers was a becoming dusky winter rose shade as she turned back to her napkin and folded it into a neat little triangle. When she finished her task, she stared at it with interest.

Following her lead, I pushed aside my plate and folded my own napkin. My attempt at a triangle was something of a disaster in my discomfited state and I gave up and dropped it in a lumpy pile on the table.

Finally, my wife broke the silence, turning back to me. "So, what is it that you hope to learn in your observatory?"

Desperate to take her unspoken offer of a less fraught conversation, I seized on the topic. "A little of everything." At her not entirely disinterested nod, I continued. "They found a comet perhaps five years ago. I did not even have the telescope yet, but you could see it with the naked eye. Perhaps you recall —though you would have been quite young—the Great Comet?"

"Not so young, I was nineteen. But I do not remember it."

"That is to be expected. It became an obsession then, I suppose. It was visible the summer after my wife died, during my recovery. It was something else to focus on. Before that, my interest was more... measured."

I was not entirely certain if she would press me for details of the accident. And I was less certain if I wanted her to. It was the first time I had mentioned it outright.

If I felt more relief or disappointment when she did not press me, was anyone's guess.

"So you had an observatory built?"

"First, I bought books, a lot of them. Then a smaller telescope—not the one you saw today. Much of the other equipment preceded the actual observatory."

"A gradual descent into madness then?" Her brow lifted, teasing.

"Oh, I was mad well before the comet." That comment earned me a laugh, relief flooding my chest at the musical sound. Perhaps that signaled the end of the palpable tension that had settled over this marriage like a thick, inky fog.

~

CHARLOTTE

There was an eagerness about him when he discussed the comet and the stars and his equipment. A delighted pride he wore like a cloak.

It was... charming. As was his proclivity for peppermints. They seemed to be the only thing that settled my stomach with any consistency. That he always had them on hand and that he retained their scent was a pleasant surprise.

This was almost nice. Perhaps we would not be husband and wife in any real way, but friendship could be attainable. If I was honest, I was in need of a friend or two. There was no rule that one's convenient, platonic husband could not be a companion and confidant.

"Do you—would you wish to see it?" Lee asked. It seemed asking about his observatory was the proper course of action with my husband. Far from horses, gaming tables, and his estate, his interests lay with the heavens.

I did not particularly care about the stars, planets, or comets. But in the interest of marital harmony, I could feign enthusiasm.

Today had been no less exhausting than the day before, but I ended this day as I meant to go forward, amicably. After all, when I had dried my tears that afternoon, I vowed once more to act as the sensible woman I knew I could be.

"That would be nice." If he could read my fib, he made no mention of it. Instead, he turned back to his plate with eagerness.

And so it was, as the clock struck ten, that I followed him out of the house and down the well-loved footpath to the observatory, trailing after the lamp in his grasp.

The night was brisk. Gooseflesh rose up my arms and the back of my neck. Fortunately, the trip was a short one and we reached the observatory before I could regret *every* one of my choices.

Lee ushered me inside and placed the lamp on the desk before making for the nearby candles. He lit only a few, leaving us cast in shadow. By the time he had finished his task, it became apparent that this room was not significantly warmer than the walk over had been. Probably owing to the large hole in the ceiling.

"I close it up in case of inclement weather," Lee said, answering my question before I gave it voice. "There are shutters."

I merely nodded, no closer to understanding his fascination than when I arrived earlier this morning.

Without a word, he nodded to the telescope. It was an impressive beast, far larger than any I could have imagined. He tipped it down, then bent his knees to look through it and moved it across the night sky.

He stepped back and gestured me to the device. It took a moment to understand, he had adjusted it for me. My husband was a tall man, quite the tallest of my acquaintance, but he had successfully set the scope for my eyes. I peered through the lens.

"What do you see?"

"A star. I think a star?"

"Altair. You can see that one easily with your naked eye. May I?" I broke away while he maneuvered the metal tube again. He brought it lower, closer to the horizon. The effort required him to bend even farther and crouch slightly.

For such a large man, my husband was quite graceful. By sheer size, he should have been clumsy and awkward, but those were words I'd never once thought in relation to him. The sheer effort required to orient the telescope for my use was astonishing.

"Here," he said, backing away again.

The image in the scope looked almost exactly like the star, perhaps less bright and more distinctly round.

"What am I looking at?"

"Jupiter."

Shocked, I pulled away and met his gaze. At my surely astounded expression, he merely nodded.

I turned back and peered at the object again. "I am looking at the planet Jupiter?"

"Yes."

"But it's so clear."

"You don't even need the telescope." He backed me away, pointing to the open ceiling. "Here, in Virgo."

"I don't know where that is."

"There, the brightest star right there, Spica. Those nine stars make up the constellation. And right—there—is Jupiter."

He pointed at a speck, perhaps the slightest bit brighter than the other specks, parted between great fluffy clouds.

When I offered no comment, he made to grab my hand only to freeze an inch or so from it.

"May I?"

I felt my brow furrow in confusion until he tipped his head toward my hand.

"Oh, yes," I replied even before understanding dawned. "I—you were not—have not been overly familiar, Lee. I promise."

His nod was relieved and a tension I hadn't noticed lifted from his shoulders. He wrapped his oversize hand around mine and adjusted my fingers to a point. His knees bent to line him up to my height, and his soft, peppermint-scented breath brushed against a curl. The warmth of him finally breaking through the chill of the room.

"How do they know it's the planet? And not another star?"

"The way it moves throughout the sky is very different."

I nodded as though that explanation made sense. His free hand had found my hip, holding me steady. Not that I was unsteady. At least, I was not before he decided to manhandle me.

He pulled my hand up, up, up, until I was pointing directly to the heavens. "Do you know what this constellation is?"

"I do not know what any of them are."

"Cassiopeia, the one your dearest friend is named after."

I pulled away from him with a laugh. "Your cat is a menace."

"She is."

Free from his grasp, I was surer, more at ease. But I was cold again.

Lee must have read my shiver because he shucked his coat without a word and draped it over my shoulders before adjusting the telescope once more.

The wool was thick and warm and smelled of peppermint and something undefinable, woody and more subtle. It was huge. The fabric drowned me, hitting my calves. When I slipped my arms in the sleeves, I had several inches left to scrunch over my wrists.

"How do you know all of this? I've never understood the constellations. They do not look like what they are named."

He huffed a laugh, still tilting and turning the tube. "No, I suppose you're right. There are maps. If you spend enough time with them... you memorize them I suppose."

Seemingly satisfied with the positioning, he wandered over to the desk and flipped through the charts. He shifted one to the top, then beckoned me over.

And there it was, the heavens made paper. He had drawn little lines between dots with labels. Virgo—as he'd mentioned, Cassiopeia, Hercules, Ursas major and minor, Draco, Lyra. Some I had heard of and some were completely new to me.

Tentatively, I lifted the paper and took it over to the open windows. I held it up, trying to match Virgo as he showed me with the chart. "Virgo." I pointed when I found it, turning for approval. He leaned back against the desk but nodded encouragingly. When I looked again at the sky, the stars all swirled into indistinguishable dots. Eventually, nearly straight up, I found one I recognized. "Ursa Minor."

"Yes."

"Most of them still look like random dots, even with the chart," I commented, returning to his side.

Lee laughed out another, "yes," before taking the map and setting it back on the desk. He had rolled up the sleeves of his shirt, leaving bare, muscular forearms dusted with light brown hair. The veins there were prominent. Those were masculine forearms. It was an inane thought, but it was true, there was nothing delicate about his arms.

"What do you hope to learn with all of this?" I repeated, gesturing to the entirety of the observatory.

"I doubt I'll discover anything new, if that's what you're asking. There are more powerful telescopes out there and people far smarter and far more dedicated than me. I just... it makes me feel small. And makes the world feel less... random."

"Really? It seems quite chaotic out there to me."

"I know, but it is not. They rise and set in a predictable pattern. It changes throughout the year and the night, but if you know where to look... they will always be there." He found a journal and flipped to a page, then directed my attention to it. In neat script were detailed notes of what he saw, what he expected to see in the coming days.

"Ordered chaos then."

"Indeed. Thank you." His tone was tentative, soft.

"For what?"

"Indulging me. I can be a little... enthusiastic about all of this."

"Yes." He huffed a quiet chuckle in response to my honesty. "But that is not to say it is not worthy of being enthusiastic about."

I turned back to him from his notes. He was closer than I'd expected, less than a foot. Lee's eyes found mine, catching there and holding. His irises were dark in the dim lighting, a shade lighter than the inky sky he was so interested in.

My breath had escaped me on finding him so close. It was hooked, caught in my throat waiting for.... something.

Midnight eyes flicked to my lips and back to meet my gaze. I had seen that look before, from men.

Before I could decide how I felt about that possibility, Lee shook himself free from our moment and stepped back. My breath returned in a disappointed rush.

"You—" He broke off and cleared his throat. "You must be tired. I'll see you back to the house."

"No need. I know the way." I lit a spare lantern he had near the door, then I stepped outside before he could protest.

It wasn't until I found myself shutting the door to my chambers that I realized I was still wrapped in his oversize, peppermint-scented coat. When I stripped it off, I was left even colder than before, and no number of logs added to the fire could match that warmth.

Chapter Seventeen
BENNET HALL, SURREY - JUNE 23, 1816

CHARLOTTE

"—TRULY will not join me at the bonfire tonight?" a lilting feminine voice questioned, disappointment lacing the words.

"You know I would love nothing more. But I cannot abandon him," a honeyed baritone answered.

I was nearly certain it was Brigsby and Eliza, one of the maids. Their overdramatic flirtation was a source of much amusement for me. She was a pretty thing, with dark hair and eyes and full lips. Truthfully, she could do far better than Brigsby, but his attentions must have held some appeal because she always encouraged them.

I had returned to the breakfast room only to fetch the book I had forgotten earlier. But the overloud-loud whispers out in the hall were far too intriguing to interrupt. Silently, I pressed closer to the door, striving to hear.

"He has a wife now. Surely she can look after him."

Lee. They were discussing Lee and me. There was no doubt now.

"Eliza... Please understand. If there were any way—"

What does that mean?

"If there were any way, you would be with me. Yes, yes. But you only have yourself to blame if I become chilled at the celebration and allow Tommy Higgins to warm me."

"You wouldn't..."

"I suppose you will never know. Because you'll be here. With him. And I'll be there. With Tommy Higgins."

"Eliza," Brigsby warned. "You know Tommy Higgins cannot kiss you the way I do."

"I know no such thing," she insisted.

"You don't want Tommy Higgins," Brigsby's voice dipped into a growl.

"You don't know that."

"I do know that. I know that very well. Because Tommy Higgins is a boy barely out of leading strings and you, you require a man."

I had to bite my lip to hold back my laughter. It was quite possibly the worst line I'd ever heard.

Eliza seemed to agree with me because she huffed, retorting, "You're right, I do. But I do not see any here." Her slippers stomped down the hall, irritation ringing in every step.

Brigsby sighed, and I waited, listening for a second set of footsteps.

Instead, the knob by my hip turned. Startled, I leaped back as Brigsby opened the door.

For a second, we both stared wide-eyed at each other. Then, he began, "My lady, how long have you—"

"Longer than you would have wished," I offered, still biting back a smile.

"Right. And I do not suppose I can persuade you to forget you heard any of that."

I shook my head, allowing the grin to bloom slowly.

He cursed before straightening, a worried gaze shooting to

mine. It was the precise moment I lost control of the giggles that threatened to overtake me.

"'A *man*...'" I quoted between bubbles of laughter.

His hand found his eyes and pressed there as his head hinged back.

After some minutes, my laughter quieted to a manageable chuckle every few seconds. "So that went well."

"Indeed, spectacular. They'll be reading the banns any day now."

I shot him a look. "Come now, you have no serious designs on that girl. And she's not truly considering you either."

"It's just nice. A bit of flirtation with a pretty girl to break up the day."

"That better be all it is. If I find out that you've compromised the girl—"

He raised his hands in surrender. "I haven't. I swear it."

"Good. See that it stays that way. Now, what is tonight?"

Finally confident he wasn't about to see his employment terminated, Brigsby leaned a hip against the doorframe and crossed one arm across his chest as he wrapped a hand around the opposite bicep.

"It's a festival. Down in the village. For St. John's Eve."

"Oh, yes, I forgot. Imogen had mentioned that. It seems like a jolly good time. Why can you not go?"

His free hand reached up to scratch the back of his neck as he straightened. "I— I have duties to attend to. Lord Champaign—"

"Will survive for a few hours without your manly assistance."

He winced. "It will be quite some time before you forget that, yes?"

"Oh, years, if ever."

"Perfect... But no, thank you. I could not possibly—"

"I have given Imogen the eve off. Surely Lee can spare you. In fact, I was considering asking him to attend with—"

"No!" He'd started toward me, his hands grabbing my upper arms. Brigsby realized his position at the precise moment I did because he released me at once, stepping back. "I beg your pardon, my lady, but no," he insisted, calmer.

"Why?" I demanded.

"That is not really—"

"I will forgive the impertinence of the scene you just caused if you tell me why. Why can I not ask my husband to accompany me to a festival in the village? Why can you not leave him?"

I could see the entirety of his thought process. Right up until the moment when he spun to the door and peered into the hall. Satisfied we were alone, he pulled the door shut.

He sighed and urged me to my usual place at the breakfast table before taking Lee's seat. His lips pursed as he considered me.

"Well..." I demanded, gesturing for him to get on with it.

"Lord Champaign—he has not told you of his scars, I assume?"

I considered lying. It was almost certainly the sort of a thing a wife ought to know about her husband. But he was not truly asking. He knew. So I nodded.

"He is—it was a fire." In retrospect, that was surely obvious to anyone with sense. His scars were clearly from a burn. Why I had not considered it, I did not know.

"It took some time, months, before he could even abide a fire in the grate. That was a cold autumn. But he managed it. Though, in truth the alternative was to freeze to death in this glacial house so it was not much of a choice."

"But a bonfire..." I continued for him.

Brigsby nodded. "A bonfire is too wild, too uncontained. And tonight—it is not a good night for Lord Champaign."

"Because of the fires?"

I watched the indecision cross his face before he leaned forward. "The combination of the many bonfires—the smell of smoke in the air..."

"Thank you for telling me." He nodded, though he wore an expression of guilt, as though he had betrayed my husband's confidence. "I think you should go tonight. To the festival. With Eliza. She is right—Lee has a wife now."

"My lady, I do not think that—"

"You should bring her flowers too. Might have a warmer reception."

His mouth was downturned and his eyes guarded when he asked, "Are you sure?"

"Yes." I buried the uncertainty down deep. "Yes."

~

I SEARCHED THE STUDY, the library, his bedroom, and the observatory without any sign of my husband after supper.

The meal itself had been stilted—more so than it had since we clarified our arrangement at any rate. Lee ate little, if anything, and contributed nothing but one-word answers to my attempts at conversation.

It was a very good thing Brigsby had informed me, or I probably would have been cross with my husband.

No sooner had I set my fork down than Lee shot from his seat and disappeared into the bowels of the house without a word.

I set out a few moments later to the observatory—expecting that to be his likely haunt—only to find it dark and shuttered in the balmy night. The fires in the nearby village left an orange cast on the horizon and acrid smoke was thick on my tongue. Brigsby hadn't undersold the scent.

Crawford and Mrs. Fitzroy were all that remained of the

staff. The rest had been given leave to laugh and dance and flirt in the village until the fires burned low. It was the first time Jack, the youngest of the footmen, had been allowed to join. He was now six and ten and his excitement had been palpable.

Crawford opened the door for me with his usual obsequious, overdone bow. Each time he did it, my annoyance lessened and it became more of an amusement.

I left him in the entry and forged ahead in my fruitless search for my husband.

Room after empty room, I wandered until all that was left was the guest wing. Crawford had—to my astonishment—been willing to leave this off the tour. Instead, he simply stated that it was a mirror of the family wing. Upon setting foot at the top of the steps, it became clear that the only significant difference was a muggy damp in the air and a dearth of light.

The candlestick in my hand chased away the dark—that and a semicircle of light spilling underneath a door—nearly the last in the hall. The one that, if I was oriented correctly, matched my own.

Outside the door, I wavered in my conviction. Whether to knock or simply enter or abandon him to his musings—questions much more fraught than they had been at the other end of the corridor.

Desperate for insight, I pressed my ear to the door in an entirely unladylike fashion, but I was met with nothing but silence.

With a bracing inhale, I turned the knob and took a single step inside.

Feminine, with light olives and slate blues accented with burnished steel rather than her favorite creams, Amelia Bennet's bedroom was elegant in a way I'd begun to picture the lady herself. And I was certain that *this* was her bedroom —not the room I had been given.

Sheer curtains draped elegantly in front of the massive

windows in the same way I'd considered for my own chamber. The bed was a large four poster that should have looked bulky, but the carvings on the headboard and the posts were so intricate and delicate it was astonishing it managed to support the canopy. The bed coverings looked as soft as a cloud but were the dark blue-gray shade the clouds grew just before a storm.

Those details, however, were secondary to the scarred profile of my husband, plopped on a rug the color of fresh rosemary with his back leaning against the foot of the bed. Either he hadn't heard my entrance or hadn't cared because he didn't turn to face me. Instead, he stared straight ahead, unblinking, at the unlit fireplace grate. One long leg was sprawled straight in front of him, the other bent at the knee. He rested a forearm on the knee, and between two fingers, he twisted a long silver chain. A ring spun from the end of the chain, glinting as it twisted back and forth in the light of the candle beside him. Next to the candle, a half-empty bottle of a clear liquor was clasped in his loose fist.

Gooseflesh rose on my arms and the back of my neck despite the tepid, clammy state of the room. "Lee?" I whispered.

I caught a flinch—nearly imperceptible—of his lip. The candlelight at his side caught on the edges of his scars, sketched captivating and intimidating lines and crevices along the blade of his cheek. His heavy hand closed around the bottle and dragged it to his lips for a lazy swig before dropping back to the floor. I received no other reply.

He wasn't drunk. I'd found Ralph collapsed drunk on the floor or the settee or the staircase more than once, and this wasn't that. But Lee wasn't *here* either. And I didn't know what to do.

Slowly, with the trepidation of approaching a wildcat in a trap, I stepped toward him. When I received no protest, I knelt next to him and set my candlestick beside his.

"Lee," I tried again, suddenly hoarse.

His throat bobbed but he didn't turn. "Shouldn't be here," he rasped out.

"But..." I began with no notion of what to follow the protestation with.

"You should go." The words were crisp and clear, without the slur of drink, but the usual warm notes of his baritone were absent. And for the first time ever, they smelled nothing of peppermint.

"I think I should help you back to your chambers."

He shook his head, eyes never leaving the fireplace even as he continued to twirl the ring—a pretty, dainty thing, with an amethyst stone.

Something glinted off his cheek and it took an embarrassingly long time for me to work out that it was a tear, dipping in and out of the divots of his skin in its trek down his face.

It was as though I was watching someone else, but it was my hand that reached for Lee's cheek, to brush the tear away.

His head shot back and he nearly fell in his attempt to get away.

The candlesticks knocked into each other as he kicked out instinctively to right himself. Both dropped to the floor in an echoing clatter and went out, casting the room into night.

"Get out!" His cold growl echoed, his gin-soaked breath harsh and ragged in the darkness.

With all the grace I could muster, I rose and strode from the room in but three purposeful steps. I followed the hall, down the steps, and out the front entry without a word to anyone.

I would not beg a man—not ever again.

Chapter Eighteen
BENNET HALL, SURREY - JUNE 24, 1816

LEE

I AWOKE TO THE STALE, musty scent of long unused bed linens and every single one of my muscles protesting even the slightest movement.

"How are you feeling?" It was Brigsby, somewhere off to the side in that smoothed-out tone he always used after an attack. It was the way one spoke to a child and I hated it a little.

It took a moment to unlock my jaw. "Like death," I croaked, my throat still scratched raw. "How bad?"

"I don't know. I found you after."

Carefully, I blinked my eyes open and found Brigs perched on a stool beside my bed—the old one. Daylight poured in from the window at his back—damn. I had a vague recollection of supper with Charlotte, then... nothing.

"Why'm I here?"

"Because you're too big to carry down the hall, down a flight of stairs, up another, and down a second corridor."

"Fair. Charlotte—did she see?"

"I neither know nor care. I found her stomping around the bonfire in a huff." There was something odd in his tone, but the throbbing in my head was too strong to concentrate on anything else.

"Would you like something to eat, my lord? You missed luncheon."

"Don't think I can manage more than toast."

"I'll return shortly. Try to rest," he rose and made for the door.

"Brigs," I started and he froze, not spinning to face me. "Thank you."

He turned, his gaze meeting mine. "Do not thank me." With that, he stepped from the room, shutting the door behind him.

After much consideration and with a great deal of effort, I flopped to my back. I laid there for some time, contemplating a crack forming in the ceiling. Fortunately, it didn't appear structural from my vantage or I would have been compelled to investigate.

The rattle of the door against the frame drew my attention. Rather than Brigsby with the toast, the door opened of its own volition—only a crack. I let my head flop back to the pillow and waited for my intruder to hop on the bed. She obliged with a quiet *mrow*, before curling up between my knees. Not a single attempted bite or scratch. It could only mean that I looked so wretched even the cat felt sympathy for me.

On occasion, Cass was willing to lay with me without her usual displays of irritation—after the accident, after and on occasion during an attack, whenever I came down with a cold. Those moments, though rare, were the primary reason I never tried particularly hard to keep her out of wherever she wished to be.

"—is he?" Charlotte's sharp whisper floated in through the door.

"Fine." Brigs's familiar tenor, hushed as well, followed.

"Is he awake?" Me—she was speaking of me. Any hope I had of keeping my attacks from her vanished. The thought had me biting back a groan that wasn't the result of physical pain.

"Yes."

"He told me to leave, Brigsby. What would you have had me do?" Charlotte's quiet voice was thick with sentiment.

"Stay with him, as you said you would."

"I did not know—you did not tell me."

"I *told* you that he struggles with fire. You insisted you could manage it. Instead, I find you wandering through the village watching the celebration without a care in the world. Leaving him to suffer alone," he hissed.

"*That* was not about the fires. Not entirely." Was it possible to die of shame? I rather thought I could manage it in that moment. What *had* she seen?

"It is not my place to share your husband's confidences if you are unable to earn them yourself."

"He asked—ordered—me to leave. Should I have stayed against his express wishes? Begged? I do not—will not—beg."

"Beg, do not beg, I care not, my lady. You left a good man to suffer alone."

"Will you please just tell me if he's all right? That is all I wish to know."

"He will be fine," Brigsby snapped, abandoning the whisper entirely. I caught the distinctive pattern of Charlotte's slippered feet on the hall rug, less jaunty than I had grown used to in the short days of our marriage.

It was followed by Brigsby's oafish stomping and a singular curse when he found the door cracked. His head peered in first, a hopeful expression across his face that immediately fell upon meeting my gaze.

"Damn cat. How much of that did you hear?"

"Enough. Brigsby, I appreciate your efforts to champion me," I began, struggling to press myself up on the pillows stacked behind my head. "But you cannot speak to my wife in that manner."

"Even if she deserves it?" he asked, handing over a tray with peppermint tea and buttered toast before resting a hip against the edge of the bed.

"She does *not* deserve it. But no, even if she did, you cannot reproach her. You may be as impertinent with me as you wish—you often are. But not Lady Champaign."

"My lord—"

"No, enough now." I didn't recall the night before. If past experience was any predictor, I never would. But I didn't doubt I had sent Charlotte away as she said.

She was saddled with me, surely that was punishment enough for any misdeeds, real or imagined.

Brigsby wore his irritation in the tension of his brow and downturned lips, but he huffed, leaving the tray and abandoning me to the anxious, melancholy exhaustion that often marked the day after an attack.

◈

I HADN'T SEEN or heard from Charlotte by the time night fell. Whether that was Brigsby's doing or hers was even odds.

The proper thing to do would be to seek her out, apologize for whatever I said or did. But every time I considered it, my heart began to race and beads of sweat welled up on the back of my neck.

So I hid. I was confident enough in my masculinity to

admit that I hid in my old bedroom until well after supper when I snuck out to my observatory like a thief in the night.

Fortunately, the sky was clear, a promising night to lose myself in the stars. Steadfast and dependable as always, they kept me company for some time until I heard the creak of the door slipping open.

Expecting Cass, I didn't bother to turn until a flood of light spilled into the room.

Charlotte, pale and ethereal hovered tentatively in the doorway, lamp in hand. My heart tripped a moment but then righted itself.

"Charlotte, I..."

She shook her head, curls flashing gold in the flickering candle. "May I come in?"

Words were certain to fail me. All I could offer was a small nod. She set the lamp on the desk. Freed of their occupation, her fingers fidgeted at her sides.

"Are you well?" Soft, with a hint of vibrato, her voice carried in the quiet distance between us.

"Well enough. I must ap—"

The shake of her head, barely more than a tremble, broke my speech. "If you are well, that is all I need to know. I shall leave you to it." She turned, reaching for the lamp.

Stay.

"You could stay," I blurted before my head could order my mouth silent. "If you want."

"Do you want?" Something about the note of the last word spoke of vulnerability, even though she didn't turn to face me and her hand still hovered an inch or so off the handle.

"He asked—ordered—me to leave." My chest tightened, aching, but this time not because of my earlier attack—at least not directly.

"I do."

Charlotte turned once more, her eyes meeting mine. "Then I will stay."

I nodded, trying desperately to keep the elation from my face. I reached into my pocket. "Peppermint?" I croaked.

"Yes, please." She stepped to me and plucked it from my palm, then popped it between full rose lips, upturned in a gentle smile that spoke of relief. A relief we could share.

Chapter Nineteen

BENNET HALL, SURREY - JULY 10, 1816

CHARLOTTE

THE BURNT-ORANGE STREAK seeped into the parchment, the finishing touch on my watercolor. Careful of the wet paint, I set it beside the chart Lee was fussing with. "Is this how it should look?"

Lee turned from his notes slowly. For the last fortnight, I had taken to joining him in the observatory. While he observed the stars, I observed my husband. He was often reluctant to abandon a thought. It was as though he had to rip his eyes from whatever was occupying him.

But he always managed—without complaint—then he devoted himself with the same singular focus to whatever had pulled him away. In this case, my painting.

"This is extraordinary. You managed all that detail from the telescope?"

"No, I cannot see all the colors from your scope, or the individual rings. But it was described in that book." I gestured to one of the texts left open to a description of Saturn. "And when you explained that they were separate, it made sense to paint them individually. Was that wrong?"

"No, not at all. It is perfect."

My teeth caught my lower lip, hiding a pleased smile from his gaze.

"You do not mind it? Helping me here?" His eyes were wide and downturned when he asked. The expression he always wore when that same question crossed his lips.

It was never a lie when I replied, "I do not mind, truly. It is something quite different." At his disbelieving expression, I added, "I find myself weary of painting floral vases and fruit."

As always, his eyes narrowed at me, searching for the lie that was not there.

Ignoring the display, I turned to his notes for the night. "Will you show me the mapping again?"

Lee nodded distractedly while reaching into a pocket for a peppermint. I held my hand out expectantly and he dropped one into it. He always brought out an extra for me now. At first, it was the only thing that settled my stomach consistently. And now... well, I just liked them. The sharp bite, just shy of painful on my tongue, was soothing in a way it had no right to be.

I reached for his sketchbook and flipped to a clean page. Then I drew the requisite circles with the compass. I sketched the lines and labeled them as he had taught me a few days before, 0–23. He quietly directed me with the sextant and explained where to plot each star on the parchment.

"Here," he murmured, pointing one line over.

I sighed and crossed out the star I'd drawn.

"Such a perfectionist," he tutted, something teasing in his grin as his mint breath washed over me.

His chuckle was warm and bemused, and I must have rolled my eyes again. He seemed to find that unfortunate habit a source of endless amusement.

The fortnight since St. John's had been quiet but illuminating. Our tacit agreement never again to mention that night served us well. It allowed me to observe my husband in his natural habitat. Here in the observatory, Lee moved with a kind of confidence he seldom displayed elsewhere. He stood even taller, was more decisive in his statements, and moved with purpose. In this room, he never faltered.

And the way he spoke to me, the soft praise, the gentle corrections—I hadn't known men were capable of such... kindness. It was a jarring juxtaposition, this massive embodiment of masculinity speaking in a tone that could only be described as tender.

Enjoyable as it was in the moment, the encouragement, the praise, and the way they made me feel—it was worrisome. It was an addiction. I could almost believe he *liked* my painting. His words nearly had me convinced that I was doing quite well with this star charting. The thoughts warmed something in my chest.

Another few stars plotted without error earned me a genuine smile. He reached out to clasp my upper arm in his hand, pausing a breath away before closing the gap. His grip was warm and pleasant, seeping into the bone beneath.

"Soon you shall outstrip me, and I will be tossed from my own observatory." Blueish gray eyes gripped my gaze, forcing me to acknowledge the comment with a small smile.

"Hardly."

I knew, I *knew* these little compliments were things he offered to keep the peace, to placate a wife he hadn't wanted. But he was so sincere when he delivered them, I could almost forget, if only for a moment.

He was so damn nice to everyone too. Even the vindictive cat who sat curled atop some piece of equipment I couldn't recall the name of. It was certainly not a place he wanted her to be, but he just shook his head and allowed her to ball up there.

Was I like the cat? Someone who pranced in and did what she wanted but whom he indulged because he was too kind to do anything else.

"It took me months to learn to do this properly. And you're perfection in a but a few nights." It was certainly another lie, but it had something flipping in my belly anyway.

Lee's sincerity made me want to be brave in a way I hadn't in years. And as I watched the boyish delight cross his face as he urged me over to look at some star or other, an idea took hold.

∽

Lee

She rolled her eyes again at the compliment. I wasn't entirely certain she was aware of the motion. Every time I saw it, I was forced to bite back a laugh. Her reaction left me desperate to offer her more praise, just for the scoff and eye roll. How had she survived in the *ton* with such an expressive face?

If I were a better man, I would stop dragging her out here each night. Women with child needed rest, not hours in a chilled observatory with their eccentric husbands.

But I quite liked her company. She was a distraction, to be sure. But a nice one—a distraction that smelled of orange blossoms and lavender. A distraction that rolled her eyes at me and painted the most stunning depiction of Saturn I had ever seen put to paper. While I was perhaps the least productive I had ever been, I was also enjoying my work in a way I had quite forgotten.

Seeing the galaxy through new eyes was invigorating. Explaining things to her brought new life to them.

Cass took that moment to hop off her perch on the scaphe and onto the floor with an irritated chirp. She pranced over to my wife and wound herself around Charlotte's legs, tangling in her skirts. And Charlotte gamely, just as she had the last three times the cat had done this, dropped her hand out for Cass to sniff.

The cat, seemingly approving, rubbed her head under the fingers before dragging her back along while Charlotte offered a few scratches down her spine. Every time before, Cass had rewarded my wife's efforts with a bite. When Cass turned around, rubbing along my wife's fingers again, I caught the edge of a flinch. But still, she did not remove her hand. And this time, to the astonishment of two humans, and probably the cat herself, she allowed a second set of gentle scratches down the spine. With a final chirp, Cass sashayed out of the observatory and into the night.

My wife turned to me, astonishment written across her face, which surely mirrored my own. "Did she just?"

"I think so."

"What does that mean?" She whispered, eyes wide and lips parted fetchingly.

"Perhaps she likes you?"

"Surely not." Charlotte shook her head. "She must be lulling me into false complacency. She will surely bite the entire hand off next time." Her tone was full of mirth while she struggled to keep her expression sincere.

I lost my fight with my own laughter, and it escaped in a huff. "You're almost certainly right. But it will be a challenge for her—even your tiny hands are bigger than her head."

"My hands are not tiny. You just have massive, beastly paws." I caught one of hers in mine and lined up our wrists.

Lord, she was right. They were beastly in comparison. Charlotte's delicate fingers and carefully maintained nails did not even reach my second knuckle.

"Perhaps these are why you're so skilled at painting—dainty hands. Probably explains the piano too."

"Yes, it's certainly the hands and not the hours of practice." Another eye roll.

I caught my lower lip, hiding my smile. "Are you suggesting that it is a lack of effort on my part? I am personally offended, you know. My mother once convinced me to sit at the bench for seven entire minutes. Is that not enough?"

"Oh certainly. In fact, it was probably three minutes too long. I've heard that too much practice can result in an overly studied air."

The desire to slip my fingers just the tiniest bit to the side, to slot them with hers and curl them around her hand was overwhelming. I broke our hands apart, turning back to her sketchbook beside us.

On top was the painting of Saturn she had done earlier, perfect rings delicately wrapped around the brightly colored sphere. "May I?"

She nodded and I flipped to the beginning. A vase filled with roses, another filled with tulips, a third filled with sunshine-yellow daisies. A bowl of fruit—she hadn't been jesting. Regardless of the subject, they were quite good to my untrained eye. She captured the light and the textures, even with the watercolor medium.

I knew ladies were expected to have accomplishments. But surely, even among the most accomplished ladies, Charlotte was extraordinary.

"We should have some of these framed. Do you have favorites?"

"Oh, that's not necessary. They're nothing compared to the paintings that are already hanging."

"They're lovely." I insisted, but I could see my protests were falling on deaf ears. With a sigh, I set the sketchbook back on the desk. I rather thought they belonged on the walls of our home—something to remember her by when she returned to town and left me behind.

Already I knew I had made a mistake. My promise to leave her to her life in town after one year... It would devastate me when she left. I knew that now. In a few short weeks, Charlotte had woven her way into my life. After a year, she would be essential to me.

I had time though. Perhaps I could convince her to let me keep the paintings—Saturn at least, and probably the daisies. They were bright and happy. And, if she still refused... I wasn't entirely above stealing from my own wife.

If I couldn't keep her, I could keep something of hers.

Chapter Twenty
BENNET HALL, SURREY - JULY 24, 1816

LEE

She was trying to kill me with the damn gowns. Why had I thought it was a good idea to have a modiste brought in from London? The woman was clearly well versed in torture.

Charlotte fussed over her barely existent belly for weeks before the curve was obvious. What *was* obvious was her bosom. Every morning it was more magnificent than the last.

It was entirely possible that I was merely so desperate for the sight of a woman's curves that my mind was running away from me. But this gown... another of her favored golden, buttery silks, plunged low on her breasts for the sole purpose of sending me to the asylum.

My wife sat primly across from me at the supper table as usual. Her nausea entirely dissipated, she dipped her spoon into the white soup with more frequency and enthusiasm than in weeks passed.

Much as it thrilled me to see her eating more, I would miss the peppermints. The first few weeks, she had asked for them politely. By the third week of marriage, she merely held out an expectant hand, waiting for me to deposit one or two. It was nice. Intimate. I still carried more than usual each day, just in case.

"How is the cloud cover tonight? Do we have any hopes of a Uranus sighting?"

And then there was that. The interest she had taken in my hobby. It was likely feigned, I *knew* that. I couldn't help but love it anyway. She had taken to listening to me babble with a bemused smile—my absolute favorite expression. It was accompanied by the littlest roll of the eyes before one side of her lips quirked up in an indulgent curl.

"Doubtful, I'm afraid. It's muggy out. I expect we'll get rain later. Though I'm beginning to suspect it is my scope and not the weather preventing us from finding her. I will probably need to upgrade my equipment if we're to have any hope."

"But you said it should be low on the horizon. Perhaps it's the terrain?"

She was acting, I knew. Truly I did. But she was so skilled I could almost believe she was interested.

"Shall I purchase another estate then?"

"Oh, certainly. Though perhaps you should wait until you receive the bill from the modiste." It was not the first time she'd delicately hinted at the coming expense. I couldn't see how she could bankrupt me with the bit of frippery she wore tonight—there was hardly enough fabric for that—but I did wonder who left her so concerned over funds. Whether it was her late husband or her father's doing was anyone's guess. If forced to put money on it, I would have leaned toward her father. Her behavior spoke of old habits, older than her first marriage.

"Worth every shilling."

Her answering laugh was bright and bold, and I caught my lip between my teeth to keep from grinning like a fool.

"Do you have need of me in the observatory tonight?"

She had proved a quick hand with the sketchbook, conquering in half the time what took me hours to accomplish, and with twice the detail I could have managed.

I shook my head. "I closed everything up before supper." With a nod, she turned back to her plate. The expression that crossed her face was a mystery to me, her brow furrowed just the tiniest bit. "How is the harp coming along?"

That brought a return to the mirth. She grinned, shaking her head simultaneously. "Precisely as poorly as the last time you asked. I thought my experience with the piano would be of more use than it has been."

"When will you allow me the privilege of hearing you play?"

"Never." She laughed.

"I'm certain you're quite good. You simply expect too much of yourself. Perfection in all things."

"Hardly."

"You do." I nudged her knee with my own.

The first time had been an accident. But she hadn't shuddered away, hadn't dressed me down. Now, at least once a meal, I brushed my knee with hers. But only once a meal—I limited the intimate gesture lest it become noticeable. Occasionally, if I was very lucky, her knee brushed mine. Those were my favorites.

Her teeth caught her lower lip, her eyes meeting mine. "I have been up to something while you've been visiting tenants and fussing with your mirrors—vain man that you are. Would you like to see?"

"Yes." The answer escaped automatically and a little more desperately than I would have preferred. Her teeth dug just a little harder into her lip before her eyes dropped from mine. "When?"

"After supper?" Her knee accidentally knocked into mine

before darting away almost immediately. My stomach flipped as I fought back the instinct to chase it with my own.

If I began shoveling the chicken into my maw a bit faster than before, who was to comment?

∼

"Where are we going?"

After the food was cleared, she sidled up to me and slipped her arm in mine without a word.

"It's a surprise." She led me down the hall toward the staircase. At the base, she hesitated. She pulled her hand away, and my heart gave a disgruntled jolt.

Then, with no warning, her little hand dipped into the pocket of my waistcoat. Several heartbeats were forgotten as she rustled around before her hand emerged grasping a peppermint. She unwrapped it and popped it into her mouth with a self-satisfied grin before depositing the wrapper back into my pocket.

My swallow was ragged and likely accompanied by a desperate sound I couldn't hear over the rushing in my ears. She settled back at my side and resumed leading me up the steps, my knees wobbly.

"Thank you," she whispered in a falsely demure tone. My wife was pleased with that little display.

"You—" my voice cracked pathetically and I cleared it desperately. "You're welcome."

At the top of the steps, she turned down the family wing, toward our chambers. The door to my bedroom was framed at the end of the long hall, making its presence felt.

Had she decided to continue the torture here? My breeches tightened uncomfortably at the thoughts of what we could do behind that door. What we could do if I were a different man, anyway.

Instead, while my thoughts had taken a lascivious turn, Charlotte stopped us a few rooms away, outside the room designated as a nursery.

Oh, I was a letch, brimming with lusty thoughts when she had done something for the babe.

She broke away from me and turned the handle before seeming to consider otherwise.

"Cover your eyes." Catching one of my arms in her hand, she guided it up to press against my eyelids. The other joined of its own volition with a laugh.

"Really?"

"Yes! Can you see? No peeking."

I pressed my palms to my lids more thoroughly, just to be sure. "I can see my palms."

A hot hand found my shoulder and I caught the grind of metal as she turned the handle. The door brushed against the floor inside with a swish. She pulled me into the room. A scent lingered in the air but I couldn't name it. It wasn't unpleasant, just... present.

"Can I open my eyes?"

Objectively, I knew I couldn't hear an eye roll, but I heard one out of her. Still, she granted me a, "Yes."

And so I did.

～

Charlotte

What was I doing? This was a horrid idea.

I'd made mistakes, a lot of them, but I learned from every single one. Yet my damn husband had lulled me into complacency.

Now that I had brought him in here, I knew this would be the moment he revealed himself to be exactly like all the others.

And like the fool I was proving myself to be, when he asked to open his eyes, I said yes.

I fought desperately to steel myself against what was sure to be derision at best, fury at worst.

Lee's gaze instantly found the mural. I could not bring myself to look away from his expression, entirely unreadable.

Objectively, I was pleased with my work—both design and execution. I had taken the grounds of the estate—the wooded area, the garden, the lake—and transposed them onto the wall. Above it all was the night sky. I had written a copy of his notes from that first night, and everything was placed more or less correctly. The constellations, the stars, Jupiter, and the other planets all had a home on the wall and up the angled ceiling on the inky blue sky of my mural. I had added a few clouds where his notes were unclear and hoped he would not notice.

Now that I was left to observe his struck face, I realized precisely how difficult this would be to correct. The midnight sky would require innumerable coats to cover.

Why had I not asked?

It felt an eternity while he stared at my wall, though it was more likely a minute, perhaps two. He stepped quietly up to the plaster without a word. His large, masculine hand brushed over Virgo and Jupiter. His touch was gentle, the barest whisper of his middle and ring fingers.

I only noticed that I had begun gnawing on my lip when my mouth flooded with the tang of copper. The urge to fidget warred with my well-rehearsed manners.

"When?" He asked without turning from the wall. His tone was unlike any I'd heard from him before, thick and tangled in his throat.

"The last few weeks."

"How?"

"I used your notes."

"Late June?"

I merely nodded, and when presented with no auditory answer, he turned to me. If I had to name his expression, I probably would have said incredulous, but there was an undercurrent.

And then he went and said precisely the thing I most needed to hear at precisely the right moment. "This is incredible."

The knot in my chest loosened and the smile came forth without guile or guise. "You are not displeased?"

"Why on earth would I be displeased? This is astonishing."

Relaying my history with murals was beyond my capabilities at the moment, not when his grin was boyish and charming and he looked so damn impressed.

"Did I get it right? I can make corrections."

"Perfect." This time he made no effort to turn his gaze to the wall. In fact, his eyes never left mine. They were a cloudy, stormy blue gray tonight, the color belying the carefree delight in the crinkles at the corners of his eyes and the quirked side of his mouth.

And then, just like that night in the observatory, his eyes dropped to my lips before flicking back up to meet mine. The knot in his throat bobbed and my lips parted involuntarily in answer.

"Charlotte?" The question—my name—escaped in a graveled whisper.

My body knew the answer, even though my head did not and my "yes" was higher, more tensile than any syllable I'd ever uttered.

It was enough for him though.

His massive hand, the one that had traced my painting, found my jaw with less delicacy. Less delicacy but more passion, infinitely more passion. He cupped my cheek, jaw, the back of my neck, his hand spanning all of it with ease, pinning me in place. And then he descended from his great height towering over me and his lips found mine.

The comforting scent of peppermint was entirely at odds with the thoroughly overwhelming experience of being kissed by this man. His hand directed me to the angle he liked, and his other arm wrapped all the way around my back, catching my hip, dragging me onto my toes. Soft lips threatened to consume me. Lee kissed like he was drowning and I was air. He kissed like he was *desperate* for me.

Fighting to regain some sort of stability, I caught his cheeks in my hands. Bristles caught against one hand as the other caressed the strangely smooth, rippled flesh of his scarred cheek. He tensed when my thumb brushed the tangled skin there, freezing for precisely as long as it took to drag my tongue along impossibly smooth lips. And then he was breathing me in again.

I dropped back down to the floor on flat feet, and his lips chased mine. He took everything, gave everything, and I never, ever wanted to stop kissing him.

His hands were restless, flitting from shoulder to hip to thigh, back to shoulder. The other fisted in my hair before finding my cheek again and repeating the cycle. When one dragged higher up to my ribcage and hovered just shy of my breast, I stifled a smile—a man like any other. Somehow, on him, the desire was endearing rather than lecherous.

He poured delicious groans into my lips with every breath and at some point, my own moans had joined in the chorus.

I wrested my lips away from his—only a desperation for air could have forced the action. Lee felt no such need, dropping to kiss my jaw with nothing but a pleased hum.

"Lee—" Words escaped me when he found the particularly sensitive divot where my jaw and neck met.

His only response was a vaguely interested "Hmm?"

"Bed."

He broke away slowly, his eyes finding mine as he breathed heavily. I was gasping in great lungfuls as well, my chest rising and falling in time with his. What, precisely, he was looking for, I had no idea, but I realized that for the first time I *needed* a man to take me to bed. I thought I had wanted Wesley, but not one of his kisses had felt like *this*.

Lee's lips, tongue, teeth, hands all left me tangled in an intoxicating combination of tetchy and sluggish with pleasure. I needed to know what else he could do to me.

Apparently, he found whatever he was looking for, because he replied with a simple, "All right."

Chapter Twenty-One
BENNET HALL, SURREY - JULY 24, 1816

LEE

SHE WORE the marks of my attentions beautifully—flushed cheeks, reddened lips, darkened eyes, and decorated jaw. My beautiful, talented wife stared up at me, waiting for me to lead her. To the bedroom. To ravish her.

In my dreams I had done so, twice a night in fact, for nearly the whole of our marriage. But more than half of those nights the dreams twisted to nightmares. And I had absolutely no way of knowing which way tonight would go. This was real —none of my nighttime visions had felt like *this*.

I hadn't been with a woman truly since Mia, and not one of our interactions had this drugging, frenzied, ardent quality. It had been years, and I wanted Charlotte with an aching, longing desperation.

With more confidence than I felt, I led her to my chambers. If she had an opinion about the location, she did not share it but permitted me to tug her along.

The click of the door settling into frame and the turn of

the lock echoed in my fingers, punctuating our breathing. Nerves twisted deep in my chest.

And then Charlotte held her arms out in supplication. Who was I to refuse her, to deny her offer to worship her? Wrapping her in my arms, burying my face into her tangled curls, was the only answer. Her hair was so damn soft, even mussed from my hands with half the pins probably splayed all over the floor of the nursery. She smelled so good, floral and something indefinably *Charlotte*.

Delicate lips brushed my cheek, right over my scar, and I wanted to weep. Instead, my lips found hers again, gentler this time. Rather than devouring, I savored her, the finest wine. My fingers caught on the knot of her spine, just below her hairline, and I dragged them down each vertebrae, drawing a shiver from her.

Nightmares drifted further from my thoughts with each brush of her lips and tongue, each delicate sigh banishing them. I could do this. All that was required of me was to worship my talented, passionate, beautiful wife. That was no difficulty at all—it was a privilege.

The magnetic pull of her lips valiantly tried to pin me there, but more silky skin needed to be explored. A constellation of freckles called this side of her shoulder home, the Diamond Cross of Carina, or perhaps Crux. No matter, they were equally worthy of adoration.

Then there was Cygnus, or part of him—perhaps missing the tail. It was difficult to tell, trapped in the curve of her bosom as it was. I wanted to find out if he was represented in his entirety. My hand found its way there of its own accord, tugging the neckline of her gown just slightly farther down. Oh yes, there he was. Tracing him with my tongue earned me a delightful moan.

My wife's clever fingers found the buttons of my waistcoat. Unfortunately, removing it meant lifting my hands from heated curves and that was less ideal. I shucked it, flinging it to the ground before caressing the contour where her hip and bottom met, every bit as luscious as her breasts, as expected.

Dimly, I became aware of a tugging sensation on the shoulders of my shirt. Then a breathy, "Off, off." Understanding crashed over me. The scars—

Lust evaporated faster than it had arrived. Every one of my nightmares was real. I had frozen, mouth ghosting over delicate lines.

"Lee?"

I broke away, stepping back. "I cannot." The words came without permission from a strangled, pitchy voice that certainly didn't belong to me. But there was no one else.

She blinked at me, comprehension slowly dawning in her eyes. Her brows drew together and her eyes slackened.

"I see." Her tone was small, tight.

"Charlotte..."

"I should go."

"Wait, stay..."

She swallowed and the sound was harsh between us. "I—no, no thank you."

"Char—"

"Good night." She turned and found the door in quick steps, then fumbled with the lock for a moment before escaping.

"I'm so sorry," I whispered, far too late, into the impossibly empty room.

∽

CHARLOTTE

Every time I thought I had learned, every damn time. Lee wasn't different. He wasn't any better than the rest of them. They were all precisely as awful as I thought.

My feet carried me, directionless, down the hall. I passed the open nursery and a pang of hateful longing knotted in my chest. My fingers itched for paints. Not tiny, detailed brushes, but big ones, designed to cover large swaths of wall. White, white was a perfectly acceptable color for a nursery.

In spite of my desperation to cover my mess tonight, I hadn't the paint or the brushes, just a few pots of the colors I'd used scattered on a drop cloth on the floor. Not enough.

I scurried down the stairs. I needed to be farther away.

The house was quiet with servants distracted elsewhere, and I slipped through the front door and down the walk. I wanted to leave, to run, to flee. The stables were just down this walk, perhaps a quarter of a mile. I could be in the saddle in mere minutes. If I waited for a carriage, I could be on the road to London in half an hour.

But even if I could ride in my condition, I had nowhere to go, no one to see. And that was the wretched truth of it. I was alone, utterly and completely. My father wouldn't have me. James Place was occupied by Ralph's heir now. Wesley was out of the question.

I changed direction and found the garden behind the hedgerows. Left to make friends with the bees.

The wrought iron bench was still there, untouched in recent weeks. Dusk was falling when I settled in.

Unlike my last trip to the garden, there were no bees, and wasn't that a lark. Even they wanted nothing to do with me. It was an irrational thought, I knew it was—half of my thoughts were these days—but I was just so... alone. Alone and unwanted, once again.

Lee's rejection stung, perhaps worse than Wesley's. I was too distracted, too frantic, too desperate when Wesley sent me away, to feel the weight of it. But now I was trapped in this house for another ten and a half months.

Another ten months in which I would grow rounder and puffier and any acquaintances I had in town would forget me entirely. I didn't have any that I would classify as friends. Wesley—I had thought—but that was gone now. The sad truth was that no one was missing me. I received no letters, nothing to indicate that anyone at all remembered my existence.

I would return to town without a reclusive husband and with a babe—too old to be that husband's. And try as we might, no one would believe the child was actually Lee's. Wesley had told too many—I would be ostracized.

And worst of all, I could not understand *why* Lee had rejected me. If I knew the reason, perhaps I could accept it. Lee may not love me, he may not even be fond of me, but he was attracted to me. That was clear before tonight from the frequency with which his gaze found my bosom. He'd kissed me like a man starved. He wanted me, carnally. It just seemed that he didn't *want* to want me.

At least as far as prisons went this was a nice one. The flowers here were lovely, even late in the season. Daisies, zinnias, and Peruvian lilies intermingled in a way that should have left half of them entirely unable to flourish. The gardener must take exceptional care with these.

I should go back inside. My husband would worry. He was too kind to do anything else. I was a mess too—halfway to tupped. But I had little interest in the sight of Lee at present. And the thought of walking passed that nursery...

Unfortunately, the sky made my decision for me. What began as a single drop of rain shifted to a downpour in seconds. The nearest shelter was the observatory, and my gown was too new and too fine to ruin, even if the silk had been besmirched by my husband's wandering hands.

I scurried into the building, slammed the door behind me, and braced against the sudden wail of the wind. Lee's observatory lay before me as I had never seen it, dark, shuttered, empty. I lit the lamp he kept by the door before finding a few additional candles.

Now bathed in a soft, flickering glow, it was a more familiar sight. But unfamiliar at the same time. Lee was always so *present* in this room, in a way he wasn't elsewhere.

Rain pounded the roof in concert with the gusts of wind. I was going to be here awhile. Thunder clapped in the distance—a long while.

My husband's equipment was too delicate and too precious to examine without his permission. With the windows shuttered there seemed little point in the endeavor anyway. But the journals, ledgers, and books—I couldn't damage those.

After opening the leather-covered folio he was always making notes in, I thumbed through a few pages. I couldn't help the huff of laughter that escaped me. It was so clear when he saw something he found particularly interesting. His writing trailed off midword and he dribbled, his hand moving faster than the quill allowed. The more perfunctory observations were written in a steady hand with an appropriate amount of ink.

My name appeared more than once in recent entries: Charlotte found, Char—did. I couldn't remember what I did that had him so excited, but he lost half of my name in his enthusiasm. His penmanship was such that I couldn't begin to guess what he was writing about.

Beneath the ledger were a few of my attempts at a star chart, my paintings as well, Saturn, Jupiter, Neptune by theoretical description only. He had those tucked into a folder for safekeeping.

Propped against the wall, the desk acted as a makeshift bookshelf. *On the Heavens*, *Sidereus Nuncius*, and other texts on astronomy. And more astonishing, he had medical texts. I slipped one free only to find a page marked with a scrap of paper. A page dealing with human development—in somewhat graphic detail I realized, feeling my face heat. Beside it was a second text on midwifery, and this one had its own scrap of paper. But it had notes on it too. In the same excited, cramped hand he used for discoveries, he had comments about swelling and joint pain. Lee had noted itching on palms and feet, and heartburn.

Farther down he had more notes. *Due November?*

And suddenly the ache in my chest that accompanied my flight from the house was just the tiniest bit less painful.

The wind still howled outside the observatory. I would need to settle in for quite a while, perhaps all night. While the astronomy texts were certain to lull me to sleep, it seemed wrong that my husband be more informed of the changes taking place inside me than I was.

I flipped back to the beginning in the midwifery text.

Chapter Twenty-Two
BENNET HALL, SURREY - JULY 25, 1816

LEE

BRIGSBY'S KNOCK the next morning was sharp, reproachful. It also signified that I had managed an entire night staring at the ceiling, unblinking.

"My lord?"

"Yes?" I sounded even more wrung out than I felt, hoarse and weak.

"I do not suppose Lady Champaign is in here by any chance?" he asked, striding in unbidden.

"No..."

"Then I do believe we may have a problem." Brigs rarely, if ever, skirted around an issue, preferring to confront it—me—with sarcasm and insults. That he was doing so now had me shooting upright in the bed. "You see, sir, she is not in her chambers."

I glanced at the clock. "She is in the breakfast room, surely."

"She is not."

The bed coverings tangled around my feet, trapping me while I flailed. "The music room."

"Empty."

"Library?" Finally free of the blankets, I made a search for my banyan.

"Also bereft of ladies." His tone belied the serious implication of his statement.

"Well where the devil is she?"

"We were hoping you might have an idea. One of the scullery maids saw her headed toward the stables in quite a hurry last evening."

Stables.

Carriage.

My Charlotte.

My knees wobbled and my stomach dropped, a familiar copper tang filling my mouth. Banyan—needed my peppermints. Not spread across the bed. Not hanging on the screen. Where was it?

Already the darkness was encroaching, my periphery dimming. I wasn't going to find it, not in time. I collapsed back on the bed, my heart palpitating without rhythm. I dragged my fingers along the bed covering, desperate to keep myself here. But I felt nothing beyond the familiar, hateful tingling sensation.

Brigs was crouched before me, still visible in the pinhole that remained free of the darkness. But I heard nothing. His hand found my knee, but there was no accompanying sensation. And then the darkness overtook everything. Just like it always did.

∾

THE BITING scent of peppermint brought me out of it, minutes, hours, days, years later.

My chest was still tight, but my heart pounded in regular time. The throbbing ache behind my eyes was always one of the first sensations upon my return.

"Breathe."

At once, my lungs obeyed his command. The air sliced along my impossibly dry throat and left me hacking desperately.

A cup of tea appeared beneath my still coughing face without a word. I took a sip and choked it down.

"How long?"

"A few minutes only."

I shook my head. "How long has she been gone?

Brigsby's expression was unimpressed. "Ten hours, perhaps twelve."

"Have my horse saddled." I threw back the bed coverings for the second time this morning before I was met with Brigsby's stern hand on my chest, pushing me back down.

"She never arrived at the stables."

"What?"

"Which word was confusing?"

"Brigs..." I broke off with a sigh. If she hadn't set off in a carriage... It had rained last night. Hard. And for a long while. She wouldn't have stayed out in that, surely. My countess was not one for discomforts.

The observatory.

It had to be. It was the only significant shelter between the house and the stables.

"I need clothing. Now."

"Of course. Will you be requiring the hairpins that were scattered across the floor as well?"

I cursed impertinent valets the world over, as was my usual practice, and shucked on my breeches before dragging a shirt over my head. I batted away the cravat in his hands. If she wasn't in the observatory... I couldn't afford to waste time dressing.

I strode around him, all but racing down the hall and stairs and out toward the other building.

The path was more mud than gravel with puddles interspersed every few feet.

The structure's exterior seemed no different than it usually did—no indication that she was inside, but no evidence that she was not either.

My breath hitched before I turned the handle, a perfunctory, involuntary effort to steel myself against disappointment.

What I found inside saw my heart clenched painfully. Charlotte was curled into a small ball on the chaise I sometimes used for precisely the same purpose. She was burrowed underneath the great coat I'd left here some time ago. Her breathing was slow, even, and shallow. And she was safe. Safe and *here*. And perfect.

∼

CHARLOTTE

He was carrying me. My ridiculous husband was carrying me like a child. Or not like a child, he had one arm under my knees and the other around my back, but my point remained. How, precisely, had he come to the conclusion that this was the better solution than waking me?

Now I was left with the absurd choice of stirring in his arms or feigning sleep the entire way back to the house. I was not particularly fond of either option.

"I can hear you rolling your eyes." His voice was a low grumble, the vibrations drumming against my cheek. I did roll them before blinking them open, this time in a conscious choice.

"What thought process, precisely, led to this course of action?"

Lee gave a thoughtful hum before replying. "Well, I assumed you would still be cross with me, and I wanted to delay the sight of the little pout you give when you're angry for as long as possible. But you looked cold." His gate was smooth. I would never admit it, not to him, but it was quite nice to be carried save for the childishness of it. "See there, pouting."

"That is merely my face. Are you going to put me down?"

"I hadn't planned on it. And while you do make that expression quite often, it is not merely your face." We were nearing the house now, within sight of the windows at least. I wriggled, trying to force his hand but he merely tightened his hold.

"Put me down. I am still cross with you."

"Charlotte, the ground is wet and muddy. You'll ruin your slippers and gown. Surely you do not wish to spite me that badly."

That was, perhaps, the only thing he could have said that would have convinced me to stay where I was. I did like the slippers and the gown. I wrapped a reluctant hand around his neck while he sidestepped a puddle.

At last we reached the house and there was Brigsby, opening the door with a smirk. "My lady, you had us worried."

"Apologies," I retorted, ensuring no apologetic note crept into my voice. I wiggled once again and finally Lee deposited me onto my feet with a put upon sigh.

"I am quite sincere, my lady. Lord Champaign was nearly *senseless* with worry." Brigsby emphasized the word in a way I couldn't quite interpret. Lee's glare at the man indicated that the comment was intended for my husband regardless.

"Yes, well, I am quite tired. I do believe I'll retire for a few more hours if you have no need of me."

Lee muttered something under his breath I couldn't quite catch beyond the words "great need." I ignored the comment in favor of my promised respite.

I trudged down the hall with far less grace than was my want. Whatever aspect of human nature was responsible for the desire to poke a bruise had me turning to peer through the cracked nursery door.

And there I saw it—tiny, yellow paw prints scattered all over the floor and the bottom foot of the painted wall.

I was a lady. I behaved with decorum. I had never once in my life screeched. But right then, in that moment, that was the only descriptor for the inhuman sound that escaped me.

Massive footsteps thudded up the stairs faster than should have been possible. Lee rounded the top of the landing and skittered to a stop mere inches from crashing into me.

"What? What is it? Where are you hurt?" The questions poured so rapidly from him, it took a minute to parse them. In the interim, his hands had found my shoulders, my sides, my face, seemingly searching for some unseen injury.

"Your cat."

"What?" He wheezed out between panted breaths.

"Your cat," I repeated, pointing into the open doorway.

His expression shifted from one of panic to one of anguish. Widened eyes downturned and the tension left his form, shoulders slumped, and lips relaxed into a loose frown.

"Charlotte..."

"I closed the paints. I know I did."

"No, I know. I'm..."

"I am not responsible for this." My tone was sharp and tight through the knot in my throat. I couldn't bring myself to set foot into the room, to catalog the damage. There must have been a hundred individual paw prints. The damn cat probably had to dip its feet more than once.

The floor was a bother in a practical sense. It would likely need to be completely refinished. But the wall... last night I had been set to paint over it, a stark, blank slate. Now that it was destroyed, and not by my hand, the tears welled up without permission.

Lee stepped past me and fell to his knees before the wall. Gently, he touched a finger to one of the prints, then pulled it away and examined his hand. From his crestfallen expression I knew the paint was dry.

My vantage from the hall offered a view of the paints I had set across the floor. And every. Single. One. Was closed. The yellow was no exception.

"If you'll excuse me, I'd like to rest for a few minutes. Since it's already dry there's no point in trying to clean it now."

"Charlotte..."

"Good night, Lee." It wasn't night or good. But I could not have this conversation with him. Or any other. Not without irrational tears and I was not willing to be irrational with him at the moment. Or any moment.

If I shut the door to my rooms harder than necessary... well, I was angry.

Chapter Twenty-Three

BENNET HALL, SURREY - JULY 26, 1816

LEE

My head gave a perfunctory throb in response to the slammed door. The pain had gotten so much worse in the last quarter of an hour.

My attacks always left me drained, shaken, and tetchy. It wasn't the worst I'd had in recent weeks—but it was still unpleasant.

I needed to speak to Charlotte, to explain. But the mere thought of that conversation left my chest tight and my mouth dry.

One problem at a time. I found a cloth my wife had used to keep her work area clean. In a predictably futile effort, I rubbed the dry cloth against the yellow prints. It produced no effect whatsoever. I was loath to dampen the cloth, unsure what effect that would have on her mural. Did it matter?

I flopped onto my backside with a sigh. Cass had been thorough in her efforts. Unbelievably thorough. From afar the prints almost resembled little flowers, admittedly less intricate than Charlotte's. Unfortunately, up close they were very clearly smeared paw prints and no amount of wishful thinking would change that.

Dragging an exhausted hand through my messy hair, I took a deep breath and blew it out in a thoroughly dramatic sigh. A shimmer caught my eye on the floor. A hairpin. Charlotte's hairpin.

All at once I was flooded with the memories of last night. How had I gotten everything so wrong? It had been progressing so well. She'd felt so *right* in my arms, soft and sweet-smelling and passionate. I'd never experienced the kind of responsiveness Charlotte had offered me with her clutching fingers and encouraging moans. It was heady, lovely, and wonderful, and I had ruined it in two words.

This was why I hadn't planned on taking another wife. I wasn't *good* at this sort of thing, even before the accident. I was practical, pragmatic, and sensible. All things wives weren't.

This sham of a marriage should have suited me well, a proper agreement between two rational adults. But Charlotte surprised me at every turn. I had no doubt she could be a doggess given half a mind—she rolled her eyes far too often to convince me she was as compassionate and considerate with everyone as she was with me. But she was. With me she had been thoughtful, generous, and enthusiastic.

It all left me befuddled, floundering for stability. And to ensure I was completely and perfectly ruined, she was so damn beautiful. Bewitchingly beautiful.

Worse still, the clock was running out, ticking away every minute of every day. It was part of our agreement. A concession I had offered without hesitance when I still had my wits. Her stay here was temporary. She would return to town, my name the only reminder of her time trapped here with me. Charlotte would find another man, less horrid than the last, and fall in love with him.

And I would be here, alone with nothing but the stars for

company. Mere months ago, I was content with that life. Now... I wasn't entirely sure how I would survive it.

A sharp rap on the doorframe announced Brigs. "Sir, you have visitors in the drawing room. Mr. Wayland and his wife."

I blinked slowly, numbly. What the devil was Wayland doing here?

Brigsby, correctly interpreting my expression, added, "He indicated that the road to his estate was flooded from the rains last night."

~

CHARLOTTE

Indistinct voices drifted into the hall from the drawing room when I woke from a fitful nap hours later. The familiar baritone of my husband, along with that of a man I didn't not recognize, and more astonishing still, a feminine lilt.

Lee did not have visitors. Not once in the whole of our marriage had anyone called. Jack slipped out of the drawing room and tried to pass me. I caught his arm and whispered, "Who is in there?"

"A Mr. Wayland and his wife." He pulled his arm free and continued down the hall, unwilling to abide any further interrogation.

Imogen hadn't said anything. She must have been unaware or she would have told me.

A quick glance at my stomach told me what I already knew. I was visibly with child, and there was no hiding it, not in this or any dress. Perhaps I could escape to the—

Lady Juliet Dalton—Wayland—stepped into the hall and shut the door behind her. I learned two things remarkably quickly. She, too, was with child, and she was entirely aware of my condition, if the lack of astonishment in her expression was any indication.

"Oh, Lady James, it's so good to see you. Lady Champaign, I mean. Forgive me."

"You as well. Forgive me for my absence. I had no idea of your visit."

She laughed, a little false note in it. "Neither did we. The road to our home was flooded. And if I'm quite honest, I suspect my husband wanted a peek at the observatory. He spoke of nothing else when we decided to see if you were receiving visitors." That explained one thing. Lady Juliet was one to be counted on to read social cues, at least. "I hate to be a bother, but I am in need of a bit of privacy. Can you direct me?"

After instructing her, I steeled myself for the drawing room and one Mr. Wayland. If I had a million years I could not say precisely how I felt about that man. He'd kept my late husband from the house at all hours of the night—certainly a note in his favor—but my husband also gambled the entirety of his annual income and more at the man's club. And of course, he had his wife's father arrested at my ball two years ago. Which, while it thoroughly disrupted my plans, did leave the evening unforgettable in the eyes of the *ton*. I considered that a wash.

I stepped inside and closed the door quietly behind me. Not quietly enough. The gentlemen—gentleman and degenerate owner of a gaming hell—noticed me instantly and stood.

"Please, do be seated. Forgive me for not being here to greet you, Mr. Wayland. Your wife indicated carriage troubles?"

"Lady Champaign, lovely to see you. It was not so much carriage troubles as road troubles. You'll have to forgive our abrupt appearance."

"Of course."

"You know Wayland?" Lee asked.

"Oh, Mr. Wayland's appearance at a ball I hosted a few years ago is infamous."

My husband merely raised a brow at his visitor.

Wayland's hand found the back of his neck in a sheepish gesture. "I, uh—I suppose I owe you an apology for that display."

"It was no worse than the viscount's," I retorted.

That earned me a choked laugh at his brother's expense, just in time for Lady Juliet to return and perch on the settee next to her husband.

Lee's gaze darted between us, searching for explanation.

"If it makes you feel any better, it is not only your closet they take advantage of," Wayland added.

"It does not. But I appreciate the sentiment."

My husband interjected, "I've missed something."

"A great many somethings," Wayland replied. "You should come to town more often."

The men proceeded to bicker about their feelings on London and society. I watched carefully as both visitors guests noted my husband's scars but made no comment or expression. Had that occurred before I arrived? Lee didn't seem any more self-conscious than he usually was. His cravat wasn't tugged up, and he hadn't shifted to one side. A small bite of tension left me with the observation.

The gentlemen soon begged off to explore the observatory. Lady Juliet smiled indulgently with a teasing appeal to enjoy playing with the toys.

At their departure, I caught her eyeing me with interest. She wasn't usually one for gossip—that was me—but her fascination was still of concern. The tenuous situation with my husband would not be improved with increased scrutiny.

Of course, she was with child too. And farther along than

I would have guessed having seen her at the masquerade a few months ago.

"So, it seems congratulations are in order," I said, unwilling to sit here in this stupid manner for any longer.

"Yes, thank you. You as well. How are you feeling?"

And now I had stepped in it. My nausea had abated after the third month, which I had confirmed last night was typical. But I was too tired to fabricate a story. "Better in the last few weeks. You?"

"Like a whale," she said, rubbing her bump with a sigh. "I suspect twins, but no one believes me."

"I'd hardly say whale. How far along are you?"

"The quickening was a few days ago."

I nodded as if I understood, but I had yet to feel the child inside me move.

"Kate made this look so easy. Not for me. The smell of everything makes me sick. I am swollen and sore. And I cry for absolutely no reason. Yesterday, Michael ate the last tart—which I told him to do—and when I went to find it and it was gone... sobbing."

"The cat got into the paint," I replied in commiseration. "Peppermint helped me with the nausea."

"It has mostly passed. And, as I have no intention of going through this again, I will have absolutely no use for that information. But I appreciate it."

My laugh surprised me. Lady Juliet and I had never been close. If I was honest, we were barely cordial. But apparently, she was quite amusing.

"Oh, never again," I agreed half-heartedly.

She raised a brow. "I can see why not. Your husband is a giant. You best hope the babe doesn't take after him."

And just like that, the tension in my shoulders eased. She knew, she had to, but she was going to confirm our story.

"He is quite tall." My agreement was distracted. I was still irritated with Lee and paying him compliments in that frame of mind chafed. Though I could hardly argue the fact that the man was a tree. A tree I'd tried to climb last night. My cheeks flushed at the memory and when I glanced up from the tea, my companion was observing me closely.

"Oh, did you hear? Celine—Lady Rycliffe—has remarried. William Hart," her bland tone belied the intrigue in her news.

I never would have expected Celine would wed again. As a fashionable widow she had much more freedom. "I do not know a Lord Hart?"

"Mr. He is a solicitor."

"How did that come about?" My interest was piqued.

"It was quite dramatic. She and Mr. Hart were investigating her late husband's murder and fell quite irrevocably in love along the way." I knew about Lord Rycliffe's murder—everyone did—but in the years since his death there hadn't been a scrap of news. I was a gossip at heart, and there was no more intriguing subject than murder.

"Did they find who was responsible?"

"Well, they found the actual killer, but he claims he was acting on the orders of another gentleman. And that man has gone into hiding. No one seems to be able to locate him." Again, her tone did not reflect the nature of her gossip. It was the kind of missive that should have been delivered behind a fan in a ballroom at a loud whisper. Lady Juliet truly must seek to improve herself in this respect.

"Who is the man?"

To my great astonishment, she set her tea aside and took my hands in hers. We did not have that sort of friendship. I did not have that sort of friendship with anyone.

She waited until my eyes abandoned our clasped hands and met hers before she continued. "Mr. Parker." Her tone was soft, gentle, and there was caring in her eyes.

She knew. She knew everything. And by the gentle way her thumb brushed the back of my hand, she knew this was the only way to relay that intelligence while maintaining our polite ruse.

I felt sick in a way I hadn't in weeks. "Are they certain?"

"They seem to be. Are you well? I know this is quite shocking news. Is there anything I can fetch you—tea perhaps?"

"I am quite well. Thank you." My tone was tinny and false, but she politely chose to ignore it.

I could not believe it of Wesley. He may have refused to take responsibility for our child, but murder? There was a huge leap from his moral failing to killing a man. And Celine's husband died seven, perhaps eight, years ago. I met Wesley less than three years ago. He was affable, funny, and charming with a sharp wit and good looks to match. He could not have been a killer that entire time.

Except, he had avoided every Rosehill function. And Wesley never once flirted with Celine. Everyone flirted with Celine. She was lovely and French and took the amorous comments in stride with a smile and a set down. But I could not recall a single instance in which he spoke to her.

Welsey—My Wesley. A murderer. I was carrying his child. He had touched me with bloodstained hands. Memories swirled red and sticky. Every whisper, every touch, every kiss.

"Charlotte?" Lady Juliet asked, overly familiar.

"I am well. Thank you for telling me," I said, finally meeting her eyes again.

"I was not certain if it would be best to tell you. Or if it might be too upsetting."

"I—It was best that I know." And then a horrifying thought struck me. "How much, do you suppose, children take after their father?" After the words escaped, I realized how fraught a direction that conversation was.

Her head tipped to the side as she considered. "Well, I would like my child to be very much like his father. Perhaps with slightly less penchant for gambling, but that is not a requirement. But... I hope I am not so very much like my father." She rubbed her free hand across her belly once again. Her father... carted away to debtor's prison in the middle of my ball. "I imagine you might feel similar? And Lord Champaign is by all accounts an excellent man, and he *will* be an excellent father, even if his child is a tiny bit shorter than he is."

Lee would be an excellent father. And he was the father of this child. In every way that mattered, he was the father.

"Thank you."

"Of course. I know we have not always been... close. But, well, we do have quite a lot in common at the moment," she said with a nod toward my stomach. "Perhaps we could start again?"

If last night had taught me anything, it was that I needed a friend. Desperately. And she was at least proving discreet and tactful, which were not the worst qualities one could have in a friend.

"I would like that."

"My friends call me Juliet, or Jules if you are feeling whimsical."

"Charlotte."

Chapter Twenty-Four
BENNET HALL, SURREY - JULY 26, 1816

LEE

"So... Lady Champaign." Michael had clearly been waiting for a lull in the conversation to introduce the topic of my wife. He was not subtle.

"What about her?" The warning was heavy in my tone. I wouldn't have my wife insulted in her own home, or anywhere else for that matter.

"Nothing... you just—when you had Summers ask me about her, I did not realize it was with marriage in mind."

"What did you think?"

He backed up a full step, hands in front of him placatingly. "Oh, no. That way lies yet another black eye."

"Bring many men to violence by insulting their wives?"

Wayland shrugged as he flipped through a book with feigned interest. "It happens, though not usually for that reason. Jules won't admit it, but I know she finds a black eye rakishly handsome. I had one the night we met."

"Yes, I'm certain she swooned."

"I apologize. I haven't been sleeping well with Juliet feeling so poorly. I seem to say precisely the wrong thing to everyone lately. I didn't mean to imply that Lady Champaign wasn't worthy of the title."

"Is Lady Juliet that unwell?"

"Yes, she's still sick often—though there has been a slight improvement. And we had two losses before this one. It feels like I've been holding my breath for months. If I release it, we'll lose this one too. And Jules is the worrier in the marriage. It's a daily wonder she's still upright."

"I'm sorry for your losses."

"She thinks she's carrying twins, and I just... childbirth is so risky. Every single thing I learn I wonder why we decided to do this in the first place. And twins..." He set the book down and turned back to me. "But we're talking about you and your marriage. You made quick work of the task, well done."

I wasn't so delusional to think he hadn't done the calculations. Wayland was nothing if not skilled with numbers. And surely Charlotte's degenerate suitor was a regular in his club. I suspected he intended the comment as an olive branch. Of course, I wasn't overly fond of my future child being referred to as a task, but I decided to let that sit.

"Yes, well. I need an heir. And the estate is entailed."

"Ah, one of the many benefits of my father's philandering. No title and I own everything outright." Michael wandered over to the telescope and peeked through it even though the shutters were closed against the daylight. "Champaign?"

"Yes?"

His eyes dragged along my scars, the ones he had been quite successful in dismissing until now. "Why did you not tell me how bad the accident was? I would have been here to help."

"There was nothing to help with," I said, dismissing the comment.

"But the burns... Surely they took months to heal. And

you didn't inform me of Lady Champaign's death until months after it happened—didn't tell me you were injured at all."

"Wayland..."

"Never mind. I just... I know we weren't the *best* of friends. But I thought we were... friends. And I didn't hear from you for years. You never responded to any of my letters."

His hangdog expression dragged a heavy sigh from me. "We were. But I wasn't in a place to have friends." I hadn't realized the truth of those words until they hung in the air, heavy between us.

"Are you in a place to have friends now?"

And wasn't that a question. "I'm fairly certain I'm not even in a position to have a wife at the moment." Half of a laugh was trapped in the answer.

He chuckled outright. "Well, you certainly picked the easiest and most biddable wife to try with."

"I really did. Do you know I thought her a practical choice? There's nothing practical about that woman. She's extraordinary."

He surveyed me with a queer, unfamiliar expression. "I think you are probably in a very good position to have a wife." There was something in his tone, approving or respectful perhaps.

"I doubt Charlotte would agree with you."

"If it's any consolation, you can't have mucked it up worse than Hugh, and his wife is quite in love with him now. Though the reason remains a mystery..."

"Shall we return for supper?" I asked, unwilling to give more thought to my failings as a husband.

"A little longer? Juliet wanted a few minutes with your wife."

"Whatever for?"

"I have no idea. Mending fences most likely."

What fences required mending, I had no idea. But that wasn't overly surprising. "Do you want to see the mirrors?"

"Of course I want to see the mirrors. What are the mirrors for?"

A bubble of laughter escaped me. "For the telescope."

"Why does the telescope need mirrors?"

～

THE SUN WAS long set when we all piled back into the observatory after an amiable supper. The ladies had seemed much more at ease when we'd returned. Whatever Lady Juliet wished to speak to my wife about had been beneficial to them both.

Lady Juliet now surveyed the room with more wonder than I'd expected. Charlotte quietly explained pieces of equipment to her while Wayland and I made for the telescope.

I set it up for him and showed him how to find various stars.

By the time I made my way to the ladies, Charlotte was giving a thorough overview of the star charts and planets we might see. Rather than interrupt, I leaned back against my worktable, watching with interest. She spoke with enthusiasm and real knowledge.

Something inside me twisted as I realized she wasn't feigning attention. At least not all of it. My wife had listened when I spoke about my interests.

I should have recognized it earlier, but something about watching her impart her knowledge with such eagerness... It was breathtaking. And frankly, seeing a woman—*my wife*—explain the use of a nocturnal had last night's lust returning in full force. It was unbearably lovely, Charlotte speaking the language of the stars.

Why had I stopped her? We could have spent last night

wrapped in and around each other, speaking an entirely different language. A language of sighs and gasps and moans and love.

I swallowed the hunger, fighting for sense. Not the time. Not the place.

Charlotte's gaze flitted to mine when Lady Juliet asked a question she didn't have an answer for. Her lips parted in a sweet pout. I had tasted those lips a mere twenty-four hours ago. I had laid claim to them. I should never have stopped.

My wife had summoned me, though. I strode to her and my hand found her waist of its own volition. Her golden bronze curls were calling to me in the candlelight and I dropped a quick kiss to the top of her head before reviewing the book she referenced. She tensed under my grasp before melting into my side.

Michael called out to his wife, drawing her over to show her something or other—it was hardly relevant at the moment. Not when I had an arm full of warm, lavender-scented Charlotte.

She popped up onto her toes and leaned into me. "I am still cross with you," she breathed against my neck before dropping down from her toes with a placating pat to the shoulder. Then she abandoned me to join her friend.

I bit back a laugh that would be difficult to explain. She had spent a great many days of our marriage cross with me. Truly, she ought to be accustomed to it by now.

~

CHARLOTTE

The exhaustion finally set in long before we bid our guests good night. Mr. Wayland proved an enthusiastic student of astronomy and Juliet was interested as well. She was more intelligent than I had given her credit for in the past. Perhaps she would not be the worst friend I could have.

Lee hovered a few steps below me at the landing separating the East and west wings.. The warmth of his form seeped in through the layers of my gown and his coat that I borrowed to ward off the chill. I was reluctant to part with it. The hall was cold as well—not for any other reason.

I turned to face him. For the first time, we were the same height. The view was different here, right in his eyeline. His lashes were a darker blond than his hair and impossibly long. That was always the way with men, long, beautifully curled eyelashes they couldn't give a fig about.

Looking up from below, his eyes had always seemed a flat, clear, grayish blue. But now I could see a darker navy ring around the outside and little flecks of silver in the irises.

The growth on his face was the same shade as his lashes, and I knew from last night's experience it was soft with just the right amount of bite against my lips.

His tongue darted out to wet his lips before he finally broke the silence. "We should talk. But not tonight."

"Not tonight," I agreed, still reluctant to give up the advantage of height now that it was mine.

Lee was quite considerate about not overwhelming me with his presence. On occasion, I even forgot I lived with a giant. But now, on the same level, I realized it wasn't just the height. It was everything. His nose, his ears, his whole head—they were all massive. I didn't usually notice since they were proportional to the rest of him, but he was simply a large man.

I tucked a wayward strand of hair behind his ear and leaned forward to press a kiss to his cheek. Sensing my plan, he turned his head and caught my lips with his. He didn't hesitate, didn't wait. His hand caressed my cheek, and he devoured me.

He tasted of peppermint and a hint of the scotch he'd

shared with Mr. Wayland, and I chased it with my tongue. I should not be doing this. I knew better. But once I started, it was so hard to stop. Impossible.

One by one, he climbed the steps between us until there were none left and he was looming over me again, engulfing me. Gently, he urged me back a pace and joined me on the landing. Once there, he directed me backward down the hall. All the while his lips claimed mine.

I needed to stop. It could not be him this time. I wouldn't survive the rejection a second time.

One more taste, one more caress, just one more. And another, and again. Kiss after kiss until I forgot why I needed to stop. Until I forgot that stopping was an option. Until I forgot the definition of the word.

My back met something hard and flat with a thunk I didn't feel. It took a moment to recognize that Lee's hand had braced my head before he pushed me back against my door. My door... There was a bed in there... We could...

Lee abandoned my lips in favor of my jaw, doing absolutely filthy things with tongue and teeth that were sure to leave me reddened and wonderfully disheveled.

"Good night, Charlotte," he breathed into my ear. And before the rejection could set in, before my heart had a chance to drop into my stomach, he added, "We'll talk tomorrow. When it's just us."

I nodded. I had left the power of speech somewhere by the landing when his teeth had caught my lower lip in a delicious nip.

He pulled away, his eyes searching my face. Whatever he found there must have pleased him because his lips found mine again with a groan.

Eventually he dragged his lips from mine. His hand found the doorknob at my side and twisted it open. Gently, he brought his hands to my shoulders, turned me around to face my firelit room, and gave me a playful shove inside.

"Sweet dreams," he added for good measure before shutting the door between us. I counted three heavy footfalls before the quiet creek of his door.

Sometime later when I crawled between the sheets, my lips still bruised from his attentions, I dreamed of peppermint and stars and Lee.

Chapter Twenty-Five
BENNET HALL, SURREY - JULY 27, 1816

LEE

OUR GUESTS LEFT the next morning, eager to finish their journey. They only had one unwelcome nighttime visitor of the feline persuasion.

The weight of the needed conversation loomed over me in the hours that followed.

I wasn't too proud to admit I was hiding. The darkness and the unavoidable delay made me brave last night. But the harsh daylight had me cowering in my study like a frightened child.

For the moment, Charlotte seemed content to pluck away at the piano keys down the hall, rather than force a conversation. I couldn't decide if I was more grateful for the reprieve or annoyed that the swirling, anxious typhoon in my stomach was to carry on indefinitely.

I could have put a stop to it at any moment, I knew that, but knowing and doing were two very different things. Unfortunately, my estate ran well, and there was little in the way of calamities to offer distraction.

She finished one song and began the next—Beethoven, if I was correct. I was struck again at just how talented my wife was. She mastered complex pieces with graceful ease.

This was ridiculous, sitting down the hall listening when I could have been there experiencing. Thought was proving to be the enemy in my marriage.

Before I could muster the necessary courage to face her, Imogen slipped into the study with a perfunctory knock. A tray overflowing with biscuits was balanced gracefully in her hand.

"My lord," she nodded, dipping to set the tray on my desk. Without a word, she moved to stack the empty plates and cups that littered my desk and the nearby bookshelves. I had noticed those disappearing more frequently than usual.

"You can leave those for Eliza or Jack, Imogen."

"If it's all the same to you, I'd rather remove them before they grow legs and walk away."

Feeling sheepish, I averted my gaze. "I—uh—after my accident, I wasn't always—I would get headaches—in here I mean. I wasn't entirely gracious with people distracting me from my work. They tend to avoid this room."

Finally, I met her eyes only to find a raised brow, the gesture seeming more of interest than judgment. "Does your head still ache, sir?"

"Only when Brigsby is particularly vexing."

She chuckled before adding to her increasingly precarious stack. "Then perhaps you might allow me to collect them at my leisure."

I nodded, noting the way her teeth caught her lower lip.

"Might I speak freely, my lord?" At my go-on gesture, she began. "I'm not certain what it is between you and Lady Champaign. You should know, she is tenacious—I expect you do know that. But that is because she has had to be. Because there was no one else. She endures."

"Yes."

"I was hired on before her first season. She wasn't... That girl dreamed of more than the hand she was dealt."

The knot making itself known in my throat wasn't at all like one of my attacks. I wasn't capable of more than a solitary head bob.

"I believe you could be more for her, something she does not need to merely endure. But if you—if that is something you do not believe yourself capable of... I would ask that you return to your previous terms."

"I—" My throat rattled and I broke off to clear it. "I would like to be more."

"Then is it perhaps time to stop hiding in your study, my lord?" Her expression was one of self-satisfaction and mirth.

I caught my eye roll only a second before I unleashed it at her, then rose wordlessly to follow her out of my study. I turned toward the music room as Imogen proceeded to the kitchens.

The piano overlooked a large window with views of the lake behind the house. It framed her, bathed her in an afternoon glow that poured around her, caressed her—my enduring wife.

At the sound of my footsteps, she broke off, the final note hanging heavy, lingering. She turned to face me with an arched brow.

"Decided to come out of hiding?"

I bit back the instinctual denial. These women... "Yes." My voice was high and tight. I cleared my throat. "Will I regret it?"

She released a single chuckle. "Probably."

"I thought I might."

A cheery whistled note sounded from down the hall, then a second and third mixed to a jaunty tune. Leaning back, I peered out only to find Crawford, oblivious to the rising tension, whistling and spinning his pocket watch on its chain as he strolled through the house.

When I turned back to her, I found my wife peering curiously at me. Her eyes narrowed slightly.

"Another venue, perhaps?"

I nodded, waiting as she crossed the room before trailing behind her. I followed along like a lovesick sop, desperately dogging her heels.

It was easier when she was ahead of me. Her floral scent was calming, and her dark honey curls were distractingly shiny. I needn't think with her here. Half the time I was incapable of coherent thought at all, my attention wrapped up in her soft skin, warm eyes, and truly magnificent breasts.

She led me into her sitting room. The one with the door that opened right into her chambers. I was capable of a great many thoughts on that proximity—none of them fit for polite company.

Mutely, she gestured toward one of the chairs, then sat on the settee opposite. Her rooms were above the music room, offering an even more spectacular view of the lake. The sun had dipped a little lower behind the trees and was a little less oppressive when I sat in its cast.

My chest tightened, but not in a concerning way—like one of my fits—but in a way that had everything to do with my proximity to Charlotte and our combined proximity to her bed.

~

CHARLOTTE

His legs were too long for the chair leaving him crunched up in his seat. I sacrificed my lip in order to keep from laughing at the picture he made, curled up like a frog.

The confident man that left me a lusty husk last night was nowhere to be seen. In his place, an awkward, gangly gentleman, tangled in a chair. Every second or so, he shifted, trying to find a comfortable position. He was never going to find it.

He was also never going to begin talking.

"It's up to me then?"

Lee didn't feign confusion. Instead his throat bobbed, drawing my gaze to the long, muscular line of his neck. I hadn't ever noticed a man's neck before. Perhaps I noticed it now because his cravat was loose and hanging uselessly and I had a better view. But it was probably just because it was *his* neck.

"Where do you wish to start?" he finally croaked.

"There are a great many options. And you would know better than I which circumstances I ought to be acquainted with."

"I didn't mean to keep secrets. I just... This isn't what I thought it would be like." Something in my expression must have given away the sinking in my stomach because he rushed to continue. "Not in a bad way. It's wonderful, truly. But you're... more than I thought you would be. I thought we would be husband and wife in name only. That you would give birth and a few months after that, you would return to town. And I would stay here, precisely as alone as I was before."

"If you did not wish for a wife, why did you agree to marry me?"

"I didn't *not* want a wife... I—I thought we understood each other. You required the protection of my name. And, well, I couldn't be a real husband to anyone. I thought at least I could be a fictitious husband to you."

There was a great deal to consider there, to press him on. But the temptation of another question, the one that had been nagging at me since the moment I learned of her existence was too much to overcome.

"What happened to the previous Lady Champaign?"

His eyes found his feet and he dragged a hand through his hair. There was sentiment in that gesture, but I couldn't name it from my vantage. "Carriage accident. She passed in a carriage accident." The notes were sunken, lifeless.

The answer was no surprise at all. I had considered as much for weeks, perhaps since our wedding day. It made a horrifying sense.

"What happened?"

"We were traveling at night, returning from a ball in town. I used to do that occasionally—it's so easy a journey. We hit a rut and my head bumped the edge of the lantern, knocked it off the hook. It landed on the floor, on Mia's dress. I've never seen anything ignite that fast. I tried to stomp it out, I ripped off the curtains trying to smother it. It just burned faster, hotter. Her screams..."

His gaze dropped to the floor as he battled against tears. It didn't work, and he wiped angrily at them.

"You don't have to—"

"No, you should know. I knocked the rod off the bracket when I yanked the curtains off. I don't know how, but it got jammed in the door. I couldn't get us out. Eventually one of the footmen got the other side open, pulled her free. Meanwhile, I managed to get the damn curtain rod—on fire—twisted in the handle and when I tried to turn it, it hit me in the face, and brushed my chest, just enough to set my shirt alight. I fell out of the carriage, backward and on fire. My leg got tangled in the seat and I broke it in the fall. I managed to put myself out. I had to crawl around the damn carriage to find her. I was too late. Mia died, horribly, while her husband did nothing."

The broken, dispassionate nature of the speech, delivered

to the rug, had tears gathering on my cheeks as well. I longed to reach for him, to touch him. But I wasn't certain it would be welcomed in that moment. The memory of his flinch from that night—from St. John's—was still fresh.

"Lee—"

"I had one job. One. And no one has ever failed as spectacularly as I have. Not only did I fail to protect her, but it was my fault."

"It wasn—"

"It was. It was why I couldn't... didn't want to—why I can't be a husband to you. I can't be a husband to anyone."

A thousand tiny moments became clear, and I hated every single one of them. More than anything I had ever wanted in my entire life, I wanted the power to take away the pain creasing his face, the empty hollow of his voice, the wretched thoughts in his head.

In that moment, I would have given him up. If I could turn back the clock, if I had a wish, Amelia Bennet never would have set foot in that carriage. Her death never would have left this man shattered and devastated.

I would be alone, unwed and with child. But Leopold Bennet's scarred face wouldn't be buried in his hands. He wouldn't be bent in half as his chest shuddered with silent sobs. And that would be worth it.

Without permission, my knees met the floor at his feet, and I wrapped my arms around him as best I could, curled up and doubled over as he was. It wasn't clear he even perceived my presence. I didn't recognize the notes of my sobs, mixed with his, until his shirt was a soaked mess in the middle of his shoulder.

The shushing sound I was making was warped and ugly between throaty breaths. My pathetic rubs of his back showed no signs of providing relief.

Lee was lost to the world. If anything, his sobs were

getting worse, harsher. His breath was ragged and desperate. Every single inhale ripped a hole in his chest. I was seconds away from rising, from pulling the bell, from summoning Brigsby or Crawford, anyone who might know how to help.

Then his hand found mine. He interlaced our fingers, tightening his grip.

"Don't go," he gasped.

"I won't. I'm here."

"Stay. Please stay." And for a second the desperate part of me, the part I refused to acknowledge, leapt at the thought that he meant something more than this moment.

He didn't, I knew he didn't. But my answer was the same either way.

"Of course."

Chapter Twenty-Six
BENNET HALL, SURREY - JULY 28, 1816

LEE

It was a disconcerting juxtaposition, waking with dry, crusted eyes, a sticky face, a sore throat, a full bladder, and the beginnings of a megrim but also wrapped safe in my wife's arms. Mostly wrapped in my wife's arms. She was small and I was large, and the hint of her growing belly pressing into my upper back made her reach even shorter.

Her boney arm was tucked between my neck and head, bent with a delicate hand laying claim to my chest—just above my thrumming heartbeat. The other arm was slung low across my waist, the hand hanging in the air.

Snores, almost imperceptibly soft, were pressed into my neck. Her breath was warm and damp against my shoulder blade.

An icy foot had found its way between my calves, so cold that frostbite was a possibility.

Every other point of contact was hot, so hot, too hot.

And I never, ever, wanted to move again.

I belonged right here, trapped under her lavender-and-orange-blossom-scented quilt, half damp with sweat and half frozen.

Never in my life had I felt so dead and so alive at the same time. I couldn't even recall making it to the bed last night. Surely I had cooperated. She couldn't have managed it on her own. But everything after I asked her to stay was blank.

Physically, this was remarkably similar to the aftermath of one of my episodes. But emotionally... It—*she*—was like nothing I had ever known.

Many long moments passed before I was able to name the feeling in my chest or, more accurately, the absence of feeling. Relief. This wrung out, exhausted, languid feeling was relief.

There was embarrassment, too, at my display of overwrought emotion. But that was familiar, almost like a friend. I felt that every time I swam to the surface after an episode.

But mostly there was a void, an empty place where some of the guilt and turmoil used to live. It was still there—I didn't expect it would ever go away—but it was lessened.

I had never told anyone before. When Mia died, Brigsby told her parents. I was still recovering from the broken leg and burns—and the subsequent infection they brought. The tenants and villagers just... knew. Gossip traveled fast and their landlord killing his wife was perhaps the best gossip in existence. As for everyone else... I avoided them. I hid in Bennett Hall and my observatory. Right until Charlotte.

Ah, there it was, the spark of guilt returning. Charlotte, who should be dancing at balls and hosting parties. Instead, I kept her locked in my tower like a beast. Someday, someone would come to slay me, to free her.

We had found a permanent solution to a temporary problem, she and I. But when she returned to town and her life... she would find someone else, someone true. I'd promised her freedom—one year for the rest of her days. The thought twisted like a knife in my gut now. Some faceless booby with grubby hands and overly waxed hair would caress her curves, taste her lips.

It wouldn't be enough for that man, the piece of her that I'd promised to leave free. The memories I kept wouldn't be enough for me either. How naive I'd been to think I could have her for a year and give her up at the end.

I would have to, though. The question was, would she let me keep the sliver we'd discussed, or would she want to give that to the one when she found him?

Divorce... I would grant her one, if she asked it, but it wouldn't free her—not entirely. The consequences would place her right back where she started before our marriage. Ostracized and shamed. But the right man, a man who loved her enough, he wouldn't mind. I wouldn't mind.

But I was a selfish man, and she would need to ask for it. Otherwise, I would cling to the sliver I was allowed to keep, alone in my empty observatory with nothing but the heavens for company.

She stirred against me, her arm tightening reflexively before loosening when consciousness returned. The hand hovering in the air near my waist moved to wipe her mouth. She must have drooled.

Something about knowing that my beautiful, accomplished, elegant wife was a little less perfect in her sleep was comforting. Had the arse that left her alone with child been allowed to see her this way? Had her husband?

Jealousy wasn't an emotion I'd spent much time with. But I knew it instantly. I swallowed, my throat still raw, and tried to shove it down. It wasn't my place.

"Good morning," she breathed into my back. Her voice was low and hoarse with sleep. I found the hand still pressed into my chest with my own and dragged it to my lips and pressed a kiss to her elegant fingers before setting it back home.

I should apologize for my display last night. I intended to, truly. Instead, a rusty, "Thank you," escaped.

"How are you feeling?"

"Like death. But also... better. I should have told you before. I'm sorry."

I felt her shake her head, her forehead pressed against my shoulder blade, rolling there. "You told me when I needed to know."

"A bit late. I did try to make you ride several hours on your wedding day. In your condition."

A sweet laugh, muffled by my shirt, rang out. "That was badly done. But I understand now."

"You do?"

"I do."

And that was enough, those two words, to make me brave. With a great inhale, I rolled over to face her.

CHARLOTTE

He was adorable, all sleep rumpled and bleary-eyed. His hair stuck straight up on one side.

I couldn't help myself, I reached up to brush it down. It sprang back up.

At my laugh, he dragged an irritated hand down it, but his efforts were futile as well.

"It always does that 'til I wet it." His voice was low and graveled, hitting deep in my lower belly.

I trapped an inappropriate sound, nodding instead. Surely I was a mess too. I had been drooling on the back of his shirt mere moments ago. But I wouldn't have moved for the world.

His hand fell down, landing on my waist over the curve of my growing belly. The move was so nonchalant, so unpracticed. As though it wasn't unbearably significant. This moment where his massive, unbearably warm hand settled on the babe that wasn't his.

The babe understood the significance too. Because they chose that precise moment to make their presence felt. It was little more than a flutter, not so different from the bubbling nausea I had experienced for several months. And yet, entirely different. Nothing had ever been more different.

A kick.

I froze, waiting, desperate to confirm it wasn't a hallucination. And then, again. Right beneath his hand. My eyes met his, wide and round to match his lips, parted in a perfect astonished circle.

"Is that—" he asked, graveled tone gone and wonder in its place.

I nodded dumbly, too filled with emotions I couldn't name to speak.

"Has that—" Apparently he had lost the ability to finish a sentence.

"I—not like that. Not so strong. I didn't know what it was before."

For the second time in less than a day, my giant of a husband folded himself in half and buried his face in my belly. He pressed a distracted kiss there, right above his hand before leaning to whisper, "'lo there. That is some truly exemplary kicking. But do not forget to be kind to your mama. You were a right terror for months. Need to earn her favor."

And for the second time in less than a day, hot tears slipped down my cheek. I laced my hand with his, and the babe gave another greeting kick. In that moment, every horrible, unkind thing I had ever thought about this child floated away. All that was left was love. Love for the child. And love for the man contorting himself to whisper nonsense into my stomach.

It was, perhaps, the most perfect moment of my life. Which was, of course, why the scratching noise at my door was entirely unsurprising. Lee didn't notice, too wrapped up in chatting with my belly. The door creaked open a crack, and I saw the tip of a tail swishing back and forth toward the bed.

It reached the edge before the tail dipped out of sight, but I knew what was coming. With a disgruntled, *merah*, Cass landed on the corner of my mattress. She chirped her way over to me, each step accompanied by a corresponding *mrow* before she found my wrist. She rubbed her head against my hand until I lifted it and let her sniff.

Satisfied with my scent, she stroked her head under my hand, stepping forward so it dragged along her back. Again. A third time. And like the mark I was, I gave her a scratch on the fourth rub and received a chomp and an irritated chirp for my trouble.

My curse was enough to draw Lee from my belly.

His eyes narrowed at the cat. "Shoo."

I laughed, full and hearty. "Has that ever once worked?"

His warm gaze met mine over my belly, accompanied by a sheepish grin. "There's a first time for everything."

I rolled my eyes. "Of course."

His grin deepened and melted into a full, brilliant smile.

I never wanted to leave. Not this house, not this room, not this bed—even with the absurdly manipulative cat. Outside the sanctuary of this quilt, the remaining months of our arrangement ticked by ever faster, each minute shorter than the last. We could stay here forever though, right?

With a feigned casualness, Cass sauntered over to the other corner of the bed by my husband, where she bit him on the calf.

Perhaps I could do without the absurdly manipulative cat.

Chapter Twenty-Seven
BENNET HALL, SURREY - JULY 28, 1816

LEE

UNBURDENED, we spent the day occupied in our usual separate pursuits. And once every minute or so, I'd remember the tiny flutters under my hand this morning and smile.

For the first time, it was clear that Charlotte wasn't quite so displeased with the child growing inside her. I still had no doubts that given another option, she wouldn't have chosen this life. But perhaps she didn't hate it here. And maybe she didn't hate the being that brought her here either.

I found myself in the nursery an hour before supper. The paw prints were not going to come off, not without destroying the mural underneath. The floor, too, would have to be sanded down and refinished. My futile efforts with a damp cloth proved entirely ineffective—not that I had expected anything different.

Something shiny winked up at me from the floor. I bent down and there was a delicate floral hairpin. I swallowed against the immediate ardor that reminder produced. Perhaps the nursery should be moved elsewhere if I couldn't manage being in this room without crumbling to a lusty heap.

A tiny beaded flower topped the pin. Five yellow beads surrounded a red one. And just beyond it in my line of sight was a paw print on the floor, four toes and a slightly larger print for the main pad. In yellow.

I couldn't. Could I? What could it hurt?

A quick search revealed Charlotte's well-closed paints, and I found a red that matched the hairpin. I considered using a brush, but that was well beyond my—nonexistent—skills. Instead, I dipped my little finger in the paint. The floor was the best starting point, at least it wouldn't make her mural worse. Gently, carefully, I tapped the center of the paw with my finger.

It didn't look like a flower. But it didn't not look like a flower either. I tried to picture it, a bit more detailing, a stem, some leaves... It certainly wasn't the worst idea I'd ever had.

For a moment, I considered forging ahead with the rest of the prints. But the mural had been Charlotte's vision, and she should have final say over any repair attempts.

A handkerchief cleaned the paint off my finger with ease.

I went to my chamber and dressed for dinner, ignoring Brigsby's usual chatter, consumed with thoughts of Charlotte. Thoughts of Charlotte and tonight...

Last night was necessary. It was painful and it was cathartic. But I had been hoping for a different kind of catharsis when the evening set out. My body still remembered her soft hands and sweet lips.

Tonight... Tonight could be a more pleasant catharsis.

Somehow, the thought was less terrifying than it had been. Charlotte was wonderful. If she could manage my broken sobs last night, she could manage my broken body.

CHARLOTTE

I kept expecting to have difficulty reaching the strings of the harp, but thus far my protruding belly proved to be no obstacle. My back, on the other hand, ached today. Sleeping curled around my husband's gigantic form was probably the culprit. But I couldn't bring myself to regret the arrangement for anything.

Learning the harp proved a challenge. I had spent years studying the pianoforte. There were tutors to teach me proper technique, and decades of practice allowed me to play relatively complex pieces well.

Such was not the case with the harp. I had no instructor for proper technique—though I had found a book in the library. Every time I found an intermediate or advanced piece, I reached for it, and every time it proved too much for my fumbling fingers.

The fastest way to build bad habits was to rush the basics, stumble through a fingering enough times and it became automatic. It was easier to learn things correctly than to fix something learned wrong. Every lecture from my piano instructor came to the forefront.

But the basic songs were so dull. There was no depth, no complexity. Even if there was satisfaction to be found in achieving a new skill.

The hours I spent trying to improve quicker than I ought left me with sore fingers and an aching back.

Pressing a hand to my lower back while Lee was occupied with his soup, I tried to stretch it subtly.

It didn't work. I should have known. Any motion that drew attention to my breasts was sure to catch every man's eye in the vicinity.

My husband's cheeks and neck flushed and his gaze flitted

toward his soup only to catch on the hand pressing against my back.

"Are you well?"

"Yes, it is nothing."

"Charlotte..." His tone was low, warning.

I relented and settled back in my seat. "My back aches slightly."

He nodded thoughtfully with nothing more than a hum before turning back to his dinner. It was unusual for him. He had a tendency to fret.

We finished the meal in relative silence. I was only slightly peeved at his unexpected nonchalance. He trailed me up the stairs.

The night was clear and the moon was a thread-thin crescent—a good night for stargazing. He would likely go to his room to change into something a bit warmer and head to the observatory. I considered whether to follow him. He'd welcomed me every time. But my back twinged at the thought and my feet were swollen in my slippers.

I opened my door, then turned to call after him, to tell him not to wait for me, but he was on my feet, awaiting entrance.

I startled, stepping back into my chamber. His hand found my waist, steadying me.

"I do not think I will join you tonight."

He blinked, his brow furrowing. "I'm not going to the observatory." The last word tipped up, questioning my meaning.

"You're not?"

"No, you're unwell."

It was my turn to blink slowly, comprehension dawning and settling into my chest, warming it.

Ralph had never, not once, cared when I felt poorly. He lived at the gaming hell, rain or shine, in sickness or health—

either of ours. If they hadn't kicked him out when he started to turn the yellow color, I suspected he would have died there.

"But you cannot—there's nothing you can do."

"Your feet hurt too. I saw you fussing with your slippers earlier."

He strolled over to the settee and settled in as if he belonged there. One night in my bed and he had claimed the room as his own. He looked at me expectantly. My expression must have reflected my confusion because he patted the space next to him.

I shut the door against wayward felines and joined him, mostly for lack of other occupations.

In spite of the knot forming in my lower back, I sat properly. He huffed before bending over and astonishing me by grabbing my calf and turning me in my seat. He draped one of my legs over his lap and his intent became clear.

When I refused to move the other leg, he merely sighed and grasped my slipper, then dropped it on the floor with a *thunk*. Without so much as a word, he lifted my foot in his large hand. I made to protest, managed to expel half a syllable even, until his thumb dug into the arch of my foot and my words turned to a desperate, unstoppable moan as I sank back against the pillows.

Convinced of the intelligence of his plan, I raised my other leg to rest in his lap for him to do as he wished. And he did, strong fingers working intently at the ball of my foot. My stockings bunched up and he grasped the tip of it, looking at me askance. When I nodded, he tugged the delicate silk from my leg, leaving my foot, ankle, and calf bare to him. He used that moment to remove the other slipper and stocking as well, then returned his attention to the first.

"How is your back? Do you need another pillow?"

I shook my head. At some point my eyes had slipped closed.

"You really gave up the stars for my feet?"

"The stars will be there tomorrow." His voice was a low rumble.

"So will my feet."

"Yes, but they hurt today. Do you want me to give your back a try?" He asked, dragging a hand down my calf.

I froze, considering the implications.

"Not like that," he rushed to add.

Feeling daring, I asked, "What if I wish for you to mean like that?"

He swallowed something that sounded like a groan. "Your back hurts."

"That is why you should rub it."

"I will. If that's what you want. But just that. I don't—not while you're hurting."

"I'm afraid that is going to be the majority of the time for the next several months."

"I do not wish to hurt you, Charlotte."

I shrugged. "It always hurts."

His hands paused, and his eyes narrowed on me. "What do you mean, 'It always hurts'?"

"Just that. It is just the way it is for women."

"No. No, it's not."

I rolled my eyes. Nothing like a man to be an expert on women.

"It's not, Charlotte. It shouldn't hurt. Did you—Did it... You had pain? Every time?"

"It's quite usual."

His eyes shut and he took a great breath, inhaling and exhaling loud enough to echo over the crackling fire. "Which one?"

"I beg your pardon?"

"Which man hurt you?"

"What does it matter?"

"If it's the one that is still alive, I'm going to kill him. And if it's the one that's dead, I'm going to spit on his grave." His tone was one I had never heard from Lee, ever patient and kind Lee.

"That is absurd."

"It was both of them. You said as much."

"Yes, yes it was both of them. But that hardly matters. And you're a man. I think, of the two of us, I have a better idea of what is usual for women."

Gently, he set my feet on the floor. A dramatic sigh accompanied the gesture. He pressed himself to stand and wordlessly began digging through my armoire.

"Can I help you with something?" I asked through a laugh.

"Night rail?"

"Left-hand side." He pulled out two, one practical and unadorned, the other a remnant of my former life. It was a lacy, frilly slip my mother had insisted on as part of my first trousseau. The one that had remained unused since my second wedding night. Lee considered it thoughtfully before shaking himself and putting it back into the armoire. He set the other one atop the bed and returned to me, holding out a hand.

I took it, and he pulled me up. He turned me to face away from him and began working on the dress hooks lining the back of my gown. His hands made quick work of them and before long, the gown pooled on the floor between us. The petticoats joined it, leaving me in nothing but stays and chemise.

His touch was gentle, soothing, but perfunctory. I wanted to question him, but I hadn't the faintest idea where to begin. He seemed almost angry at me, but not quite. Usually when I peeved him, he snapped back—just a little. But he was restrained, tight.

The knot on my stays loosened. My rushed inhale echoed in the space between us. "Why do you have this so tight?"

"I'm not used to the belly. I do not like it."

A large arm found its way around my shoulder and tugged me back into his chest. The other hand found the rounded bump in question. His hand was so large it spanned my entire belly with ease.

"I do."

"You do not."

"I do. It brought you to me." His lips found my temple, and he pressed a dry kiss there. "Stop lacing it so tight. It's just me here."

He was more than enough reason to put effort into being beautiful.

Before I could argue that point—or the part of it I was willing to admit to—he added, "Please." All I could do was nod in answer. "Thank you."

The stays fell between us in a *thump* that matched the pounding of my heart.

"Can you manage the chemise?" I nodded again and he withdrew. For a moment I thought he would leave—leave me bereft after accustoming me to his touch. But he merely turned to face the door.

I undressed and redressed quickly. "All right."

He faced me again, his gaze flitting down my form then back up again. A flush creeped from under his cravat.

Instead of reaching for me, kissing me, caressing me, dragging me to the bed, he went over and turned down the coverings. This wasn't precisely the romantic consummation I'd hoped for, but he was clearly nervous.

He pressed me back to sit on the bed, then bent to lift my feet. This was truly the most bizarre... His footsteps padded on the carpeting before he settled at the foot of the bed, pulled off one boot, then the other. He yanked off his cravat and waistcoat as well and dropped them into the pile of my things at the foot of the bed.

Silent, he stood and rounded the bed, then crawled in the other side. This was it. Now we would... He urged me onto my side and slid his arm under my head. The bed shook slightly as he pressed up behind me. This wasn't how I imagined it, but...

His other arm wrapped around my waist and settled on my belly. Wisps of hair tickled my cheek as he breathed.

The silence stretched for a minute, two, three. "I can hear you thinking," he murmured from behind me.

"What are you doing?" I whispered.

"Holding you," he said in a tone that indicated he thought it was quite obvious and I was oblivious. "Does the warmth feel better on your back?"

I considered it. The heat of his chest and belly against my back settled into the aching muscles pleasantly. "Yes."

"Good. Go to sleep."

I stared through the window—he had left the curtains undrawn—and out at the stars. "You needn't stay. You can go to your observatory."

His arms tightened in response.

"Really, Lee. The conditions are perfect."

"And they will be again. I have everything I need right here."

"But..."

"I can see the stars from here. Look, what's that?" His hand left my belly and extended to point at the sky through the window.

There was a familiar friend, winking back at us. "Saturn."

A kiss found the top of my head. "Precisely, and what constellation is it in?"

"Capricornus."

"Perfect."

"But your telescope…"

"Will still be there tomorrow. Now, do you want to look at the stars or do you wish to sleep?"

I quite liked the stars now. From my limited vantage on the bed, through a closed window, they were lovely but less interesting than they were through the telescope.

I was tetchy though, wound up from what I'd thought was an awkward seduction.

"Tell me a story?"

I felt more than heard his laugh against my back. "What kind of story?"

"Something with a happy ending, please."

He hummed thoughtfully, the low rumble vibrating down my spine. "Once upon a time, in a kingdom about two hours on horseback from London, there lived a beautiful princess."

I rewarded his effort with a soft giggle. He continued on, whispering in his low tenor about the princess trapped in the kingdom by an adorable but mischievous guard cat.

Occasionally his hand would drift to my back, rubbing the exact source of the ache even at the awkward angle, before returning to my belly. And as he told increasingly ridiculous yet believable tales of the cat's misbehaviors, I drifted off.

Chapter Twenty-Eight
BENNET HALL, SURREY - JULY 28, 1816

LEE

Her breathing evened into slow and steady rhythms around the same time her frigid feet made their way between my calves. I trailed off in the midst of an increasingly absurd story after the entirely fictitious cat used various household objects to barricade the princess in the tower.

The snoring began shortly thereafter—little sounds, quiet enough to be amusing rather than annoying. I dropped a kiss to her temple. My hand traced along the curves of her side, up her shoulder and down to her hip and back.

Fury unlike any I'd ever known still swirled through my veins at the thought of her late husband and the arse at the masquerade. Every man she'd ever met or thought about meeting made it onto my list.

But I also felt tenderness like I had never experienced. That was overpowering the rage at the moment. Now that I had her wrapped in my arms where she was safe and warm—mostly, the feet seemed to still be a problem—nothing could hurt her. I wouldn't allow it.

Hovering just out of reach was the memory of Mia, another woman I'd vowed to protect. Mia had far fewer people trying to cause her harm. And still, I'd failed her.

Reflexively, my arms tightened. Charlotte's snores broke off for a moment, but she didn't wake. Under my hand, the babe gave a little kick, nothing hard enough to interrupt its mother's rest.

"Hush, little one. Let your mama sleep." The words were more breath than whisper, and neither babe nor mother stirred.

I couldn't decide if wedding Charlotte was the best or worst decision of my life. If I hadn't agreed, if I'd refused... She would have found someone else, and all I would have was the memory of a single dance. That thought was so painful I could hardly imagine it.

Except the future would come, the one where I had a year to accustom myself to Charlotte's musical laugh, lavender scent, and silky curls. And then I had to say goodbye to her. *That* would be unbearable, and it was inevitable at this point.

But there was one more possibility, almost certainly an inevitability itself. The version of this story where I showed her that love, physical love, didn't have to be painful. In that version, I spent the next several months worshiping her. And wouldn't that be worse still? To have had her, truly had her, in *almost* every way that counted, and then set her free. Or was it worse to know with absolute certainty that this woman, my Charlotte, was moving through life thinking love and pain were one and the same?

It hardly mattered because I was a beggar, and I would feast on whatever scraps she deigned to give me. I would subsist on them until there was nothing left. And then I would live on the memories. Now I just had to make sure they were good ones. The best.

∽

By the next evening, we had entered into something of a standoff. One I hadn't the slightest idea of how to break. Well, I had a great number of ideas on how I might go about that. But those were fantasies in which I was the world's greatest lover, and Charlotte was waiting on my advances with bated breath.

In reality, we hovered around each other—or I was at any rate—hoping for the slightest indication that she wished me to ravish her.

Nothing of the sort had arrived at the breakfast table.

She'd made no hint that she wished for my attentions at tea.

Supper, too, was bereft of significant glances.

Now she peered up at me, her brow arched, as she stood beside my telescope. Her soft lips requested assistance in adjusting it. That was the moment I realized that there were, perhaps, indications I had missed.

A lingering glance across the breakfast dishes.

A brushed hand when passing the tea.

Knees sliding between one another under the table.

Now she begged for my help with a task she'd mastered a month ago. And she did so without backing away in the slightest. She forced me into her orbit, trapping me there forever.

"Lee?"

"Yes?"

"I should like to retire now."

Blast and damnation! I had missed the signs and now it was too late. "Is it your back again?"

I grabbed the lantern and blew out the nearby candles.

"No, my back is perfectly well."

"Tired?"

She tucked herself against my side as we made the short climb back to the house. "Not in the slightest."

"I don't—*Oh*..."

"Caught up now?"

"I—yes. I believe so."

We reached the house, and Brigsby was there to see us in. I asked him to close up the observatory while Charlotte started up the steps without me.

Task disposed of, I raced after her like an overeager puppy, catching her around the waist and spinning her to face me a few steps before the landing. I liked kissing her here, where she was an inch or two taller than me. Loved it, in point of fact.

The change in angle left her kisses bolder. Her hands were greedier, her whimpers a little more demanding.

She pulled away, chuckling quietly when my lips chased hers. "Do we understand each other?"

"Yes?" I panted out before recognizing the questioning lilt. "Yes. Yes. We understand each other."

"Good." Her lips crashed onto mine, her hands spearing in my hair. I took a step, then another, crowding her down the hall in a repeat of the other night. Only this time, there was purpose behind the action. Determination. This kiss wouldn't end outside her door.

And it didn't.

Who was responsible for the actual turning of the knob would forever remain a mystery, but we stumbled into the room in an ungainly tangle of limbs. Well, mine were ungainly. Hers were elegant and poised as always—probably—I was too busy with the dress hooks to truly notice.

They were easier for the previous night's practice. The petticoats, too, were simple work to remove.

Charlotte's hands were nearly as greedy as mine. Shoving off my waistcoat, tugging at my cravat—with only a light strangulation—yanking my shirt from my breeches.

Ice raced through my veins at that.

"Wait." The word escaped without permission, and I ripped my lips from hers.

"Leeee," she whined. It was quite possibly the sweetest sound I'd ever heard.

"I... there are scars."

She blinked, owlish, in response before comprehension slid over her face. The distance I had gained evaporated with her single step. Wordlessly, she returned to her task with more reverence and less ardor than I would have liked. Gently, she dragged her palms along my flank, the shirt moving with them.

She could not manage the entire task without my assistance. When the linen caught on my arms, I lifted them with a trepidation I hadn't felt since the night of the masquerade. Summoning my courage, I caught it behind my neck and tugged it up and over.

And then I stood there, allowing—enduring—her perusal. My gaze settled on something over her head, but I wasn't actually seeing it. Every second without a word was agonizing. My chest tightened and my heart plucked an irregular beat, squeezed too tight by too much and not enough air in my lungs.

She stepped away and turned toward her bedside table. I found myself floating above the scene. My body motionless there with a mottled, gnarled, twisted chest. And Charlotte's delicate form, prim and perfect and too polite to scream.

It was ten, perhaps twenty seconds between when she stepped away and when she returned. And I died in them. My chest cracked open and my heart poured out, still tripping along half-heartedly.

I fought to remember, to consider. Linen stitches in the shirt, still clenched in one hand. There weren't enough things to touch, to center, and my feet weren't working. Dimly, I was aware of her return, but I was too lost to recognize it. And then... peppermint.

I gasped, my lungs finding purchase again as the crisp scent of peppermint wafting up from somewhere. Delicate hands found my empty one and pressed something into it—a mint. Charlotte. Charlotte had brought me a peppermint. The stinging burn of it on my tongue cut through the panic in a way nothing else could. The razor-edged aura of mint freed the breath trapped in my chest while I had been desperately gulping more with no space. And my heart, still pounding, echoing in my chest, returning to an even tempo.

"Better?"

I nodded, certain any words would come out shrill and thready.

"Is this why you've been so... reluctant?"

Another nod, accompanied by a swallow of mint. I could sense the moment it hit my stomach, stilling the raging ocean in my belly.

"Lee... you're beautiful."

"What?" The word escaped me in a choked half gasp, half cough.

"You are. I've always thought so." *Lies.*

"You do not have to—"

"I am not lying. Truly. You're the most beautiful man I've ever seen."

"Charlotte—"

And because she was my Charlotte, she rolled her eyes. Nothing in the world could have made me laugh in that moment—except for that. My chuckle earned me another eye roll before she shocked me into silent stupor.

She stepped even closer, rose up onto her toes, and pressed a kiss to the worst of the scars, right above my heart. It had taken years to stop paining me, that particular scar. I still occasionally had a strange, constricting sensation alone in bed—so alone. Always alone.

And Charlotte was kissing it.

As a rule, I touched my chest as little as possible. The skin under her touch was thicker, an odd juxtaposition of numb and too sensitive. The impression of her lips on my raised flesh was unlike any I had ever experienced. I couldn't feel it the same way I felt her hand on my unmarred shoulder—instant, exact, hot, and soft except for the very tips of her fingers, calloused from her harp practice. But my skin knew *something* was there and her touch tingled, singed, in a way that was entirely new. And what I lacked in sensation, I was able to fill in with the visual.

And, *oh*, what a visual. She had dropped back down to her toes and was making her way along the angry marks, kissing each one. The sharper, more distinct line where the rod had landed and the freeform, abstract ripples where the fabric had caught.

I stood there stupidly staring at her with my hands hovering about her shoulders, desperate to touch her but too afraid to shatter this illusion. And it was surely an illusion. She would not—could not—look upon the evidence of my disgrace and see beauty there, something worthy of her touch.

Except, I never could have imagined the dual thrill of the hand dragging down my unmarred left side and its twin on the left matching it. The moment was surreal. And wonderful. And I was not nearly clever enough to contrive it. Which meant this was happening.

And that meant *I* could touch *her*. My hands settled, one on her waist, the other on the back of her messy curls. Itchy fingers longed to sink into the silky strands.

Pins—must remove pins. The other hand joined in the pursuit, but she paid no heed, working her way along the wound that curved around my rib cage.

When she found the edge of the scar, a groan ripped from me. Everything was different there, *more*. Too much. Not enough.

My hand tightened involuntarily in her—mostly free—curls, pulling her up to catch her lips in mine. Whatever restraint I once had was gone, forgotten. I was entirely incapable of it.

Stays—looser today—fell to the floor between us with one firm yank on the laces. I stepped over them, directing her back toward the bed between desperate, heady kisses.

There were things I was supposed to remember. I knew they existed. But what they were... It was anyone's guess.

When her knees hit the bed, Charlotte broke away and fell back to land in a disheveled heap on the bed. Perfection.

I knelt before her, too wrung out for guise or artifice. Because I was going to convince her to stay here, stay with me, tonight. Right now.

A slipper came free easily and I tossed it away with a *thunk*. The stocking, silk and lovely, followed over my shoulder, floating down like stardust in my periphery. Then their twins.

"Lee?" Nothing but the slight apprehension in her voice could have compelled me back to reason.

Still, the fetching knee was *right there* in desperate need of a kiss before I dragged that leg over my shoulder. I leaned back, meeting her gaze with a raised brow.

"What are you doing?" she whispered, a mix of trepidation, curiosity, and lust in her voice.

That was it, the thing I was supposed to remember. Every single man she had ever met had been a selfish arse. I couldn't decide whether I hated the men who came before or loved them for allowing me to be the first one to do this for her—to show her pleasure.

But then Charlotte's lip caught between her teeth warily

and I settled firmly on hate. I pushed it down, it wouldn't help in this. Instead, I summoned the memory of her lips on my chest, vanishing everything except the adoration I felt for her.

"Do you trust me?" My voice was ragged, ripped apart and put together into a graveled, shredded mockery of my usual tone.

"What?"

I pressed another kiss to the side of her knee, still *right there*. "Charlotte... Let me love you."

Her eyes widened, considering. That was the moment I realized what I was asking—and my heart cracked in two.

The "please" poured out of me, thoughtless and desperate. This wasn't about her pleasure—not yet. She was opening herself for me, risking pain, rejection, every awful thing that had ever happened to her.

I was asking her to show me her scars.

When she nodded, a tentative, shy movement, I loved her all the more for it.

Chapter Twenty-Nine
BENNET HALL, SURREY - JULY 29, 1816

CHARLOTTE

NO ONE, not one single person, had ever looked at me the way Lee was. A sliver of blue silver ringed his pupils. The lust was familiar, but the adoration—that was entirely *Lee*. His bitten lips were parted, allowing for panted breaths to drag into his heaving chest.

Every concern I'd had about him not wanting me, not finding me attractive, was well and truly shattered on the floor between us. His throat bobbed, his gaze flitting between mine and the rather vulgar view in front of him. I had the inane desire to bite that shifting knot.

And he asked me if I trusted him. With what, I had no idea. But for some ridiculous reason, I did. It would haunt me later—trusting a man always did—but I could deny him nothing. And I did not want to.

When he asked me to let him love me... How could I do anything else?

My nod was met with a groan that shook the walls. But he didn't do any of the things I had come to expect. He didn't rise and strip off his breeches. He didn't fall atop me in a heavy heap. He didn't order me to turn over.

Instead, he dropped an eager, open-mouthed kiss to my thigh laying across his shoulder. Then another on the opposite leg. It was a filthy, harsh action, his teeth grazing my flesh. And I loved it.

Unfamiliar sensations twisted deep in my center. They carried a vague resemblance to the heat I'd felt when Wesley made promises, when he spoke of how it would be between us. But the stirrings were amplified to such an extent as to be nearly unrecognizable.

My hand reached for his scarred shoulder, scrambling for purchase, to pull him up. His hand found mine, pulled it from his shoulder, and laced our fingers together as he placed another kiss, higher up my thigh. A foreign ache formed where we would join. A need.

"Lee," escaped in a whine.

Why was he dragging this out?

He shushed me and my eyes rolled thoughtlessly. He chuckled and whispered, "I have you... You're safe with me." Then, without another word of warning, his mouth fell *there*.

My heart stopped. My stomach dropped. In the time it took to comprehend his actions, sensation had taken over. And *oh*.

This was... it was...

Magnificent.

For a moment, perhaps two, the sensation was awkward and strange. And then he did *something* with his tongue and I couldn't breathe. The air left the room. I was lightheaded and swirly, and I never wanted him to stop.

Fortunately, he seemed to have no intention of ceasing. Once he started whatever he was doing with his tongue, he kept at it with the same single-minded determination with which he searched the skies every night.

And then Lee—wonderful, beautiful Lee—slipped a finger inside my channel, slow and tentative. When he met with no resistance, he started moving it in a rhythm that matched his tongue's, working me over and higher.

At some point my hand had found his hair and I realized, dimly, that I was tugging rather hard and ought to stop. But my fingers wouldn't obey my commands. Then he made a circling motion with his tongue as he curled his finger and hit *something*, and I no longer cared.

My desperate, whimpered pants echoed through the room, harmonizing so beautifully with his groans that to hush them would have been a travesty I could not abide.

He added a second finger and I realized his efforts were building to... something. Like one of his meteors, I found myself in his atmosphere and I was bursting into smoldering flames. We were on a collision course and the resultant explosion would shatter my world.

His tongue made another circuit before changing direction while he twisted his fingers and that was it—my vision went white and I ceased to exist.

∽

When the world reformed, Lee was propped on his side trailing a finger around one of my breasts with fascination in his gaze.

He wore nothing but a well-deserved, smug expression and his breeches.

"Good morning," he said with a teasing grin. I was forced to check the window to be sure he was teasing. It was still night.

I rolled my eyes.

His answer was a half snort. The laughter was entirely contagious, and my giggles joined his.

My head lolled to the side to face him. That he hadn't put his shirt back on was a surprise. He had been so uneasy displaying his scars before.

I pressed a kiss to the worst of them, the one above his heart. With a groan, he rolled onto his back, and I followed, propping my chin on his unburned shoulder.

I trailed a hand along the seam where scar and unmarred flesh met. His hand caught mine, and for the briefest moment I thought I had misstepped. But he raised it to his lips for a kiss before setting it on his chest, pressing it there.

"Does it hurt?" I asked.

"Not so much any longer. But it's not quite the same as the rest of me. Itches sometimes, and it can feel tight when I move certain ways."

The discomfort hadn't kept him from whatever labor was responsible for the firm, defined muscles underneath.

He pressed a kiss on top of my head and wrapped his arm tighter around me. "Can I ask a question?"

I hummed my agreement.

"Did that hurt?"

My head popped up with alarm. "No!"

"Good." He lifted our joined hands from his chest and considered them with a thoughtful expression as his fingers traced mine.

"I-I didn't know you could do... that," I added.

His eyes crinkled with a smile that was grander than his quirked lips implied. "I've been wanting to do that for weeks."

"Really?"

"Oh yes." Something about the tone he used, low and sensual, had my center clenching on nothing. "Did you... Was it something you'd like to do again?"

He chuckled at my enthusiastic nod and set my hand back on his chest, then reached up to adjust the pillow behind him.

The movement emphasized the taught muscles in his arm and chest in a way that had my cheeks heating.

I dragged a thumb along his chest. "Earlier, when you took off your shirt..."

"Yes?"

"You... went away for a moment."

His throat bobbed. The only answer he was capable of giving.

"Is it just that you didn't want me to see? Or was it something more?"

His entire chest rose and fell with his sigh, and me along with it. "Both. Mia died years ago. I tried to find... companionship once. It didn't end well."

I wasn't entirely certain what that meant, but I had suspicions—none of them pleasant.

He continued, "And it was you. You're... important to me. I want..." He was silent for a moment, and I understood what remained unsaid. I had wanted him to find me attractive, and he wanted the same.

"I know I explained what happened with Mia. But knowing and seeing the evidence of my failings with your own eyes are different."

There it was again, "failings." "You didn't fail her, Lee."

He said nothing but flopped his head back on the pillow to stare at the ceiling.

Entirely unconvinced.

It wasn't the sort of belief I could undo in moments, and I was reluctant to shatter the soft contentment surrounding us like candlelight.

"You didn't seem to mind me touching them."

Stormy eyes found mine again. "No, I didn't mind. It was —no one has ever—it felt... nice."

"Perfectly polished mirror nice? Or found-a-new-planet nice?"

"Found-a-new-planet nice." He grinned.

What a lovely feeling. My chest warmed with pride. I trailed fingers along the shelves of muscles lining his lower abdomen. They were stacked neatly atop each other with a trail of dark blond hair leading to an intriguing hardness under his breeches.

I'd never found a man's... manhood of much interest. Until I was married in any event.

I knew it was there, a part of them the same way arms and legs were a part of them. And that was that. But then I wed Ralph. And a great deal of my life was consumed with whether or not his manhood was satisfied. That was an exhausting, thankless, onerous task. When he occasionally redistributed the job to a lady of easy virtue, I was grateful for the reprieve.

Wesley had boasted a great deal about his manhood. He said it was the largest and thickest of any gentleman in the *ton* and I would experience such ecstasy when I beheld it that I would weep when he buttoned his falls again.

My eyes rolled of their own volition at the thought. My husband chuckled.

I rather suspected Wesley was very, very wrong in his assessment. Because Lee was certainly more impressive, if the tenting beneath the buckskin was any indication. Although, to be quite honest, Ralph may have been more impressive. It had been difficult to see Wesley during our single tryst in a darkened corridor.

"What on earth are you thinking of?"

My gaze shot to Lee's and my cheeks burned.

Bright laughter spilled into the room. "Oh, now I must know."

I shook my head, burying it into his chest. A warm hand came up to cup the back of my head.

"Tell me."

"I don't think I will." My prim reply was muffled into the coarse hair and silken planes of his chest.

"Fine, keep your secrets." The hand on my head slid into my hair and threaded through it from root to end before beginning again.

The hardness in his breeches made its presence felt against my thigh when I shifted, breathing in his scent. The peppermint was still there, but something masculine was underneath it.

I was dawdling. I knew that. But Lee made no move to rush me. He didn't take my hand and place it on his member, didn't reach to unbutton his falls, made no snappish comments. And the horrid part of me was wondering... just how long would he allow me to feign ignorance of his situation?

"Charlotte?" And there it was. At least he would ask rather than telling, or worse, just shoving me into whatever position he desired.

"Hmm?"

"I do not wish to return to my own bed. Would you mind terribly if I stayed here again tonight?"

∼

Lee

My heart clenched pitifully on the silence that followed my question. It was too much, too far, too fast. Allowing me to be with her had required a great deal of trust. And I could not content myself with that. I was greedy, asking for more than she was willing to offer.

Her "Stay" breathed against my skin was nearly inaudible. Relief flooded my chest in a great rush of blood and air. My arm tightened around her bare form involuntarily.

Permission granted, I ought to move, to draw back the

covers and settle her beneath them. Surely she was cold. And a chill would be bad for both her and the baby. But a languid warmth had settled into my bones and my limbs weren't obeying commands. At least none of the commands that involved relinquishing my hold on Charlotte.

Charlotte, who hadn't relaxed back into my arms after my question. She hadn't moved, not really, but she held herself stiff and uneasy. Perhaps her back again?

Disentangling my fingers from her curls was a disappointment and a challenge. I'd made quite the mess. Once freed from the tousled, silken chaos, I dragged my hand down to her lower back—the place that had ached the previous night—and rubbed gently there.

Her hand resumed its distracting pattern along my chest, weaving in and out of the scarred areas at random. She didn't shy away. Not that she ever had. But my chest was the absolute worst of it and she endured the sight with grace.

My cock was steadfastly refusing to forget that I had my beautiful, *naked* wife in my arms, and was making his presence far too known. Fortunately, Charlotte seemed content in her aimless tracing for the moment.

The angle was wrong, but I pressed a thumb into the line of her spine, swirling it in the space between vertebrae. She relaxed the littlest bit with each circle.

Suddenly, she tensed again.

"What's wr—" My question broke off in a pathetic, hysterical choke.

Without warning, the hand that had been chiefly occupied tracing my chest dipped its way down my abdomen and slipped into my breeches to wrap around my shaft.

My wife's hand moved in a practiced rhythm, one designed for efficiency. It was incredible. Warm, soft hands twisted with the intention to bring about a swift climax—of course it was wonderful. And that was not even considering that I hadn't felt a touch other than my own in years.

But... it was exactly that. Practiced, requisite, perfunctory. Instinctively, I caught her wrist in my hand, biting back the groan when I pulled her hand away, and cursing every instinct that told me this wasn't desire but duty.

"Lee?"

I pressed a kiss to the hand I'd captured. "That is not what this was about."

"But... you're..."

"I do not know if you've noticed, but you're naked, darling. It's just... how my body reacts when my beautiful wife lies naked in my arms. What we did, it wasn't so you would reciprocate. I just wanted to make you feel pleasure. I thought that might be a good way to go about it, minimal penetration, limited opportunities for pain."

"And you do not want..."

"I do—I do not wish for you to think otherwise or to retake the silly notion that I do not desire you. But I only want it when you desire it too. Because you wish to, not because you feel that you are supposed to. Not because you believe you owe me, but because you want nothing more."

She hesitated, considering her next sentence in starts and stops. When it finally escaped her, I understood. "What if I never wish to?"

I sighed, swallowing the strange combination of longing and pride. That question—it would not have been easy for my Charlotte to ask. That she felt comfortable—safe enough—to ask it... An odd sort of warmth filled my chest at the evidence of her bravery. It was enough to overwhelm any other emotion.

"Then you never want to. I never expected you to let me touch you, let alone the reverse. I'm far from disappointed."

Finally, her head propped up on my chest once again, her

lip caught between her teeth. "Thank you." So much sentiment was wrapped in those two words. I never could have named her feelings.

"Do not thank me, not for that. Now, I need you to move over just a bit so I can wrap us in the coverings before you freeze to death."

"I am hardly going to freeze to death."

"Well, your feet tell a different story." I squeezed her frosty toes between my stockinged calves.

Her eye roll was all the sweeter when I earned it.

Chapter Thirty
BENNET HALL, SURREY - SEPTEMBER 4, 1816

CHARLOTTE

I MISSED MY HUSBAND. It was so strange a notion that it had taken several days to worm its way into my understanding. Not once in the entirety of our marriage had I missed Ralph. In fact, I wasn't certain I'd ever wished him by my side.

But Lee—just as we'd grown closer the harvest began nearly a month ago and occupied all of his time. And the babe occupied nearly all of my energy. I woke exhausted, went about my day exhausted, and fell into bed exhausted.

I sighed as Imogen ran a brush through my curls. It seemed a waste to dress with such care for a man who wouldn't even see my efforts.

"Something amiss, my lady?"

"No, everything is fine."

"Because if you were missing that husband of yours, I wouldn't blame you."

I met her eyes in the mirror. "You've been spending too much time with Brigsby. You're becoming impertinent."

"I've always been a little impertinent. It does not make me wrong."

I handed her a peachy silk ribbon that matched the flowers lining the hem of my dress. "I suppose it's *possible* I miss Lord Champaign. Only because I am without the diversions of London, of course."

"Of course," she nodded solemnly, entirely unconvinced if her tone was any indication.

"It is a good thing you're off to see your sister soon. You've grown entirely too comfortable here."

"Not as comfortable as you have," she teased with a look toward my bed chamber where the coverings remained rumpled on both sides.

Before I could retort, an expectant hand appeared before me, awaiting a pin. She tucked a curl easily.

"It seems a waste. Such a lovely gown, and my hair is behaving so well today—and my husband isn't available to appreciate either."

She hummed, hand held out for another pin. "If I were to make another impertinent suggestion, would I be risking my employment?"

"It depends on precisely how impertinent," I said, knowing there was absolutely no amount of insolence I would not tolerate from Imogen. I was already dreading her absence when she left to see her sister through her confinement.

"Well, as you said, your dress and hair are quite fetching. It is a particularly fine day. And, I have it on good authority that your husband is working on the Geller field just one plot over today."

"What are you suggesting?"

"I'm suggesting that you take the picnic I helped Mrs. Fitzroy pack this morning and see if your husband wishes to have luncheon with you."

"You did?"

"I did. Jack helped as well and was adamant that he receive credit for his efforts."

"That does sound lovely, but I wouldn't wish to interrupt."

"He's been scything and picking for days. I rather think he would welcome an interruption from his beautiful wife."

"Imogen..."

"What is the worst that could happen?" she asked, leaning down so we were level in the glass, her hands pressing on my shoulders comfortingly.

"He could send me away."

She shot me a look that told me precisely how absurd she found that notion.

"He could!" I insisted.

"I suppose you're right. But he would never be cruel about it—and you know that."

I took a steadying breath. "It is already packed?"

"Yes, a picnic for two."

"Fine."

"Good," she retorted, rising and pinning the final curl with a jab to punctuate it.

~

I COULDN'T EXPLAIN PRECISELY what had apprehension seeping into my bones. Imogen was right. Above all, Lee was kind.

Kind and tall. His was the first head I spotted over the massive stacks of wheat. Head. Shoulders. Back. Bottom. Thighs. Calves. *Holy...*

Unlike the men he was chatting with as he worked beside them, Lee had kept his shirt on—that wasn't a surprise. But it was entirely irrelevant. He'd still stripped his coat and waistcoat, and the linen of his shirt was nearly transparent with sweat, his hair damp and curling around his neck.

My husband was a handsome man. He was also incredibly muscular, powerful, in a way that was easy to forget when presented only with his kind heart.

A dampness grew between my thighs that had nothing to do with the heat.

Lee laughed at something one of the men said. Brigsby noted me first, the sun turning his chest a shade that matched his hair. He nudged Lee's shoulder.

"You just had a break Brigs," Lee muttered, still swishing the long pole side to side.

One of the lads I wasn't acquainted with noticed me before Brisgby could reply, his scything ceasing. "Lord Champaign..." he interjected tentatively, his gaze flicking to the curve of my belly.

At once, my trepidation, temporarily eased by lust, came roaring back.

"What, Geller?" Lee asked, never pausing.

The third and fourth man ceased their efforts and turned to stare at me as well. All of a sudden instead of fresh-cut wheat, I could scent stale ale and piss. *That* was the source of my worry—the last time I'd approached a group of men unasked and unannounced.

"Lady Champaign," Brigsby directed to me with a bow.

"What about her?"

I could endure the stares no longer. "My lord?"

Lee froze before spinning on his heels, nearly taking off the Geller lad's ankle with the scythe had the boy not jumped out of the way. Lee tossed the thing to his near victim and reached for me instantly.

"Charlotte? Are you well? What is it?"

One damp hand found my waist, the other my cheek, his gaze

frantically searching my person. "I didn't mean to worry you. I just... I was wondering if you might be in need of a break soon? I brought some food." I lifted the basket pathetically by way of clarification. My stomach was tied in such tight knots, I was nearly too distracted to appreciate the open neckline of his shirt.

"You brought me luncheon?"

I nodded, my gaze finding the ground so I need not see the inevitable rejection.

Instead of a polite dismissal, warm lips found the crown of my head in a gentle kiss. My eyes shot to his.

"Take a break," he called to the men behind him without turning their way.

"Yes, my lord," they answered, Brisgby with his usual impish note accompanying the title.

"Lee? I—"

The men filed past us, Lee didn't spare them a glance.

"Is there a blanket?" he asked, reaching for the basket. "Oh, damn—"

"What?" Warriness crashed over me with the curse.

"I'm so sorry, Charlotte. I ruined your pretty frock." He dipped his head toward my waist where a perfect, oversize dirt handprint remained.

"It is no matter—"

"But you look so lovely. I'll see about having another one made."

"I'm certain Imogen can work some magic with it. And besides, you paid for it. In truth it is yours."

"Charlotte..." An unfamiliar note slipped into his voice. My eyes flicked to his. "*This* is not how I wish to ruin your dresses."

"Pardon? I don't—*Oh*..."

He chuckled, hands cupping my cheeks and pulling my lips to his. My belly and the basket ended up trapped between us as he offered me an entirely inappropriate kiss that I accepted gladly.

Once he pulled away, he finally tugged the basket from my hands and withdrew the blanket tucked on top. Eagerly, he spread it out right across the break in the row before urging me beside him.

I set about arranging the various fruits, cheeses, and cold meats between us when another chuckle broke from him.

"Come here."

I scooted closer, and he pulled a handkerchief from his pocket and wiped at my cheeks. "Perfect," he added once satisfied before working on his own hands.

He laughed when he presented me with the results of his efforts. "I'm afraid to say this might be as presentable as I come without a bath."

Absolutely every bit of tension I'd felt before I arrived melted away at the bright sound of his laughter. This was nothing like the boxing match. And there was nothing at all of Wesley in my Lee.

"It is no problem," I explained, coy coquettishness in my tone.

I grabbed a slice of apple off a plate and offered it to my husband. With a raised brow, he leaned forward slowly, giving me time to pull away, then took a bite of the slice in my hand.

Cheekily, I popped the rest of it in my mouth.

"Thief," he cried.

The grapes were next. I held one out. When he leaned to take it, I shook my head. "Open."

His grin was infectious as he obliged. Gently, I tossed it toward his open mouth and hit him in the eye.

Far from annoyed, my husband laughed, delight spreading across his face before being replaced by mischief.

"If you cannot manage it, I shall have to take over," he warned. I plucked another grape off the plate and held it out expectantly. Rather than opening again, Lee's hand wrapped around my forearm, holding me steady as he wrapped his lips around it. It and my fingers.

Dampness grew between my thighs when his tongue teased the pads of my fingers before pulling back impossibly slowly. "Lee..."

He pulled his hand away, his gaze lingering on the handprint left behind. When his eyes met mine, the earlier mirth was gone, replaced with a lust to match mine.

I caught him around the back of the neck and pulled his lips to mine. He obliged easily, clamoring over to my side before throwing a leg over my thighs. Lee met my ardor with his own and eased me down, down, down to the blanket beneath us. Laughter and kisses swirled in the balmy air.

~

IMOGEN TOOK one look at me and nearly fell over laughing before arranging a bath. I settled before the mirror as maids and footmen worked around me. One look was all I needed to confirm that it was even worse than I'd thought.

Clear fingerprints and even entire dirty handprints traced the edge of the bodice and curve of my belly beneath my husband's coat. Smudged stains lined the folds of my skirt where Lee had tugged it up with eager joy. Seeds, stems, and Lord knew what else littered my hair, which tumbled out of my coiffure.

Strangest of all was the smile on my face beneath the dirt. I was happy—truly, wonderfully—happy in a way I couldn't recall ever being. It was nothing like the practiced, elegant smiles I'd offered the *ton*. Lines creased the corners of my eyes. My cheeks ached from smiles. Hell, my chest actually hurt from laughter—I hadn't known that was possible.

After a refreshing bath, I wandered downstairs for a lonely

supper, a less unpleasant prospect for having enjoyed my husband's company earlier.

I floated along to the barren table that had been a source of my despondency until that very afternoon. Settling into my usual spot, I sent only a brief longing glance toward Lee's empty place.

No sooner had I dipped a spoon into the squash soup than Crawford arrived carrying a silver tray.

"A letter for you, my lady."

"Thank you," I replied distractedly, then set down my spoon and took it from him.

Dread crashed over me, a rockslide crushing me beneath grit and boulders when I touched it. I didn't know how. I didn't know why. But I knew it was from Wesley.

There was no sender. I'd seen his handwriting once, maybe twice. But in my soul, I knew that masculine slant was his.

At some point, Crawford wandered off, leaving me to my correspondence.

My heart pounded so rapidly it threatened to rip right out of my chest.

With trembling hands, I abandoned my plate. I shoved away from the table and strode through the house, filled with purpose—and nearly crashed into Imogen.

"My lady?" she cried.

"Not feeling well," I called back, not turning as I rounded to ascend the stairs. They were a bit more effort in my current state, but at last I was flicking the lock on my bedroom door.

Carefully, I uncrumpled the parchment and stared at it through blurry eyes.

The mere sight of it made my comment to Imogen no lie, I did feel sick.

I collapsed on the settee and stared at the letter for an impossibly long moment, trying to will myself to open it, to slip a finger beneath the wafer.

A knock sounded, echoing through the room.

"My lady?" Imogen asked, tentative.

Without conscious decision, I shot up and cast the letter into the fire. The sight of parchment curling and blackening before flaking upward transfixed me.

"My lady?" she repeated.

I broke away from the fire and turned to the door to let her in.

"Oh, you do not look well. Would you like to turn in early?"

At my nod, she set about finding a night dress. My gaze turned back to the fire. No remnant of my letter survived the flames.

After Imogen helped me undress, I laid on the bed, curled on my side as night fell through the window. The moon had long cast its glow when I felt Lee's familiar form curve around me. Silently, his hand found my belly and was greeted with a kick from the babe.

"Stop that," he breathed toward my belly while I feigned sleep.

He dropped a kiss on my temple. "Thank you for today. It was perfect," he whispered before his breathing evened out around me.

It had been—it was. I wouldn't, couldn't allow Wesley to take this from me. There was nothing, absolutely nothing in that letter that I cared to read.

Still, sleep refused to come, even as I lay wrapped safe and warm in my husband's arms. Not until I felt him rise to ready for another day of harvest. And even when it came, it was fitful and full of wretched dreams.

Chapter Thirty-One

BENNET HALL, SURREY - OCTOBER 2, 1816

CHARLOTTE

THE WRITING DESK tilted precariously on my belly. Juliet had been kind enough to send me a few recommendations of accoucheurs and wet nurses she was considering. Now, I was left with the onerous task of writing to convince them to travel here for the birth.

I had met the village midwife, but she was a stern, no-nonsense woman, and I wasn't certain we would suit. And besides, women of my station hired an accoucheur. It was the done thing.

Cassiopeia had settled herself next to me and fell asleep with a paw resting on the bump of my belly. She had taken to doing that on occasion and only bit or scratched me one out of every two or three interactions. I had no choice but to consider it progress.

Lee had finished the harvest but had taken to assisting the tenants with preparations for winter. While I could appreciate my husband's work ethic, I missed the midsummer nights basking under the stars.

Imogen knocked on the open door frame with a sheepish expression. The noise woke the sleeping beast who pressed herself up with an angry chirp and stretched languidly. Another *mrroww* followed as she bounced to the floor and flounced out to cause mischief elsewhere.

"Go chirp at your human," I called after her.

Imogen hovered in the doorway, watching as the cat strolled past.

"Come in."

Wordlessly, she took a seat on the nearby chair. The lines of her forehead were tight.

"What is it?" I asked, unwilling to wade through a sea of small talk before we reached the point.

She sighed, wringing her hands. "There are rumors."

"What kind of rumors?" It was an unnecessary question. I knew precisely which kind. The inevitable kind.

"That you're too far along for the babe to be Lord Champaign's."

I felt resignation settle into my bones. I deserved the censure, the comments, the shame. But my heart hurt for Lee —Lee who had done nothing but come to my aid. And he would be humiliated in his home.

"Brigsby is valiantly trying to quiet them," Imogen added. "But I believe several of the tenants have relations in town. The harvest had them chatting."

My stomach sank in a way that had nothing to do with the babe. "So the whole of London, then?"

"It seems that way."

"I do not suppose we can convince them that Lord Champaign and I anticipated our vows?"

"I believe that is the angle Brigsby has taken. But... Lord Champaign is known to go to town so rarely. There was little opportunity."

Cursing my reclusive husband, I flicked my quill away with no heed for the parchment beneath.

"Well, it is not as though we didn't foresee this probability. They may gossip all they like. The child is my husband's in the eyes of the law."

"There's another problem."

"What is that?"

"Rumor has it that Mr. Parker has gotten himself into a spot of trouble. And has made himself scarce."

"I'd heard something to that effect. Surely that is a good thing."

She quirked her head questioningly. When I didn't respond, she forged ahead. "The rumors also say he is the father of your child. And that you are sheltering him."

I choked on air and hacked pitifully. "I beg your pardon?" spilled out between coughs.

"They're saying Mr. Parker is the father of your child. That he murdered Lord Rycliffe years ago. And that you are in love with him and harboring him."

My stomach jolted in a way it hadn't in weeks, rolling disgruntledly.

"He told all and sundry that he was not the father. Told anyone who would listen that I had enjoyed the company of every man in town. Why is he now receiving credit for his efforts?"

"I don't rightly know."

"What am I to do about it?" I whined, pathetic even to my ears.

"I do not know that either. But I thought you ought to hear it."

"Where do they say I'm keeping him?"

"Some secret love nest the two of you shared." That deserved an eye roll. The only love nest we'd shared was an empty hall outside the music room during the Countess of

Canton's ball. Hardly a place one could hide unnoticed indefinitely.

"Thank you for informing me, I suppose."

"Of course." She stood and turned for the door but hesitated before taking another step. She glanced back at me. "My lady?" Her tone was tentative, considering.

"Yes?"

"I know you wanted him. That you loved him. But I'm glad you found Lord Champaign instead. He's a better man."

I ought to scold her for her impertinence. But it was such an accurate assessment of my own feelings that I couldn't bring myself to.

"He is."

Chapter Thirty-Two

BENNET HALL, SURREY - OCTOBER 23, 1816

LEE

"MY SOLICITOR IS COMING TODAY. I expect he'll arrive sometime this afternoon."

Charlotte looked up between tentative bites of toast and nodded before returning silently to her breakfast. She had been unusually stoic the last several days, at least during the incredibly brief moments we had spent together.

Will had written a few weeks ago, asking to meet to go over some paperwork or other. The harvest had put me so far behind in correspondence that it was shameful. Fortunately, he was still free. His letter offered some additional intelligence of interest as well.

"I believe he is bringing his new wife."

"Shall I have the blue room readied?"

"That would be nice. Thank you."

Something was wrong with my wife. Not a single eye roll. This agreeable, formal woman before me was not her.

"I believe you know her. Lady Celine Rycliffe?"

That earned me a mere blink before she returned to her

food. The news had knocked me back into my chair when I read it. But Charlotte... nothing.

Entirely without ideas, I continued breaking my fast in silence before retreating to hide in my study. It was a good use of my time. I had plenty of letters to catch up on this time of year.

When Brigsby alerted me to Will's arrival, trepidation swirled in my stomach. It was the first time that Celine—now Mrs. Hart—would see my scars and, though the idea bothered me less than it would have a few months ago, I did loathe the thought. She had once considered me as a marital prospect, after all.

When I arrived in the drawing room, I found Will and his wife, but no hint of Charlotte. Brigs whispered, "Headache," at my confused expression. I caught my own eye roll after the fact. Charlotte's habits were catching.

Will was no stranger to the mottled lines of my face. Astonishingly, he had a new scar of his own across his right brow. Smaller and cleaner than mine, of course, but curious all the same.

Celine's eyes widened at the sight of me, but she was too poised for anything more demonstrative.

Perfunctory greetings delivered, I was left to satisfy my curiosity. "So... I assume you were caught on a veranda again?" I directed my question toward Celine.

"It was a balcony. And we were not caught." She replied primly, leaning back with a self-satisfied grin when the laugh burst from me.

Will's groan nearly overshadowed the laughter, and he removed his spectacles, dragging an exhausted hand over his face. Never would I have paired practical Will with socialite Celine. But they moved together in a way that spoke of real intimacy.

"He's my client, love," he grumbled at her, flushing.

"I'm happy for you, both of you," I added. And I genuinely was. No one deserved a good man more than Celine, and I would have difficulty naming a better man than William Hart.

"I understand I am to wish you joy as well?" she asked.

"Yes, my wife is feeling unwell at the moment."

"Oh, I do hope she recovers soon." I recognized that tone out of Celine, slightly higher pitched with the accent just a touch thicker than was natural. She was putting on airs.

"I'm certain she'll be devastated to have missed you." I added a hint of warning in my tone. Nothing Will would have caught. But Celine understood my meaning instantly and caught my gaze with a nearly imperceptible nod.

"Well, I shall let you two gentlemen get to your work. I will take a few moments to refresh myself."

I handed her over to Eliza and took Will to the study with me.

He was familiar with the room and made himself at home in the chair opposite mine across the desk.

"I cannot believe you let Kit handle the marriage settlements instead of me. I thought we were friends."

"You were busy. Apparently finding a wife of your own."

"Yes," he breathed with a pleased sigh.

"It agrees with you."

"It really does. You as well."

It did. Waking curled around her soft warm body with frozen toes trapped between my legs was its own kind of peace.

"What happened to your eye?" I asked.

"That is a long story. The short version is that my wife saved me."

"She would."

"Of course, the longer version is that she is the reason I required saving in the first place."

"That... also fits."

His answer was a pleased chuckle. He then dug a sheet of parchment from his attaché, his usual method for moving the discourse along. "Now, about my visit. We had a small fire at the offices. Some of the paperwork has seen better days, unfortunately. If you don't mind, I'd like to sort through your ledgers—make certain everything matches."

"A fire? Is everyone well?"

"Yes, yes. Paperwork suffered more than anyone else."

Relief seeped into my bones. "I am glad of it."

He nodded and dug into my ledgers with his usual attention to detail.

I sought out a pot of tea and biscuits to accompany our efforts before falling back into the seat behind my desk. We'd been working in relative silence for more than an hour when I broke.

"Will?"

"Yes?" he asked, head popping up, eyes wide behind his spectacles.

"I've—I heard some rumors. I..." Now that the time had come to speak the words, I didn't want to give voice to them. But it was a necessary evil. "What have you heard about my wife?"

"I am certain she's quite lovely—"

"The truth, Will."

His sigh filled the room. "Cee may have used the word *shrew*. And Kit's sister had an impressive list of complaints to lay at her feet as well."

"I meant more recently."

He could not hide his wince. "Oh, that rumor."

"Yes, that rumor."

"No idea what you mean," he replied with a cheeky grin that became a chuckle when I rolled my eyes.

"Is there anything to be done about it? The babe is mine,

of course. But I hate to think of Charlotte subjected to such talk."

He sighed and pulled off his spectacles, then folded them on top of his ledger. "Probably not. Not without making everything worse in the process."

"That is what I worried about."

"Cee, though, she might be able to help. She's a bit less popular since she married yours truly, but she still has the ear of everyone who matters."

"How could she help?"

"I suppose I should ask... The concern is that the rumor says you are not the father of the child, yes? More so than the number of days between your wedding and the presumptive date of birth?"

"Yes," I replied tersely.

"Well, suppose she saw the two of you having a tryst somewhere." He snapped his fingers performatively. "In fact, I recall she said as much. She caught you two in a lover's embrace six months ago at the... Cavendish party."

There was one gaping flaw with his plan. "How do you suppose I attended a party and no one noticed me? You may have missed it, but I am, in fact, quite tall and scarred like the devil."

"Right. The theatre?"

I gestured toward my face again with an irritated hand.

"It is quite dark!" That earned him another look. "Well, I'd leave it up to Cee."

"I'll consider it. You are certain she would help a 'shrew'?"

"She's a forgiving sort," he said with a shrug.

CHARLOTTE

I was hiding. Like a coward. I had been for days.

Lee ought to be informed of the rumors swirling. And, ideally, the person to inform him would be me. But the reality of that prospect left my chest on fire. Though that may have been the babe.

Every time I closed my eyes, the warmth in Lee's gaze and the indulgent curl of his lips was branded there. I couldn't bear to see that expression turn to disdain. Which it absolutely would when he was reminded of why he never should have wed me in the first place.

Oh, he would be nice about it. Lee was kind about everything. But just a hint of contempt would creep into the corner of his lips. It was inevitable. It happened with Ralph, and it happened with Wesley—though more suddenly.

And it would happen with Lee—it would begin with informing him of the rumors.

So I hid like a coward, and now time had run out. Because Lady Rycliffe was here. A newly married—and to a solicitor—Lady Rycliffe. Well, Mrs. Hart. Ordinarily that would have interested me. But the gossip would not have missed her. And she would report it.

I could still remember the first time I saw her, Lady Celine Hasket, Marchioness of Rycliffe, draped in mauve silk that clung in the most flattering ways. It was my debut. There, she flirted with the handsomest man in the room—a notorious rake, if memory served. But she smiled, laughed, teased in a delicate French accent, and then sauntered off leaving him gaping after her as if he could not believe he had breathed the same air. And I wanted to *be* her.

Celine did all the things my mother warned me never to do—flirt, wear low-cut gowns, and speak with passion on inappropriate subjects. She even wore the solemnity of widowhood well and still managed to ensure every single person she met adored her for her easy manners and bright smile.

I could not fathom a single secret in the *ton* she was not privy to. One flutter of her lashes and any man would tell her anything she wanted.

And she loathed me.

It was not an unfair assessment, truly. Celine was popular, in part, because she was kind. I hadn't recognized that at first. When my engagement fell through with Rosehill—Celine's brother-in-law—the rumors began to swirl. And every single one of them had *him* finding *me* wanting. Where one gentleman went, the rest followed. At once, I was left with the dregs of society. I was left with Ralph.

For weeks after my wedding, I watched from the wall—Ralph too preoccupied at Wayland's to attend—as she danced and smiled and laughed and the men flocked to her, entranced by her beauty.

And that was where Wesley had found me, in my darkened corner, sad and unwanted. I could not even recollect the precise comment now. Something about her pug nose. And his answering laugh felt good. It soothed the bruises left by my fall from grace. My second observation regarding her sun-leathered skin earned a chuckle from him, and that felt even better. Genuine giddy delight had welled within me. When he called another gentleman over for me to repeat it, I added a note about the nasal quality of her voice—something I had long admired for its sensual tone—which earned me a snicker, and the attention of yet another gentleman.

So it continued. I earned what I thought was the respect of the gentlemen in Wesley's circle. I knew now how wrong I was. It wasn't anything like respect. It merely amused them to watch us snipe among each other. Or to watch me take pathetic swipes against a woman who neither felt the impact nor cared for my efforts. She was too far above me for my arms to reach.

But she knew, and she knew about the other hits that had landed—the targets that had been within my grasp. Miss Kate Summers, whose only mistake was accepting a dance from the man who had rejected me. Lady Juliet, who had later managed to engage herself to him. Dozens of others who incurred my ire.

And she would tell Lee. Sweet Lee, who had no idea who the woman he married truly was. When she finished telling him of my past, she would divulge the current rumors. Oh, it would be for his own good. She would never think he had married me knowing the full truth—who would?

He would know then. He would know and revile me. And I would deserve it.

Chapter Thirty-Three
BENNET HALL, SURREY - OCTOBER 23, 1816

CHARLOTTE

By supper, my desire for food outweighed my better judgment. I dressed with more care than usual, directing Imogen to tug my stays tighter than they had been in weeks—a vain, ineffectual effort.

I stepped into the hall and began puttering down the long rug toward the landing. Only to meet Lady Rycliffe right there.

I had thought her lovely before. And she was. But marriage, it seemed, agreed with her—even marriage to a solicitor. She was more radiant than the sun, beaming with her golden hair and skin. Her eyes were brighter, more emerald than the olive I remembered. And as usual, the mauve silk caressed her form like a lover. Years later and I *still* wanted to be her.

Instead of lovely, I was round, puffy, achy, and splotchy. She offered a delicate, dainty curtsy, while I struggled to manage an acceptable one on swollen ankles. Her greeting was polite, not that I expected anything less from her. My only reprieve was that she didn't comment on my new, more rotund form.

We made the usual remarks on the weather, her trip, my headache as we traversed the stairs together. When we approached the drawing room, I caught two masculine murmurs. Lee and the one belonging to the solicitor. I gestured for her to precede me, and after a deep breath for courage, I slipped in behind her.

Feeling very much like I had all those years ago, I slinked along the wall, holding myself there while I observed.

I would not have chosen a solicitor for myself, but I could see the appeal. He was shorter than Lee. His light brown hair was dusted with gray at the temples, lending him a distinguished appearance. But it was his cheekbones and eyes that set him apart. I'd never considered a man's cheeks before, but I did now. Honed like a knife's edge, they drew the gaze to his eyes. Those eyes were a shade of blue so bright I didn't have a name for it—cobalt, sky, royal were all lacking. A fresh scar cut through one brow, which left him seeming dangerous rather than studious. And he wore the utterly besotted expression that was so common among the men in Lady Rycliffe's orbit. It was naked adoration with just a hint of disbelief that she deigned to grace him with her presence.

A massive open palm with a singular peppermint slid into view. I took it, popped it in my mouth, and relished the answering bite. After turning, I found Lee close enough that I had to tip my head back a bit to meet his gaze. His eyes were lovely too, a crystal navy shade with concern clear in the tilt.

"Feeling better?"

"Yes, thank you."

"You look beautiful," he said, then dropped a kiss to my temple. "Cee, I believe you know Charlotte? Will, this is my wife. Charlotte, this is William Hart, my solicitor."

Cee? Cee? Any comfort I had drawn from the kiss and the peppermint left in a rush along with all the air in the room.

"I wasn't aware you knew each other." My voice was pathetically shrill and desperate.

"Oh, we've known each other for ages," Celine replied from her husband's arms with a languid smile. "You know, there was a time when I was almost Lady Champaign."

My answering hum of acknowledgment was thready and high, almost a whimper. I cleared my throat, desperately hoping for stability. "I was not aware of that. What happened?"

"Nothing worth mentioning," Lee said. Oh, that was worse than knowing. I had managed to concoct at least three scenarios in the seconds since I learned of the arrangement. Without intelligence, I would be left to create thousands. Hundreds of thousands.

"Oh, come now! It is certainly a tale worth telling. Besides, it paints you in a most gallant light," she teased, then turned to me. "Your husband had the misfortune of courting me in my misspent youth. Before I wed Lord Rycliffe, I was adored by the *ton*. And bored out of my mind. Your poor husband was the least objectionable option while I was trying to coerce Gabriel into giving up his rakish ways."

"What evidence do you have that I had serious designs on you?" Lee asked with a mischievous smile.

"You did offer for me."

"Well, I could not leave you to Rycliffe without at least providing you an alternative. I was fairly certain he would make a terrible husband."

Mr. Hart's burst of laughter startled the room. When all eyes found him, he clarified, "I've never agreed with a statement more." Lady Rycliffe—Mrs. Hart—Celine—if Lee could use her Christian name so could I—gave his shoulder a playful slap with her fingertips.

I loathed this feeling, where everyone referenced events I had not been present for. Now I was a child while the adults spoke of adult things around me. These people shared a pleasant history. I shared a moderately acrimonious one with only Celine.

Lee's hand settled on my lower back, which helped a little, soothing the ache. He took pity on me as well and whispered into my ear, "Will and Lord Rycliffe had a less than pleasant history before his passing." It seemed likely to be the only explanation I would receive so I took it gratefully.

Jack chose that moment to announce supper. The other newlyweds filed out, but Lee found my hand and kept me back.

He tucked a curl behind my ear. "How are you feeling?"

"I am well. I will not join you in the observatory though." He nodded and wrapped one arm around my shoulders to pull me into his embrace. For a moment, I simply breathed in his bright scent.

"Come now, you must be hungry." He broke away and guided me into the dining room. If our guests noted our absence, they said nothing.

Our meal began with less circular talk, and instead the usual polite discussions occupied us. What followed was a lively recitation of our guests' rather unconventional courtship. Celine was an incredible storyteller, jesting in the right places, offering significant, suspenseful glances in others. And her entirely besotted husband added details at precisely the right moment. It was a dance, one with steps only they knew.

"And how did you two meet?" she finally asked. There it was, the moment I had been dreading. Any hope I'd had that the subject had been covered while I was resting was well and truly shot.

Then Mr. Hart did the strangest thing. With a significant

glance at his wife, he interjected. "You know this one, Cee. You told me yourself. You invited Lady James to a tour of Vauxhall Gardens. A widow's gathering, if you will. There, you happened upon your dear friend Lord Champaign."

With an enthusiastic breath, she took up the torch. "Oh, that's right. How silly of me. I remember—I caught the two of you alone on one of the dark walks! Not that I could blame either of you. Clearly it was true love."

My husband nodded in agreement while I stared at the three of them in astonishment. Celine widened her eyes significantly.

"It's true. I could not stay away from her. Not when she was so lovely and vivacious," Lee added.

Realization crashed over me in a wave, tears flooding my eyes and pooling on the lower lashes.

She was going to help me.

"Yes, I was just telling Davina how in love you two were when you met all those months ago. And how it's absolutely no surprise to anyone who saw you that you will be blessed with a child so quickly. The passion..." she sighed the last word for dramatic effect.

I swallowed thickly before joining in. "Yes, it was love at first sight."

"Precisely. Which is what I shall be reporting to anyone who has a misunderstanding of the facts."

A single tear escaped, and I brushed it away furiously. The rumors might remain, but if Celine told my fictitious story with a fraction of the enthusiasm she gave her real story... The entire *ton* would know about our famous love match. There were still holes. But it might sow enough doubt...

"Thank you," I replied with more significance than I had ever given those two words.

"But of course. I do love the best gossip. I know just the people who would adore such a story."

We returned to less fraught topics. And eventually Lee took our guests to the observatory, and I, desperate to be out of shoes and stays, retired for the evening.

∽

Lee

The three of us trailed Cass down to the observatory as she chirped every few steps.

"You really rescued a cat?" Cee asked, incredulity clear in her tone. "I thought that to be mere rumor."

"Why would anyone lie about such a thing?"

"Well, I do not know. It was just more evidence of how you were too good to court me, and I would have ruined you if we'd wed." That was patently ridiculous in so many ways I couldn't possibly enumerate them.

I settled on, "I am not that good."

"You are. Far too good, really. But you are not foolish about it, and so I approve."

"Oh, because I knew you were a self-satisfied hellion when I courted you I meet with approval? Wonderful."

Will trapped his chuckle behind pressed lips as he slipped passed me and into the observatory. He was appropriately awestruck once he stepped inside, his gaze wide-eyed at the telescope. Celine, on the other hand, made herself comfortable on the edge of the desk, flipping through books with disinterest.

I gave Will a tour while Cee busied herself, and finally we reached her. She was elbow deep into some of Charlotte's paintings. "I had no idea your wife was so talented. I thought her only skills lay in gossip and petty squabbles."

"Love..." Will's warning tone cut through the setback I was preparing to deliver.

"Apologies. I forgot you have a soft spot for petty women

who make unfortunate romantic choices." She gestured to herself deprecatingly. "I assume this marital arrangement was another charitable endeavor?"

"Have care how you speak of my wife," I snapped.

"You've actually become fond of her? I apologize then. I believe you should be evaluated by a physician. But I am sorry."

The only sound I was capable of was the growl that escaped. Cee's response was a raised brow—not nearly as fetching as an eye roll.

"Parker is the father I presume? He was a favorite of hers." The venom she injected in the two syllables of the man's name was truly something impressive.

I said nothing, unwilling to speak at the moment.

"He killed Gabriel," she added, setting down the paintings with a grace that belied the severity of her words.

"I beg your pardon?"

"Well, he was responsible. Gabriel was involved in…"

"A great many illegal activities," I filled in.

"Yes," she snapped. "One of them was fixing races. Parker was one of the unlucky beneficiaries of his efforts. He called Gabriel out the morning he was killed. When Parker failed to arrive, Gabriel returned home, only to be stabbed on our front steps."

A slow blink was the only reaction I could manage. I knew he had been killed. But on their steps… Stabbed… Poor Celine. Even now her voice was thick when she relayed the story.

Will chimed in, relieving his wife of the burden of the rest of the story. "His brother has since confessed to the actual stabbing. But no one can locate Parker."

"And you think she…"

"If she doesn't know his whereabouts, she may have a good idea," Celine insisted.

"She doesn't. Cee... Charlotte has not had a visitor since she arrived."

"You're certain?" Will asked.

"Yes."

Cee sighed and picked up a sextant before returning it to the desk with a perfunctory pat. When she finally spoke, it was in a flat tone that brokered no argument. "It's my condition. I will spin whatever lie you wish. By the time I'm through, every single member of the *ton* will be convinced beyond a doubt that you two are more in love than anyone has ever been. That you've known each other since birth. That I caught the two of you fornicating in the rose bushes for all I care. But I want her cooperation."

"I won't have her put in danger."

Her gaze narrowed. "Then I'm afraid I saw your introduction at the masquerade. And she is scandalously far along for the length of your marriage. What is it, three? Four months?"

"Cee, please," Will begged.

"Charlotte has been a spiteful shrew for years. Do you even know all that she's done to poor Kate?"

"Kate is a viscountess and happily married. Whatever it was cannot be so bad," Will answered.

She ground her teeth, arms crossed over each other. I was certain it was the least elegant expression she had ever made. The wrinkling frown suited her poorly.

I had a card to play in negotiations. "You owe me. I could have ruined you with what I saw on that veranda."

"Gabriel wed me days later. I would hardly have been ruined."

Will's hand found the bridge of his nose, and he pinched away at a burgeoning headache, no doubt.

Cass, apparently determined to join the discussion, trotted over with a chirp and wrapped herself around Celine's legs.

With a performative sigh, Cee reached down to give the cat a scratch. Only to be met with teeth and claws.

She straightened in a flurry of French curses, inspecting her hand. Will crowded her.

Eventually, I was able to glean that there were only one or two superficial scratches. "Why did you save that beast?"

"What can I say?" I asked, leaning a hip against the desk and crossing my arms. "I have a soft spot for rescuing shrewish women in unfortunate situations. Are you going to help me?"

"Are you going to ask her to help me find Wesley Parker?"

I considered it. Charlotte and I did not speak of him. In truth, I had no real notion of her feelings on the man at present. Would it hurt her to ask? Surely she was unaware of his dealings.

"I will *ask*. But not while she's still with child. I won't place that burden on her. Nor for a few months after while she's healing."

"One month after the birth."

"Love, be reasonable," Will pleaded.

"Three. And only if she agrees," I replied.

"Two," she shot back.

"Three. Or you're on your own with Parker."

"She will be ruined," she argued.

"And Wesley Parker will still be out there, swanning around the streets of London, free."

"Fine," she grit out. "Three months. *And* she comes to town to assist."

"If she agrees. And nothing dangerous."

"Yes, yes. I'm certain she would rather face ruination than poke around her lover's haunts."

She stuck her hand out, waiting for me to shake it. Will merely eyed the entire process warily. Agreement completed, she straightened.

"I'll leave the two of you to your stars." Cee pressed a kiss to Will's cheek, then strode from the observatory to make her way toward the house.

He turned to me with a sheepish expression. "She tends to be a little... intense, regarding the subject of Gabriel's murder."

"You do not say."

Chapter Thirty-Four
BENNET HALL, SURREY - OCTOBER 24, 1816

CHARLOTTE

I LAID, still and staring, in Lee's arms that night. My mind refused to quiet until long after he came to bed.

When the clock finally struck a nearly acceptable hour, I rose, leaving my husband to his much-needed rest.

The only occupant of the breakfast room was Lady Celine. She swallowed a bite of toast with a letter in her hand.

"Oh, good morning," she trilled.

"Good morning. I trust you slept well?"

"Quite. Are you recovered?"

"Yes, quite," I lied.

"Oh, good," she replied. Celine studied me with more interest than my breakfast selection warranted, and it left me feeling disquieted.

"I was wondering..." she started, trailing off.

"Yes?" I asked as I sat down with a slice of pound cake.

"If I remember correctly, you are fond of Mr. Wesley Parker?" Her voice ticked up at the end, marking it as a question. But I had no doubt it was a statement.

"We've parted ways," I replied flatly.

"Yes. Of course. It's just... we suspect he may have been involved in my late husband's murder."

I was much too tired to feign shock at this intelligence. "As I said, I no longer have contact with Mr. Parker."

"Certainly." Celine was not content though. "But you, perhaps, know how to locate him. Where he might go."

The fictitious headache from yesterday threatened to become factual today. "I'm certain I have no idea."

"Surely you could draw him out with a bit of effort," she insisted.

A dull throb began to form behind my eye.

"Truly, I have no idea where he might have gone or how to draw him out." I replied through a thready throat. It had taken weeks for me to find him when he was only hiding from me—did she suppose me a magician?

I heard him before I saw him—my husband. He was graceful for a man of his size, but he was still large and the floor sometimes protested his presence.

"Celine," he snapped from behind me.

She straightened and turned back to her letter with feigned interest.

My interest, however, was peaked. I wasn't entirely certain my husband had ever taken that tone, not that I could recall anyway. He settled in the seat beside me, but his gaze was still directed at our guest, sharp below a furrowed brow.

He stared her down for another moment before turning to me. Bright navy eyes traced my form, surveying me with concern.

Mr. Hart arrived before I could question it, and we turned to more perfunctory breakfast conversation.

After we broke our fast, Celine's husband all but dragged her to the carriage.

"What on earth was that about?" I asked Lee from where we stood waving them off in the doorway.

"No idea," he replied, something off in his tone. "I need to pick up some things in the village. You should rest. I know you slept poorly last night." He tucked a loose curl behind my ear.

I nodded, feeling the exhaustion settle in. Whatever this morning was, whatever he had discussed with the pair, my husband wasn't outwardly angry with me.

"Do you need anything?"

"No, thank you." Lee caught my chin between his thumb and forefinger and tipped my head back for a gentle kiss that had my heart melting. I loved our kisses—the passionate ones, the tender ones, but this one, this was... habitual. As though it was a mere fact that he could not go about his day without it. My eyes filled with tears—the babe had turned me into a fusspot. I dipped my gaze to the ground, refusing to worry him over my nonsense.

After a brief respite, I woke feeling refreshed enough to take on the onerous task of correspondence. In the months since I'd arrived, I had received five letters. One reply from Lady Juliet with a list of accoucheurs and wet nurses she had considered who might be available to assist me. Two responses from those physicians—one quite rude and one available, for the right price. And a single letter from a wet nurse, and not one of the ones I had written to. And the other one... the one turned to ash in my fireplace.

I wrote to accept the accoucheur, offering an obscene sum in order to cut down on the back and forth.

Mrs. Hyde, the wet nurse, had heard of my search and reached out to me proactively. It didn't seem the way of things, but then I'd never hired a nurse before. A few women in the village were available who might suit, but I hadn't the fortitude to risk a face-to-face rejection, so I wrote to accept her as well with an equally obscene sum.

I handed off the letters to Crawford to be sent express. He left with only the requisite muttering about the cost. It took all my restraint to nod solemnly instead of suggesting the termination of a butler to offset the costs of postage. Much as he was an irritating little man, I'd grown to enjoy the amusement provided by his complaints.

Task completed, I was left feeling aimless. I missed my husband—the harvest season had only recently wrapped and, if I was honest, I had been avoiding the rumors, and avoiding him by extension.

Without any particular destination in mind, I decided to enjoy one of the last fine days we might see before winter. The sun was warm and bright against my face as I wandered past the lake and to my favorite bench. Most of the flowers had ceased to bloom, leaving only the goldenrod.

The babe alternated kicking the various vital organs he or she shared a home with as I sat down, a hand pressed on my lower back.

Bees worked, busily gathering the pollen that was left among the remaining flowers. A bird I couldn't see chirped a happy song somewhere overhead.

The sun beat down on me for some time before I heard the sound of hoofbeats signaling Lee's return. He tossed the reins to a stable hand, then turned to his observatory, a parcel in hand, without noticing me between the blooms.

I loved the way he moved, confident and certain with his long, strong limbs. At some point, he'd abandoned the hat he usually wore to the village, allowing the sun to caress his face.

I rose, slower than I would have liked because absolutely every movement took too long at present, to follow him down to the observatory.

He hadn't made the effort to close the door by the time I arrived, but he had stripped off his coat and was fussing with a book I didn't recognize. It was always a bit messy here, but it was an ordered chaos, and I enjoyed watching him struggle to find a place for his new purchase while I leaned against the doorframe.

He startled upon finally glancing up, his hand coming to his chest. "Charlotte!"

I bit back a grin. "Enjoyable trip?"

"Yes, very." His gaze flicked up and down my form. "You seem refreshed."

"Yes, thank you."

Lee shifted uneasily on his heels, one hand tapping the desk in front of him.

"*You* seem unsettled," I added.

He chuckled, seemingly to himself, as a hand rose to scratch the back of his neck. "It has come to my attention that I've been remiss in my duties as a husband."

"On that, I cannot agree."

Graceful hands grabbed a file off the desk as he rounded it in two easy steps. "I have, though," he said, stepping in front of me and pressing the file into my hand.

"What is this?"

I smiled at the sight of his eye roll. "Open it."

"You're stealing the worst of my habits, sir."

"Charlotte..." His free hand cupped my cheek, fingers wrapping around my neck. "Do as you're told for once."

I raised a challenging brow but flipped open the file. Inside, I found pages upon pages of sheet music—for both the harp and piano.

My heart tripped. A gift. My husband brought me a gift. I couldn't recall the last time I had received a gift—it wouldn't have been appropriate from Wesley, and Ralph—never. But Lee, the man who was supposed to be my husband in name only...

"Lee..." I choked out in a hoarse whisper. "This is too much."

"'On that, I cannot agree,'" he quoted in a teasing tone and dropped a kiss to the crown of my head. The gesture was so sweet, so affectionate, so unassuming. It overwhelmed me.

With my free hand, I tugged on the ends of his cravat and pulled his lips down to mine—my ankles were far too swollen for tip toes. He allowed one kiss, two, before he drew back when I tried to deepen it.

"You're welcome. But that wasn't why I brought it."

"I know..." When my hand on his chest gave a nudge, he stepped back, following my guidance willingly, eagerly—too strong for me to have forced him. His thighs—his tight, muscular thighs—hit the back of the desk, and he stumbled, falling half atop it.

"Charlotte... What do you want?"

"For you to do as you're told for once."

I pulled him back down by a shoulder to crush his lips onto mine. It took a moment for his smile to melt into our kiss, but eventually he obeyed with a hot arm banding about my waist, supporting me. His other hand curved around my neck.

When that hand slipped down to trace the line of my collarbone, I pulled back.

"Stop trying to distract me."

"Distract you from what?" he asked, genuine confusion in the divot between his brows.

I swallowed, assessing myself one last time. My heart was pounding, but not in distress. Butterflies danced in my belly—happily. My limbs were jittery, nervous, but not unpleasantly so. And my center ached in the best possible way. "May I...I wish to try something."

His eyes darted between my own, searching. "Anything." He broke off, clearing his throat. "Anything."

Between one breath and the next, without giving myself another second for a volte-face, I knelt before him. In my head, it was an elegant, dainty maneuver. Of course, I hadn't accounted for my shifting weight, and I nearly collapsed, face-first, into his lap. Praying he would allow it to pass without commentary, I moved my hands to the falls of his breeches, his member pressed against them in interest..

"Charlotte?" he choked, reaching down to grab my hands. "I didn't—that's not—I—" His eyes slipped shut with a deep inhale. After the exhale, dark eyes fluttered open again. A pink tongue darted out before he attempted speech. "You want this?"

I nodded, my eyes never leaving his. "I do." And I did. It was the strangest thing, but this moment felt like nothing I had ever experienced. There was no tawdry tightness in my spine, no revulsion in my belly. Nothing but anticipation and *want*.

"Hell." He cupped my cheeks with both hands. "Stop at any moment, for any reason. Promise?"

"I will," I vowed.

"I just—this isn't—it's not about the music?"

I knew only one response would put him at ease. I rolled my eyes.

His head hinged back on a breathless laugh as I started working the buttons. "Fuck... I lo—just—not here." He hauled me up by the arms.

"What?"

"Not the floor."

"But—"

Lee ignored my words as he helped me to my feet, then guiding me to the settee that lined the wall. "Sit."

While I was annoyed with the questioning and the change of venue, my knees were grateful and I plopped onto the settee. If I was honest, the angle was better too.

"Any other demands?" I asked, entirely rhetorically, as I

again reached for the buttons of his fall flap. The familiar hardness pushed against the fabric as I worked.

"None at all." He swallowed, harsh in the stillness of the observatory. "I am yours to command."

Chapter Thirty-Five
BENNET HALL, SURREY - OCTOBER 24, 1816

LEE

CHRIST, this woman was lovely, heartachingly so. Her full lower lip was trapped between her teeth. Whiskey eyes focused on the place where normally dexterous fingers fumbled with the buttons on my breeches.

My heart was set to fly right out of my chest.

With one notable exception, my cock hadn't known the touch of another in years. And it more than remembered Charlotte's too brief touch a few weeks ago.

I'd thought recent weeks had been a beautiful torture, bringing my breathtaking wife to climax after climax, sleeping with her cocooned in my arms. But this—watching her slowly work each silver button through the hole with the sort of concentration she typically only dedicated to a star chart was something else entirely. It was surely the most exquisite suffering known to heaven or hell.

The need to assure her that this was unnecessary warred with the desire to pull her hands away and rip the fabric off entirely, but before I could make a decision, she freed the last one.

She was nervous, that was clear in the way she bit her lip, in the way her eyes flicked up to mine—questioning—before returning to where her fingers hovered over the loosened falls. I knew my wife well enough to recognize the determined set of her shoulders.

Carefully, she set her hands on my hips and dragged my trousers down to tangle around my thighs. My breathing was ragged and unsure, like an attack, but also not. There were no worries here. I was entirely present in this moment.

My cock was still mostly covered by my shirt, though it tented the fabric absurdly.

"Off," she demanded, nodding toward my remaining layers. Dutifully, I stripped the simple, yellow waistcoat and tossed it aside. The cravat took a moment since my wife's industrious little hands had knotted it quite severely. But I managed. The shirt quickly followed, leaving me bare before her.

Far from the familiar panic, I had no hesitation in displaying my form for her. Charlotte had seen the worst of my scars, and she'd never so much as blinked. And she didn't now—no, now her perfect pink tongue darted between her lips in a way that had me groaning as her amber-honey eyes skimmed up and down my naked body.

Then, her pretty little hand wrapped confidently around the base of my cock and I died.

Death hadn't actually befallen me, but the air abandoned the room, and I required great heaving gasps to continue living.

My eyes had slammed shut involuntarily, and I forced them open, unwilling to waste another single second of the sight. And thank Christ I did because Charlotte, my Charlotte, never did what I expected. Instead of that hand sliding up my shaft in a less obligatory version of what she had begun that night weeks ago, her eyes caught mine as her lips parted and she leaned forward.

"Fuck—" escaped me without permission as sweet, flawless lips kissed the tip of my cock.

I'd never—no one had ever—I didn't even—*fuck!*

It wasn't until my chest began to work again that I realized it had stopped. Then it broke again when her luscious little mouth opened and she took me inside.

I hadn't expected—hadn't thought—I'd assumed I was agreeing to her delicate fingers topped with harp-induced calluses running along my length. That would have been more than enough. But this—

Dimly, I was aware that ragged half breath, half groans were coming from my throat but I wasn't capable of giving full consideration to anything beyond the goddess before me with the exquisite, heavenly mouth.

Then, in yet another attempt to end my life, Charlotte's clever tongue traced the vein running along the underside of my cock. I was forced to close my eyes against the sight lest it end prematurely. My fingers tangled in the silken curls twisted elegantly at the back of her head.

Charlotte coughed and pulled back, releasing me. I had to blink my dizzy gaze back into focus to meet her suddenly sad eyes. My heart stopped again and I froze.

"Don't grab my hair?" she whispered, her voice soft and small.

Wha... Oh.

I fought back tears at the understanding. "No, sweetheart. I'm sorry. Never again." It was a strange juxtaposition, icy sorrow for what she'd endured, warm pride at her bravery, burning rage at those who came before. "Do you wish to stop?"

She shook her head, her gaze returning to my flagging member. Without warning, she swallowed me down and I choked on nothing.

My fingers, desperate to ground myself to the world—to her—clenched and unclenched as she brought my arousal soaring back.

"Hand," I gasped. Her brow furrowed before she moved the hand cupping the base of my cock lower to cup my bollocks. Pleasure tightened in the base of my spine, sharp and imminent. Desperately, I shook my head. I reached down, carefully with trembling fingers, and tugged the fingers of the hand resting on my thigh. "Yes?"

In response, Charlotte slotted our fingers together. Then she doubled her efforts to suck my soul out of my cock with the kind of determination that would have been terrifying in any other context.

Pleasure, as I understood it, was a simple matter. Or it had been. Now, I knew differently. *That* had been a pale imitation of pleasure. This was entirely new, a layered, complex cosmos of sight, sound, sensation, and sentiment.

There was something so heartbreakingly beautiful in the knowledge that this was Charlotte. My breathtaking, vulnerable, courageous, damaged, fierce Charlotte was doing this for me. Tears welled in my eyes again even as I fought to blink them away, unwilling to miss even a second.

I loved this woman. I was so in love with this woman that it ached to breathe. She had been hurt, so many different times, in so many different ways.

Slowly, giving her time to stop me, I brushed a finger along her cheek before cupping it. Love and pleasure—a potent drug. If I hadn't been addicted before, I surely was now.

The only stupid thought swirling in my addled head was the desperate desire to propose to her. *Marry me! Marry me.*

My heart sang—as though this incredible woman wasn't already my wife.

But I was greedy and selfish, and I wanted more. I wanted it all—everything she had agreed to give and everything she hadn't. The next months were mine, but I wanted all the ones to come. I wanted every laugh, every tear, every smile, and every eye roll. I wanted the babe in her belly and any others that came along. I wanted her in my house and in my life, so steeped there that it was as if she'd never been anywhere else. I wanted—needed—her to be mine.

Verbal communication had long since escaped me. Our laced hands were the only method left to me. I squeezed in desperate warning as pleasure tightened into a sharp knot. Desperately, I forced out an unintelligible, "Cha—*mgh*," of warning.

Shockingly, she understood whatever that was and pulled back, her hand continuing to work my length. There was nothing perfunctory about her movements—at least nothing I could see. Her eyes were darkened, her lips swollen and gorgeous, her cheeks flushed, and her delectable bosom swelled with every breath.

One quick turn of the wrist was all it took before I spilled, my free hand moving without permission to keep from making a mess of her.

My breath was harsh and ragged, but no matter how my chest heaved, my lungs were never satiated. Weak-kneed, I fell to the settee beside her with a pathetic flop, half on, half off.

Charlotte bent down, my brain too wrecked to make sense of it. When she returned with the handkerchief from my pocket and reached for my hand, I understood. Task disposed of, she curled up along my side with a delicate kiss to my heaving chest—right over my scar.

I wrapped my arm around her shoulder, pulling her in closer.

"Was that all right?" I asked, sounding pathetic even to my own ears.

The edges of her smile brushed along my chest. "I do believe that is my question."

"*You* already know the answer."

She buried her head in my chest in an adorably shy manner—a word I'd never associated with her before.

"Charlotte... Tell me how you feel."

Eventually, her head popped back up and she dropped a kiss to my lips. The first was just a gentle press. The second... There was intent behind that kiss, lips slotting together, her tongue dripping along the seam of my lips.

It took me until the moment her thighs rubbed together before comprehension dawned. *Oh... Oh, yes.*

I allowed my lips the pleasure of tracing along her jaw and down her neck before moving to the delicious bounty of her breasts, offered up by the neckline of her gown. Reluctantly, I pulled away, sliding down her graceful form.

"Lee?" she asked in a tone that was not at all what I was aiming for. "I don't—not that."

"What?" My heart stopped. There was something nervous in her expression.

"I can't..." Charlotte flopped back to stare at the ceiling. "I cannot see you—I want to—I do not like that I cannot see you. Over my belly—I mean."

At once, my heartbeat kicked back in. My smile felt crooked. I pressed a lingering kiss to the side of her clothed breast. "That is easily remedied."

"It is?"

I dragged one hand along her thigh, pulling her dress up, before raising it in front of her, fingers dancing, offering their pleasure. At the same time, I nudged my bare thigh between hers, up, up, up until it met her sweet, soaked center, providing a second option. She arched prettily in response with a charming little moan. The angle was a bit awkward with her belly, but I wasn't at all willing to complain.

"Do you have a preference?"

"Both," she whispered. "Is both an option?"

"Anything I have to give is an option." I inched the fabric out of my way before my lips descended back on hers. And the afternoon's words gave way to moans, whimpers, and sighs.

Chapter Thirty-Six
BENNET HALL, SURREY - NOVEMBER 6, 1816

CHARLOTTE

My back ached when I woke and didn't relent when I pulled away from Lee's prone form. His only response was a sleep-heavy grumble while he rolled over to his back.

Sleep wouldn't be returning so I rose and grabbed my wrap, unable to abide anything more substantial. The knot on the base of my spine twisted as I made my way down the stairs. I fought back a cry. My knuckles turned white and cold on the railing as I dug my nails in. Fortunately, the pain was short-lived and released as quickly as it arrived a few moments later.

My stomach gave a disgruntled roll at the sight of the day's breakfast selection. It seemed toast was the only option I could manage.

The knot began to build in my lower back again, a dull ache this time. I sat and struggled to spread the currant jam as the ache sharpened, coming to a knifepoint and holding there. My breath caught, paused by the pain and my refusal to display it.

It faded again and I quickly took a bite. The toast was

unappetizing, but I could not manage anything more substantial.

My husband's footsteps preceded his arrival. His first task upon setting foot in the room was to kiss the crown of my head.

I took a half-hearted bite of toast and stared at the bread askance when it was just as unpalatable as the first bite.

Wordlessly, the back of Lee's hand found my forehead. I slapped it away performatively. "I am well."

"You do not look it."

"Thank you," I replied with as much bite as I could muster.

"I just meant that you look like you feel poorly. Do you have a headache?"

"No, it is merely my back again."

Lee hummed, still searching for an unseen ailment.

"Truly. It is my back only."

"All right," he said, then turned to the sideboard to locate his own breakfast.

The kink began to tighten once more. The pain was bearable, not much more significant than a particularly bad day during my courses. But it sharpened to something different, less familiar and less tolerable. It was enough to, not quite knock my breath from my body, but to trap it in my lungs once again.

"Charlotte?" Lee's concerned voice came from my side.

I forced my lungs to release. My questioned, "Yes," was tepid and pathetic, even to my ears. The tightness loosened slower than the last time.

"Your back?"

I nodded. "Yes, but it's better now."

"How long has this been going on?"

"I'm not certain."

"How often?" His tone was unreadable, and his eyes gave nothing away either.

"Every few minutes or so? It's merely a cramp, stop fussing."

Quietly, he slipped his pocket watch out and glanced at it, saying nothing. Brigsby entered and greeted Lee with a smile, me with a polite nod, then leaned over to speak with his employer.

With a sigh, I contemplated my toast once again. The task of eating seemed all but insurmountable, and the sideboard held no more interest than it had earlier. It seemed tea was all I could manage this morning. I took a tentative sip and swallowed with trepidation. Fortunately, when it hit my stomach, there was no reaction.

Conversation continued beside me. I contributed nothing as I was entirely incapable of listening between tiny sips of tea.

Just as before, the ache began to return. My eyes fluttered shut without my notice, my lips pressing together. When the knife finally left my spine, I raised my lids to two sets of eyes staring at me with varying combinations of interest and worry.

"Charlotte?" Lee asked with a glance at his watch once again.

"Yes?"

"I believe it may be time."

"Time for what?" I asked distractedly, considering my toast once more.

"Time."

"Time for—oh. No, of course not. It cannot be time. It is too early. It is merely a cramp."

Brigsby took that moment to excuse himself with alacrity, backing out of the room the way one would to avoid an advancing predator.

"They're coming regularly," Lee said.

"It is my back. Not my womb," I protested.

"I do not believe that's entirely uncommon. That book said—"

"It is too early," I insisted.

"Not so early, darling." He offered a placating smile and came to stand by my side. It was a tone I would typically have found sweet but was utterly irritating at the moment.

"The nursery is not finished. I have not received a response from the accoucheur. The chambers are not prepared. We have not even discussed names. It is too early."

"I do not believe the babe knows or cares. Now, can you stand?"

"Of course I can stand, because the babe is not coming." His hand found my waist when I pressed myself up.

"All right. Now, how are you feeling about the stairs?" he asked, completely ignoring my valid points.

Not once in our marriage had I ever wanted to knock this man upside the head, but right now... "Do you really suppose that you know my body better than I do?" I snapped.

"Of course not. But I think you are frightened. I am frightened. And sometimes when things are very, very frightening, it can be tempting to pretend that they're not happening."

"Of all the condescend—" The next cramp broke the end of my sentence.

"Well then, if it is not time, then what do you suppose these very regular *cramps* you are experiencing mean?"

"Well, I do not know that." I bit out between clenched teeth. His hand found mine and I crushed it in my grasp. It was painful, surely it was. I watched as my knuckles turned first red, then white with the force of my grip. He didn't so much as grunt as he guided me down the hall.

Even as the cramp dissipated, a small hope was growing—that this was the beginning of childbirth. Because if it was not... if this was something else... How much more painful would the actual event be? Could I survive that? Did I want to?

"Has there been any... fluid?" he asked, running his free hand along my back.

"You did not just ask me that."

Jack stumbled into the hall, both arms filled with pitchers to be brought upstairs. With one look at the two of us, he paled, swaying slightly. Lee fought to free his hand and grabbed the footman by the upper arm.

"Steady, lad. I need you to run and tell Mrs. Fitzroy that it is time."

"It is *not* time," I protested.

"It *might* be time," Lee corrected.

Jack's gaze flitted between us before he seemingly deciding to follow my husband's instructions. He skirted along the wall beside us—leaving a wide berth—before breaking into a run toward the kitchens. He sloshed water from the pitchers all down the hall along the way. My eyes rolled of their own volition.

"Look, there is your fluid," I bit out.

Lee paused our trek, huffing a snort of laughter before dropping a kiss to my temple. "There is my wife." The note of affection in his tone was impossible to miss.

The compliment warmed my heart enough for me to push onward. A few feet more and I was faced, once again, with the stairs.

So many steps. Too many. An infinite, impossible number of them.

Another cramp crashed through my middle.

One moment, I was vertical with my feet firmly planted on the floor. The next, I was horizontal, my feet swaying in the air. My arm found Lee's neck on instinct and clutched it with a desperation I had never known. The linen of his shirt was soft and fine and peppermint-scented when I buried my face there.

"Lee?"

I felt the rumbled, "Yes, darling?" from deep in his chest along my side.

"I think it may be time."

His lips found my forehead again with a distracted hum as he navigated the stairs for me.

"I am frightened," I whispered into his chest. I sensed each step, but he was careful not to jostle me.

"I am too."

"I know men are not to be in the birthing chamber, but would you stay? Just for a little while?"

"I'll stay as long as you like," he whispered from just above my ear.

"Forever?"

"Forever." This time, it was my heart and not my back that clenched.

Chapter Thirty-Seven
BENNET HALL, SURREY - NOVEMBER 7, 1816

LEE

THE HOURS after I carried Charlotte upstairs were long and horrid. I had only felt this impotent once in my life, and I had hoped never to experience it again.

Someone had fetched the midwife, Mrs. Griffith—much to Charlotte's protest. She arrived quickly and set about her tasks with a businesslike efficiency that was honestly terrifying. Someone else had been sent to town to fetch the accoucheur and wet nurse Charlotte had engaged. Vaguely, I wondered whom I owed thanks to for the fetching, Brigs and Jack most likely.

The smallest bit of my tension eased at the midwife's arrival, in spite of the woman's complaints about our lack of preparedness. My eye roll matched my wife's. As if we had expected an arrival weeks early.

The night grew so late that it was actually early morning, long after word came that Brigsby had returned with the nurse and no accoucheur, when Mrs. Griffith urged Charlotte into position on her side. And by the time the sun rose, a squalling cry came from near the foot of the bed.

My wife, sweaty, disheveled, and triumphant, collapsed back against me as Mrs. Griffith placed the babe in her exhausted arms. I brought a hand to each forearm to steady them.

"A beautiful boy," the midwife announced.

And he was beautiful. He was the most beautiful thing I'd ever seen—with a shock of dark hair, ruddy cheeks, and the tiniest fist in the world, trapped between my wife's thumb and forefinger.

"He's... perfect," she breathed in exhausted awe.

"He is," I agreed, then placed a kiss to her damp curls. "We never did talk about names." I traced his cheek with a single finger.

"Leopold," Charlotte said, then added softly, "Leo."

And just like that, I was in love with my son. Leo. And he was—my son. My perfect, sweet son. And my brave, beautiful wife. They were mine.

"Leopold Bennet. It's a good name. Do you not think?"

"Perfect," I agreed.

"Do you wish to hold him?" Rather than wait for a reply, she shifted, nearly dumping the boy in my arms. He gave a short, disgruntled cry, his face scrunching in disapproval, and I did not blame him. I wanted to cry too.

The terror that had dissipated when Charlotte relaxed following the birth returned in full force. This was my son. I was responsible for him. And my hand was larger than his entire body. I was going to crush him with my oafish paws.

"Relax, you will not break him," Charlotte teased, reading my expression with ease.

"I might."

"You won't. You will be an amazing father." Something about her tone drew my gaze away from my grumpy Leo and to my exhausted Charlotte. Relief was there in her expression, fatigue, and something else... trepidation perhaps. It took a moment to place the source, but once I did, it snapped into place. She was still worried I would reject her, reject them, that I wouldn't want a son who wasn't from my seed to inherit. That I didn't wish to be this boy's father.

"I hope so." He was mine in every single way that was worth anything.

I pressed a kiss on his forehead before returning him to his mother's arms. Gently, I tugged her back against my chest and settled my chin against her shoulder where I could support her —prop up her exhausted form—and watch him.

"Lee?"

"Hmm?"

"I..." She trailed off into nothingness.

"You?"

"I... Never mind. I must admit, I am quite exhausted."

"Let me take him for a while. You have earned a rest."

Her nod was grateful, but there was still reluctance in her gaze when she handed Leo to me. Precious bundle in hand, I slipped out the door and down the hall. To the nursery.

The footmen did an exceptional job furnishing it during the chaos of the afternoon. A rocking chair sat by the window near a bassinet. An oversize Scotch carpet covered some of them, but yellow paw prints still lined the floor and lower walls, save the one I had altered weeks before.

My son fussed for a moment when I slid into the rocker. He made a sleepy snuffling noise before settling back down. Quietly, so as not to wake him, I hummed the tune to a song my mother used to sing. I had long forgotten the lyrics, but it seemed right in the moment.

Never before had I felt such instant possessiveness. Maybe it was a natural facet of becoming a father. Or perhaps, it was my burgeoning feelings for my wife. The source of the feeling was no matter. It had burrowed its way into my very being, the swell in my heart and the tumultuous sea in my belly were certainly permanent. I loved this boy, I loved him and his mother and, when they returned to town—

Tap, tap, tap.

The underside of a tiny paw tugged against the door. Nothing in the world could have induced me to move, though, not even to scold the beast. The paw disappeared and the sound shifted to a *scratch, scratch, scratch* where the door meant the frame.

Cass possessed magical powers, and the door swung open, creaking heavily on its hinges. She chirped her way into the room while I eyed her warily. First, she perused the perimeter, stopping to inspect my handiwork with the paint and tossing me a look. Then she trotted over to the rocking chair.

"If you so much as think of scratching or biting him, I'll have you sent to Wales in a donkey cart. Do not for one second think I will restrain myself."

She added another chirp, hopped up onto her back legs, and dragged her front paws along my shin. Her claws remained sheathed.

"Understand?"

Chirp.

Tentatively, I shifted my arms out, allowing her to smell the blankets swaddling my infant son. Her front paw caught one of my hands, gently guiding the bundle lower. I obliged, filled with curious trepidation. She settled both paws on my hand and peered over the edge of the blanket to see Leo's face.

After a moment of contemplation, she offered a nearly silent chirp and rubbed her cheek against my hand and the edge of the blanket before dropping back onto four paws.

Unwilling to press my luck, I pulled Leo back into my lap while Cass ran figure eights around my legs, soundless chirps accompanying her movements.

Convinced that the cat would behave for at least another half minute, I spoke to my son. "Leopold Bennet... I did not know it was possible to love someone so completely nor so quickly." His face scrunched and he wrestled a little fist out from his blankets. I thought Charlotte's hands were small, but Leo's... I ran a finger along each one. His entire fist was barely wider than my thumb.

We were suspended here, the two of us, frozen in the time between breaths. And there, I waited for the moment when he would inevitably decide that he wished for his mother or his nurse. I was determined to enjoy every single second with him. Today, tomorrow, and every day between now and when they inevitably left me.

When I had made this arrangement with Charlotte, I had been so certain that the part I would regret was wedding her in the first place. Never could I have imagined how much I would hate the mere thought of the end of it. But that day ticked ever closer, the moment when I would send her back to London, this babe in her arms. Off to live their lives, dance, laugh, grow up, grow old, and fall in love...

An abrasive knock sounded, startling all three of us. The boy let out a disgruntled cry, and a woman, presumably the wet nurse, peeked her head in. Cass offered little more than a hiss in response.

"I just came to take the little lord off for a feeding, and it sounds as though I'm just in ti—Oh, good heavens!" The motherly, doting tone slipped from her voice and her hand flew to her chest.

It had been so long since anyone had reacted to my scars that it took me a moment to comprehend her reaction. The petite woman, whose dark hair was a shock against her pale skin—paler for the sight of me—pressed herself against the wall with something akin to terror.

Ordinarily, I would have been bothered by her reaction. I

should have been, to be honest. But I was so full of love for my wife and my son and so astonished at the realization that I hadn't immediately understood the cause of her fright—that I hadn't thought to hide my face before she entered—that I couldn't bring myself to care.

"Mrs. Hyde, yes?" I asked, keeping my tone soft in an attempt to prevent her from fainting. "You are the nurse my wife hired, I believe?"

"Y-yes." She braved a step into the room.

I rose, standing to offer the quivering woman my crying son. He *was* probably quite hungry. He'd had a busy day after all. But at my movement, she scurried back into the wall once again.

I rolled my eyes, but otherwise refused to acknowledge the absurd display. With the utmost reluctance, I stepped farther into her orbit, holding my boy out for a moment before she finally reached for him.

Leo's cries increased at the change in arms, and it broke my heart a little to take my hands from underneath him. Turning Leo over to her was physically painful, the fist around my heart tightening nearly more than I could bear.

"Thank you," I muttered, more out of habit than actual gratitude as I backed away. She scurried out of the nursery, my son in her stiff arms and Cass right on her heels. Leo's wails grew ever louder with each step.

Finally, she must have reached a distance where I could no longer hear his cries. That understanding left me tetchy and on edge. Desperate for some purpose, any purpose, I found Charlotte's paints, tucked away in the top drawer. With no other useful occupation, I set about adding stamens and leaves to the rest of the paw prints. I could hardly make them worse after all.

Chapter Thirty-Eight

BENNET HALL, SURREY - NOVEMBER 7, 1816

CHARLOTTE

It was midday when I woke again, groggy, disoriented, sore, and still exhausted in my usual chambers. Worse still, missing both of my Leopolds.

Neither of the whisperers in the adjoining sitting room were Lee's. Mrs. Griffith's stern directives swirled with the voice of the other woman—not *my* nurse, but the wet nurse—I loathed her.

The sniveling, obsequious, nasal tone of her unintelligible words set my teeth on edge. Something about her—I couldn't abide her after a single meeting. I had already vowed to see her returned to London as soon as was feasible.

The midwife murmured something I couldn't make out. The words clearly upset the nurse. Her volume rose, frustration clear.

"That is precisely why he should not hold the babe. The child was screeching at the mere sight of him. And who can blame the boy? I wanted to scream at the sight of—"

"Mrs. Hyde," Mrs. Griffith interrupted. "Try to maintain a little bit of professionalism please."

"I am stating facts. It took me forever to get the little one settled. And—"

A sharp rap on my door interrupted her hateful spittle. Lee popped his head into my room with a relieved grin.

The sitting room door snicked closed from the side wall. Apparently the knock was enough to alert them to the cracked door.

Once Lee confirmed I was awake, he strode across the room and settled beside me at the side of the bed. Gingerly, he helped me press up to sit back against the headboard.

"There you are!" he murmured. "I did not anticipate they would move you back to your chambers. I probably should have, but... I apologize."

"Do not apologize. I did not think either. Where is Leo?"

"The wet nurse took him. Do you wish for me to find him?"

Yes. I shook my head. "I am sure he's quite all right."

"How are you feeling?"

I rolled my eyes. "Tired, sore, hungry, thirsty. Need I go on?"

He chuckled at my list of ailments and dropped a kiss on my forehead.

"Food and tea are on the way. I'm not certain what help I can offer with the rest of that."

I shrugged. Lee had a talent for solving a great many of my problems, even the ones I previously thought unsolvable. But he was not capable of miracles.

Without warning, his hand caught mine and pulled it up to his lips. There, he pressed a gentle kiss to the back of my knuckles. If my insides hadn't so very recently been ripped out by Leo, I might have felt that gesture in more than just my heart. As it stood, my husband still left me giddy and missish.

He made to let go of my hand, but I tangled our fingers together. I dragged him over to my side, encouraging him to prop his back against the headboard next to me. He made a token protest about his boots on the bed coverings that I shushed away. Obliging me, he draped his free arm along my shoulders and tugged me gently into his chest. The moment was nearly perfect. So very close. It was only missing little Leo.

"I know it is not proper..." I began, unsure of how to voice my desires.

"Very little about you is," he replied, a teasing grin etched across his face. I turned to his free hand, distracting myself with inspecting it. Oh, his hands were lovely. Big and strong, soft and warm, and—green?

"Why do you have paint on your hand?"

Lee made to pull his hand back, but I held fast, thoroughly distracted now. "I was—I did a... thing."

"You did a thing?" I drew the syllables out, hoping they would become sensical as they hung in the air.

"Do not worry about it. What were you saying?"

I rather thought I would worry about it. But unless he had painted Leo, this was his home. What he chose to do to it on the day I brought a child into this world was not entirely my business.

I dropped my voice to a low whisper, barely audible even to me. "I know there is a proper way to do things... With Mrs. Hyde and such. But I just... I do not like Leo being so far from us, from me. I..."

"You wish to... nurse him yourself?" He joined in my whisper.

I nodded slowly, even though I could not read his expression—shocked, disapproving, ambivalent? He was inscrutable. "I... yes."

"Very well, if you're certain. Do you wish to try it a time or two first? Rather than dismiss Mrs. Hyde and be left bereft?"

That was—he was... "That is a good notion. I do not suppose—could we look into others, if I'm unable? I... there's something about her."

The tiniest bit of tension, so small I hadn't noticed its presence, evaporated. Leaving him freer in its wake. "If you wish it. Anything you wish."

Before I could reply, Mrs. Griffith entered from the hall, her arms laden with a tray overfilled with tea cakes and the last of the fresh fruits.

She froze at the sight of us, curled together on the bed, heads dipped conspiratorially. "You best not be trying anything, Lord Champaign. She won't be well enough for some time, and you won't be anticipating this the way you did your vows."

Lee blinked slowly at her. Then I caught the edge of a bit-off smile while he stared at her with the entire force of his scarred, stern, wealthy, earlish countenance. It should have been foreboding, but she scoffed and strode easily to my side and setting the tray atop my lap. Her efforts broke my husband's stern expression, and he let out a delighted chuckle.

"Yes, you frighten everyone into submission, I'm sure. But you're a harmless pup compared to some of the ladies I order about during the worst pain of their lives."

And wasn't that thought enough to make even the burliest man blanche, my massive husband included.

"That's what I thought, my lord."

Lee cast his gaze away shiftily, unwilling to give the intuitive woman any further insight into the state of our marriage bed.

She made to shoo him out of the room to examine me. An unpleasant prospect, certainly, and not one I particularly wanted Lee to witness. His support had been wonderful for the birth, but I could avoid any further traumatic images for the both of us.

"Can you bring Leo? I find myself missing him."

He nodded with alacrity and slipped into the sitting room eagerly. Mrs. Griffith watched him go with a wistful sort of expression.

"Lord, he is an attentive one. Handsome too," she commented once Lee had shut the door. "He seems a good man, if you don't mind me saying. No truer test of a man's character than a birth. I've had more than a few I wanted to clop 'round the head. *That* man loves you something fierce."

It was impossible to know how to feel about that. I quite agreed that he was handsome. It was an understatement. But that Lee loved me... Perhaps she merely thought those words would offer comfort to her patient. He was fond enough of me. Attracted. But in love... No.

"You don't believe me?" she asked while she fussed with her examination. "Ah well, you'll learn someday. When a man looks at a woman the way that one looks at you, he's in too deep to claw his way out."

No sooner had she settled the bed coverings back around me than a rap sounded on the door. Lee walked inside with a sleeping bundle in his arms. He strode over and deposited our son into my arms. This man was a natural with a babe, gentle, but unhesitating and confident.

And then I peered at the bundle of perfection in my arms. With the blanket covering his dark shock of hair—no, Lee *was* his father. The color of his hair made no difference. Besides, *my* hair was dark—in the right light. It certainly could not always be described as blonde.

Lee settled back on the bed beside me and wrapped his arm around my shoulder. The limb was heavy, warm, strong, and supportive. I felt more than saw his fingers tangled in the bedraggled ends of my braid.

And then I glanced up. And his eyes met mine. Stormy sky irises were filled with so much feeling. Sentiment? Surely it wasn't love. I was an obligation, a favor he happened to find pleasant. But there was *something* there. And it looked a lot like love. Giving it another name didn't make his expression any less tender.

Before I could find words, little Leo woke and began to wriggle irritably.

"I know you've employed Mrs. Hyde, but if you'd like to try feeding him, I'd be happy to explain," Mrs. Griffith interjected. I had entirely forgotten her presence and, given the slight jolt that shot through Lee's arm, he had as well.

"That's not really the... done thing. Is it?" I hesitated.

"Whatever pleases you is the 'done thing' my dear. And also, I told you." She tipped her head in Lee's direction, and my cheeks heated uncomfortably.

My husband's head swung back and forth between us, searching for an explanation *I* wouldn't be sharing. And Mrs. Griffith better not be sharing either if she wished to retain her employment.

A combination of genuine desire for instruction from the capable woman and desperation to avoid the subject of whatever feelings Lee may or may not have for me drove my answer.

"Yes, please."

Lee started to pull away, to leave us to privacy, but Mrs. Griffith tutted, saying, "Oh please. This is the least horrifying thing you've seen all day, my lord." And he settled back down in chastened silence with flushed cheeks.

In the crisp, businesslike way she managed everything except comments about the state of my marriage, she explained the process and helped me convince an increasingly more irate Leo to latch on.

Once he did, she bade us adieu and left our little family in peaceful, loving solitude.

Chapter Thirty-Nine
BENNET HALL, SURREY - NOVEMBER 7, 1816

LEE

CHARLOTTE RELUCTANTLY AGREED to let Mrs. Hyde take Leo for the night feedings. I suspected her decision was made primarily to avoid the scene that would surely result from her refusal.

I resolved to dismiss the woman first thing in the morning, rather than subject my wife to the confrontation. The nurse was terrified of me. I may as well put my hideous countenance to use.

It was a jarring realization. Months ago, her clear disquiet at my appearance would have been devastating. I would have hidden away in my observatory for weeks, refusing to subject anyone to the sight of me. But now... Somehow, entirely without notice, I didn't *feel* hideous any longer. And not once had Charlotte expressed displeasure, quite the opposite. She only noted the scars so as to offer me the absolution of her soft fingers and sweet lips.

In fact, the length of her—significantly less round than she'd been this morning—was pressed along the knotted flesh of my side. I had almost forgotten what it was like to have her this close. As soon as we had reached a level of comfort with each other, Leo made his presence felt instead. His home in her belly forced a physical distance between Charlotte and me.

A sleep-heavy sigh escaped her when she shifted.

"Uncomfortable?"

"Sore. Too exhausted to rest," she replied.

"Can I help?"

"No, I'm afraid not."

The only reply I could offer was a hum.

After a stretch so long I had begun to suspect she had drifted off, she spoke. "You should go see the stars. Make sure to chart Leo Minor for me." My heart offered a jolt at the affectionate tone in her weary voice.

"Are you sure? I do not want to leave you."

"Please? I want it framed, for his birth."

I nodded. "I won't stay long."

"Perfect," she said with a smile.

I began to rise, but she pulled me back down for a quick kiss that shouldn't have been nearly as affecting as it was.

The hall was silent when I slipped into it. As I passed the nursery, I paused to peer in only to find it empty. Across from the nursery, a candle burned under the closed door. Disappointed to find my son with Mrs. Hyde and unavailable for a quick cuddle, I continued down the stairs and out into the brisk night air.

∼

CHARLOTTE

As soon as Lee stepped out, I flopped across the bed, spread out as wide as possible. I wouldn't sleep—I was too exhausted for it. And I was regretting letting Leo out of my sight with every passing moment.

I understood that one of a wet nurse's duties was to keep the child quiet. And Leo had proved, thus far, to be a remarkably tranquil child. But I hadn't heard a peep out of either of them in some time. Certainly this feeling, whatever it was, would be tempered by the sound of his cry. I missed him, my son, but it was more than that. It was as though I had lost a limb, and I kept making to use it, only to remember it wasn't there.

I shifted to sit up with more effort than anyone should have to make, then punched the pillows in irritation and flopped back down. As I sprawled across the sheets, it occurred to me that Leo was what was missing. There was no weight of him, pressing against my spine, my organs, stretching my skin. My body was my own once again, more or less, if my aching breasts had an opinion on the subject.

I curled up onto my side, the only position that had been bearable for months. But it was wrong, somehow. It left me bereft, wanting.

Finally, I accepted the obvious solution. Forcing myself upright again was a chore, and standing required even greater effort. I was weak and shaky as I padded over to the door and down the hall to the nursery.

The door was cracked open. Leo wasn't in the empty bassinet. A glance across the hall revealed a flicker of candlelight from under Mrs. Hyde's door.

Out of the corner of my eye, I caught them—Cass's yellow footprints. The beast and I had entered into a truce in recent weeks, and I had mostly forgiven her for her artwork. But they weren't footprints any longer. Not really. Oh, I could see the prints along the wooden boards because I knew what they were. But they had been transformed. Every single one.

Stamens and leaves had been added, details, too, turning

each little paw pad into a flower petal. There was but one possible culprit.

I didn't realize it until I caught sight of a drop landing beside a flower, but tears were slipping down my cheeks.

They were beautiful. Lee made them beautiful. He took a mess, and he made it lovely. Just like he did with me.

My chest could barely contain the pounding of my heart. I would go to him in the observatory. I would explain that our marriage hadn't been a sham to me, not for months, perhaps not ever. I would tell him how I felt—that I loved him so much I couldn't contain it. I would beg him to let me stay here, to let me be his lovely mess.

Across the hall, a disgruntled *rowll-mrow* came from behind the closed door. Mrs. Hyde was a brave woman to trap that beast in the room with her.

A paw appeared underneath the door, digging and scratching. I sighed. It would be best to free the menace before she maimed the woman in order to win her freedom.

As quietly as I could, I turned the knob, nudging the door open. Cass spilled out, rubbing herself along my legs with a disgruntled *mrawl-rawl*. Something about that sound...

Icy dread filled my veins. I didn't know how. Or why. But I knew.

I thrust the door open all the way, letting it smack against the wall with a cacophonous clang.

The room was empty, silent but for a flickering candle, burned nearly to the holder, and a letter.

Chapter Forty
BENNET HALL, SURREY - NOVEMBER 7, 1816

LEE

THE WEATHER WAS COOPERATIVE. The lake was like glass, mirroring the stars. Only the reeds and lily pads broke the reflection. The brisk night air chased away the clouds. And the moon was but the tiniest sliver, a suggestion more than anything.

When I'd set out for the observatory, I intended to take the time only to chart Leo Minor, as Charlotte suggested. But once I arrived and began, I decided the entire night sky was a more worthy gift for my sweet son.

The walk back to the house wasn't quite frigid enough to be termed cold, but it was a near it. Snow would be upon us sooner than I wished. Perhaps the winter would be treacherous enough to keep Charlotte and Leo here a few weeks more. Maybe even a month.

Eager to see my favorite lady and little gentleman, I charged up the steps two at a time. It wasn't until I reached the landing that I recognized something might be amiss. As it was, my gut understood before my head.

The nursery door was ajar, the bassinet still empty. When I peered over the side, I saw it wasn't only empty—it was untouched. Not a wrinkle to be found. The longer I stared, the less sense it made. But my blood recognized the truth, frozen solid in my veins.

A frantic glance across the hall revealed another open door. Mrs. Hyde's room.

Also empty.

Empty but for a burned-down candle on the table next to a piece of parchment.

One, two, three steps to rip it from the polished wood desk.

Charlotte,

> *I have the child. Bring £5,000 and meet me at 36 Earlham Street as early as possible. We'll leave and start our life together at last, my love.*
> *W*

The letter shook with my trembling hand and the periphery dimmed. Not the way it did in one of my attacks. No. This was something entirely different. This was a rage the likes of which I had never experienced.

I was going to rip that spineless little weasel apart with my bare hands.

A thousand needs welled up inside me, each fighting for precedence. I needed to vomit, but a scream caught in my throat, pushing the bile back down. My lungs had no interest in performing their intended function. My hands itched to shred the letter into dust and crush beneath my feet.

And worst of all was the tiny, miniscule part of me that wondered if Charlotte wanted to go with him.

Clammy hands grabbed my shoulders, turned me around, and shoved something into my grasp.

"—to London!"

The voice registered midsentence, finally reaching a pitch that drowned out the ringing I'd just noticed.

"What?"

"Lady Champaign—she's ordered a carriage to London right this moment!" I finally recognized Brigsby's distressed tone.

Lady... "Charlotte?"

My limbs unfurled, allowing me to stumble toward the room I'd left her in.

Fumbling at the door, I slung it open only to stare uncomprehendingly at the tossed bed coverings. At the pile of night clothes at the foot of the bed.

She was... gone.

Instinctively, my hand rose to my mouth, a peppermint falling in. Someone—Brigsby—had shoved it there. The burst of mint restarted my mind. Charlotte wasn't gone. She wasn't —she hadn't left me—she wouldn't. She was going after *our* son.

"Has she left yet?" I blurted.

"No, not yet. She sent me to find you."

Relief flooded me, leaving my limbs loose and ungainly. My back found the wall without thought and I was grateful for its support.

Precious seconds we didn't have ticked away while I caught my breath. Finally, my lungs stopped hitching with every breath.

Charlotte needed me. Leo needed me.

I shook away the rising darkness. "Pack a set of warm clothes for us both. Wake Mrs. Griffith. Find out what Charlotte requires to travel safely, then have her follow us at first light."

Brigsby blinked at me slowly for a moment, then two, then snapped into action. I couldn't blame the man. I, too, was astonished at my own sudden coherence.

I stumbled down the stairs, two, three at a time and out the side door closest to the stables. Seconds that felt like days passed before I reached her.

She was an apparition in white against the inky night sky, directing every man she had found to hitch the carriage. Her appearance belied the commanding tone as she ordered the men.

I could no more have stopped myself from wrapping her in my arms than I could have stopped the sun from rising. Small, so small, and trembling, she burrowed into my chest.

Words intended to comfort poured from me, but I only heard vague murmurs, entirely drowned out by the sob that escaped her. Objectively, I understood it to be a quiet, contained sound, but it echoed in my chest, a staccato ache in my heart.

"Stop gawking and hand me that tack," came from one of the men—Jack. I nodded my thanks to his back. He had already turned to the horse.

"Lee..." Charlotte whispered, wresting her head free from where I'd pressed her close. "Lee... he's going to... he has..."

"He's not going to do anything. He won't hurt Leo. Hell, she's probably not more than an hour or so ahead— Who readied her carriage?" I shouted.

All but Jack froze, suddenly remembering I was massive and scarred to hell. In the tepid glow of the lanterns, I was certainly terrifying.

"No one, sir," Jack piped in, tossing the lines over a horse's back where they slapped a petrified stable boy in the face.

"I didn't say stop. I asked who readied her carriage!" The men flinched simultaneously before jumping back into action.

"Best I can figure, she had one waiting for her just out of

sight, around the bend. Either a hack or someone picked her up."

"Thank you, Jack," I replied. After pressing my lips to Charlotte's temple, I added, "She had to sneak out and walk around the bend. She can't be more than an hour ahead."

"Halfway to Lond—" Charlotte broke on the word, another sob escaping.

My reassurances were interrupted by Brigsby with a small trunk bouncing at his side as he jogged to us.

"Thank you, Brigs."

He hefted the trunk onto the back of the carriage and strapped it down. Then he turned back, brushing his hands off before shoving them in a satchel. Without a word, he shoved an entire bag of peppermints directly into my pocket.

"Do you want your mount saddled?" he asked, trepidation echoing in the quake of his voice.

Until that second, I hadn't realized what I was about to do. I was about to climb into a carriage that I would push to the absolute limits. At night. Lit only by lantern.

Instinctive horror ripped through me, but I fought it back with everything I had. Charlotte needed me. Leo needed me. She couldn't ride, not in her condition. And I couldn't—wouldn't—abandon her to the carriage alone. It wasn't an option. Not this time.

"No," I said, shaky and tentative. "No." This time it was clearer, brighter, certain. Determined.

An infinitesimal fraction of the tension left Charlotte's body.

I shoved another peppermint in my dry mouth and crunched until my teeth gnashed the shards.

Mrs. Griffith came panting up the gently sloping hill, her arms laden with blankets and who knew what else. Wordlessly, she shoved the items into the carriage before rounding on me.

"If you ordered her to stay, would she?"

"What?"

"She shouldn't go—has no business going. It's dangerous. She's at a delicate time—there could be infection, and she'll be in unbelievable pain. But she won't listen to me. I've learned that much of her resolve and will in the birthing bed. Do you think she would listen to you?"

I shook my head. Never in my life had I been so certain. Nothing would keep her from Leo. She would square off against the devil himself if need be, and not even a directive from Christ could stop her.

"Help her stay clean. I know you won't stop the carriage, but when you arrive have her walk around a bit. There's pillows and blankets to cushion things for her. As well as items to help her clean up. We've discussed how to use them already. I'll follow at first light."

"All right."

"Lord Champaign?"

"Yes?"

"Tear him apart," she ordered.

"I beg your pardon?"

"You heard me. I've never—this is the worst thing that's ever—" Her words weren't behaving. But I knew what she meant. What Parker had done... It was a level of cruelty that was unfathomable.

Charlotte shivered in my arms. I ripped my coat off and tugged it around her shoulders before tucking her against me once again. The boys were almost finished with the carriage.

Sensing my wariness, Charlotte dipped her hand into the coat pocket, pulled free a peppermint, and held it out to me, her palm trapped between our bodies. Gratefully, I took it.

And then I watched, heart in my throat, as the stable hands hung the lit lanterns in the carriage. The first one rocked on its hook, swaying back and forth innocently. It was almost polite as it threw fractals of light along the dark velvet seat. One beam shone through the window, directly into my eye, taunting me, challenging me. I pulled in a deep breath.

Jack set about placing the other lantern on the opposite side, that one no less worrisome for its steadiness.

Without a word, the stable hand, still eyeing me warily, opened the door beside us.

Charlotte pulled away and gingerly climbed into the conveyance. I was left alone in the pitched, charred night.

With valor I pulled from an unknown reserve, I strode to the carriage. I couldn't give myself time to pause, time to think. Instead, I ducked and stepped inside, my breath trapped in my throat, my eyes caught on the wavering, deadly flame.

Chapter Forty-One
CARRIAGE TO LONDON - NOVEMBER 8, 1816

CHARLOTTE

HE WAS TORTURING himself for my sake. I knew that. But I couldn't bring myself to be brave about this. Selflessness was beyond me.

The scent of peppermint filled the carriage, and I caught the crunch of another. He busied himself settling the blankets before dragging me over to them. To him.

His arm, warm and steady, pulled me against his stiff shoulder, his fingers attempting to rub a soothing pattern along my shoulder and upper arm. It was an odd juxtaposition, the conscious comfort and the unconscious terror. Whether the latter was due to our missing son or the flames flickering beside us... I doubt he knew himself.

"Lee..." His name seemed to be the only word I was capable of now.

"Can you try to rest?"

My curls caught on the beginnings of his beard when I shook my head.

"All right. That's all right. When we get to town, we'll—"

The carriage jolted forward, and both lanterns swung precariously on their hooks. And Lee... he broke off with a choked gasp.

In my entire life, I'd never once considered the perilous nature of the lanterns. I pulled free from him, flipped open the nearest one, and blew it out. I had no need of sight for this trip. What good would it possibly do?

Lee followed suit with the other and a relieved sigh, and when I settled against him again, he was steadier, more solid.

"Right," he breathed out in a rush. "We'll go straight to Wayland's... Or Hudson's? I suppose it will depend on the time."

"Why there?"

His fingers tangled in the loose ends of my half-braided hair. "The gaming hell is the only place to find that high a sum quickly. I doubt Parker will accept a bank note. Ainsley knows I'm good for it. But he might be at the bakery that time of morning."

"You're—we're—going to pay him?"

"If it comes to that. Though I'd rather not have him learn that he can simply kidnap our son whenever his funds run dry. After that, we'll stop by Cee's."

"Why?"

"More hands. It's possible there are more involved—beyond Parker and Mrs. Hyde. But Celine is out for blood, Parker's specifically."

"Is there time for all of that?"

"We'll make time. Send Jack to Cee's if need be."

"Jack?"

He merely pointed out the back window. The boy must have come with us.

Our vague plan, if it could even be termed as such, came together over the miles. We found a numb kind of calm, trapped in the carriage as the night sky rushed by outside. My body ached more with each passing mile. There was little strength left in my abdomen after my ordeal.

It lasted right until the moment the carriage wheel dipped into a rut, hurling us to the side violently.

Lee's reaction was sharp and swift. Beneath and around me, he became stone. Immovable, breathless, inhuman marble.

"Lee?"

My eyes hadn't entirely adjusted to the inky black inside the carriage. I couldn't see the look of terror I was certain consumed his face.

"Lee?" I repeated. Catching his textured cheek with my hand, I tried to pull him down to face me. It was a fruitless endeavor. "Lee, please. I need you. Leo needs you."

Underneath the pulse of my wrist, I felt it. The slightest dip in his jaw as he swallowed. My own heart restarted in a pounding rush.

"Char—"

"It's me. I'm here."

"Sor—"

"Don't apologize. Just come back to me. Stay with me."

His nod was shaky and tentative, whiskers dragging along my palm still caressing his cheek. "Peppermint?"

With trembling hands, I dug into his pocket and grabbed two. I unwrapped one and handed it to him, then the second went to me.

The bright scent filled the muggy, dark carriage, wrapping us both in its comforting blanket. He shuddered, his forehead dropping to my shoulder.

"I..." he trailed off, too exhausted or overwhelmed to finish the thought. My fingers tangled in his overgrown hair, my thumb dragging along the back of his neck.

"Another?" I asked, already fishing it out of his pocket and pressing it into his hand with my free one. He didn't move from his place on my shoulder as he crushed it in between his teeth.

"I warned you I would be a terrible husband."

"You're the best husband."

Lee scoffed and turning his head to the side to rest his temple before inhaling, quick and rough through his nose. Though he didn't reply to my comment, I could *feel* the disagreement lapping over him.

"You are," I insisted.

A massive palm dragged along my back, soothing the ache his absence caused as he pulled away.

And there, in the moonless night of carriage, he shattered me. "I swear to you, I will get Leo back to you. But... You do not have to come back to the manor. You and Leo. I will not hold you to our agreement. I will get him back to you, and the two of you can start building your life in town."

"What?" The word ripped from me, breathless and pained. "I don't..." He was so solemn, sincere, certain, and I didn't—couldn't... "I do not understand. You want me to—"

"Stay in town. I think it's for the best. Once we have him back."

"But I..." *want to stay with you. Don't want to leave. Love you.*

"You'll be safe, the two of you. And no matter what anyone says, Leo is legitimate in the eyes of the law. You won't need me anymore."

Why was he doing this? How could he do this to me? Here? Now?

Before I could give voice to the questions, before I could slap him, before I could reach behind him, yank open the door, and shove him out, the carriage shuddered to a halt.

Lee blanched at the motion before recognizing we were at one of our destinations. He peered out of the curtain, leaving it open before turning back to me.

"Wait here. I'll be back shortly."

As if I could do anything else. Physically, I wanted to die. Emotionally, I wanted to die. And practically, I knew I had bled through my dress quite thoroughly.

Lee grabbed his coat and donned it after he stepped out of the carriage and strode into the gaming hell.

The anguish I felt at the realization that Leo was missing returned full force, as if Lee's presence had been the only thing keeping the wrenching of my heart at bay. The distraction of his episode had dulled the edge of the terror but his exit had pulled it back. Now the knifeblade stabbed into my chest with every breath, with every heartbeat.

I wasn't entirely lost to sense. I knew Lee's offer was likely due more to his episode than any particular desire to be rid of me. Or Leo. But... I could not think on that now. There wasn't time, and I hadn't the energy.

I needed to conserve both for my babe. Once Leo was back in my arms, safe, then I could decide what to do with my lout of a husband. At the moment, abandoning him to his solitary sad existence seemed the least punishment he deserved for choosing *now* to have his crisis of conscience.

The carriage shifted, the door creaked open, and Lee wearily eyed the seat he'd vacated with his absurd, slappable face.

"Good news. Augie had more than enough on hand," he said, patting his bulging pocket distractedly. Comprehension dawned slowly, slipping through thick, soupy exhaustion and worry to the forefront. My husband, right this moment, had hundreds of pounds casually tucked in his pocket. That was...

"This is a terrible idea."

"Yes," he replied with a decisive nod. "Unfortunately, I've nothing better."

Neither did I.

He climbed across from me and with a jolt, the carriage set

off again. Lee's hand found a peppermint in his other pocket, the one not packed to bursting with life-changing sums of money. He tipped his head back and tossed the mint in his mouth, gnashing on it with gritted teeth.

His eyes slipped shut. For a moment, I worried over another attack, but his breathing remained steady. Too steady. He was concentrating, slipping his palms across the velvet covered seats at his sides. His concentration entirely spent, he was focused on fighting back another episode.

Lee continued in this fashion until we pulled up outside a stylish white house on Grosvenor's Street.

"Right. Cee's. Do you want to come in?" he asked, distractedly reaching for the handle.

"I cannot," I replied tersely.

Lee froze, his hand hovering just above the door. "Why?"

"I'm bleeding."

His eyes widened, and he paled even further.

"What?"

"It is normal," I bit out.

"But..."

"It is normal. I gave birth this morning."

"I don't..."

I rolled my eyes and thrust out my hand. "Your coat. Please."

He shucked it unquestioningly, and as I stepped from the carriage with a handful of supplies, he wrapped it around my shoulders.

We climbed the few steps to the door, Lee hovering behind me the entire way. Rather than step to the side, he merely curved his arm around my shoulder and pounded on the door, rattling it in the frame.

His knock was too loud and too long to be anything but an emergency and we waited only a minute before a soot-covered scullery maid answered the door. The sun hadn't yet hinted at its arrival, and presumably she was the only one awake.

She blinked blearily at me for a moment before her head tipped back. And back. And back, to find Lee. Her only reaction to his scars was a wince.

"I need your employers. It's urgent—life and death," Lee rushed to explain. The fury in his tone sent her dipping into a tremulous curtsy before scurrying down the back hall. Not up the stairs directly in front of the open door.

Lee sighed and urged me inside even though we'd received no invitation.

"Gone for the butler, almost certainly. I've half a mind to drag the two of them out myself," he muttered.

One minute, two, three passed with no sign of the maid, the butler, or the family. Lee turned to me and rubbed his hands along my arms. "How are you feeling?"

Before I could reply, we were interrupted by returning footsteps. Lee's gaze shot from me to the rumpled butler stumbling down the hall. He was hastily half dressed.

"Who the devil are you? What is the meaning of this? Barging in here, and in the middle of the night!"

Lee looked around him at the silent maid. "I said your employers."

The butter interrupted. "You'll speak to me, and me alone."

A curse escaped my husband and he dragged a hand through his ragged hair. "It's about Rycliffe's murderer."

That stopped the butler in his tracks, still halfway down the hall. He considered my husband thoughtfully, his gaze catching on his scars. I couldn't contain my eye roll.

"How am I to believe that?" the man protested, slower and with infinitely less fury, as he came to stand before us.

In that moment it all transferred to me. Fury. Rage. The

fires of hell sang through my blood. Before I made the choice to do it, I had yanked him down to me by the collar.

"Get me your employers in the next minute or so help me, you will be wearing your bawbels as a hat. I have done the impossible today, and I can do something as simple as that with my bare hands and not even flinch."

He froze midflinch before wide, horrified eyes tipped behind me, presumably to where Lee stood.

"Do not look at him! He is not the frightening one here. I am. Get me your employers. Now. Am I understood?"

"What is the meaning of this?" The shrill voice came from above.

Celine. Finally.

∾

LEE

My wife had clearly lost her tenuous grip on her temper, possibly her sanity as well. And, of course, that was the precise moment Cee saw fit to join us. Entirely abandoning her French accent in her upset.

Charlotte released her grasp on the sniveling little worm of a butler, and he scurried to the side.

Now I was left to explain why my wife was accosting the household staff.

I began, "Cee—"

"Do you want my help finding Parker?" Charlotte cut in, not bothering to face me.

That had Celine rushing down the stairs, two at a time.

Will followed—they were both still in dressing gowns—and caught her arm with a tut before she could accost my wife in the same way Charlotte had the butler.

"What do you know?" Celine ordered more than asked. "And why are you no longer with child?"

"He has my son." Charlotte's words were low, solemn, snapped through gritted teeth and filled with more hatred than should be possible to fit inside her.

The butler took that opportunity to creep back down the hall, facing my wife in his retreat, with the scullery maid in tow.

"What?" Celine demanded.

"He took my son. And I have an address. Are you coming?"

"Yes," Celine replied. "Now?"

"Wait just a minute, love," Will interjected, grabbing his wife's elbow.

Both women spun toward him, feral. He tripped back a step, arms raised warily.

I started to explain and slide closer to my wife, but Charlotte rounded on me. "Are you helping?"

"Wh-what?"

"Help or get out. I do not have time for you to send me away for my own protection or whatever ridiculous scheme you've concocted where I'm left here while you swan off and get yourself or Leo killed."

"Charlotte—"

"Tell me I am lying. Tell me that wasn't what the speech in the carriage was. That whore's pipe has my son, the babe I birthed this morning. I do not have the time or energy to deal with whatever noble, self-sacrificing, asinine shite you've worked up. If your plan involves me sitting here—*waiting*—I have no interest in it. And you can leave."

That was... precisely what my plan involved. I was even willing to send Celine in Charlotte's place if need be. At least she hadn't given birth some three and twenty hours ago. But I wasn't dim enough to tell her that at the moment, not after what she'd threatened the butler with.

This woman was not my wife, but also... she was. *This* was the woman I'd met at the masquerade, the one who was willing to seduce a perfect stranger to secure a future for herself and her child.

"All right, no plan. Can I convince you to sit down before you make me wear my ballocks as a hat?"

Eventually, Will managed to coax everyone to a seated position in the drawing room, easing the tiniest bit of the tension.

Time ticked slowly by as the women argued over the scraps that would be left of Mr. Wesley Parker when they were finished with him. Will and I eyed each other warily through discussions of pistols, swords, and even an umbrella.

"From a legal perspective, I really should not be here for this," he muttered under his breath toward me. "Kit is going to have a devil of a time keeping us all from the hangman."

I wasn't overly thrilled with the idea of leaving our fate to Will's overworked partner—a solicitor who did not even specialize in criminal matters.

But... I was also fond of all my parts. "You're welcome to interject," I whispered back.

He sighed. "This would be much easier if I drank as a rule." Turning toward our wives, he spoke up. "Ladies, would you be amenable to a plan that doesn't involve execution as a likely consequence?"

Their synchronized nods were slower and less enthusiastic than I would have liked.

"Right. If I might propose an alternative to flaying the man."

Again, a reluctant, almost petulant, nod from each of the ladies.

"Now my plan does, in fact, hinge on Lady Champaign

maintaining her calm and not murdering the man in cold blood. Is that feasible?"

"What about me?" Celine interrupted.

"You, I know, will murder the man in cold blood. You'd only need a piece of string and some shoe polish."

"Will..."

"Fine. Go grab your maid's outfit. I'm certain you've still got that thrown somewhere in your drawers."

I could feel the puzzled expression twisting along my face, pulling against the scars. Nonetheless, Celine seemed to understand the meaning of his bizarre request and shot up the stairs.

"The dagger, too, love," he called after her.

"You say that as though I don't already have it on my person," she yelled back. And wasn't that terrifying.

Will only raised a brow and turned back to use. "Well then... How comfortable are you with acting, Lady Champaign?"

"Charlotte, please. We're plotting a murder. It seems only fitting."

"Charlotte," Will replied

"I'm adequate," she answered in a strained tone. I tried to remember back to when she was trying to seduce me.

"She's better than adequate," I protested.

"Good. Here's what we'll do..."

Chapter Forty-Two

EARLHAM STREET, LONDON - NOVEMBER 8, 1816

CHARLOTTE

Celine had sacrificed her lowest-cut gown for this fraught endeavor. It was too tight and uncomfortable against my aching breasts. The lady herself was draped elegantly draped across the opposite carriage seat in an ill-fitting maid's uniform looking every bit as lovely as she did in a ballroom. Even though I was cleaned up, I still *felt* wretched. Sore, disgusting, and nauseated.

Celine's sickly sweet perfume wasn't helping at all, and I missed Lee's bright, comforting peppermint essence.

My heart hammered so hard it was a wonder it stayed contained.

"You look unwell. This won't work if you cast up your accounts on his shoes."

"I'm fine."

"You're certain neither of them know your maid?"

"Yes. Imogen has been visiting family since before Mrs. Hyde arrived, and Wesley never concerned himself with such things."

"Good. You must relax though. You're in love. Remember? You must put him at ease, flirt with him, get him to talk." If she reminded me one more time...

"My maid is much quieter. In case you were looking for performance notes."

The carriage trundled out of Celine's fashionable neighborhood and toward the warehouse district.

"That was funny, actually. Have you always been funny?" she asked.

"It's usually at your expense," I replied, distracted by the beginnings of the early morning bustle. "We should have taken a hack."

"Where would you have arranged a hack in time in Surrey?"

"We stand out." The hour was early, but seamstresses, chimney sweeps, fishmongers, and everyone in between who was about turned to watch the fine carriage roll along on their way to work.

"Charlotte, it will be fine. The worst that can happen is the bloodshed we've already discussed."

"Yes, shots fired around my newborn babe. What could I possibly have to worry about?"

"I apologize. I'm being insensitive. It's possible you may be the only person who hates him more than I do."

"I apologize as well. I did not know about Lord Rycliffe, I swear."

"No, I didn't think you did," she said, entirely sincere.

The carriage turned onto Earlham Street and eased to a stop. Celine drew up her cloak, covering the golden curls her cap couldn't hide.

After a deep breath, I made to leave the carriage, but Celine's cool hand found my wrist. "We'll get him back. I promise."

I nodded, feigning more confidence than I felt as I clambered out into the light. Celine stepped out after me, far too elegant for a maid. I was about to hiss a correction when a hack pulled aside down the street, and an impossibly tall figure stepped out.

Lee.

Three men followed him, the shorter, wiry form of Will, a similarly short, broader man with dark curls, and another man with a medium build and graying hair. I knew the other two only by their roles in this.

Will and the second unknown man stepped forward, crossed the street, and disappeared down an alley with a nod. That gentleman was the constable then.

Lee and the final man waited by the carriage. His eyes burned into mine, comforting even from such a distance. Much too far to make out the blue-gray color, but I took strength from its memory.

"Kit," Celine explained, identifying the final gentleman as she tugged me toward the warehouse doors. Pulling me from Lee.

The brick building was long shuttered, windows broken and re-boarded several times over. The roof had seen better days, and holes were visible even from outside.

Apparently, Wesley's family had been in textiles—procurement and shipping, if the sign was any indication. How little I had known the man I fancied myself in love with. He clearly hadn't taken over his father's efforts.

With a deep breath and a roll of my shoulders, I slid the door open and stepped inside.

The sweetest sound in the entire universe kissed my ears. Leo's cries.

Celine pinched me low on the back of my arm before I could rush toward the side room where the sound came from.

Massive rolls of silks, wools, and cottons in every color of the rainbow—ruined by time, elements, and insects—lined one side of the room. They were stacked nearly to the ceiling and were surely blocking a back entrance. My stomach gave a jolt.

It was fine. Will and the constable could listen and come in the front entrance just as well. It was fine. Perhaps there was a third door I couldn't see.

From the side room, I heard the hateful murmurs of Mrs. Hyde cooing at my Leo. Trying and failing to soothe him.

A few more rooms lined the other side of the space, farther from my son.

The entire place smelled of mildew and excrement. The only source of natural light came through several holes in the roof. The early morning sun fought its way through years of neglect and grime to wash, patchily, over the concrete floor.

And then an icy, smooth voice reached me from the far corner. "You made it."

I whirled around with a breathless grin. It felt false and misshapen, but I was fairly certain I'd arranged my face correctly. "Wesley!" I cried, rushing toward him as quickly as I could given my situation.

He was disheveled, sooty, and worn in a way I'd never seen him. His usually close-cropped dark hair was overgrown and scraggly. The beard lining his jaw was unfamiliar and unflattering. And his eyes... There was something wild in those eyes I'd once admired. It was terrifying.

Cool, reptilian hands found mine. "Did you get it?"

"I did," I replied. "And you, are you well? I cannot believe you've been living like this."

From the other room, another frustrated cry escaped my son. The only reaction I permitted was a harsh grinding of my teeth.

"The money, Charlotte?"

I reached a trembling hand toward my reticule, shaking it

at him. This was wrong. I was supposed to delay until he confessed.

Wesley grabbed for it, trying to snatch it off my wrist.

"Wesley! I brought it. Don't be rude."

His desperation was growing far too quickly. I opened the bag and slipped my hand inside. The massive roll of bills caught on the closure and I fumbled, tugging it free. He ripped it from my hand, unfurling the cash.

"Good, you didn't bring a bank note."

"I'm not a fool, Wesley," I snapped.

Of course, he thought I was a fool, a mindless whore he could use, abandon, and then fleece when funds ran dry. Informing him that *his* plan was blatantly obvious to all but the most simpleminded twits who were desperately in love with him was not part of *my* plan.

His hand found my waist and pulled me closer. Like the rest of the place, he smelled of mildew and decay and I had to force down a heave.

"I'm sorry, my love. It has just been a trying time. Trapped here, and without the comfort of your love. I'm eager to start our new life together."

Not for the first time since I read his note, I wondered if he actually meant to take Leo and me with him. He may have planned to run with the money. But... he was a man who enjoyed intimate relations and, once upon a time, I was a willing participant.

"As am I. I've waited so long. When do we leave?"

"The next ship departs the docks at noon."

Leo gave another irate cry. "Can't you stop him crying?" Wesley shouted at, presumably, Mrs. Hyde.

Her identity was confirmed a second later when she came out from the side room, my son in her arms. Tears pricked at my eyes and my throat knotted. He was the sweetest sight I'd ever beheld. It took absolutely everything in me not to rush for him, snatch him into my arms, hold him forever, and never, ever let go.

"He won't hush," she complained.

"May I?" I asked, breathless. This wasn't part of the plan, but God himself couldn't have stopped me from reaching for my son.

Wesley's smooth voice had me aborting my efforts. "I didn't realize you were so attached." There was no room for misinterpretation in that frozen tone. Skepticism. He was catching on.

Swallowing the desperation for my wailing son, I turned back to Wesley.

"I just—"

"It's the crying m'lord." I was floundering for an explanation when Celine cut in. "It's grating for mothers especially."

"And who are you?" he asked, eyeing her in a way that was simultaneously suspicious and appreciative. How had I found this charming?

"Imogen, m'lord. I couldn't let my lady travel alone. An' I din' want to stay when that beast found out his wife and son was gone." Celine was overdoing it quite a lot. And rather poorly. But I was suddenly grateful that he seemed distracted by her figure, disguised in ill-fitting maid's garb as it was.

"It is true, dearest. The cries—they are just upsetting. And he might stop if he recognizes me," I said, perhaps a touch too enthusiastically. The sound of my voice seemed to have Leo quieting a little. *Just a few more minutes, my sweet boy.*

Wesley glanced over at me, distracted, before returning to Celine. "Right, well, it's a good thing we're to leave him here then."

"We are?"

"Of course we are."

"But..." Why was I protesting?

"A ship is no place for a babe, Charlotte. And besides, your husband might come for the child. He won't come for you."

Wrong. I may be furious with my husband, but Lee would burn the world down for either of us. He'd risk even more scars without hesitation. I knew it in my bones.

"Of course, you're right," I agreed.

He hummed in acknowledgment. "Is your maid coming with us?"

Celine smiled flirtatiously at him. In the past, I would have thought it true, but now, having seen her with Will, I knew the falsehood in the set of her jaw and the fire of her eyes.

She was envisioning this man's blood flooding the floor. And relishing in it.

"If you wish it, m'lord," she replied with an eyelash flutter, her tone coy. "Anything to get away from that beast. He's nothing like you. You're such a handsome man. I know the rumors aren't true. You couldn't possibly—"

"What rumors?"

"I heard rumors from that vile Juliet Dalton—Wayland. She said they're saying you killed a man?" I asked, trying to keep my tone fretting and not accusatory. "But that's absurd. You wouldn't hurt a fly."

On cue, the door slammed open with a heaving clash. The scent of peppermint cut through the filth. Framed there, silhouetted in the morning light, was a great, hulking beast of a man. Far more than six feet tall, broad and strong and *perfect*.

Lee.

The pitiful light from the ceiling caught the edges of his scars menacingly. He wore nothing but his shirtsleeves and trousers, the shirt hanging pitifully off him to display more of the ragged flesh.

Wesley gasped pitifully and a terrified cry escaped Mrs. Hyde.

Leo gave a more sedate coo, unafraid.

"Parker," Lee said simply. His voice was low and menacing, but he didn't shout. Instead, he was quieter than usual. If I hadn't heard the same tone grumbled in my ear every morning, it might have been frightening.

"Champaign," Wesley replied, a slight quake in the word.

"I believe you have a few things that belong to me." Lee stalked forward a step with every word, and Wesley stepped back, a dance that ended abruptly when Wesley's backside hit a table. Lee crowded against him, towered over him.

"They're mine," Wesley protested pitifully, more stubborn and desperate than intelligent.

"What's yours?" Lee asked, false nonchalance in his voice.

"That's my son," Wesley argued again, finding a pathetic well of courage somewhere.

"No. He bears *my* name. He was born of *my* wife."

"Everyone knows it's not yours. Your name doesn't make it so."

"I think you will find it does. And he, not *it*." Somehow, Lee found a reserve of height, straightening even farther over Wesley. The man's head was hinged as far as it would go, and he could still only see chin.

"You know I have to kill you for this." Lee added simply, as though it was a mere chore.

"You can't. You'll lose." Wesley said in a half whimper.

"I can. Besides, the women think you couldn't hurt a fly. Do you suppose I could squash you like one?"

I had to bite back a delirious laugh. If my husband was any less physically imposing, if the situation was any less terrifying, his threats would be amusing.

"I've killed a man before. I'll do it again," Wesley threatened, and relief washed over me.

Finally.

"Oh, really? *You've* killed a man?"

"I have, and for less than what you're doing right now."

"Do tell," Lee said with dark interest.

"Rycliffe. He cheated me so I had him killed. I tricked him into meeting me. And then I had him stabbed," Wesley bit out.. Pitiful even in this.

But there it was. The final truth. I could only hope the constable had heard. An astonished cry left Mrs. Hyde.

Lee continued, undeterred. "Oh, you *had* him killed? Couldn't even manage that yourself. Pathetic."

"Just because I'm not fool enough to kill a peer in cold blood, doesn't mean it wasn't my doing. In a fair fight there's a chance to lose, so why would I fight fair?"

"It's the gentlemanly thing to do," Lee replied.

"I'm not a gentleman," Wesley bit out, finding his anger. "I am no gentleman. *This* is my estate," he gestured toward the rain- and piss-soaked room. "I'm not a gentleman, and no one will ever let me forget it. So, why, pray tell, should I abide by gentlemanly rules?"

"So you don't end up right here," a smooth voice replied.

Celine. I was so distracted by the argument, I hadn't noticed her slipping around Lee to get closer to Wesley. I caught a flash of silver in her hand.

She pointed a dagger at Wesley's lower back. He flinched when she pressed it harder against his flank.

"I'm not like you," she added. "I finish my own battles."

"Who are you?" he asked.

"You don't recognize me?" She nodded to Lee. He grabbed Wesley by the shoulders and spun him to face her. Celine tossed the cloak off her head and pulled the cap free. It was the kind of dramatic gesture I never could have managed even with years of practice. "How about now?"

"La-Lady R-Rycliffe," he stammered.

"You killed my husband."

"No—No, I... My brother—"

"Oh, but you just said—for everyone to hear—that

ordering the kill was the same as performing it yourself." Those words were whispered, hissed with so much venom it was a wonder they alone didn't kill him.

"I—"

"Hand the child to his mother," she ordered.

Everyone's gaze except Celine's found Mrs. Hyde and Leo. Reluctantly, the nurse stepped toward me and passed him into my arms.

The rest of the world dimmed, faded away, and it was the two of us. He reached a tiny hand out of the blanket, and I gave him a finger to grasp. My son was unharmed. Still soft and ruddy cheeked and sweet smelling, in spite of the filth. My tears dropped to catch on his dimples.

In my periphery, I caught distant curses and a scuffle.

Then a massive, warm hand found my lower back, so, so familiar and just as comforting. Lee's other hand cradled his son's head beneath mine. He pressed in close, shielding us from whatever fray was occurring behind him. Gently he guided me back and out of the way.

Lee caged us against the wall, his arms on either side of me. I peered around his shoulder when another curse rose.

Will had Wesley restrained by the arms, holding him back. Wesley was now bleeding from a wound on his lower side. He presumably owed the injury to Celine's bloody dagger—*when had that happened?*

The other solicitor had Mrs. Hyde in a half-hearted grasp. She wailed and flailed about, but her efforts were mostly performative.

The constable merely stood between them all. His befuddled gaze flicked between the parties with a lost, haunted expression.

When it became apparent that the man hadn't the foggiest idea what to do, Will sighed in frustration. "The shackles, sir."

"Oh, right. I'll be back in a tick."

Will's head hinged back in frustration until Wesley gave a little wriggle and he tightened his hold.

"What do you want? I'll give you anything," Wesley pleaded.

"You do not possess a single thing that I want," Celine answered, exhaustion and hatred warring for prominence.

"Charlotte, dearest, please. You don't want the father of your son hanged," he called to me.

I slipped smoothly under Lee's arm. He turned to follow my movements. Silently, I passed Leo over to my husband before approaching Wesley.

Now that Leo was safe, the pains of birth and travel, dimmed by fear and anger, were welling inside. It took several painful steps to reach my former lover.

Once the handsomest man I'd ever seen, his hair was almost black with grime and sweat, and he smelled of filth and copper. His clothes were torn, dirty, and blood-soaked. He was... disgusting.

"Charlotte, tell them. Tell them I need a doctor," he whined.

"You're right—"

"Thank God. Tell them to let me—"

Unwilling to listen to more of his pathetic pleadings, I interrupted him. "You're right. I do not wish to see the father of my son hanged. So it is a very, very good thing that he is not bound for the noose. In fact, he's right over there—with his son."

Wesley turned, his eyes bleary with desperation and pain, toward where my husband held Leo, safe in his arms.

"You're more foolish than I thought if you think anyone is going to accept *that* hideous beast. Or that the *ton* will see the child as anything other than a bastard. The *ton* never forgets. Everyone knows what you are."

"And what is that, Wesley?" I was goading him now,

pressing him into saying something that would give me leave to hit him, just once.

And he obliged. "A filthy whore."

It wasn't precisely ladylike what I did next, but it was entirely satisfying. With every ounce of strength I possessed, I thrust my knee into his groin. Will, seeming to anticipate my maneuver, pushed Wesley out, shoving him into the contact.

Wesley doubled over, held upright only by Will's grip on his arms. His whimpering cries hit an unfathomable pitch, and he retched pathetically. Good, he deserved to experience that as well, Lord knew I had.

"Well done," Celine said from behind me.

I spun toward her. "You as well," I said, gesturing toward the knife.

She nodded, wearily. "Not as cathartic as I thought it would be. But you three should go. We can manage from here. It's not safe for you or the babe here."

She certainly wasn't wrong about that.

"Charlotte? Let's go home," Lee added from my side. We made for the door and stepped aside to allow the constable to enter with two sets of shackles.

At last, Lee guided me out into the blinding sun with one hand on my back and the other cradling our son.

Chapter Forty-Three
84 BROOK STREET, LONDON - NOVEMBER 8, 1816

LEE

It wasn't until the carriage halted outside the house that I realized I had managed the entire trip without a hint of panic. Before I had a moment to revel in my accomplishment, nearly every servant in our employ spilled out onto the pavement.

A half-asleep Charlotte, still clinging to Leo, and I were greeted by a cacophony of relieved exclamations. Brigs, Crawford, and Jack—delight poured from them all.

Finally, Mrs. Griffith's sharp tone cut through the noise, directing everyone inside to see to their duties so she could take care of Charlotte.

Charlotte slumped against me in exhausted, pained silence while we mounted the steps into the house. Inside, with the door shut against the harsh world, her head found my shoulder.

"Come now. We'll get you cleaned up and do a quick exam on you and the babe. Have you tried to feed him?" Mrs. Griffith questioned.

"No—I didn't even think..." Charlotte said.

"Hush now, that's all right. We'll clean you both up and you can try. I take it Mrs. Hyde was there?"

"She was," I answered.

"At least he's probably been fed then."

"It was filthy though and smelled of mold," I explained while I guided Charlotte to the stairs.

We reached the first step and my wife stared up with trepidation.

Right. "You have him?"

She nodded, still eyeing the steps. Without a word, I leaned over and slid my arms under her knees and shoulders. Leo gave an irritated snuffle and nuzzled back into her while I climbed the steps.

"Tired," my wife murmured into my chest.

"I know. We're almost done."

Mrs. Griffith followed us into my chambers where a bath awaited. I set my wife on her feet before the tub, my hands hovering at her waist to ensure she was steady.

"I'll examine the little lord while you get cleaned up, Lady Champaign," the midwife directed.

Charlotte released a distressed cry when the woman reached for Leo.

"May I hold him while you examine him?" I asked.

Mrs. Griffith sighed before agreeing.

"Is that all right?" I questioned Charlotte. She nodded wearily and handed Leo to me with only a slight hesitation.

I helped clean the boy with a damp linen while the midwife examined him.

She pronounced him well enough. His lungs showed no sign of illness now, but she worried he might develop it in the days to come. All things considered, it was the best outcome we could have hoped for given the circumstances.

As soon as Charlotte left the water, she reached for Leo, refusing to let him go while she was examined. In short enough order, my wife was also pronounced as well as could be expected with warnings of possible infection in the days to come.

Finally, Charlotte was settled into bed, Leo at her breast, and Mrs. Griffith left us. Both mother and child fell asleep in mere minutes.

Sleep, however, was far from my grasp, and I spent the next hours guarding them both.

~

I MUST HAVE DRIFTED off because I woke to some truly impressive cursing, both in creativity and duration, from my beautiful wife.

The problem was immediately apparent when I opened my eyes and found her crouched over the end of the bed, Leo upon it. Apparently, ladies' education did not cover the changing of infants. I barely managed to catch the laugh before it escaped, and I received a rather scathing look for my effort.

"Don't you dare laugh at me, Leopold Bennet."

"Which one?" I asked.

"Both of you. I'm not certain he knows how yet, but I can tell that he'd like to. And I *know* you would."

"May I ask why you haven't called for a servant?"

She turned away from Leo and met my gaze with a glare that informed me, more thoroughly than words ever could, that I was, in fact, an infuriating lout. Likely that was a nicer version of what she wished to say to me.

"I understand. But we may need someone to take him eventually, though, for some things."

"Not yet," she replied primly, returning to fuss with the clout with gritted teeth.

"I think that bit—"

"If you attempt to correct me, I will not be held responsible for what I do to you." Well, this adventure had been nothing short of eye opening. I was beginning to understand why Celine had called my wife a shrew. An astonishing, incredible, impossibly brave shrew though.

"I think you're doing a remarkable job and it is perfection itself."

"Thank you," she replied with an eye roll that had me biting back an indulgent smile.

She managed to get the clout and pilch wrapped in some sort of vague semblance of the way Mrs. Griffith had done it a few hours ago, before she tied it in a messy knot I was sure would have to be cut.

Charlotte shuffled back to the head of the bed, Leo wrapped in her arms. After she'd settled back in, her head dropped onto my shoulder with a sigh.

"I am still cross with you," she murmured.

"Any particular reason?"

"We are not staying here, not without you."

The temptation was there to feign ignorance, to allow her an escape when she felt well and remembered my poor showing in the carriage. But I was a weak man, and the future she seemed to be presenting... It was more than I could have dreamed.

She continued, "I know that is not what we agreed on. But... I didn't think I'd fall in love with you."

My heart gave a desperate thump before ceasing entirely. "You... you love me?" I asked on an exhale, more breath than sentence.

Carefully, so as not to wake our son, she turned to meet my gaze. "Yes, in spite of all your best efforts, I am, in fact, in love with you." There was no lie in her whiskey eyes, just affection such as I had never known.

My lids slipped shut for a moment. I was overwhelmed.

The sight of her, earnest and brave, threatened to stop my heart. When they opened again, my lashes were damp.

Matching tears fell across Charlotte's cheeks. My hands found her jaw, my thumbs brushing away the drops before they fell on our son. "I love you too—*both* of you. More than anything. I've spent weeks, months, trying to determine how I was to live without you when you left."

"Fortunately, you shall not have to. Because I am entirely uninterested in a future without you." Charlotte shifted our babe and cupped my cheek with one hand. Her eyes were soft, forgiving, and so loving.

My chest filled with so much devotion for this woman and this babe that it physically ached.

"It is fortunate," I agreed and pressed a kiss on her forehead. Her free hand caught my shirt and tugged me down to her lips, careful not to crush Leo.

And I kissed her. I kissed her so gently, so softly, that my heart seemingly forgot to beat—too full and distracted by joy and peace and love.

Chapter Forty-Four
84 BROOK STREET, LONDON - DECEMBER 18, 1816

CHARLOTTE

"That is tight enough, Imogen. Thank you."

She nodded and looped off the corset strings before gathering the gown for tonight's soiree.

Leo was comfortably settled in his bassinet under the window, chewing on his own foot. He'd discovered them a week or so ago and they were his favorite things.

Imogen helped me into the gown, a new one for the occasion. It was a delicate, spun gold with a split skirt that revealed a white silk underskirt, embroidered with matching gold stars along the hem and lines of the skirt. The waist was fuller than fashionable but nothing compared to my masquerade dress.

After Imogen fretted for a few minutes, adjusting the skirts, it laid properly.

"I won't need you tonight," I said when she stepped away.

She gave me a knowing smirk and a wink.

Leo made an irritated sound, and I went to him, kneeling beside the bassinet. It seemed he had gummed a bit too hard on his toe but hadn't figured out how to let the appendage go.

"Now you know how it feels," I told him, pulling his foot free.

My efforts lasted all of a few seconds before he merely switched to the other.

"Serves you right then."

"What's that?" A masculine voice called from the doorway, the scent of peppermint enveloping me.

"Chewing on his feet again."

"Tasty," Lee replied with a grin in his voice. "You know, I know he's the most perfect child in the entire world, but—"

"Hush," I scolded. When I straightened and turned around, my husband was fussing in the mirror with whatever ridiculous knot Brigsby had used for his cravat. He tossed a distracted glance my way and returned instantly to the mirror before his hand froze on the fabric. Slowly, he turned and dropped his hand from his neck to my waist, eyes raking my form.

"Charlotte..."

"Good?"

He chuckled, his lips finding my bare shoulder. "We could always... not attend. Begin the more enjoyable parts of the evening early." His finger traced the neckline of my gown with interest.

That was more tempting than I was willing to admit. But I rather thought he ought to attend tonight. And besides, the anticipation that had been humming for weeks, growing steadily since Mrs. Griffith finished her examination that morning with a wink—was its own kind of enjoyment.

This massive, powerful, intimidating man was all but on his knees before me. Metaphorically, of course. Though I had little doubt it would be literally as well before night's end.

"Just an hour or two?" I asked, my eyes wide and hopeful.

"Fine," he muttered into my collarbone. Pulling away, he

added, "Except in the very likely event that a lady requires smelling salts at the sight of me."

My eye roll had him biting back a grin. "I highly doubt that."

"And you're sure it's not a masquerade?"

"No masks allowed," I added with false contrition.

"One hour? Please?"

"One hour. I'll even agree to leave early *and* take the blame if you need to escape. We'll need some sort of signal."

"I adore you..." His smile was bright and full of easy affection as he dropped a kiss to my forehead. "I could hand you a peppermint?"

"I suppose that will do," I said with a laugh.

He grabbed my wrap from the nearby table while I bent down to drop a kiss on Leo's forehead. Lee rubbed the boy's hair fondly.

We stepped into the hall and knocked on the nursery door. Jack popped his head out. "Off to the ball?" he asked, stepping into the hall.

"Yes, you'll mind him?"

"Of course! Leo, Adrina, and I shall play peek-a-boo until one of us falls asleep. And then we'll bother Crawford while he complains about how much work he has than he does actual work."

Adrina herself rounded the corner at the top of the stairs, her own boy on her hip. Imogen's sister had been willing to come serve as wet nurse. Much to my disappointment, I wasn't always able to produce enough to satisfy the little foot gnawer in the other room.

She was quietly understanding about the fact that she was never, ever left alone with Leo. In fact, she even refrained from comment when she was often accompanied by a footman barely out of leading strings himself. Of course, she was also paid handsomely for her tact.

"We'll be at Cadieux House on Grosvenor's Street. Brigs has the address."

"I've been there, remember?" Jack was less quiet in his understanding, though he seemed to enjoy his new role watching Leo more than he had his footman duties.

I trailed Lee down the stairs and out into the night. In front of the steps was a horsed phaeton. Lee froze, comically glancing up and down the street searching for his carriage.

"I borrowed it from Cee," I said from behind him. "I thought we could try it."

The open top was entirely impractical. It would be freezing. We would certainly attract attention. But... I rather hoped it would make the trip a tiny bit easier on my husband.

"Char—Thank you." His voice was thick with sentiments I couldn't name for certain.

He considered me and the phaeton in equal measure, his head bouncing between us. Abruptly, he stripped his great coat off and wrapped it around me before guiding me to the conveyance. Beside it, he grabbed me by the waist and lifted me straight in, ignoring the step entirely. He clambered in after me.

The pocket of his coat was filled with peppermints, and I snagged two as we set off. One for him and one for myself.

"Is this a signal that you no longer wish to attend?" he asked teasingly.

I rolled my eyes and bit into my own mint, nodding toward the reigns. Reluctantly, my husband grabbed them and urged the horses into action.

"I do not know if I mentioned it, but Mrs. Griffith examined me this morning."

"Are you well?" There was real worry in his tone and eyes, darker than their usual navy in the dim streetlight, as he turned my way.

"Quite. In fact, she has no concerns about *any* activities I may wish to partake in going forward."

He blinked slowly, parsing my meaning. "Truly?" he choked out.

"Truly."

"*Any?*"

"Any."

"Then what the devil are we going to this ball for?"

"Because I wish to go, and you love me. Besides, anticipation is a good thing."

"Anticipation! I've barely been able to touch you for weeks." Our touches had been limited by my recovery, slower for my early overexertion. But he'd found more than a few loopholes in Mrs. Griffith's rules.

"Oh, you've touched me plenty."

"How am I meant to dance knowing that?" he whined.

I glanced at his lap before meeting his gaze with a raised brow. He wasn't wrong, dancing in that state might be a challenge. "Think of Lyra." I suggested, nodding back at the road.

As expected, he began his usual litany of complaints. "It looks nothing like a harp. It's poorly named."

"I know."

"I just—I would've made a better choice."

"Of course, darling. Left here," I directed.

My distraction worked and he was still offering better suggestions between my quiet directions when we pulled up outside Cadieux House. The phaeton slowed to a stop, and my husband looked around us, confused.

His gaze found me again, settling with an indulgent smile. "Clever minx."

"Precisely. Glad you recognize that. Come now, time to go inside before we freeze."

Lee sighed and allowed me to drag him up the steps and inside.

A PROPERLY CONDUCTED SHAM

LEE

Charlotte pulled me up the steps and into the house, eager and sweet-smelling with little yellow flowers in her hair.

The halls weren't filled with the usual bustle of hiding wallflowers, tipsy chaperones, and couples looking for a quiet corner. In fact, we found only the butler at the door. He blanched at the sight of my wife before wordlessly pointing toward the hall.

Instead of the usual dull roar I remembered from these fêtes, the orchestra was held at a tasteful volume. Charlotte's tiny hand guided me along and into the ballroom.

At the entrance, Will and Celine greeted us. We hadn't seen them since they called—nearly a week after the events at the warehouse—to let us know that Wesley Parker had died from an infection in the gaol the day before.

She wore her usual shade of purple, and there was a lightness to her that hadn't been present even before Gabriel. When she turned to Will, she looked at him as though he hung the stars and the moon.

After the usual greeting, Charlotte pulled me deeper into the ballroom. The moment I'd been dreading. Far from a crush, there were but a few couples. Wayland and Lady Juliet, not much longer from the birthing bed than us, waltzed—though the tune was a cotillion. Ainsley and his wife chatted easily with Lord and Lady Grayson. A few other couples I could not name laughed or danced gaily. It was no more than seven, perhaps eight in total, and a few single stragglers.

Ainsley caught sight of us and waved us over.

And not a single person so much as blinked at the sight of me.

Charlotte tugged on my hand, moving toward them.

When she met with no success, she turned to me with wide, concerned eyes.

"Lee?"

"Did you..."

She smiled, soft and adoring. "I thought this might be an easier first step. And Celine was pleased when I suggested it. She was desperate to host, but she was worried about how Will would be received. I hope it is all right?"

"All right? Charlotte, I... This is the nicest thing anyone has ever done for me."

"I birthed you a child."

"Second nicest," I corrected quickly.

She gave a gentle jerk on my hand where it was clasped in hers. "Shall we?"

This time, I allowed her to guide me to the group. Once there, Ainsley performed the necessary introductions.

Lord Grayson was familiar. With our estates so near each other, we had more than a few connections and challenges in common.

At my side, Charlotte leaned toward Lady Grayson. "May I have a moment?" she asked, gesturing toward a private corner. "No beverages," she added, displaying empty palms.

I wasn't entirely certain what that meant, but her countenance was easy as they wandered the short distance toward the wall.

Lord Grayson trailed off midsentence, watching with concern.

The two ladies spoke easily, hand gestures tentative, before returning to us. Lord Grayson inspected his wife thoroughly. Upon finding her in precisely the same condition as when she left mere moments ago, he tucked her diminutive form tight into his side.

I caught my favorite soft brown eyes with a raised brow. She merely shook her head.

Convinced of his wife's safety, Lord Grayson turned back to chat at me about various improvements he was making to his estate.

Finished with their improvised waltz, Wayland and his wife made their way over. Reunited, the ladies wandered off to discuss whatever it was ladies discussed while one of the gentlemen pulled a scotch from lord only knew where. We passed the bottle around in the corner of the ballroom like schoolboys before Will trotted over with a disapproving furrow.

And every time I sought Charlotte, her eyes were on mine. Warm and affectionate sometimes, low and lustful others.

When the actual waltz began, I wandered over to claim my wife.

"You seemed to be enjoying yourself?" she asked, settling into my arms with an ease that certainly hadn't been there the night we met.

"Yes, thank you. I-I'd forgotten how to be a person, I think. Stars do not judge. But they do not care either."

"I think they care a little. I read a theory in one of your books. We are all made of little bits and pieces of stardust. I do not know if it's true, but it is a rather romantic notion."

"It is, isn't it."

Her hand slipped from its proper place on my shoulder to curl in the ends of my hair. Permission granted to be improper, I dipped my hand scandalously low on her waist and pulled her closer.

There was something about her smile, about the spark of her gaze, the sensual way she carded her fingers through my hair. Tonight was different. There was something in the air.

I didn't even feel it, her other hand sliding into my pocket. But when her outstretched hand appeared between us, two peppermints in her palm, it was all I could do to laugh—laugh and let her lead us out to the phaeton and the starry night.

Chapter Forty-Five

84 BROOK STREET, LONDON - DECEMBER 18. 1816

LEE

A LUST-FILLED tension found a home in my spine, settling low and simmering. It carried through the drive home. It remained as we stepped into the house. It accompanied me as I trailed Charlotte up the stairs to check on a soundly sleeping Leo, splayed atop an equally unconscious Jack. It followed all the way until I heard the click of our bedroom door latching. Then and only then, did it break.

Hours of anticipation, weeks of desperation, months of longing, years of celibacy—it all washed over me, a tidal wave threatening to sweep me out to sea. I was going to drown in Charlotte, or without her. It wasn't clear. It didn't matter. Her lips were the only things that mattered, had ever, would ever again matter.

And if the sweet whines and disoriented, needy tugs to the buttons of my waistcoat were any indication, my wife felt the same. She managed quite a few, her dexterous fingers working tirelessly between us to undress me. Patience wasn't my wife's strong suit, so it shouldn't have been a surprise when, quite without warning, she grabbed the edges of the garment and tugged, sending a button or two pinging to the floor. *That* was certainly the most arousing moment of my entire life.

In a pathetic bid to keep from embarrassing myself, I spun her around, stripping her of my great coat to reach the line of buttons fastening her gown. Five delicate circles lined her spine, wrapped in the same gold thread of her dress. They were all that separated me from my wife. And likely additional layers, but those were a problem for future Lee.

The temptation to grab and yank was there, certainly, and stronger than any urge I'd had thus far. But when I dropped a kiss to the delicate freckle at the nape of her neck, she shuddered. And that shudder gave me ideas.

Impossibly slowly, I worked the topmost button free. Pleased to have revealed more skin and another tiny freckle, I dragged my finger along the new landscape. Charlotte swallowed. A second button earned me a clenched fist. The third revealed chemise or petticoat or whatever ridiculous underthings she wore. To make amends for the absence of porcelain flesh, I received a whine of my name.

"Yes, darling?"

"Do you suppose you might hurry this along?" she asked, irritation swirling with the lust in her tone.

"Hurry what along?"

She spun around, glaring at me before grabbing a fistful of my shirt and tugging my lips down to hers. Her lips and tongue were greedy, and in seconds, my entire objective was lost. One hand found her waist, the other the side of her neck, tangling curls I'd already mussed.

As quickly as the kiss started, she pulled away, leaving my lips chasing pathetically after hers. She hovered, just out of reach, smirking at my own needy whine. "We've had months to build the anticipation, Lee. I'm finished with slow."

It took my lust-drugged brain a moment to grasp her

meaning. When it dawned at last, I could not have held back my groan for the world.

My hand still on her waist spun her back around. In no time at all, I was yanking her gown to pool on the floor between us.

"That's better," she purred.

The ties on the petticoat protested my rough treatment, the sharp snap of stitches popping carrying over our harsh breaths. The sound was heavy and significant with implication.

Still, I had a directive from my lovely, imperious wife, and I half-heartedly shoved the material down to join its friend on the floor. It caught between my waist where it was pressed in tight against her bottom without my permission or notice. That obstruction was irrelevant when I was faced with the challenge of stays.

My fingers, too large, fumbled on the lacings in a doltish refusal to obey my head's commands. I had the rather inane wonder what sort of undergarments she'd worn with that dress she'd donned the night we met. The one that offered up her luscious breasts for adoration.

At last, I managed to free her from that layer too.

"Well done."

I rolled my eyes in response to the praise, even as I bit back a grin at her satirical commentary. The ties of her delicate, threadbare chemise snapped under my fingers. It was her own doing. I wouldn't apologize for my responses to her provocation.

With a gentle grip, I turned her around. Then, gentleness abandoned me. My fingers twisted in her curls, dragging her onto her toes and up to my lips with bruising intensity.

Far from intimidated, Charlotte gave as much as she received. One tiny hand caught in my hair and yanked me down farther when she dropped to flat feet. The other worked ineffectively at the fall of my breeches. I sacrificed the hand on her waist to assist in her efforts.

"Lee," she panted when she drew away for breath.

"Hmm," I answered into the delicate skin of her jaw.

"Breeches off."

"Not as easy as it seems, is it?"

"Smug and self-satisfied are not attractive qualities," she retorted.

I bit back a smile, abandoning her collarbone in favor of following her instructions in a timely fashion, lest she decide not to bestow her favors.

I divested them quickly, tossing my shirt away at the same time. Task completed, I reached for her again.

She shook her head, instead giving me a gentle shove toward the bed. Charlotte's hand, still pressed in the center of my chest, shoved just a bit harder, directing me to sit.

No sooner had I done so than my arms and lap were full of my lovely, lavender-scented wife.

"Hello."

"Hello," she replied distractedly. Her hands dragged freely across my torso, brushing across scarred flesh. My chest tightened at the realization—not that she was touching my damaged skin—but that I had forgotten its existence entirely.

Through the months, I had grown so used to her appreciative glances, her nonchalant brushes, her purposeful touches, that when we were alone, I only considered the scars in so much as her touches there *felt* different.

As wonderful as that realization was, sentimental blubbering was not what either of us wanted for tonight.

Taking charge, I dragged her lips back to mine and pulled her with me as I laid back on the bed.

She was a tiny little thing, my wife. Sprawled entirely atop me, it was clear how delicate she truly was, how dangerous our race to London had been.

Shaking that horrifying thought away, I caught her waist and tugged her up my frame. We'd managed to work this position out in the months before she gave birth, when everything was uncomfortable for her. And... I rather liked it.

Charlotte's hand dropped down in the center of my chest, halting my efforts.

"What's wrong?"

"I want to try something..." She trailed off with a raised brow. I hadn't the faintest idea what she wanted to try. But it was Charlotte, naked Charlotte, and I couldn't fathom anything she could want that I wouldn't.

"By all means," I said, flopping back. "Where do you want me?"

"Right there," she said, something sultry in her tone.

And then, then, she slid her leg over my waist and sat back on my thighs. Her entrance, lovely and damp, right beneath my painfully hard cock.

Christ, I loved this woman.

～

CHARLOTTE

Lee was wrecked, his pupils blown so wide his eyes were black. And I hadn't even done anything.

Watching this man, this massive, powerful, damaged, gentle man fall to pieces at the thought of my touch was a heady thing. Arousal and interest settled low in my belly. It was a familiar sensation around my husband but unfamiliar in the context of this activity.

One hand fisted in the sheets, tangling and untangling, while I gathered my nerve. He seemed to sense my need for control in this and was perfectly willing to allow me to set the pace.

The cool fingers of his free hand traced my side, dragging across the unattractive marks our son left behind.

"What?" he asked. My expression must have revealed my discomfort because he continued. "You flinched."

"There are marks, I don't..." *Want you to touch them* remained unsaid.

"Oh, well, as I am a perfect specimen..." he retorted, his grin sardonic.

"That's different," I protested. "You were injured being heroic."

He hummed, most likely biting back a protest of his heroism. "You were injured bringing our child into this world. There is nothing more heroic, and nothing more beautiful."

With that, he rose up to kiss one mark, then another, and another. There was no difference in sensation, but the sight... The vision of Lee worshiping curves and lines I hadn't yet come to terms with—it was enough to overwhelm. There was no warning before the tears came, a passive process in a way they had never been before. They merely seeped from my eyes, flowing freely.

Sensing my overflowing sentiment, he dragged himself back up to kiss away the stray tears.

"What do you want tonight, Charlotte?"

And that might have been the easiest answer I'd ever given. "You. Us. As one."

Before he could distract me with his earnest gaze and soft words, I dragged his lips to mine. Lee responded the way he always did, fully, completely, without hesitation. He kissed with his entire body. It was the same way he loved me.

His deft hands worked around me and then inside me. He set about stripping me of sense—left to clutch desperately at broad shoulders and a muscular chest as he readied me for him.

Reluctantly, I separated our lips and wandering hands

before urging his torso back to the bed and dragging my splayed fingers down the intriguing planes of his chest. Carefully, I pressed my palms to his abdominals to rise above him.

His hands found my thighs, offering eager assistance. Lee held my weight easily as I sank down, down, down on his hard shaft with a sigh.

Whether Lee surged up or I pulled his lips to mine, I neither knew nor cared. The entirety of my being was focused on his sinful lips and more sinful cock. Gently, tentatively, he rocked up into me. And I knew nothing but pleasure and bubbling joy.

Lee dragged his lips away, cupping my cheek to prevent me from following. "Is it all right?" he whispered, so quiet I wasn't entirely certain I understood the words. But the sentiment was so clear in his eyes.

"Yes," I nodded.

He melted in relief, his hand catching the back of my neck as he fell back against the pillows, tongue tangling with mine.

With the other hand clenching on my waist, he helped me set a rhythm that suited us both.

Thanks to Lee, I wasn't a stranger to pleasure. I could sense it building low in my spine as I worked above him while his hands traced curves and his hips met mine.

In the delicate firelight, I—we—discovered something entirely new. Somewhere in the space between us, stars were formed and lived and died and were reborn. They swirled, orbiting around us, bathing us in twinkling light.

Lee was quiet and gentle. His eyes caught mine with determination. He'd never said as much to me, but I knew he would abide nothing but breathtaking, earth-shattering pleasure. Our bed, our little slice of paradise, had no room for self-doubt or pain. The luxurious, sensual joy burned everything else away.

Somewhere in the midst of our heaven, Lee found a place inside me that had my toes curling and my breath catching.

"There!" One of us breathed it, whether it was him or me or the stars was anyone's guess. And white-hot bliss danced along my spine.

Seconds, minutes, hours later the pleasure began to recede and awareness dawned once more.

Sense returned slowly, around the time Lee pulled me against him with a kiss to my forehead. I answered with one to the scar over his heart.

"Charlotte?"

I hummed, still incapable of actual words.

"I... you enjoyed that, I believe?"

That was enough to startle me up a bit to meet his gaze. "It was perfect."

"Good," he replied, trying to tug me back down.

I resisted. "Did you not find it so?"

A smile tugged at the corner of his lips as he caught a tangled curl between his thumb and forefinger, twirling it thoughtfully.

"Perfect is too inadequate a word," he assured me. "But you said in the past, it was not always enjoyable. I merely wanted to be sure."

"With you, everything is different."

His smile was bright and accompanied by a breathless laugh. I finally allowed him to tug me down for a kiss.

When we broke apart he added, "Good, because as soon as I regain feeling in my extremities, I'd like to do that again—if you're amenable, of course."

"I am. Amenable. Very amenable." I curled my head on his chest.

A quiet cry from the other room interrupted our basking. I knew Leo well enough by now to know it was his general dissatisfied with life cry and nothing more serious.

My husband stretched with a slight groan before rolling out of bed and grabbing his banyan. He picked up a nightdress off the floor and tossed it to me with a teasing smile.

No sooner had I managed to convince my limbs to cooperate in pulling the garment on, than Lee returned with our son bundled in his arms.

"Well, I frightened Jack beyond his wits. We'll need to increase his pay to compensate for the years I took off his life."

Between chuckles, I asked, "What did you do to that lad?"

"He thought someone had come to steal the boy. Was ready to stab me with a fire poker."

"That should more than double his wages." I reached up for Leo. My husband deposited our son safely into my arms as he slid into bed.

Lee curled around us, letting me use him as a pillow while I rubbed our son's belly in the way that usually soothed.

Leo settled a bit, grabbing his foot in both hands and trying to drag it into his mouth.

With a chuckle, Lee stole the foot away, placing it back beside its brother and offering his finger for inspection instead.

"I don't know what I did to deserve you two," Lee murmured.

"It is strange, I was thinking the exact same thing."

He considered us for a moment. "Perhaps we should just enjoy it, rather than trying to find an explanation for it."

"I quite like the sound of that."

Course of action decided, Lee dropped his usual kiss on my forehead and another one on his son's dark head. And together, our little family drifted off to sleep.

Epilogue

BENNET HALL, SURREY - JUNE 4, 1820

LEE

WATCHING the sunset by the lake had been peaceful once. No company but the dragonflies dragging the water and the bees hard at work among the flowers.

Peaceful was certainly not a word for this evening. Not with Henry Grayson and Leo chasing after Sophie Wayland with a toad they'd found lord only knew where.

And I couldn't be happier about the change.

Emma and Georgiana Hudson, Lizzie Wayland, and my second son, Charles, were a little more subdued, sharing tea with dolls, wooden horses, tin soldiers, and anything else they could find. They even had Rose Grayson propped against a pile of blankets, happily gumming a biscuit—only slightly more animated than the toys.

"Leo..." Charlotte called with a warning in her tone. She was propped against me. Her belly, growing once more, often caused her back to ache.

My eldest son trotted over, looking sheepish, leaving the

young Grayson heir to taunt his younger cousin with the amphibian alone.

Neither the Wayland nor the Grayson families seemed overly inclined to intervene. Living so close to one another and so near a creek, I suspected toad wars weren't an uncommon occurrence.

"Yes, Mama?"

"You must be kind to our guests."

"But Henry start—"

I cut him off with a cleared throat and a raised brow.

Suitably chastened, he wandered over to the eldest Wayland twin to apologize.

With dark hair and eyes, there was nothing to call mine in Leo's physical appearance, but when he helped a tripped Sophie to her feet with a sincere apology and an offer to help her find a toad of her own—one she eagerly accepted—I saw something of myself in his actions.

Henry Grayson, without anyone to chase or be chased by, set the frog beside the lake and sulked back over to the blanket and his mother.

He whined something to Kate, who answered entirely without sympathy. "Well then, you shouldn't be teasing. No one will want to play with you if you do."

Cass, sensing a vulnerable amphibian, stalked through the reeds. She lined up her pounce and waited for precisely the right moment—a moment she missed by half a second when she landed with two paws on the empty rock.

Not having anticipated failure, she slipped and slid off the rock and into the lake.

I was laughing too hard when she escaped the watery torture and angrily chirped her way over to me, to pull my hand away before she clamped it between her teeth. The bite didn't have the slightest impact on my chuckles as she strode off with all the fury her diminutive size could convey.

Delighted by the incident, the Grayson boy settled on the blanket with a giggle.

No sooner had he reached for a handful of biscuits than three forms appeared over the hill. Will, Celine, and Hugh, their arms laden with lengthy sticks, returned to our picnic.

"Who wants to learn to fence?" Cee called.

The eldest rapscallions all shot to their feet, leaving only those too small to walk to our care. Just Rose and Charles. Sweet Charles, barely over a year old and already the vision of perfection. His blonde curls were just beginning to come in. His eyes were the same honey brown as his mother's.

The Ainsley children, Emma and Georgiana, were by far the most sensible of the heathens running amok in our gardens, with Lizzie Wayland displaying some decorum.

But my little lion, Henry Grayson, and Sophie Wayland were overly energetic menaces to society, and allowing them to beat each other with sticks was likely the only way to achieve a modicum of peace when they explored the stars that night.

With a sigh, I leaned back on a palm. "I should go set up the observatory so they don't have to wait for me after supper." I stood, stretching out my aging back. "Try to keep them from killing each other," I directed toward Ainsley and his wife—the only ones capable of such a feat.

"I make no promises," Ainsley called after me.

"Your best effort is all anyone could ask of you."

When I stepped inside the observatory, silence and darkness enveloped me. I waited for a moment for familiar relief to come.

But there was nothing.

If anything the solitude irked more than soothed. If I could tell the Lee of five years ago what I knew now, how much better life could be...

A sliver of light poured in from the cracked door, expanding as it opened before disappearing entirely.

The delicate scent of lavender and peppermint washed over me at the same time that delicate arms banded about my waist.

Charlotte pressed against my back with a pleased hum.

"Well, hello there," I greeted, wrapping my arms around hers.

"Your son is thrashing the Grayson boy. I think Lord Grayson may have a fit."

"Quite right. What did you do with Charlie?"

"Jules wanted a few minutes of cuddling."

I hummed, turning in her arms and throwing one of my own around her shoulder.

"We do not get much time in here any longer, do we?" she asked.

"No, we don't."

"Do you miss it?"

"No, not really. It turns out, wives and children are better company than stars."

She smiled and pulled out of my arms to circle the room. "Not too chaotic?"

"Precisely the right amount of chaotic." She dragged her finger along equipment she was now intimately familiar with. The movement was exploratory, as it had been in the first days of our marriage. "I'll need to polish one of the mirrors, they'll be tarnished."

"Beyond use?" she asked.

"No, just not as they ought to be."

"Hmm, what if you... didn't." A suggestive note filled her voice that had my interest thoroughly peaked.

"And what would I do instead?"

She finished her circuit and returned to face me. One interested hand caught my cravat, and the other caught my scarred cheek. Gently she tugged me down, down, down until only an inch remained between our lips.

"You could show *me* the stars."
"But it's daytime," I teased.
"Lee?"
"Yes, Charlotte?"
"More kissing and less talking, if you please."
"Yes, dearest wife."

No force in the world could have stopped the gravitational pull between our lips.

The End

The Most Imprudent Matches series will continue with *The Scottish Scheme*.

Enjoy a bonus second epilogue here: https://www.allyhudson.com/bonus-scenes.

Support the Author by leaving a review.

Acknowledgments

Thank you to Laura Linn for your feedback and services as a sounding board while I whined about this for months on end.

As always, thank you to my friends and family.

A special thanks to my mother for not saying I told you so as often as you should.

Thank you to Martha for reminding me to touch grass occasionally.

Thank you to Bryton, Mariah, and Ali for making me smile.

Thank you to Holly Perret at *The Swoonies Romance Art* for my beautiful cover.

About the Author

Ally Hudson is an Amazon bestselling author of steamy Regency romance, crafting captivating tales of love, healing, hope, and family. Her debut series, *Most Imprudent Matches*, weaves together eight unforgettable love stories spanning decades, blending humor and heart with devoted heroes and capable heroines. Ally's stories celebrate the countless forms love can take, each one deserving its moment to shine.

When she's not writing, Ally can be found embroidering, baking, or catering to the every whim of her charming dog, Darcy.

Also by Ally Hudson

MOST IMPRUDENT MATCHES

Courting Scandal - Book One

Michael and Juliet

The Baker and the Bookmaker - Book Two

Augie and Anna

Winning My Wife - Book Three

Hugh and Kate

Devil of Mine - A Prequel Novella

Gabriel and Celine

Angel of Mine - Book Four

Will and Celine

A Properly Conducted Sham - Book Five

Lee and Charlotte

COMING SOON

The Scottish Scheme - June 2025

A Lady's Guide to Abduction (And Other Legal Matters) - Fall 2025

Made in the USA
Monee, IL
04 February 2025